The Pumpkin Bride

The Pumpkin Bride

FIONA BUTTERCUP

MIRA

MIRA™

ISBN-13: 978-0-7783-3266-4

The Pumpkin Bride

MIRA
22 Adelaide St. West, 41st Floor
Toronto, Ontario M5H 4E3, Canada
MIRABooks.com

HarperCollins Publishers
Macken House, 39/40 Mayor Street Upper,
Dublin 1, D01 C9W8, Ireland
www.HarperCollins.com

Printed in United Kingdom

26 27 28 29 CPI 10 9 8 7 6 5 4 3 2

To my husband, who starts counting down to Halloween on November 1st, and is the reason we own four fog machines.

Chapter 1

Deep in the hinterlands of Harvest Hollow, Sir Bram Duncan led a lance of knights through Windfall Woods. A tang of pine clung to the chilly night air. And . . . *sniff* . . . if he wasn't mistaken, ripening pumpkins. He raised an eyebrow. A dense wood like this should be too full of shade and roots to sustain a vine-based crop. But this was no time to worry about agricultural oddities. Not when curious glowing eyes peeped from between the trees.

"How much farther?" Bram called back to Prince Crispin.

"Just up ahead," Crispin said. "It's impossible to miss."

"How did you find this treasure tree anyway, sire?" Bram asked.

"It's called the Lantern Oak." Crispin grunted as they climbed over an enormous rotting log. "And I found it because I'm brilliant."

"Obviously." Bram clasped a thick-necked knight, Fergus, by the forearm to help him up and over the log. Kevin followed unaided. Points to him for his strength, but Bram immediately deducted those points for his lack of stealth. The man's brigandine clanged like church bells on Sunday morning. How had he made such a racket when the small plates were riveted *inside* his padded jacket?

Lack of training, that was how.

In the years since Bram arrived in this realm to earn prestige and a plot of land, he'd concluded the education for pages, squires, and knights in Harvest Hollow was lax. But if he was being candid, he'd call it a death sentence for the men who believed themselves prepared to square up to an invading army.

This was a boon to him, though.

Thanks to his foster father's firm training, Bram handily won several tournaments. These victories gained Prince Crispin's notice, which opened the door to his royal inner circle. Crispin claimed surrounding himself with handsome champions reflected well on him. In Bram's experience, it also increased the number of maidens tossing their favors at his crew.

Bram, happily in a romance, declined all such favors.

He rubbed his half of a locket anchored on a silver chain that lay nestled against his chest. Princess Marigold's portrait had been with him during every journey, quest, and step he'd taken since departing Thornwick. After tonight's adventure, he would finally have enough coin to return home and make an impressive offer for his true love's hand.

"You can do this," he called to Crispin's squire, young Coby.

The adolescent scrambled up and over the massive log with the agility of a squirrel. Impressive for a lad with only two years' training, especially since he'd kept his lantern level. The squire was sharp of mind, too—he could memorize instruction and repeat it back verbatim.

Unlike Sir Kevin over there.

"Well done," Bram said. Crispin rarely offered positive feedback to the boy, so he tried to fill in the gaps. "Help me with these?"

Together, they laid three thick limbs across a gurgling brook.

"How will we know the tree?" Bram asked.

Crispin tapped his foot impatiently. "By the lights. It's called the Lantern Oak for a reason."

Bram tested the hasty bridge. Solid.

As he crossed, he asked, "What should we know about the magic?"

The command in Bram's voice belied the pit in his stomach. Unlike battle plans, magic provided too many opportunities for misinterpretation. Like when he was small and his parents flipped a coin into the Whispering Well. New to the kingdom of Thornwick, Harvest Hollow's neighboring realm, they'd wished for their child to become a knight. Magic twisted the simple request. Instead, his parents had disappeared and Sir Patrick Duncan stumbled upon him, alone and crying in the square, clutching his wooden sword. The only thing he had to remember them lo these twenty years were his mother's eyes and his father's face, which he saw in his reflection.

"So many questions, Sir Bram," Crispin said warily. His blond hair gleamed silver, the moonlight marking him a sovereign. "Where's your sense of adventure?"

Bram wouldn't let it go. "It's present. And the magic? What are we facing?"

The prince walked the sturdy limbs over the brook. The longer he held his tongue, the more the pit in Bram's stomach widened. Crispin's presence was unusual, so there must've been more to tonight's jaunt than met the eye. Bram was game for anything so long as the quest paid. He sought information to prepare for danger. Fortune favored him when luck met preparation and increased his chances of returning home to his childhood sweetheart.

He *ached* for Princess Marigold of Thornwick.

She was his true love, his true north, his heart's desire. Her red curls, eyes that flashed like sapphires in firelight when he'd been particularly annoying, soft curves that tempted him like candied apples . . . He could write epic poems about her wondrous body. Above all, he missed their conversation, their laughter, and their understanding of each other. Like they were in a private bubble, where nothing they said or did flowed into the cesspools of courtly intrigue.

Letters had kept them in contact, but it was no replacement for holding each other. Another of her cherished missives had arrived this morning, bearing news that her beloved uncle, the king of Thornwick, had fallen ill with the posy fever. While she was an optimist, the fever was almost always a death sentence. Her sadness had leaked into some of her words as well as the uncertainty about what this meant for her branch of the royal family tree.

After tonight, he'd return to the kingdom of Thornwick to comfort her.

"There's nothing special about it." Crispin hopped over the muddy bank and onto solid grass. "The acorns at the top of the Lantern Oak turn to gold between midnight and dawn. Once plucked, they remain in their precious state."

Bram turned the information over in his brain. His muscles tensed, the same way they did while walking home late after a night at the Laughing Gourd. If collecting a fortune was that simple, Crispin would've stripped this tree bare. The prince had held something back.

"Where's the barb on this lance?" Bram asked.

"Well asked, Sir Bram. A sprite guards the Lantern Oak's riches. If you wake him, he'll ask you a riddle. A minor roadblock, but I don't doubt our success."

"A sprite?" Bram groaned as he crossed the brook.

Much as he distrusted magic, a party his size should be able to contend with a lone tree sprite. Unlike the situation at Thornwick's northern borders. Marigold had written with news of mountain-sprite incursions at the foothills of the Gildfall Mountains. Her twin brother and Bram's best friend, Rowan, had been dispatched to protect their northern villages. Her younger brother, Beckett, was in training but expected to join the fray soon. Yet another incentive for Bram to end his service here and return to his home realm.

At Crispin's side, he murmured, "You should've told me about the sprite before now."

The prince arched an eyebrow. "Careful, Knight. You assume too much familiarity."

Indignation tangled with his need to remain in Crispin's favor. The prince was correct—a knight should not question his sovereign. But if he was to serve Crispin well, Bram needed to work with a full understanding of potential dangers. He swallowed the rough words he was tempted to say and turned his attention to the squire crossing the makeshift bridge.

Even with the load Coby bore on his back, the limbs barely bounced under his slight frame as he followed. The lad whispered to him, "If you don't mind my asking, what's fearsome about a sprite?"

Bram hushed the remaining members of their party. He, Coby, and Crispin were light-footed, but saints, Kevin and Fergus might as well have beat a drum with the noise they made. He'd never met knights so determined to give away their advantage.

"Size-wise, nothing," Bram said in a low voice. "Wits-wise, their riddles are notoriously confusing. If you succeed, they often twist the terms of the agreement. But most interactions end with a curse. Sprites aren't merciless—every curse comes with a loophole. But overall, it's best to avoid them. They aren't trustworthy."

"But not to worry, Squire. Neither am I," Crispin said, overhearing them. He pointed to a scrim of willows undulating in the sharp fall wind. "Our destination should be through those trees. Hurry. Tonight is the last night we can harvest—tomorrow's the full Hunter's Moon. Upon the next day's sunrise the sprite and his gold acorns disappear until next year's equinox."

Papery leaves scraped against his wool brigandine as Bram pushed through the switches. In the mossy meadow beyond, he stopped, awed by the Lantern Oak.

Ancient and massive, Bram could not see its top. The broad, knotted trunk was the size of a respectable cottage, and the sprawling limbs spread out in all directions. He did not doubt it could carry the weight of the world if asked. Dozens of glowing amber orbs dotted the tree as though it was decorated for Yule.

"Whoa." Fergus gasped. "Look at the size of that thing."

Obviously, Bram traveled with poets.

"Are we supposed to cut it down or something?" Kevin asked. The knight was five years Bram's senior, but his voice had aged faster. Low and slightly strangled, it sounded like his thick neck muscles fought the words.

Crispin clearly had favored brawn over wits when he assembled this quest.

"What? Why would you . . ." Bram pinched the bridge of his nose. "Clearly not, Kevin. We didn't bring saws. I'd wager we climb and gather the gold acorns, right, sir?"

"Mostly correct." The prince snapped his fingers at Coby for the haversack, then tossed it to Bram. "Not we. You."

The buttery leather was smooth in his hands. "It would be faster with more of us harvesting the nuts."

"And more opportunity to tangle with the sprite. With speed and stealth, we may escape his notice, so this must be a solo journey. Large-framed as you are, you're the best climber. It'll take you ten minutes to reach the top. Fergus, Kevin, Coby and I will stand watch down here."

Bram shifted his weight. All of that had the benefit of being true. So why did Crispin's close inspection of him make his guts slither? Bram ran his hands through his hair. His instincts were rarely wrong, but this was silly. Crispin wanted him to succeed, and despite the occasional tension, he and the prince were brothers-in-arms. The magical aspect of tonight's quest had thrown him, that was all.

As ever, he'd master his doubt. Humbly.

"Ten minutes? Bet I can do it in nine."

He stripped off his pauldrons and brigandine to ease his climb, then handed them to Coby. The boy's spark of silver hair above his temple gleamed in the Lantern Oak's glow. Bram called it a wisdom mark when they'd first met, earning Coby's adoration.

Briefly, Bram touched the half locket. That wasn't his only memento of her—in his pocket he carried her handkerchief, the favor she'd given him when he'd left, and the small wood unicorn he'd carved for her eighth birthday, which she'd insisted he take as a good luck charm. "Soon," he whispered.

With an easy heave, he pulled himself into the Lantern Tree. Crouched upon the lowest bough, he locked gazes with Crispin standing below. The glowing orbs restored some of the prince's color, but his eyes were still black as midnight.

With the grace of a pirate atop a mast, Bram leaned against the trunk. "I'll return with enough gold to fill Harvest Hollow's coffers."

"A grandiose boast," Crispin challenged. "But succeed, and I'll grant you a title."

"You will?" A title was beyond his dreams. Marigold's parents would *surely* grant their permission for her to wed *Lord* Bram Duncan. Possibly earl?

"I swear it." The prince placed his hand over his heart and bowed his head. In Harvest Hollow, that signaled a solemn and unbreakable promise. "Now, go. The castle needs repair, and Harvest Hollow will revolt if I raise taxes again."

Hmph. Repaving the crumbling trade roads or plugging

the leaking aqueducts would be a better use of the money, but Crispin had made it clear it was not Bram's—or anyone's—place to question his decisions. Sir Patrick had taught Bram that a confident person welcomed a challenge. Not so with Crispin, as the heir apparent was still finding his feet in his regency.

Three years ago, King Clovis, Crispin's father, had fallen into his dotage and could no longer serve as king of Harvest Hollow. Princess Rosamund, Crispin's older sister, should've taken up the mantle. From what Bram pieced together, Rosamund—overwhelmed by grief and responsibility—had taken to the seaside to balance her humors. This left the regency to the ambitious prince.

It had cost Bram, a Thornwick-trained knight, many pints at the Laughing Gourd to learn the intricacies of Harvest Hollow's royal intrigues and palace gossip. The investment had served him well, though, as understanding the tensions in the balance of power had helped him win a place in the palace guard and, eventually, a spot in Crispin's privy guard.

"Tick tock, Bram," Crispin called from below.

Branches twined around him, providing a plethora of routes to the top. Despite the bark roughing his calloused palms, the tree proved easy enough to climb. Much as he appreciated the amber orbs lighting his way, he wished he could see the Lantern Oak during the day. In full sun its crimson, orange, and bright yellow leaves must've resembled fire.

With a final step upward, his head and shoulders breached the canopy.

Dozens, no, *hundreds* of gold acorns winked between the light of the moon and orbs. Bram swiveled the haversack to his front, then plucked the gold free from the branches. He made quick work of his task, tugging and snapping the acorns free. Once the sack was full, he stuffed a fistful into his pocket with Marigold's handkerchief and unicorn.

"How're you getting on, then?" a cheerful voice called to him.

A chubby winged creature who stood three apples tall fluttered above the treetop. The sprite's wispy clementine-colored hair waved around his head like a shimmering halo. His overalls were neatly tailored soft yellow leaves, though he wore no shoes. Above Bram, he blew clove-scented smoke rings from a pipe the size of Bram's little finger.

Bram pressed his lips together and stuffed down his surprise at the friendly sprite's question. As a knight of two realms, he'd encountered plenty of magical creatures. Fairies, werewolves, banshees, basilisks—they all dove for the throat first. Unlike this hovering sprite, whose eyes sparkled with kind curiosity. But he couldn't be trusted.

"I'm well," Bram said carefully. "And you?"

"Grand, thanks for asking." He drew another long pull on his pipe. "So, young fella, how'd you like to proceed?"

"Proceed with what?" Bram asked.

"Ah, now, the battle of wits, of course. I can't be letting you walk off with forty pounds of gold without putting a riddle to you first. So what'll it be—up here, or down below?" He gestured toward the earth with his pipe.

"Is there an advantage to moving?"

"No, not really, but I enjoy giving you poor humans the notion that you're in charge of something. Can't help myself. Big heart, that's my trouble. Ready so?"

Bram snapped another acorn from a nearby branch. "For what?"

"Sure and everyone knows riddles are a sprite's business." He wiggled his fingers, then drank deeply from a tankard that appeared next to him. "Get it right, and you walk away with the gold. Get it wrong, and I'll more than likely turn you into some class of fierce unfortunate creature. Standard enough."

"If I'm cursed, is there a cure?" Bram dropped another acorn into the haversack.

The sprite blew a smoke ring into the air. "Ah, now, I always leave a little door open, so I do. True love, more often than not. It's my soft spot."

Bram stroked the locket. "There, I'm well set."

"Fair play to you." The sprite flitted closer. "She's lovely, so she is."

"Correction, Sprite. She's beautiful, inside and out."

"Here's hoping so. What are you called, handsome?"

"Bram." He stripped more acorns and filled his back pocket.

"Well now, Bram. *Pleased to meet you* I cannot say, not with you robbing me blind like this." The sprite winked. "But you've got an earnest look about you, so I'll tell you truly—this curse is a desperate one. Once you've transformed, your identity is your secret to keep forever. Breathe your name, past, or family line to another soul and that soul is gone. Just like that. You can be with your loved ones, aye, but as a stranger to them. Always. A living death, if you will. So. Still want it? Or will you leave my gold and return from whence you came?"

Bram's pulse thudded harder than a blacksmith's hammer. It was time for him to couch his lance. All or nothing. No half measures.

"Do your worst." The acorn he dropped clinked against the others in his sack.

The branch before him bowed under the sprite's weight. "I admire your confidence. Now, listen close:

I am not claw nor tooth nor spell,
Yet I've tripped more knights than roots that swell.
I puff your chest and steal your sense—
Name me, shiny man of dents."

Nerves bubbled in Bram's gut as he repeated the first lines to himself. He should've paid better attention to the last bit, but he'd been too busy trying to memorize it all. Marigold had often accused him of this, paying attention to the first part of what she was saying to the exclusion of the rest.

"One more time?" Bram asked.

The autumn sprite flipped his palms skyward. "That's your lot. What's your answer, then, handsome?"

Bram closed his eyes to let the rhyme play back in his mind. *Not claw . . . tripped nights . . . steal sense . . .*

The answer clicked.

He snapped his eyes open. "Pride."

"Hmph." Orange glitter trailed the autumn sprite as he flitted to the edge of the tree's canopy. "Here now, Crispin," he called down to the prince. "Your man got it right. What'll I do with him?"

Bram narrowed his eyes. "What's going on?"

"Curse him anyway," Crispin shouted from below.

Fear sliced through Bram. The prince was in cahoots with the sprite? This would not end well for him. Unless he could slip away. As he stretched his foot down to the next weight-bearing limb, the velvety leaves tickled his ears.

"But he got it right, so he did!" the sprite shouted. "The curse won't take as well."

Crispin's voice cut sharper than a dagger between the ribs. "I said do it anyway! And make sure he can't leave this land, either. I don't want him seeking a mage's counsel."

The autumn sprite appeared directly in front of him. "Sorry, handsome. This one's out of my hands."

He tapped Bram's forehead.

Hot pain forked from the spot, eagerly arrowing from his head to his limbs, setting his skin and veins aflame. Bram's vision blurred as he gritted his teeth and held fast to the branches. He closed his eyes, breathed deeply, trying to ride it out until the agony subsided, but it was no use. He swayed.

As he fell, twigs and branches snapped along with his bones.

The earth met him with a mighty thump.

And blessedly, the stabbed-with-molten-metal sensation abated. His trial was over. He opened his eyes and found his questing party standing over him. Crispin smiled, Fergus had paled, and Kevin scratched his head. Coby, in the glimmer of the lamplight, wept.

"Have I died?" Bram sat up slowly.

His voice was strange in his ears, like he'd gargled prickly burrs and tar.

"No, but you'll wish you had." Crispin handed him one of the pauldrons he'd discarded before climbing the tree. "Look."

As he reached for the shining metal, cold washed over Bram. His enlarged hand was a deep mossy green. But there was no mistaking this was indeed his hand. The fleshy pad at the base of his thumb bore the shiny scar he'd earned when his blade had slipped while carving Marigold's unicorn charm.

Trembling, he looked at his reflection. The change was undeniable: green skin, two small tusks rising from his bottom jaw, pointy ears, black hair.

An orc.

He twisted onto his knees to retch. The sprite's orange glow hovered nearby. He was talking—something about true love and a list—before nausea overtook Bram again.

"Avoid my boots, please." Crispin crouched next to him. "I wish it hadn't come to this, but you pushed too much, too fast. I surround myself with beautiful people, yes, but I refuse to be outshone. At our last tournament, the cheers for you nearly met the volume of mine."

"They were louder," Bram growled.

Saints, this voice was more animal than man.

"Agree to disagree." Crispin tore the locket from Bram's neck. "Never fear. We'll be sure to tell your woman of your demise. Marigold is further evidence of your delusions of grandeur. As if a princess would marry a common fool like you. Kevin, the haversack."

As Kevin scooped up the gold-stuffed pack, Bram struggled to rise to his feet, then collapsed back to his knees. The metamorphosis rendered him as helpless as a newborn fawn. Fatigued him to the point of passing out.

"I'm not dead," Bram said as the stars spun above him.

"Might as well be." Crispin shook his head as he tsked. "Remember the condition of your curse—you can't reveal your identity to anyone, or they will die. From this point on, you are tethered to this plot of land. You'll live out your days on Grimroot Farm's forty hectares, known only as Jask Bone-Cracker. Sir Bram Duncan is no more."

Chapter 2

Three years later

Princess Marigold Ashford of Thornwick ducked under a low-hanging branch. *Pthht.* She spit out the pine needles that rained down on her and brushed away a speckling of sap.

Saints, she hated it out here.

Conceptually, forests were lovely. In practice they were riddled with bugs, monsters, and mud. She was more of an *herb garden and hedgerow maze* kind of naturalist. Horticulture was a refined, nature-adjacent activity which she vastly preferred to tramping through the deep forest on a moonless night.

The ghost of a cobweb slithered over her face.

"Ew, ew, ew," escaped her as she raked it away.

Revulsion pooled at the back of her throat. She refused to ponder the size of the spider that spun this drawbridge-sized trap. With clenched teeth, she bit back the shriek bubbling in her chest. Letting it rip would give away her location. The sound of nearby crackling meant she wasn't alone. She stilled, and the crunching grew quieter as whatever it was moved away.

The pounding of her heart threatened her ribs, but she walked on. At least there were no thunderstorms, which meant no death by lightning. Still, there was a chance she'd die out here. But she'd rather risk a fight with Windfall Woods' wildest creatures on her journey to the sanctuary in Mareval than march down the Briarveil Cathedral's aisle in three weeks' time.

Where Prince Crispin of Harvest Hollow would wait at the altar.

No, thank you. She liked him . . . not.

Despite her better instincts, she'd talked herself into accepting his proposal for the sake of her home kingdom of Thornwick. For three years after Bram died, she'd withdrawn from public life and immersed in the comfort of books. Until the day in the library where she, tucked in a quiet nook, overheard her parents' frustration that she wasn't doing her part to serve Thornwick. The mountain sprites were gaining northern territory, and both her brothers, Rowan and Beckett, were battling them on the frontier. The once-wealthy kingdom of Thornwick was hobbled as it devoted resources to the expensive war on the northern borders.

Then Crispin made his offer of marriage.

A union between them would be more than a familial alliance—it would be political, too. Crispin pledged defense support as well as food security and reserves. Harvest Hollow, known as the breadbasket for the five kingdoms of the Lunara Peninsula, could protect and feed Thornwick as it defended itself against the mountain sprites.

So, with one simple yes, she'd finally done her part to protect the kingdom.

During Prince Crispin's brief visit to Thornwick to finalize the financial and political terms of their marriage with her advisors, Marigold granted him a private audience. Not *too* private, mind. Her former nursemaid, now companion, Bess, waited outside the door. While their representatives negotiated the remaining details of the dower, succession rights of any children they produced, and her responsibilities once she joined his household, they commenced their first private conversation. All very pleasant and polite. Lacking sizzle, but tolerable.

Until, over a glass of claret, he said, "There's a rumor you possess a magical gift."

A rumor, if acknowledged, would land her in an oubliette. Though her hand trembled, her training kept a smile on her face. Thornwick banned magic fifty years ago, after a collective of wielders banded together in a secret plot to usurp her grandfather's crown. So it was *most* inconvenient when she, second in line to the throne, manifested a magical ability five years ago. In all the Lunara Peninsula, two people knew her secret—Bess, who'd never betray her, and Vera, the cunning woman who'd taught her to control the magic.

Unless . . . were spies in Thornwick Castle?

"Rumors are often false," she said. "Tell me more about your last hunt."

He set his empty glass on the table between them, then moved his king on the chessboard. The game was his suggestion, not hers. She much preferred Tables as there was an element of chance. Chess was all strategy, deep thought, and zero fun. Entertainment should not leave you with a tension headache.

"Let's not be coy, Marigold," he said smoothly. "The contracts are signed, and the wedding will proceed regardless. Harvest Hollow has a more progressive attitude toward magic than Thornwick. Truly, along with your stature, I hope my future children are charmed."

As though she were a broodmare, selected to contribute height and magic?

The firelight flickered in Crispin's beautiful eyes. Had she never met Bram, she might have been held in thrall by the prince's green gaze, his boyish grin, or the dimple that punctured his left cheek. But she *had* met Bram and knew all too well what sincere interest and admiration looked like. They were absent from Crispin's face.

"That's wonderfully tolerant of you, but I have no magic." She circled her gaze around the board to avoid his inspection and evaluated her gameplay options. *Ah—there.* With a fluid motion, she moved her queen into position. "Checkmate."

Satisfaction coiled through her. She might not love the game, but saints, she loved to win.

Crispin's gaze dropped to the board. "I haven't lost in years. Are you a master?"

"Hardly." Marigold lifted a shoulder. "My brothers like to play."

His laugh didn't reach his eyes. "My wife-to-be is clever, then. Good to know. At the risk of sounding indelicate, there's another rumor to discuss."

Another thing she missed about Bram—he'd always said what he meant, plainly. No hints or dramatic half statements. Innuendo especially prickled her skin, and she'd taken to bluntness to avoid misunderstandings.

"Oh?" She sorted the pieces into their appropriate places in the velvet-lined chess box, starting with the pawns. "And what might that be?"

From inside his jerkin, he withdrew a silver chain. "This. Found at the Lantern Oak, deep in the forest. A knight who died in my service several years ago wore it. Your knight, I believe? He spoke highly of your beauty, wit, and faithfulness. His worshipful adoration is what drew my attention to you, Princess. When my squire brought word of his demise, I did not send this with him. I thought to keep the affection a secret, to protect your modesty."

He dribbled the links onto the chessboard. As her younger

face smiled up at her from the open locket, Marigold's chest pinched. With much difficulty, she schooled her features. She shouldn't appear too eager to gather the necklace in front of her fiancé.

With the queen clenched in her fist, she said, "Thank you."

"I've said nothing about it. So, you see, I can keep a secret, if you can learn to trust me." The normally well-mannered prince shoved back abruptly from the gaming table. "Rest well, Princess Marigold. I enjoyed our match and look forward to your arrival at Brambleton Castle."

Wordlessly, she nodded.

Was he showing kindness? Or dominance?

A thought she'd pondered often as they'd packed her trousseau for her move to his home, where she'd learn the management of Brambleton Castle as their wedding date approached. During these last few weeks in Harvest Hollow, however, it became clearer than the waters of Amberglen Lake that Prince Crispin was obsessed with perfection, beauty, and her family's holdings—especially Thornwick's mineral-rich northern territories.

Missing from that list?

Her.

Opportunity abounded for Crispin to learn about her. Despite his endless talking, he asked her few questions. At first, she was grateful he let the topic of her rumored magical ability rest. Then, as their conversations droned on, she realized he asked her nothing about her upbringing, her thoughts on current affairs, her philosophies on life. No, his questions centered on when the dowry might arrive and if she needed a more fashionable hairdresser.

Clearly, his woo-pitching game needed work.

One of many examples—upon her arrival, he'd invited her to a candlelight supper. A good start, she'd thought. But as the evening wore on, it became clear his idea of conversation was enumerating his accomplishments as regent and pausing at the appropriate moments to allow her to swoon. Instead, she was tempted to swallow thorns to keep herself awake.

"It's as though he's never had to earn someone's interest," she'd complained to her companion, Bess. The older woman had initially served as her nursemaid but had become more of a chaperone since Marigold came of age.

"Give it time," Bess counseled as she turned down Marigold's bed. "He's a handsome fellow, isn't he? All those gold curls?"

"Yes," she'd agreed. Bram had been fair as well, but his flaxen hair had been long and thick, with the most enviable swoop at the ends. "But there's something vacant in his eyes. When he's looking at me, it's as though he's appraising me."

"You ponder much, child." Bess had blown out the bedside candle. "Tomorrow's another day to find common ground and learn to love him. You'll get there."

Bess could not have been more wrong, and what Marigold had overheard last evening proved it.

Which was why she was in the forest at the equinox's witching hour.

Spiders and mysterious cracklings aside, Windfall Woods possessed an ethereal beauty she hadn't appreciated in the first hours of her mad scramble. Fragmented moonlight scattered on the forest's floor like wish coins, and the trees' silvered bark served as signposts. In the distance, though it was not the right season for fireflies, golden orbs bobbed, beckoning to her as though the forest itself was determined to guide her through to safety.

Onward.

The duration of her travels was impossible to know, but her legs screamed at her to stop and take a break. Instead, she climbed over a fallen log and splashed in a mud puddle on the other side. Tired, hungry, and anxious as she was, she giggled as an unbidden memory popped into mind. During their first breakfast together, Crispin *had* asked her a personal question.

When do you prefer to perambulate? He feasted on egg whites and a foul-smelling green juice. *The chill fall air is good for the humors. Me? In addition to my training, I walk several times per day to keep my waist trim.*

He then pointedly sketched his glance between *her* waist and her breakfast of simple toast, butter, and blackberry jam. *Message received, Prince.* She'd certainly perambulated her ass away from Brambleton Castle, hadn't she?

Saints, he was so different from her true love.

She rubbed at the ache Bram's memory conjured in her chest. Long ago she'd felt lucky to have found him at such a young age. He'd fallen for her when she was awkward and less self-assured. At the time, it had seemed a blessing, because she could trust he'd loved *her.* Not the beauty she'd grown into or the title that had increased in importance. But now she wondered if it wasn't a curse. In comparison to Bram, all men were lacking.

A hooting owl flew overhead.

Her knees wobbled as she started, and she sprawled across the path. A bramble scratched her cheek. With a hiss, she pressed her palm to the spot to ease the sting. From the inner pocket of her dowdy cloak, her cat, Fuzzle yowled.

"Sorry, Fuzz." She reached inside to scratch behind his tiny ear.

During her second week in Harvest Hollow, she was still willing to try to find common ground with Crispin. Pets seemed a safe topic. In addition to his stables and the farm animals, the prince kept at least a dozen hounds and as many falcons.

"Animals make such lovely companions, don't you think?" she'd asked.

They'd paused to enjoy the late-blooming roses, which was where she'd noted the servant's gate that would eventually lead to her freedom.

"I do." Crispin had nodded. "My gyrfalcons are the envy of Harvest Hollow. Second only to my stag hounds. No one can believe the quality of their pedigree."

Saints, this man turned every conversation back to rank.

"Do they keep you company, though?" She plucked a rose to dry and steep in her morning tisanes.

"Only when I'm hosting nobles. They make an excellent backdrop."

Vile to use creatures for scenery.

"Don't you find them to be comforting? If it weren't for my cat, Fuzzle, after . . ."

She'd stopped herself before confiding that Fuzzle's warm cuddles kept her sane while she grieved for Bram. Instinct told her she couldn't trust Crispin with that level of intimacy. Not yet. Maybe if he—

"About the cat. You'll need to quarter it in the barn. They make me sneeze."

That was it. That was *the* moment she'd hatched her plan to leave Harvest Hollow. She'd spent the last week dodging Bess in the markets to assemble her escape kit.

Her first plan, the forthright one, was to have a discreet—but honest—conversation with Crispin. She would admit she held no affection for him and allow him to confess the same. Though the marriage contracts were signed, they could agree to lead married but separate lives. This discussion could not go through third parties, however, and it would be best to surprise him with it. As she entered the servants' hallway she'd learned to navigate since she arrived, she approached the hidden entrance to Crispin's privy chamber.

The conversation she overheard shocked her to her core.

With her fingers pressed to her mouth to stifle a gasp, she learned the awful truth. As he clinked glasses with Kevin, his man-at-arms, Crispin celebrated the wedding banns to be announced during tomorrow's services at Briarveil Cathedral.

"Years of planning, Kevin, and it's all tumbling into place," Crispin said triumphantly. "After the wedding, the mountain sprites will rend Rowan and Beckett Ashford limb from limb, leaving Marigold the undisputed heir to the Thornwick throne. Her grief will consume her, and I'll put her away at Scarlet Spire to take the sea air, leaving me, per the marriage negotiations, to rule both Harvest Hollow and Thornwick as one sovereign. What says the spy?"

"The House of Ashford is all crest and no coin." Sir Kevin's voice reminded her of the dank and dark catacombs of Thornwick. "The wars have stripped their coffers to the bone. This marriage and your support pull them from the fire."

"Excellent. The deeper in debt they are, the less likely her parents will be to contest Marigold's placement by the sea. I'll finally have unfettered access to Thornwick's minerals and boot the peasants who live atop that fortune."

Marigold backed away from the door and forced herself to hurry back to her rooms on quiet feet. Thankfully, Bess was sleeping, leaving Marigold to devise her escape. With Fuzzle in her lap, she lifted her quill to draft a warning letter to her parents.

No—Crispin said he had a spy.

Surely any correspondence betwixt she and her family at Thornwick would be read by his operative, if delivered at all. Instead, she drafted a coded letter to her twin, Rowan, who was stationed at the Gildfall Mountains, to the north. Spies might surround him as well, but a benefit of twinhood was the indecipherable secret language they shared.

She tapped her chin as she worked through the logistics.

The letter might not reach him for ages since he currently served on the northern borders. Even if he sailed the Sea of Red Tides on the *Orvale*, the navy's fastest ship, she couldn't expect a speedy escort home. The marriage contracts were in place, it was true, but she and Crispin were not yet married. Once they spoke their vows, she would have no leverage.

Marigold shivered. No, she'd need to hide elsewhere. *Aha!* She knew just the place.

With hasty strokes of her quill, she explained to Rowan in code that he and Beckett were in danger at Crispin's hand. Then, she outlined her plan—she'd slip the castle and seek sanctuary at their distant cousin's hermitage in Mareval. The smallest of the Lunara Peninsula's five kingdoms, Mareval shared Harvest Hollow's southern border. It served as the region's religious seat, and through the Lunaran Treaty, none of the other kingdoms could invade it. She'd need to cross the Shivering Dales to get there, but once through, Rowan could escort her home.

Yes, this was a good strategy.

Her—*blech*—betrothed would think her likely to bolt directly to Thornwick. She'd avoid main roads and ports, as Crispin would have eyes there. Working most in her favor was how she famously hated the out-of-doors. He'd never anticipate she'd choose a path through heavily wooded landscapes.

Her plan must succeed. For her brothers, herself, and the whole of Thornwick.

Three generations ago, overzealous mining had turned the Marches into a noxious, barren landscape. The frontier dividing Harvest Hollow and Thornwick still had not recovered from the devastation. Her grandfather enacted laws preventing such looting, but Crispin clearly did not care about laws, her people, or the earth itself.

After a sleepless night, she escaped Bess's company long enough to hire a private messenger to spirit the letter to Rowan. After that, all she could do was bide her time at Brambleton Castle, waiting for an escape.

Luck presented an opportunity three days later. While the attendants Crispin assigned to Marigold smoothed ointments into her skin and brushed her hair until it shone like copper before her slumber, they revealed Crispin had summoned the exchequer for an urgent meeting about the cost of his extensive renovation efforts.

He'd be in counsel for hours.

After the attendants left, she and Bess drank their usual bedtime blackberry-and-mint tisane as they discussed the next day's itinerary. While her companion ticked things on the list, Marigold feigned interest and *might* have slipped five drops of her precious poppy sap into Bess's cup. She regretted drugging her, but with her brothers' lives on the line, she couldn't risk tipping her hand to anyone.

Marigold inspected her companion's features. Was she Crispin's spy? Either way, the less she knew, the better. A solo escape was Marigold's only choice.

With an apologetic yawn, Bess disappeared through their adjoining door. Marigold turned the skeleton key, then hurried to her armoire.

First, packing.

Five chaotic minutes later, Fuzzle climbed into her half-filled trunk. Beneath the marmalade cat's tummy lay three kirtles, her herbal-remedy kit, a brush, a looking glass, ribbons, a week's worth of undergarments, linen shifts, hose, and a few meals she'd scavenged from the dinner buffets.

"Don't you fall asleep in there," she warned the cat.

Next, her disguise.

From their hiding place in the armoire, Marigold shook out

a doll-sized homespun dress and cloak. With a snap of her fingers, blue sparks fell toward the garments. As the clothing grew to full size, she shed her fine sleeping gown and slipped into the homespun. *Hmm.* The apothecary's wife, with whom she traded a volume of romantic poetry for these clothes, must've been a few inches shorter than she was. A scandalous amount of her ankle peeped from under the hem.

Nothing to do about it now.

Her minimancy magic only shrank things or restored them to their natural size. No enlarging. Vera, Thornwick's cunning woman, taught her how to wield this gift when it first emerged five years ago. She hadn't dared write of it to Bram, knowing his suspicions of magic.

After securing her sheathed pruning knife and leather bourse to her belt, she circled her gaze around this room for the last time. Her heart skipped a beat when she landed on the book of fairy tales. Had she really almost left it behind?

She traced its embossed leather cover with her fingers.

Parting with these pages was impossible. Her father had given her the book when she'd turned eight, the same year Bram had given her the unicorn charm. Her two greatest treasures, and one was already lost to her forever.

Marigold hugged the volume to her chest.

Grief unspooled inside her, fast and familiar. She wiped a trickle from her face. Tears were good. Better than the sludgy numbness that had wrapped around her when Bram died, which still hadn't relaxed its grip years later when Crispin offered for her hand. Hence her resigned pragmatism when she accepted the offer for the good of Thornwick.

Marigold's parents, before accepting on her behalf, asked if she might love Crispin one day, and she shrugged with a noncommittal *Perhaps.* Truthfully, she wasn't greedy enough to expect true love to visit her again.

As the time grew nearer to relocate to Harvest Hollow, much to her surprise, her frozen emotions began to thaw. In the kingdom where Bram spent his last days, she could almost make memories with him again as she ate the cider doughnuts, drank the ale, and visited the bookshop he'd described in his letters.

Ooh, his letters.

She'd pack the tidy bundle of those, too. Rescued from their hiding place inside the leg of her riding boots, she tossed them into the trunk, along with the book. Fuzzle, perturbed by the disturbance, hopped out. Alas, she'd need to leave the large portrait of her family behind. Another snap, more sparks, and her trunk reduced to the size of a pot of face cream. She slipped it into her bourse.

"I'm sorry, Fuzz." She knelt to peep under the bed. "I can't carry you long distances at this size."

Yellow eyes blinked at her. She understood the cat's resistance. Minimizing was easy, but returning to full size caused nausea, fatigue, and a headache. Not unlike befuddlement caused by overindulging in cheap wine, so, best left to emergencies.

Which this was, of course.

"It's the last time, I promise." She snagged the cat by the collar, then snapped her fingers. The blue sparks rendered the tabby the size of a mouse. An angry, hissing mouse. After scooping him up, she pocketed him.

One final thing to collect—the locket she'd shared with Bram. On Bess's advice, she'd stopped wearing it when they'd left for Thornwick. Wearing her dead true love's portrait could send the wrong signal to her betrothed. She clasped it at her nape, then dropped the now-whole pendant below her neckline.

Last step, the decoy.

From the chest at the foot of her bed, she withdrew linens,

then stuffed them into a dress Crispin had given her upon her arrival. She'd worn it once and promised herself it would never touch her body again. The bodice was cut far too low for her taste, and the skirts were shot through with stiff gold thread. As with most things crafted at Crispin's behest, this was gaudy, showy, and impractical.

But the dress would make a fine dummy.

After tucking the false princess under the coverlet, she pinched her chin between her thumb and forefinger and surveyed her work. Not bad. By the glow of the fireplace's banked coals, the figure in her bed might fool Bess if she woke from her drugged slumber. With luck, this would buy her an eight-hour lead.

From the atlas her parents sent with her, she tore the map of the Lunara Peninsula and its five kingdoms that formed a star—Thornwick to the north, Harvest Hollow to the west, Mareval in the center, Rashemba to the south, and Cinderfield to the east. She measured out the journey to the monastery in Mareval. Barring sudden storms or other interference, on foot, she'd arrive in three days' time.

Now, escape.

With a dramatic flourish, she shrouded herself in the humble cloak. She checked her reflection in the vanity's looking glass. Oh, *that* would never do. Her wild red curls cascaded from the hood like she was bearing a standard that screamed, *Marigold, Princess of Thornwick, is under here!* Her nimble fingers thatched it into a braid, then twisted that into a thick bun.

This time when she looked in the glass, a giddy bubble expanded in her chest.

Now she could pass for a non-royal.

On hinges that she'd oiled with excess beauty ointments, she eased open her door. No guards stood in the hall this evening, as though destiny itself wanted her to flee. In her well-worn gardening turn shoes, Marigold tiptoed twenty paces, then slipped down the servants' stairs to the kitchen. At this time of night, the only person present was the dozing scullery maid. Marigold smiled at the sweet-faced young lady.

She'd always been more comfortable around regular folk than royalty.

How could she not? Her father had been the third son of a king and entertained zero expectations that he'd take the throne. She and her brothers were allowed to play with the children of their noble house's servants. Then, death and abdication eliminated first Thornwick's heir, then the spare, and Papa ascended in a surprise twist after Bram left.

More food would make for a more pleasant journey, but Marigold left the loaf of bread untouched. This young one would catch the blame for any stolen food. On fleet feet, the princess escaped through the kitchen door to the service yard, then through the postern and toward the garden exit.

That was both many hours and a lifetime ago.

Fuzzle meowed another complaint. Nothing that couldn't be cured with a snack. Luckily, she carried a treat container in her bourse. From her cloak's inner pocket, he raised his kitten-sized head. As she fed him small cut of cubed chicken, she booped his pink triangle of a nose.

The cat narrowed its eyes, then retreated to her pocket.

She laughed at his annoyance. "Don't be such a sourpuss, Fuzz."

Marigold glanced skyward. The North Star winked like they had a secret between them. According to the overall star pattern, she was headed southeast, toward the border where she'd cross the Shivering Dales and into Mareval, where she'd shelter with her cousin until Rowan arrived to escort her home to inform her family of Crispin's plot.

Surely, she was almost through the Windfall Woods? On

the map they'd seemed small and contained, but the scale might have been off. Or her skill at quickly crossing vast territory on foot had dulled with disuse? The reason didn't matter—she had no choice but to press on. To cross a bubbling brook, she hopped on large lichen-coated stones, then pushed through a scrim of willow branches.

She gasped.

A gorgeous, stout oak stood in front of her. This must have been what she'd mistaken for fireflies in the distance. Floating amber orbs glowed among its limbs, illuminating its immense size. Families could make a home in each of its larger branches. Given the width of its trunk, it must've been ancient. What must this tree have seen in all its years? Battles, deaths, weddings, births. And now at least one runaway princess.

She pressed her hands to the rough trunk. "You're a special one, aren't you?"

Goose bumps slid along Marigold's nape as the tree's energy hummed through her. Saints, she was tired. She'd sit here, in the crook of this tree's roots for a quick minute. Gnarled as they were, the crenelated pockets were cozier than a hammock in the springtime. Five minutes of resting her feet and eyes. That was all she needed to tackle the rest of the journey back to Thornwick.

She drew her knees to her chest, then rested her forehead against them.

Five minutes.

Hunting dogs' howls startled her awake.

Oh, shite, the sky had pinked. That five minutes might have been five hours. Every damned mile she'd gained between Brambleton and here was lost. Those must've been Crispin's stag hounds. Except they were not foxing, no—they were looking for a russet creature of a different sort.

The air screamed in her lungs as she ran.

She would *not* be caught, not by a man like him, and not when her brothers' lives were at risk. The longer she stayed out of Crispin's grasp, the better.

Abruptly, the woods ended in a meadow. She picked up her skirts and sprinted across the flat green field bordered by a blaze of sunflowers. Beyond those tall happy yellow blossoms lay a collection of tidy pumpkin fields. In the cool morning air, the rich scent of the gourds and . . . apples, maybe? . . . graced the wind.

Were she not the subject of a hunt, she'd stop to appreciate the adorable farm.

Instead, Marigold focused her attention on the cottage beyond the fields. Its windows glowed with cozy firelight. Whoever lived there was home and hopefully awake enough to answer the door.

"Please be sympathetic to a damsel in distress," she whispered.

With the dogs wilding in the distance, Marigold ran toward her salvation.

Chapter 3

Bram tossed another log onto the fire.

Outside, Barnaby the rooster greeted dawn like a long-lost friend. As well timed as the shriek was, the rooster did not reserve it for sunrise. Midday, midnight—the actual clock mattered not to Barnaby. This past night, however, Bram hadn't minded. Had he not been awake, he might not have felt the shivers that signaled someone crossing the borders of Grimroot Farm.

Did the autumn sprite know that the same magic that restricted Bram to this large patch of land also warned him of trespassers? Since the wheel of the year had turned again to autumn, he could hike over to the Lantern Oak and ask the sprite, but he preferred not to twist this curse further.

No, he'd stay right here on the farm proper.

Most trespassers ran off at the mere sight of his immense green body and under tusks. The only person who hadn't been frightened off in the three years since "Jask" arrived was Alfred the Carter. The wizened delivery man claimed to have seen it all, wasn't bothered by orcs, and they'd struck up an amiable acquaintanceship.

Bram missed people, but he didn't relish people screaming in fear.

Thus, he'd learned to keep his own company well.

The fresh log popped in the hearth. *Hmph, must not have*

dried that properly. More pops and—*wait*—that wasn't the log. Someone was knocking at his door. He'd ignore it. It was too early for screams.

The divan he'd built for himself protested as he flopped onto it.

The knocking continued. Persistent wretch, whoever it was. Bram set his feet on the trunk next to his carving knife and the menagerie of forest creatures he'd carved, then sipped his chicory. Though he preferred coffee, a beverage he'd enjoyed on a journey with Crispin, it was hard to come by out here in the hinterlands. So, chicory it was. Bitter and brown as the earth it sprang from, the beverage was smoky on the tongue.

Saints, could the person knocking not take a hint?

The last thing he wanted to do was frighten another poor soul, but he was running out of options. Mustering his best, deepest, dangerous orc voice, he yelled, "Go away!"

The knocking stopped.

"No?" The woodpeckerish knocking redoubled. "I will not."

He raked his hand down his face and set his mug on the crate. As he stomped toward his sizable door, the floorboards rattled under his feet. Through the wood, he growled, "Go away if you know what's good for you."

"Please, sir, I have nowhere to go."

The *sir* was a nice assumption. An ill-informed one, though. Likely naivete, because, based on the voice, either a woman or child stood on the other side of the door. Bram pressed his forehead to the oak. *Dammit.* No matter his intentions, he'd frighten them off. He'd open the door, they'd scream or faint, and once again he'd be reminded of the monster he'd become.

Might as well rip off the bandage.

"Not my problem." With a mighty heave, he raised the bar, then whipped open the door. "Leave, or I'll—"

On a gasp, Bram's knees buckled.

His sweet Marigold.

Behind her, the rising sun gilded the furrowed farmland that spread like a chessboard from the cottage. That same sun sent a strategic beam directly to his porch. Though she was pale, dawn blessed her with an angelic glow. The mischievous smile that curved her lips, however, belied the halo.

"Or you'll what?" she asked.

He caught the doorframe to hold himself upright. It *couldn't* be her. He must have fallen asleep after all, and dreams tortured him yet again. That was the only explanation. But this Marigold did not match his memory. Instead of the silks that were her custom, she wore an ordinary homespun dress and cloak. Both revealed a scandalous amount of the ankles he'd caressed and massaged after she'd spent an uncomfortable day in fine new shoes.

He glanced at his hand, the one that threatened to splinter the frame.

Still green. This was no dream.

Another shiver rolled through him, making him tremble. If it was the magic that signaled a trespasser or a desire to sweep this woman into his arms, he couldn't say. But he kept his grip on the solid wood to stay his determined hands. He imagined Marigold's reaction at being unexpectedly embraced by an enormous orc. Terror would be the only logical response, and the last thing he wanted was to terrorize his true love.

"Are you all right?" She reached toward his shoulder, but he jerked away. Her touch would be too much to bear.

"Leave off," he growled. Air refused to come in the amount he wanted, so he was forced to gulp like a fish that had flung itself on shore.

She glanced over her shoulder. "Will you invite me in?"

Saints, her melodic voice was a balm to his soul. In his time here, he worried he'd forgotten her particular timbre. He had not. Honey and fizz by day; whiskey at night when she was overcome with desire. Which he should *not* think about.

"Kind sir?" She locked her blue gaze on his. "Seeing as how you haven't objected to my request, I'll take that as a yes."

She ducked under his arm and pushed her way to the middle of the cottage. He swooned a second time as her scent, like a breeze through an orchard, carried him back to their days in Thornwick. As children, romping in the paddocks and meadows. Then, as they grew older and the seeds of their childhood affection blossomed, sneaking off into hideaways that would allow them to love each other.

Chivalrously, of course.

Even before he was a knight, he was unfailingly courteous. After the curse turned him, he'd tried to remain the same. As strangers rambled across Grimroot Farm, he'd attempt a pleasant exchange, but they scampered away in fear. With his additional foot of height, thickened proportions, pointy ears, tusks, and deep green skin, they assumed him a murderous barbarian. Eventually, he decided to play the role. Much easier to live down to people's expectations than set himself up for disappointment.

But Marigold hadn't run.

Ironic, that. She was the one person in the five kingdoms that should keep her distance.

The secret of his identity stuck in his throat. All he wanted to do was shout that he was her Bram, returned to her after too many torturous years. But the curse meant the truth would kill her. He'd lost much in this life already—his name, his form, his place in the world. He'd lost Marigold as well, but because of the curse, she was not safe with him.

She must go.

"You can't come in," he growled.

"I already have." Marigold popped her hands onto her hips. "It seems we're at an impasse."

Even on his moodiest days, the juicy curve of her lips could magic a smile from him. He was a sunflower to her sun, basking in her levity. For her sake, though, he would glower and shout and stomp and scare her into leaving. Even if the playful sparks in her eye made him want to fall to his knees and beg for mercy.

"Go." He jabbed at the door. "Now."

"Oh, honestly, good sir, would you turn a princess out into the wild?" She pressed her palm to her chest. "I've traveled all night and am dead on my feet. I won't be a bother. Is your wife at home? Perhaps she and I can speak."

Marigold scanned the room as she rotated on her heel, presumably looking for another more reasonable person to charm. What did she see as she turned from where he stood in front of the door? With a hummingbird's speed, her gaze alit on the kitchen, then the dining area tucked under the loft, the stairs, the back door, and the hearth around which he'd arranged the divan, a rocking chair, and large, soft reading chair.

Her silence chafed like poison ivy between his shoulder blades.

What did she think of his humble home? Half the furniture was built by his hands; the rest he'd found here and since repaired. To his eye, it was quaint and rustic. The Marigold he'd known would think the same. But perhaps she'd changed in the last five years, and now she'd consider it shabby? Marigold remained silent, tapping her chin, as she ventured toward the shelves lining the wall on either side of the fireplace.

He should've guessed the books would attract her attention first.

"I have no wife," he grumbled to the woman to whom he'd pledged undying love.

"But you have so many books." Marigold ran her index finger along the spines.

Through Alfred, his lifeline to the markets of Harvest Hollow, he'd arranged with Brumet's Books to deliver a fresh tale each week. Along with his other hobbies, reading helped stave off boredom during the past three years he'd been chained to Grimroot Farm.

"What do books have to do with a wife?"

"In my experience, more women read for pleasure. Were these a collection of instruction manuals or atlases or religious texts, that would be one thing. But they are all novels, poems, and philosophies."

As she tipped her head back to read the titles among the stacked shelves, her hood fell back. His chest tightened as his past cannonballed into his present. Marigold fashioned her hair in a long braid tucked into a bun, the same style she preferred when they adventured in the woods as children. But her rebellious curls, the ones he'd spent hours running his fingers through, would not be tamed. They leapt free and framed her face.

In much the same way he'd like to with his hands.

"Oh, this is a good one." She pulled a volume from the shelf, flipped through it, then returned it. "The lack of a wife explains the mess," she remarked, looking around the room.

"What mess?" He'd done the dishes and tidied up after supper.

"I mean . . ." She circled her hands as she revolved on her heel. "Your home is charming, I'll grant you. Especially the outside, with the intricately carved jack-o'-lanterns. They were a beacon to the stairs. But inside? Every surface is cluttered. The chest is covered in wooden carvings, the chair possesses a library's worth of reading material, the kitchen table is full of farming tools, and the counters are stacked with bakeware."

"Apologies, Princess. I wasn't expecting company." He folded his arms and leaned against a support beam, tracking her movements around the cottage. She moved with grace, more confident than the last time they'd been together.

She lifted a carved squirrel from the surface covered in shavings. After turning it around and inspecting its tail, she set it back down. "My lady's companion always said a tidy room is the sign of an organized mind."

That companion, Bess, also often said, *Clay does not mix with gold.* Implying he and Marigold should not be friends, let alone true loves. So, her advice on that or any other topic wasn't worth a split pumpkin to him.

"Duly noted. Now leave."

She *must* go. The longer she remained, the greater the torture.

"First, kind sir, do I smell pumpkin pie?" She splayed her fingers across her midsection. "Apple as well, if I'm not mistaken. My favorites, and I'm famished after my long journey."

Her nose was as excellent as ever. "Get out."

She lifted a shoulder. "Come now, surely you can do better than that for a princess."

Do not *smile.* He did his best to exude grumpiness.

"On my honor, I'll consider leaving if you feed me any morsel you have to spare." She closed the distance between them, then stuck out her hand. "But first, an introduction. I'm Princess Marigold of Thornwick. And you are?"

He crossed his arms. "Displeased. Go before I eat you."

"I can't recommend it. I'm sure I'm gamey. Also, it's rude to leave me aloft." She waggled her hand. "Please, let's be friends."

If wisdom prevailed, he'd keep his hands neatly tucked under his arms. This body changed the way he interacted with the world, with its sensitive ears and nose and ability to see in the dark. But Bram had never been accused of being wise, and this might be his last chance in this life to touch her. As he wrapped his large warm green hand around her smaller, cooler one, relief flooded him. His memory matched the soft and strong reality of her, like she was steel wrapped in velvet.

With an arched eyebrow, she said, "Now that we're friends, about that pie . . ."

That was his Marigold. Large of appetite, especially for sweets. She'd once destroyed an entire pumpkin loaf he'd purchased after winning a purse at his first knight's tournament. Feeding her would go faster than arguing with her, but he'd make it unpleasant.

"We're not friends." He dished out a slice of each while she sat in his rocking chair. "But I'll trade food for information. How did you end up on this farm?"

"That's a long story." She unlaced her boots. "May I have a drink as well? I'm parched."

Hmph. Removing shoes was not a sign of someone expecting to depart after breakfast. In her stockinged feet, she padded into the kitchen. After two heaves of the spring water pump he'd installed in the kitchen, she washed her hands in the basin.

He poured a mug of chicory, then set it next to her plate. "Tell it, fast."

"Curious, aren't you?" She elegantly sat on the stool at the butcher's block. "Well, congratulations. You're the first person to learn I've run away from my betrothed."

Her betrothed? Bram's guts twisted like he'd eaten rotten meat. His under tusks pressed sharply into his lip as he clamped his mouth shut. Only a fool would expect her to be enduringly faithful to a ghost. Wait, though—she said she was running away.

So maybe she hadn't found true love again?

"Who is he?" Stupid of him to ask. He truly did not want to know who'd made a play for the heart of his sweet Marigold.

"I'll keep that to myself—thank you." She closed her eyes as she sampled the apple pie.

Her low, satisfied moan stirred him. He held tight to the counter and tried not to stare at her luscious mouth. Another problem with this orc body—in it, his temper flared hotter, as did his passions.

"Saints, that's perfection. Just like the apple pie from home." She pounded a delicate fist on the table. "Are you a baker?"

He grunted without answering, though warmth spread through his chest. After the first six months of barely leaving his bed, he'd thrown himself into his hobbies. It helped. After tending the farm and his animals, those hobbies—whittling, reading, and baking—occupied most nights. It had taken him ages to figure out the Thornwick recipe.

"You should sell these at the market." She cut another bite from the apple wedge, then sampled the pumpkin pie. Her low moan returned, this time accompanied by a dramatic swoon. "That may be better than the apple. What do I taste in the pumpkin? It has a warm, herbal backbone."

Everything in him wanted to boast that he'd infused the cream with bay leaf to balance the sweetness—another Thornwick-style trick. But if he spilled that secret, who knew what else she'd ask and where he'd stop? Much better to keep up with the grunting.

"I'm going to assume your grunting is grudging agreement with my appreciation of your culinary skills." She sipped her chicory, then pulled a face. "Unlike the pies, this is vile. Did you brew it from the hearth's ashes?"

"It's chicory," he answered. Alfred had recommended it, and Bram also thought it vile when he'd first tried it. "It's an acquired taste."

"It tastes like a skunk's ass."

He turned his snort-laugh into another grunt.

"Don't worry, though," she said. "My herbal blends will change your life. I'll make one for breakfast tomorrow."

His mouth turned to cotton. As much as he wanted her at his side until the end of time, the temptation to reveal his identity would be too great. One slipup would be fatal to her. No, he couldn't chance it. She had to go.

"The deal was pie, then you hit the road." He jerked his thumb over his shoulder. "Nothing but crumbs on your plate, and the door's that way."

Unfazed, Marigold sipped her chicory, frowned, then put it down again. "No, the deal was I'd *consider* leaving. After careful consideration, I decided I will not. How lucky are you?"

From the yard, Barnaby crowed at the early-morning sun.

"You can't stay." Maybe if he said it enough, she'd believe it.

She set her fork down, then folded her hands. "I must. Not for long—I swear it. I have a good plan, but I need a moment to regroup. Allow me to stay while I sort out my next step. I promise I won't be a bother. You won't even notice I'm here."

Oh, he'd notice. "No."

"No?" She knit her russet brows in confusion. "No one's ever . . . Look, I hate to pull the sovereign card, but I *am* a princess, and you're duty-bound to chivalrously protect me."

In Thornwick, she'd quizzed him on the chivalric code to help him study. What she'd quoted was true. However . . .

"Only knights must be chivalrous. As you can see, I'm a humble pumpkin farmer. Therefore, exempt from the code. And you need to go."

"But you—"

Dogs brayed outside.

Her fork clattered against her plate. She whipped her gaze toward the door, eyes widened. Anger sizzled through Bram. Not at her—*never* at her—but the person responsible for her fear. He squeezed his fists at his sides. Allowing Marigold to stay was impossible. She'd be safer with the villain on the other side of the door than here with him. Protecting her had always been his top priority, even if it meant protecting her from himself.

In a whirl of homespun cotton, she hid behind his chair. "Help me. Please."

The *please* twisted his heart. He should not do this.

And yet.

"Will you leave me be afterward?"

She nodded. "Yes, I swear on my father's crown."

"Hide."

With a grunt he buckled himself into his boots, then opened the door. The chill air on the porch was welcome against his heated skin. Unwelcome, on the other hand, were the braying dogs and half dozen knights on horseback who bore a crest he'd once worn but now loathed. A tall, well-dressed blond man dismounted.

Prince Crispin.

He was Marigold's betrothed?

Blood and bones, *no.* Not him. *Anyone* but him. Bram would lay down his life to stop her from marrying this evil, preening pumpkin-skull. He shut the door behind him, unwilling to take the chance that Marigold could overhear any part of this long overdue conversation.

The knights surrounded his porch. The gold hoops in Bram's left ear jingled as he twitched it. The slide of steel from sheath was unmistakable. Even with his augmented strength, he was outnumbered. Still, he flexed his fingers.

Crispin dismounted, then approached with wide-open arms and a wolfish grin. "Jask, my old friend! How do you fare this morning?"

Bram leaned against the porch pillar. "Full of piss and vinegar. You?"

"Distressed." Crispin pouted. "My betrothed has lost her way in the Windfall Wood."

Bram would bet his boulder-sized pumpkin Crispin practiced his expressions in the looking glass.

"Oh?" He inspected his fingernails. "Too bad, though I'd choose dangers of the wood over marrying you if I were her."

The prince glared. "Where is she, orc?"

"How should I know?" Bram shrugged.

"Liar." Crispin pointed to the dogs bounding over the pumpkins in the patch. "My hounds have traced Princess Marigold's scent here. To you."

He dropped his jaw in false surprise. "My Marigold?"

Please let him buy this. Bram was no actor, but he'd wager Crispin was unpracticed at reading an orc's reactions.

"Correction," Crispin said. "*My* Marigold. The banns have been announced."

Bram dramatically closed his eyes and punched the pillar. Something cracked in his knuckles. Huh, he thought orc strength would've splintered the pillar. Also—*ow.* But his bloodied knuckles reminded him of a plausible reason Crispin's best-in-class dogs tracked Marigold here. From his pocket, he withdrew a cotton handkerchief edged with lace. In the corner, Marigold had embroidered her initials and family crest in Thornwick's violet hue.

He waved it like a white flag.

"Of course they traced her here. You've stolen my life and my love." He growled more than spoke. Might as well give them the *real* orc show. "Now you want to steal my last memento of her? She gave me this favor during my last tournament in Thornwick."

Crispin, a predictably petty bully, snatched it from him, then held it to his nose.

"It carries her scent," the prince said.

Bram hated parting with it, but if it encouraged Crispin to leave, it was a worthy sacrifice.

"But . . ." Crispin tucked the kerchief into his brigandine's sleeve. "It does not explain the trail the hounds picked up in the woods. Men, search the house."

The knights knocked Bram aside and streamed into the cottage. Much as he wanted to clap their skulls together with a satisfying thwack, he kept his hands at his sides. Anything else would raise Crispin's suspicion.

Please let Marigold be as good at hiding as she'd been as a child.

Chapter 4

From her vantage point behind the darning basket, the ransacking knights looked huge. Well, they *were* huge. Compared to her anyway. Right after jamming her feet back into her turn shoes, she'd snapped herself down to squirrel size. Fuzzle had wakened, and in his double-shrunken state, she was able to satisfy him with a cheese crumb she'd found next to the chair.

This grumpy orc really could use a few housekeeping lessons.

"Shh," she whispered to Fuzzle. "We must be patient."

For ten minutes, she held her breath behind the collection of shirts and hose that needed to be mended while the knights thrashed and tossed the orc's belongings. She brought this upon him like a diseased blanket. Had she bypassed his cottage, had she not strong-armed him into feeding her, he'd be out picking pumpkins and tending his animals. Not watching the prince's personal guard ransack his home.

She fisted her hands in apologetic anger.

Crispin's sadistic and disproportionate responses were yet another reason to run away and seek sanctuary with allies. She felt terrible about inflicting wanton destruction on an innocent person's life.

To calm her breathing, she listed the actions she'd undertake as soon as Crispin and his poxy knights cleared out. First, help the orc set the cottage to rights. Second, evaluate if she'd veered off course, and if so, how far. Third, plot her new path toward Mareval. Fourth, beg the orc for a horse to speed her journey. Fifth, run like hell.

The smashing slowed.

Amid the flying feathers, a knight crunched through the pottery bits scattered on the floor. She ducked under the rocking chair as he paused nearby. His shiny greaves were close enough to see her reflection from where she'd hidden in the basket.

"Oi, she's not here," he groused. "Clear the home."

The ill-mannered knights left the door open as they clanged outside in their light armor. The disturbed air in the cottage drifted back to calm. She pressed her palms to her eyes and drank a deep breath to relax her pounding pulse. Her unsatisfied and unaware stomach growled.

Hopefully, the pies were unscathed.

Outside, Crispin's voice rose above the din. "My guard will continue patrolling the hinterlands until my betrothed is found. I'm sure she's been kidnapped by blackguards. Speak to no one about this, orc."

"Who would I talk to out here?" the orc grumbled.

She covered her mouth to mask her giggle.

"If she arrives on your doorstep, signal immediately."

The orc grunted—neither a yes nor a no.

His preferred way of communicating, it would seem. Honestly, with Crispin? That was the only appropriate response. From her first day at Harvest Hollow, she should've grunted at him instead of trying to talk. But then he'd probably would have already shipped her off to the Sea of Red Tides to "take the air" as he had his older sister, Princess Rosamund.

His staff gossiped far too much during evening ablutions.

Hoofbeats rattled the floorboards as the company pounded away from the cottage. The orc returned and closed the door, then slowly scanned the damage. Marigold remained in her minimized state. At this size, she had the advantage. She hadn't been able to properly look at her host.

Not without being rude anyway.

People staring at her like she was an animal in a menagerie was a professional princess hazard. She'd never wish to do that to another person, but this was her first time meeting an orc. She'd read about his kind in the broadsheets, of course, but she assumed the paper's contents were at least half fiction, bait intended to hook a reader's eyes and sell more copies. For example, they'd said orcs were of low intelligence, and that was already provably false. And the renderings were frightening, all jagged teeth and small red eyes.

Not so with this fellow.

He *was* large and green. That, they'd gotten right. *Green* was insufficient, however. His skin matched the dark rich tone of an emerald, like those in her father's crown. His jet hair fell past his shoulders and gleamed like obsidian. The pointed ears—another true thing from the stories—poked through the strands, and two small gold hoops decorated the left lobe. As he returned the massive divan to its upright position, controlled strength rippled his arms, broad chest, and thick thighs.

All from many hours working the land, no doubt.

"It's safe to come out," he called. "They're gone."

She skittered from behind the basket. After making sure the area was clear, she snapped herself back to full-sized Marigold. As her stomach swam, he stumbled backward in surprise and into the butcher's block counter.

"Blood and bones," he exclaimed, rubbing his hip. "That'll leave a mark."

"Sorry." Despite the nausea, she giggled through her fingers. That she of all people could frighten a creature like this was hilarious. The only person she'd ever intimidated in her life was Bram the first time she'd kissed him. "I should've warned you."

With eyes flared, he clutched the butcher block to steady himself. "You can glimmer step?"

"No, not at all. I wasn't invisible." She lifted a ruined pillow from the floor and placed it on the divan. "My power is minimancy. I can shrink things and set them back to normal size. Including myself."

"Hmph." He furrowed his brow. "I don't like it."

Neither did she, at first. "It's immensely useful. I'm well in control, if it worries you."

The orc pressed his lips together, then rubbed his stubbled jaw. "Is it dangerous?"

Mercy, he was nervous about her abilities. Typical in Thornwick, but she'd thought a creature rumored to have heightened abilities might be more understanding. Ordinarily she'd playfully snap back with a jokey answer to lighten tensions. But if she wanted to stay here—and what better place was there to stay than one that had already been searched by the palace guard?—she should answer him sincerely.

"No. There are side effects on living things, but nothing too terrible." Fuzzle mewled in her pocket. "Here, I'll show you it's nothing to fear."

She withdrew the mouse-sized cat and set him on the cushion.

"Stop." The orc flashed his palm. "Is that your—"

She snapped her fingers. Fuzzle blinked back to his full size. Which, if she was being honest, was a few pounds more than he ought to be.

"Cat!" the orc shouted.

She should not laugh, but she couldn't help it. Her signature bray, the one that Bess fussed about and called most unladylike, snagged his attention from Fuzzle.

"Are you afraid of cats?" she asked.

He'd hidden behind the butcher's block, his lively brown eyes peering over the edge. "It's well-known that orcs loathe cats."

Marigold lifted the mewling tabby into her arms and rewarded him with a scratch below the chin. "Why?"

"I have no idea." The orc kept his eyes trained on Fuzzle. "They're sneaky."

"They're helpful. Don't all farms have cats to keep the rodents at bay?" She stepped away from the kitchen and back toward the cozy hearth. "We can put him to work. Do you have any pumpkin puree, perchance? It helps with his tummy upset after resizing."

"No. And what do you know about farm life?" The mountain of green pursed his mouth as he watched Fuzzle prance through the wreckage. The cat made it five steps before sitting to groom his paw.

"I read a lot." She sat to adjust her laces. Revolting as it was to wear outdoor shoes in the house after pulling an all-night run in them, there was no sense cutting her feet on pottery shards.

"Reading isn't the same as doing, Princess."

"Marigold, please." She looped and knotted the laces. "And what might I call you?"

The orc stilled. "Nothing. You're leaving. Tomorrow, after the search dies down."

Saints, he was intractable. "Be that as it may, when the royal poets write an epic about my hero, he'll need a name."

Finally, he muttered, "Jask. Jask Bone-Cracker."

He spat it out like she'd spat out the bitter chicory.

Orc naming conventions were intriguing. Imagine looking at a newborn creature and naming it something like "bonecracker." Although that was his surname, so perhaps they also used professions as surnames, like tradespeople such as Miller or Chandler. Was bone-cracking an orc profession?

Ah, her thoughts were running away again, as Bess would say.

She dusted her hands together. "Well, that's a colorful name, Jask Bone-Cracker. Do you have a broom?"

"I don't need help." He righted the table in the kitchen.

"I can see that, but I'm heartily sorry I brought them to your door." She surveyed the destruction. "Consider it my penance. Anything that can be mended, we'll put on the divan; anything that's wrecked beyond repair goes into the bin."

"That'll be half of it, I'd wager."

"Absolute thugs," she agreed. "You tackle the kitchen; I'll take the living room."

"Do what you want," he grunted.

As he tidied, something about his movements were familiar. She could not explain, for the life of her, why she was comfortable in his presence. Tusks were not known to reassure humans, but strangely, she was at ease.

Jask, however, was not. Mostly because Fuzzle twined through the orc's ankles like a child skating eights on a frozen pond.

"Keep the cat away from me, or I'll turn him into slippers." He gently shooed a meowing Fuzzle away with his boot.

She leaned the broom against the support beam and scooped the tabby into her arms. "Have you met a cat? They sense who doesn't like them and then lavish affection on them until they come around. I regret to inform you that he won't give you peace until you're hopelessly infatuated with him."

The orc made a sound low in his throat as he flipped the kitchen table's bench upright as easily as she might right an errant shoe.

They worked in silence through midmorning. Jask carted

away all the broken bits in a barrow, and between them, they'd swept up three neat mounds of hay, cotton fluff, and feathers.

With her hands on her hips, Marigold surveyed the size of the piles. "I'd guess your mattress and pillows are no more."

She hadn't ventured up the stairs and into the loft where she presumed he slept. Everything else about this cottage suggested he kept the same habits as humans. Did orcs sleep in night clothes? An image of him without a shirt flashed in her mind, and she shoved it away.

"I never should've opened the door to you," he snarled. "This is your fault."

That stung, but he was right. Alas, regret was wisdom that arrived fashionably late. In his cottage, the damage was literally already done. All she could do now was help fix it. The orc scowled as he swiveled his gaze, as though he was stuck deciding his next move. Fortunately for him, her royal training featured many a lesson on soothing prickly egos, which mostly involved suggestions and compliments delivered with more sparkling bubbles than mountain water.

"Go assess the damage." She shooed him toward the stairs. "If anything else needs to be mended, use your considerable strength to toss it down."

He rolled his large shoulders, then stomped up the stairs. Once the rattling stopped, Jask let loose a scorching stream of curses. If she hadn't been permitted to gallivant with lads as a child, her ears might have burned.

"Is it bad?" she called.

"It's not great," he huffed.

Feathers rained down from the loft, then Jask returned with a bundle of torn linens. After depositing them atop the pile on the divan, he frowned at the size of the mending pile.

"We should repair these first," she said. "So you have something to sleep upon."

"Half the day's gone." He ran his hand down his face. "I don't have time for this. I've chickens to feed, a cow to milk, and fields to plow."

She dusted her hands together. "I'll help with the animals."

"No, Princess. You've done enough." He opened the back door, revealing a charming courtyard situated among a byre, a chicken coop, a pig pen, and a few other things she couldn't name. "Stay inside. The last thing I need is for Crispin and his men to come back this way, find you and toss me into Dreadmoor."

As much as she wanted to feel the sun on her face, his caution was wise.

"Still, I'd like to be useful." She pushed back curls that had slipped from her braid. "Where's your sewing kit?"

The first casualty atop the pile was a pillow bleeding fluff. One of the knights had run it through with a sword. Kevin, if she remembered correctly. Why murder a pillow? She shook her head. Wisdom often chased Kevin, but he was faster.

"In the darning basket." Jask hovered at the open door. "But I don't need any favors."

"Not a favor—an apology." She held up a hand to stop him from protesting. "I'd like to earn my keep. Should I prepare anything for our midday meal? I imagine we'll both work up an appetite."

He paused. "A princess who cooks?"

"Earning my keep, remember?" She lifted a shoulder. "To be truthful, I can't cook much, but I can make a sandwich."

"I don't care what you do. Just stay inside." Jask's mouth rippled as though words tried to escape him, then blew out a breath. "I must go while the weather holds."

She raised her eyebrow. Was the weather likely to turn? Beyond the door, the sky was a perfect cornflower blue. A glorious fall day, in fact. Chirping birds, buzzing bees visiting their final flowers for the season, and temperatures warm enough to leave her cloak on the hook. But maybe the climate was different in the hinterlands?

More likely, he wanted to escape her company. But another skill she'd learned in her princess training—for some, candor formed alliances better than flattery. She'd wager the orc fell into that category.

"Thank you for helping me," she said. "I am not your princess, nor a friend. You have no reason to risk your safety on my behalf. I am grateful."

His hand tensed around the doorknob. "You're wrong, Princess. It's everyone's duty to help someone in a difficult situation. Even if we're repulsed by them."

Not exactly a sonnet, but she'd take it if it meant he wasn't flinging her in front of Crispin. What was it about the prince that had changed the orc's mind? Before her betrothed darkened the orc's doorstep, he'd threatened to turn her out. When they were better friends, she might dare to ask. For now, she'd be content with light teasing.

With the sewing kit in hand, she settled herself on the divan. "For someone who denied being a knight, that's a courtly thing to say, Jask Bone-Cracker. Aside from the repulsion bit."

He crossed the threshold. "Tonight only, Princess. Tomorrow, you're gone."

The door rattled in its frame. Add that to the pile of things the broadsheets and books got wrong about orcs—they possessed integrity. Deftly, she threaded a needle from the kit, then stitched the split pillow closed. Soothing, this kind of work. Rewarding, too, making order from chaos.

And as for leaving tomorrow?

She thought not.

Chapter 5

By midday, Bram had been out of the cottage for hours. Inside, his sweet Marigold was currently darning sheets and pillows. Tonight she'd sleep on them, likely feet away from him. Bram tapped his forehead with the blunt side of the hatchet's head. Maybe if he tapped hard enough, he'd beat sense into himself.

What on earth had he done?

Nothing smart, that was for sure. He paced thirty yards down the fence line to cool his heated blood. Between his true love and his nemesis arriving within minutes of each other, it was a miracle he'd kept his wits about him. Though if he'd had *more* wits, to protect her from the curse, he should've immediately orcked out and sent her screaming away from his doorstep.

Now he was stuck with her.

Crispin was a puffed-up rogue, and Bram had no regrets about hiding Marigold from him. But harboring her? If Marigold was caught, Jask Bone-Cracker was as good as vivisected. Had he listened to her five years ago, all this might have been avoided.

The prince, the curse, everything.

They were both twenty-three then, and she'd fought with him tooth and claw over his plan to find his fortune in Harvest Hollow. Sir Patrick, the knight who raised him, had breathed his last, and Bram's social status was tenuous at best. Marigold was convinced her parents would allow a love match between them since her father had received special permission to marry her mother. Magical thinking, that. Love match? A silver lining. Marigold's mother, Queen Elowen, belonged to the realm's wealthiest merchant family. With her, she brought Thornwick's coffers a welcome infusion of gold.

He—the fostered child of a mid-level knight—did not.

But he had potential. At least, he used to.

A few paces away, Barnaby stretched his neck, then split Bram's brain with an impressive shriek.

"Really, Barnaby?" Bram wiggled his pinky in his ear. "It's almost noon."

As the rooster strutted away, Bram hacked at the sapling that threatened the fence post's integrity. In his quest to avoid the woman in his cottage, he'd blazed through his routine chores. He'd watered, fed, and milked the cow; scattered feed for the chickens and collected their eggs; then let the pig out to forage in the forest. Normally, the mundane work helped him sort through his growing list of problems, which included:

1. Marigold required safe passage back to Thornwick.
2. He couldn't leave the farm.
3. Jask Bone-Cracker had no friends to tap for help. Unless he counted Alfred the Carter or Barnaby, which he did not.
4. If he revealed himself to Marigold, she would die.

He ached to reveal himself to Marigold. His favorite person in the world was *right* there, no farther away than a ten-year-old could throw a mid-sized pumpkin. The funniest, smartest, most empathetic, and beautiful person he'd known in his twenty-eight years. She was stitched into the very fabric of his soul, his heart, his body.

His very excitable body.

Which meant he needed to stay out here. Perhaps forever. Discipline was a core value of knighthood, but this was beyond him. The root cellar might be an alternative place to lay his head. After watering the pumpkin patch and vegetable garden, he was no closer to a solution for escorting Marigold to safety when he himself could not escort her. The growl in his stomach begged him to stop for a meal.

But then he'd be back in the cottage. With her.

He ran his hand down his face. Perhaps there was something in the root cellar besides cider, onions, and carrots? As he headed toward the cellar door, an urgent bell clanged in the distance. What was that? Had Alfred gotten a new bell that sounded like the one that called fire brigade? He glanced over his shoulder. No—this ringing came from the front of the cottage.

Marigold.

The world bounced and shifted as he sprinted through the courtyard and around to the front of his home. There she stood, on the porch, shielding her eyes as she scanned the horizon.

"What's wrong?" he panted.

She dropped the bell pull. "Nothing's wrong. Why do you ask?"

"You rang the bell." He jabbed his finger toward it.

"Because I made sandwiches."

"I said don't bother." For the first time, Bram noticed Crispin's knights had smashed his artfully carved porch pumpkins. Knaves, all. The pumpkins weren't works of art, but there was no reason for this gourd carnage.

"But I did worry about it, and I made them anyway." She entered the house, then beckoned to him. "I hope you like salted-ham-and-brie sandwiches."

He left the hatchet on the porch. "I had salted ham and brie?"

"No, *I* had salted ham and brie," she said. "In my trunk."

Bram wrinkled his brow as he unbuckled his boots and traded them for his house shoes. "What trunk?"

"That one over there." She gestured toward a steamer trunk the size of his chicken coop. "I minimized it for easier carrying. It contains my essentials."

"Brie isn't essential."

"Never question the essentiality of cheese." She lifted a kettle from the cooking hearth and poured fragrant steaming water into a mug. "And I made my honey-lemon-ginger tisane. As promised, it'll change your life. So will the petit fours."

"Princess, I've no time for a leisurely meal."

"Neither do I. I'm very busy." She sat at an expertly laid table covered with a floral tablecloth. "Now, wash your hands and sit."

He had table coverings?

Not the point. He had two options: continue to fight with her and drag this out, or do as she said and eat with her for five minutes. Unaccustomed as she was to not getting her way, Marigold would likely follow him if he simply turned on his heel. The goal was to keep her hidden, at least for this first day.

With a sigh, he pumped spring water onto his hands and lathered with the pine-scented soap he'd made earlier this month. With the muck scrubbed free, he thumped his ass onto the bench across from her.

He picked the ham from the sandwich and flung it to the floor near Fuzzle. "I don't eat meat."

"An orc who doesn't eat meat?" She tilted her head. "Fascinating. Why not?"

Because the creatures here were his only company, and he couldn't stomach eating his friends. If he shared that, though, he'd need to explain he couldn't leave the farm, leading to the reveal that he was cursed, and . . . No. Too dangerous.

Secrets and lies it would be.

"Doesn't agree with me," he said.

"But you have a pig," she said. "She's not intended for the spit?"

Paloma, on a spit? The very idea hurt his heart.

"She forages truffles. Everyone here works, Princess."

As he took an enormous bite of the brie sandwich, he murmured appreciatively. "Jam?"

"Blackberry preserves. I brought that, too." She sipped from her mug. "By the way, I'll take the divan tonight."

Tonight. Where they'd sleep under the same roof since . . . never.

Naps in the hayloft aplenty. But a full night together? Between Bess and his foster father, they'd never managed it in Thornwick.

"Take the loft." He fixed his gaze on his plate. The sound of his chewing rivaled Paloma at her trough. Deliberate, because Marigold hated loud chewing. "I'll take the couch. I barely sleep, and I'm up early for chores. Better if I'm down here so I won't disturb your sleep."

Do not *think of her in your bed.* In her shift, betwixt his sheets.

Absently, he gulped his beverage, then spluttered the hellish liquid back into his mug.

"Are you okay?" she asked.

His mouth was on fire. "It's scalding."

"You did see me *just* pour it from the steaming kettle, didn't you?" She shook her head. "You must blow on it to cool it. Or have patience and wait."

With another bite, half his sandwich was gone.

She stared at him. "I've never seen someone swallow a sandwich whole."

Couldn't she pretend he wasn't here? He didn't enjoy being observed.

He drummed his fingers on the table. "That's how orcs eat."

"Noted. What if I change my scent?"

He cocked his head. "What now?"

This, at least, was unchanged about Marigold. She leapt from topic to topic like a tumbler at a fair. The constancy of her conversational acrobatics were oddly comforting.

"I'm slathered in stupidly expensive creams and ointments and have a trunk full of clothes that have been cleaned and pressed in the royal laundry. I hadn't thought about Crispin's hounds and their sharp sense of smell. He extolled their perfection over one particularly long meal." She sighed and rested her cheek on her fist. "I should bathe with your soaps and shampoo and wear your clothes. To reduce the concentration of trackable scents. Tonight, perhaps?"

"No," he said through clenched teeth.

Did she not realize the power of her words? Thinking about her in her shift caused him to burn his tongue. If he pictured her in a bath, he might impale himself on a fork.

She wrinkled her forehead. "You don't bathe?"

"Didn't say that." He blew on the volcanic beverage before drinking. "I wash in Coldpress Lake."

"But it's autumn," she said. "It must be freezing."

He wished. "Orcs run hot."

She drummed her fingers. "Then I shall bathe in the river, too."

"No." He shook his head. "Too risky."

"Then find me a basin—I'll take anything. Laundry tub, a particularly large soup pot." She flipped her palms toward the thatched roof. "As long as those hounds can track me, I'm a sitting target. A forest-filthy target."

He rolled his neck. Her strategy was sound, but he did not have *locate a bathtub* among his tasks for today. A tub in which a naked Marigold would rub soap and . . . No. The way it stoked his imagination was not welcome.

"I'll try," he gritted out.

She rested her chin on her latticed hands. "Thank you."

There, that was five minutes. As he shoved back from the table, he popped a petit four into his mouth, and damn, if those weren't tasty little sugar bombs. Life-changing? No, but he welcomed the treat and could eat a dozen more.

"Leaving so soon?" She dabbed her lips with a napkin. "I'd prefer your company if you can spare the minutes."

Ah, shite. How had he not noticed her tired eyes and taut shoulders earlier? Marigold was troubled. Her confident sunshine had blinded him at first, but now her distress was all he could see. Something dreadful must have prompted her to jilt Crispin. Shirking royal responsibility was not a choice Marigold made lightly—at least, not the Marigold he'd known.

He clamped his jaw shut. No good could come from asking her what happened. If she reported a bitter argument between her and Crispin—or worse, a lover's quarrel from which she'd recover—he'd want to rip that preening fool apart. Bram did not need to fan his vengeance flames further.

"Farm work never stops." He drained his mug, and the belch that escaped him was legendary.

Marigold straightened her shoulders. "Charming. Until I figure out my next step and revise my plan, Jask, I pledge I won't make your life harder."

"Too late," he said as he slammed the door behind him.

Even if it was best for her, he hated playing the asshole.

None of this—the separation, the curse, the loneliness—was Marigold's fault. *He'd* left Thornwick's safety. Bess might have suggested it, but he'd acted on it. Then he'd accepted Crispin's invitation to his privy circle and chose to stay despite repeated dishonorable acts on the prince's part. Convinced the prince would never turn on him, Sir Bram Duncan overrode his conscience like it was an obstacle on a road.

Most damning, he'd climbed the Lantern Oak, oozing hubris. Only a young fool would believe he could tangle with the autumn sprite and emerge the victor. As a result, he'd abandoned the woman sitting at his table, which set her on the path to her regretful engagement to Crispin.

For all of this and more, he had only himself to blame.

Desperate, he searched the yard for his next chore. Something to fully occupy his body and mind to soothe the itching in his soul. Ah—there. Chopping wood. A low priority on a temperate day like today, but a decent solution.

The round of wood was rough in his hands.

He'd no sooner set it on the chopping block than Marigold's cat, Fuzzle, jumped onto it. The cat had a habit of stalking him in Thornwick, too. Streams of giggles had poured from Marigold whenever the tabby leapt onto Bram's shoulder in the castle or on his ass while they were in the hayloft. As a man, he'd been mildly annoyed by the cat's sudden appearance.

As an orc, the suspicious dread was like he'd eaten a hemlock salad and the shakiness had kicked in. There was much lore about orcs and cats and how they mixed as well as sparks and dry hay. Bram rubbed at the spot where Marigold's locket once laid above his heart, his normal move to soothe his nerves. Fascinating to feel the distrust in this green skin.

But Bram was not in the mood to be fascinated.

He nudged the cat with his toe. "Are you trying to cash in a life, cat? You can't have many left at this point. Shoo."

Fuzzle crouched and locked in on Bram, then meowed.

Bram squatted. "What's your problem, Fuzz? Don't you want to be warm tonight? We need wood for the hearth."

After plopping his orange butt to the block, Fuzzle twisted

his head to the side. Bram flinched as the cat gently touched his front paws to Bram's cheeks, kneaded the flesh like he was making biscuits, then bopped his head against Bram's chin. The bop was Fuzzle's preferred way of greeting Bram.

For a moment, the orc froze.

Perhaps cats weren't so terrible.

He scratched Fuzzle behind the ears. "Do you know me, then?"

With a quick meow, the cat leapt from the chopping block and pranced toward the porch. Bram followed the tabby's movements. Perhaps he could find the time to fish for the feline. The barnyard animals were off-limits, but Coldpress Lake was stuffed with perch and pike. Bonus—the activity would keep him from the cottage.

As he set up a round to split, he pricked up his ears.

A horse and cart—oh, shite. Alfred. The first week after his transformation, the carter arrived, asking if the new tenant of Grimroot Farms had produce to sell. Alfred wasn't a farmer himself but owned a reliable horse and cart. With it, he delivered fresh vegetables and fruit to the homesteads pocketed between the hinterlands and Harvest Hollow's main market. Remainders were often purchased by Brambleton Castle's cooks, then Alfred circled back with anything Jask had ordered, along with earnings.

Minus Alfred's cut, of course.

Bram had forgotten about the pumpkin pickup today. Unlike strangers and villains who crossed the boundaries of Grimroot Farm, Alfred came and went with no warning. Once Bram gave him permission to visit, the shivers had stopped. Bram slammed the axe into the stump, then ventured from the side yard to greet his friend. Perhaps "friend" was wishful thinking on his part, he reflected dolefully.

"Ho there, Alfred." He raised his hand in greeting.

"Jask, my man." Alfred's gaze slid to the ruined pumpkins as he handed Bram his weekly delivery of a book, broadsheets, and a sack of flour. "Rough day?"

"I've had better."

Crispin's voice replayed in his mind—*Speak to no one about this, orc.* Much as he loathed following the prince's commands, this one made good sense. Alfred trafficked in Harvest Hollow gossip as much, if not more, than in fresh foods. Unless Bram wanted a repeat visit from the palace guard, it was best to withhold the tale of the missing princess and the vain prince's search for her.

"Paloma got loose in the night," he lied. "I haven't harvested the pumpkins for the market. Sorry about that. Any chance you could come back tomorrow?"

Alfred tipped his straw hat backward, scratched his scalp, then nodded. "Yeah, that'll work. Hey, when did you get a cat?"

"I . . ." The warm brush of tabby fur against his leather boots stopped him. "He showed up this morning."

The best lies were cousins to truth.

"Never thought I'd see an orc with a pet cat." Alfred slapped his knee. "Doesn't that beat all?"

Bram lifted a shoulder. "I'm not your typical orc."

"Couldn't agree more." Alfred fished his corncob pipe out of his pocket. "Speaking of . . . you ever want to come into town to sell your wares yourself? I like my share of the business—don't misunderstand. But you'd rake it in hand over fist with folks wanting to get a look at you. Even more if you growled at 'em."

Bram's stomach turned. Even if he could leave the farm, he'd never try to profit from this predicament. "I can't think of anything worse."

"Suit yourself." Alfred flicked his reins. "Not my business if you're leaving money on the table. I'll be back 'round this time tomorrow."

As the horse clopped away, Bram raised his hand in farewell.

Tomorrow would be easier, because Marigold would be gone.

Chapter 6

Thick, overwhelming silence pressed on Marigold in the night-dark cottage.

Castle life meant noise. Even at its quietest, staff whispered, carts rolled, and guards' footsteps echoed against stones. Church bells tolled, too. In the country, however, none of the comforting sounds that signaled human company could be heard.

This was a symphony of a different sort.

Above her, the thatch shifted. Outside, dry stalks whispered in the wind as well. In the distance, a hooting, but she wasn't versed enough in bird calls to discern the type of owl. Fuzzle's purring as she stroked his back was a roar in this silence. Mystery rustling perked her ears. Over time, she might be able to pick out the different noises. But for now—

Her thoughts scattered like startled birds as a scream cut through the courtyard.

The breath left her lungs, and cold seeped through her veins. Jask hadn't stirred on the sofa below, however. Or maybe Jask *caused* the scream? But it was quiet again, save for the pounding blood in her ears. Maybe she'd imagined it? Nope, wait, there it was again. She flicked back the covers and lit her bedside candle. Marigold of Thornwick did not sit idly by as murder sat at the threshold.

"It's only a fox," Jask called, guessing her concern. "They

get territorial in the fall as the young ones leave their dens. Nothing to worry about."

She edged to the loft railing and peered at the shadowy lump on the divan. "Aren't foxes cute and inquisitive? And not prone to banshee shrieking?"

"No to cute, yes to inquisitive and shrieking. And it's already gone."

This was the most he'd spoken since their humble meal together. The afternoon had gone much like the morning. Jask tackled chores outside while she repaired every textile and sorted everything within her reach. *Then* she dragged one of his big kitchen chairs around the cottage and tidied everything else. When he still hadn't finished his long list of outdoor work, she reorganized his books in their proper alphabetical-by-author order.

In a desperate moment, she minimized herself and dashed across the courtyard to the privy. Had he told her to stay indoors? Yes, but she would have been mortified if he returned to an overflowing chamber pot.

At twilight, Jask popped inside to soak dried beans for the next day's midday meal, then walked off with a stack of oatcakes, a towel, and a change of clothes. She put together a satisfying meal of bread, cheese, dried fruit and nuts, then inspected the contents of the bookcases' lower cabinets. An hour later, the orc returned damp and smelling of warm pine and cloves, the same scent that surrounded her in his large bed. It suffused the pillow, the mattress, the linens.

It was familiar to her nose, but she couldn't place it.

"Jask? Do you wear cologne?"

"No," he said, scoffing at the suggestion. His eyes remained closed.

In the dark of the loft, she frowned. Where had she smelled

the scent before? She hated when she couldn't place something. The missing information nibbled at her mind, but experience taught her not to force it. If she let the mystery simmer, eventually the answer would reveal itself.

The hearth fire crackled and gasped.

The flickering light played on Jask's stretched-out shape under a quilt. She'd rather be down there, chatting face to face. His expressions were difficult to read in full sunshine. In the dark, they were impossible.

She fiddled with a curl.

Despite brushing the twigs from her tresses and giving herself a bird bath while Jask was gone, she ached for a deep scrub. To rid herself of grime, yes. Also to cleanse herself of the castle, Crispin, and every moment between her escape last night and her arrival here.

Why had she agreed to marry Prince Crispin?

She wasn't fully back to who she was before Bram's death, but she was closer. *That* Marigold would've sussed out Crispin's viperous intentions and flatly declined his offer, no matter what the boon to Thornwick. She was not a jewel to be traded between thrones.

Here, in this taciturn orc's cottage, she was finally beginning to remember who the hell she was. If she stayed out of the prince's clutches, her brothers were safe from his plot. She hadn't yet worked out how to get to the sanctuary in Mareval and then how to inform her parents of the need to break the alliance with Harvest Hollow, but the solution would come to her.

Tonight she was simply giddy about her freedom from a terrible man.

And a giddy Marigold was a chatty Marigold.

"When can you find me a bath?" she asked.

A grunt sounded in the dark. His way of closing a subject, apparently.

A draft whisked through the thatch, pebbling her skin. That wouldn't do for a good night's sleep. The best combination was a cool room and a cozy pile of blankets. Cool she had, cozy pile she did not, and Fuzzle was a poor substitute for a warming pan.

"Do you have another quilt? It's chilly up here."

His sigh ballooned the walls of the cottage. "Chest at the foot of the bed."

Wax rolled down the candle and into the chamberstick's saucer as she navigated the loft. "How long have you lived here?"

Jask wiped his hands down his face. His palms muffled his voice as he shouted, "I'm trying to sleep."

The gesture tugged at her memory. Like before, the ghost of . . . something half-recollected . . . remained stuck below the surface.

"Sorry." She rested her forearms on the railing. "I don't mean to bother you. Or maybe I do, but only because earlier you said you don't sleep, and I want to know you better."

He opened his eyes and locked gazes with her. "You don't need to know me. And I didn't say I don't sleep—I have *trouble* sleeping. Big difference, Princess."

"Marigold." She picked at the soft dribbles of wax. "Do you want me to hush?"

"Very much."

She pursed her lips. "I have trouble sleeping, too. Talking helps."

With another cottage-rattling sigh, he tucked his arm behind his head. "Three questions, then silence. Morning comes early."

That was fair. "How long have you lived here?"

"On the farm?" His big lower teeth pointed toward her as he yawned. "Three years."

Not long, then. Odd. Who took up pumpkin farming on new land?

"Why pumpkins?" she asked. "Like, does anyone really *need* pumpkins? They're more decoration than anything else, aren't they?"

"Your ivory tower must be nice," he said. "Pumpkins are cheap and multipurpose. Hard on the outside, soft on the inside, they grow fast, store well, and feed many. In a pinch, they can be used as a projectile weapon."

He might have just described himself. Except . . . with vines that sprawl along the ground in green and gold, pumpkins flowered and bore fruit in clusters. They don't grow or survive alone, which is what Jask seemed to prefer.

"Where's your family?"

He closed his eyes again. "Elsewhere. That's three. Try not to snore."

"That's cheating. You didn't fully answer that last question."

"Devil's in the details." He rolled to his side. "I never agreed I'd answer to your satisfaction. A valuable lesson if you ever enter a bargain with a sprite."

Like she needed him to teach her about bad bargains or magical creatures. "It's still cheating."

"Good night, Princess."

"Well, bad night to you, Cheater MacCheaterpants."

His grumble vibrated the loft as she flopped back into his bedding. After kissing the picture of Bram in her pendant, she curled around Fuzzle. In the snug embrace of the fire-warmed cottage, she offered up thanks that she'd found a soft place to land.

Even if she hadn't yet had a bath.

A tortured scream startled Marigold awake. Her heart slammed against her ribcage. Was it the fox again? Had she dreamed it? Powerful, realistic night visions had haunted her before. The kind when Bram visited her, so close but untouchable.

Though she'd be thrilled if it wasn't real and she'd imagined that noise. Why were the hinterlands so unnecessarily scary? In the dark, she listened for Jask. Company made scary noises tolerable. Nothing from him, either.

She jolted at a fresh screech.

Not the fox, but her heart settled. The rooster—what had Jask called him? Barnaby?—announced the start of a new day. She slipped from the nest she'd made of the blankets and into the brisk morning. As her bare feet touched the cold floorboards, she flinched.

This room needed a rug. She added it to the mental list of things the cottage could use from the market the next time Jask visited town. No, scratch that—she wouldn't be here long enough to justify home decor. Just until the palace guard presence died down, or . . . Wait. A key clicked in her mind. She bounced on her cold toes. Oh, *brilliant*.

Finally, an idea worth having.

She'd offer the orc coin to spirit her to Mareval. Given the worn state of his furniture, he was bound to accept for pay. She'd minimize herself, and much like she'd carried Fuzzle here, Jask could pocket her and venture across the Shivering Dales and deliver her to the sanctuary without attracting notice.

She tapped her chin. Would the revised plan require another coded letter to Rowan?

Possibly, if she tarried more than a few days. She'd need to travel to the town center to hire a messenger. Dangerous, that. If only she had the costume she wore when visiting the markets in Thornwick. A simple dress, false nose, and a wig allowed her to peruse wares without palace guards hovering and driving up the price. That all stopped when Papa had been crowned, though.

As had lots of things.

She brushed her hair from her face. Or perhaps she could

convince Jask to go on his own to post a message? And shop a bit while he was there. Yes, for house slippers, and she'd strongly recommend a rug. Ooh, also for the list—pomegranates. They were in season.

Although . . .

She hadn't seen a horse. Harvest Hollow proper was a fair distance from here. How did he go to the markets? After pulling on her green kirtle and cursing the difficult-to-reach lacings, she rubbed her teeth with a piece of frayed sage twig from her herbal remedy kit, then rinsed with cold water from the jug. She attached her pruning knife to her belt, then glanced in her looking glass. The small mirror was sufficient for face only, but it would have to do. His room held none larger.

"Good morning," she trilled as she leaned over the railing.

To no one, apparently. Only a divot remained where Jask had slept, along with the quilt. She descended the stairs and ventured into the kitchen. The cooking hearth was lit, but there was no food upon it. From the nearby window, she peered into the yard.

Ah, there he was, feeding the clucking bundles of feathers.

His coarse linen shirt hugged his back, his sleeves pushed up for a day's work. No cloak, though, which meant the weather was fine. She pulled on her gardening turn shoes, then swung open the door to the cool air. The earth was fresh, and the sky held a fragile quality, a pale dove gray met by a growing pink.

"Morning!" she called.

Jask startled. "Blood and bones! Where did you come from?"

"The house?" She gestured toward the feed pail. "Let me help with that."

"No." He turned and scattered more grain for the pecking birds.

She curled her fists and glowered at his broad back. Stubborn orc. She'd inundate him with bubbly helpfulness. He'd rue the day he rebuffed her.

"I'm sure you don't need my help." She wrapped her fingers around the pail's handle, dangerously close to his, and beamed her most brilliant smile. "But I insist. Have you eaten?"

He flinched and let go of the handle like she'd thrown fire at him.

Disconcerting, but she'd take the win.

He lifted the latch on the chicken-yard gate, then let himself out into the courtyard. "I tend the animals before I break my fast."

"What else does 'tending the animals' entail?" she asked.

He disappeared into the dairy. Fantastic. She loved when someone left a conversation. The last scoop of feed plinked against the patches of dirt amid the straw. A beautiful brown hen beat its wings and hopped over the others to gobble up the feed. Marigold respected her ambition.

Jask returned with a large milk pail, then headed toward the byre.

Marigold exited the coop, then held the pail high like a lantern. "Where does this go?"

"Hook above the feed barrel, next to the kitchen door."

The metallic scrape of the pail's handle on the hook sent a shiver down her spine. Feed dust covered her hands, and she brushed them together. "What about the horses?" she asked. "Or donkeys? Anything to do for them?"

"I have neither." He opened the byre door.

She squished her eyebrows together. "No beasts of burden?"

"*I* am the beast of burden." His hand, flattened over his heart, covered a third of his chest. "Easier for me to push the plow than to harness creatures."

"Oh, I—oh." She stared at his thick shoulders, imagining

them straining with effort. Which was *not* a welcome or necessary thought at daybreak. He was her unwilling host for mercy's sake, not an object. He had a soul. An irritating grumpy one, but a soul nonetheless.

"I'll . . ." The word stuck. She cleared her throat. "I'll handle the eggs?"

He lifted an eyebrow. "Was that a question or an offer?"

Must he make everything so difficult? She wasn't amused by his needling. Far from it. Flustered was more like it.

"An offer." She let herself back into the chicken yard. The birds' excited clucking made her raise her voice. "I'm capable of collecting eggs."

He twirled the pail on his index finger. "If you insist."

"I do. Go." She shooed him. "Cow. Milk."

He cocked his head and continued twirling. "You surprise me."

She popped her fist on her hip. "Why, because princesses don't do chores?"

"No, because you used to—" His pail slipped his finger and spiraled over the fence and into the pig's sty.

"I used to what?" she asked.

He palmed his neck. "Hand out chores to servants. But that's an assumption, and I hate it when people make assumptions about me. I shouldn't have made them about you."

She narrowed her eyes. All she knew of this orc was built upon the last twenty-four hours. But something in what he'd said—or, more accurately, *hadn't* said—was the shape and weight of a lie. This was not a time to challenge, however. This was a time to build bridges, so he'd allow her to stay or, better yet, help her get to Mareval.

"I may surprise you yet, Jask Bone-Cracker."

He'd headed back to the dairy for a fresh pail. She wasn't sure, but she swore he muttered that she already had.

Chapter 7

With the animals tended, Bram would normally break his fast. Except Marigold would flit around him like a horsefly, asking a thousand questions as he cooked. After a sleepless night spent listening to her sweet sighs, powerfully aware she was mere feet away but forever out of reach . . . he needed distance from her.

Despite the strong rumble in his stomach, he strapped on his carpentry belt and grabbed a spare jagged board from the cast-off pile. Earlier, while releasing Paloma to forage, he noticed a cracked rail on the north side of her pen. His lumber supply was running low after crafting the rocking chairs from the shattered remains of the orchard's rootstock tree's heartwood. Until he chopped down another tree for fresh planks, he'd attach a support as a short-term solution.

"Alas, my love, you do me wrong . . ." Marigold's light voice carried across the courtyard as she sang. Many a time she'd break into song while they hiked through woods, insisting it made the journey shorter. "To cast me off discourteously . . ."

He twisted toward her, ready to shout at her to stop. The word dried in his throat. Saints, she was beautiful. A little paler than he remembered, but magnetic all the same. She'd flung open the door to the root cellar, and as her fingers drifted over the jarred vegetables and braided onions, the morning breeze played with her loose curls. For one second—one brief, glorious, irresponsible second—he let himself fantasize a long future of days like this.

His jaw ached with his clenching.

Fantasy, indeed. She was here for today and today only.

Bram, however, would remain at Grimroot Farm. Forever. What he'd told Marigold about people staring had been true, but the curse also kept him rooted here as surely as a shackle. The sprite's magic clamped invisible walls around the farm, impenetrable only to him. He'd tried crossing the borders in every way possible—walking, running, leaping, hacking with an axe, flinging himself skyward with a makeshift trebuchet, swimming across Coldpress Lake, digging deeper than any of the graves at Kindlewood Garden of Rest next door.

Escape eluded him at every turn.

During his three years here, he'd cycled through the fruitless feelings of shock, anger, and melancholy, and finally landed on acceptance. Then, with one knock on his door, Marigold upended his resolve. Hard-won peace with his situation evaporated. To be near her without her knowing him would drive him mad. He needed distance—feet, fields, forests—between them.

Much as she might protest, her departure must be today.

After a long, slow blink, he pivoted toward Paloma's sty. Even with his eyes focused elsewhere, his awareness of Marigold's location prickled his spine. She was the sun, and he was her sunflower, tracking her movements around the farm.

A farm where she'd never put down roots.

No, while he was stuck here, she could have a big, beautiful life wherever and with whomever she chose. A nobler knight would wish her well, but it stung worse than a fury of hornets that she'd forgotten about him and accepted a marriage proposal from another.

Bram let the churlish feelings flow.

If he didn't, they'd out in less productive ways. Like drowning his sorrows in cider or losing a battle of fisticuffs with one of his apple trees. Two opposing things could be true—he could wish Marigold every happiness, which might entail marriage to another, and he could want to drive a nail into the skull of any man she married other than him.

Bram grunted as he paused at the fractured rail.

But how had she been drawn in by *Crispin*? He spat bile into the dirt. Had the prince's good looks mesmerized her? Or was it his crown and the life of ease it promised? The would-be king playacted at gravitas, and Marigold had mocked such men ruthlessly in their youth. Had she changed so radically in the five years since they parted? No, not his carefree Marigold. Look at her over there, singing a courtly lament to the chickens.

With a snort, he drew his hammer from his belt.

The why of it all didn't matter. She was not, in fact, *his* Marigold, and she had clearly moved on. To him, a century seemed like a more respectable period of mourning for true love. Perhaps their love had not been true after all and he'd risked everything for a fantasy. Bram grunted. These fractious, prickly feelings were unwelcome.

The sooner Marigold left Grimroot Farm, the better.

As he readied his hammer, Bram plotted how to send Marigold away. Evicting her from the farm would protect her from the curse and preserve his fragile sanity. The hitch was he wanted to see her *safely* on her journey. Starvation, cold, knaves, wolves, spoiled food, cliffs—all would easily kill an untrained person traveling on her own.

He raked his hand through his hair.

Clearly, releasing her to the hinterlands alone was reckless. Minimancy wouldn't save her. At a diminished size, she'd be a target for more predators. A falcon could scoop her up for a tasty snack in two heartbeats. He'd seen their speed with his own eyes. Garrick, Harvest Hollow's royal falconer, had trained birds to swoop faster than a meteor strike.

Bram's throat thickened as he pulled a nail from his work belt.

Ah, hell. Garrick.

While Marigold had been Bram's deepest loss since he'd been cursed, his best friend was a close second. Bram longed for the nights at the Laughing Gourd while he and the falconer attempted to best Laurent the tailor and Martin the haberdasher at the tavern's Riddle Night. He was sure Garrick would've been game to help Sir Bram Duncan in his time of need.

Jask Bone-Cracker, however, could take his noise elsewhere.

There was no denying it. He personally could not see Marigold safely to Thornwick. His last resort was to ask Alfred to find a respectable, decent guide to take her safely home to her family. The carter was such a gossip that looping him in might bring the palace guard back to his doorstep, but the risk might be worth it.

The sooner she was gone, the better.

Because if his bitter heart didn't kill him, his attraction to her would.

The constellation of freckles sprinkled on her cheeks, the delicate shell of her ear, the way her kirtle hugged her curves . . . He'd slay a dragon to explore the ways she'd bloomed since they last knew each other. All the more reason to avoid eye contact. He was sure she'd read desire on his green face and be horrified. To avoid that scenario, all last night and this morning he focused his disrespectful eyes above her head or turned his back to her. Common beliefs about orcs' rudeness gave him some cover, but these tactics wouldn't last forever.

As she sauntered back toward the cottage, she bowed to Barnaby. "Alas, my love, that you should own a heart of wanton vanity . . ."

Saints, she was distracting.

Back to the fence and the mind-numbing focus it required. The rail's crack was in an awkward spot, requiring him to hammer with his left hand and hold the board with his right. Bram pounded the nail, drowning out Marigold's singing. Was today too soon to ask Alfred to find a discreet guide? Her absence was the only way to quell the vexing desire that had roared back to life the moment he clapped eyes on her.

But they could never—

He hissed as a sharp sting tore across his right palm. The nail had slipped and gouged his flesh. Blood welled from the jagged wound and trickled to the earth. Rough splinters pricked the cut like nettles. Curse his clumsiness. He yanked a handkerchief from his breeches and pressed the linen to the fresh gash.

"What happened?" Marigold appeared next to him.

He jerked back in surprise. "Nothing. You should wear a bell."

Bram winced as she laughed.

"Are you always this jumpy?" she asked. "You quailed like Fuzzle at a bath. What happened? I heard you—"

He followed her blue gaze to the linen. Red blossomed on the ivory. As his vision went gray at the edges, he swayed on his feet. Fresh blood was his Achilles' heel. A knight of the realm should be able to stomach it, but he'd never mastered his aversion. Good thing he hadn't eaten, or he'd have lost his breakfast.

"That's not nothing." Quicker than a squirrel, she dashed into the byre and returned with the milking stool. "Sit."

The legs scraped the fieldstones as he slammed onto the stool. "I'm fine."

"Liar." Gently, she lifted his hand above his head.

Her touch sizzled through him, lighting up long dormant parts of him. His heart, his hips, his . . . This was bad. So, so bad. Her fingers possessed the same soft, strong skill that had roamed Bram's body in their secret meeting places in Thornwick. His very soul awoke, and he might never lull it to sleep again.

"Orcs bleed red," she murmured as though to herself.

"Of course we bleed red. We're mammals."

"Right." She shook her head. "That was stupid of me. Keep your hand above your head. I'll be right back."

She disappeared into the cottage. He stayed upright through sheer force of will. Barnaby, ever curious, meandered toward him.

"Barnaby, don't do it."

The rooster lifted his head high, then puffed his chest.

"If you know what's good for you, Barn—"

Blood and bones, the Battle of Three Fords hadn't been as loud as this rooster. On the bright side, he was no longer about to keel over. The jolt might've cost him his hearing, but he'd take it if Marigold wouldn't find him indignantly sprawled in the courtyard.

"I'm here!" She crashed back through the door carrying a leather satchel, linen, and several bottles cradled in her arms' crook. Her footsteps were soft and sure as she crossed the courtyard.

"And I'm still fine."

"Sure you are." She set everything on the ground.

As she knelt in front of him and spread a clean linen square next to her, his vision cleared. To have Princess Marigold of Thornwick on her knees before him sent a dangerous amount of blood to other parts of his body. Although, for the sake of his hand, that was likely for the best.

"Hand, please."

"Princess, I—"

"Marigold." She held out her hand. "Please . . . let me help you."

Reluctantly, he lowered his hand. As she peeled the soiled linen away, she raised her russet eyebrows. He kept his eyes trained on her. He was no longer worried about fainting, but vomit was still a concern. He wasn't sure which was the greater indignity.

"Is it bad?" he asked.

"I've seen worse."

When had she seen worse?

"The bleeding's stopped." She withdrew pincers from the roll, then held his hand firmly. "For anything that hurts, I'm sorry. For anything that heals, you're welcome. I'll try not to dig too much as I remove the splinters."

"Have at it." His voice was braver than he felt.

With great precision, she ferreted out bits of wood. As she worked, a gaggle of honking geese flew overhead. By the time he'd turned his direction to them, then back to Marigold's hair, she'd set her pincers on the linen.

"These next parts won't be as pleasant," she said. "I need to clean it with vinegar, and you'll need a few stitches."

He enjoyed her hand cupping his far too much. "No stitches."

"Jask, they'll help it close and heal properly." She slid her warm and steady hand up his forearm, then squeezed. "I promise it'll be quick."

It better be, or he'd have to fling himself into Coldpress Lake to cool his blood.

"Do it," he said.

Marigold nodded, then uncapped the vinegar. "First, I'll clean the wound. This will sting. Badly. But it discourages corruption."

He'd survived this long. He refused to let a festering wound take him down.

With great care, she poured a thin stream of sharp-smelling

vinegar into the wound. No, that couldn't be vinegar—she must have placed stinging fire ants on his flesh. He hissed, but his discipline kicked in and he held still.

"Well done, Jask." She squeezed his forearm. "I'm sure that was terrible. Also, here."

He took the strip of leather she offered him. "What's this for?"

"The pain. You bite on it."

As though this would withstand an orc's bite.

He tossed it back to her roll. "I'll be fine."

"Your choice." From the surgeon's roll, she took up a long, curved needle, then guided a shimmering thread through its eye. "You're lucky I visited the seamstress recently. My intuition told me I might need silk thread for my kit."

"You're clairvoyant as well, then."

"No." She clipped the end of the thread. "I'm a woman who prepares."

"And a princess."

"Princesses aren't women?" The needle gleamed in the golden morning light as she wiped it with a linen soaked in vinegar. "Don't tell me you're one of those people who put princesses on pedestals, Jask. Pedestals are as much a prison as Dreadmoor."

"Princesses aren't *surgeons*."

"Do you know all princesses?" She poured vinegar onto her hands, then dried them on clean linen. "But I wouldn't call myself a surgeon. I dabble."

"Enough to do this capably, I hope?"

"I excel at everything to which I put my mind. Like palmistry." She turned his hand slightly to get a better angle on the gash. "The wound bisects your heart line, which is deep and well-defined. That would indicate a deep, true love. Have you found her yet, Jask?"

That question hurt more than the nail had.

Marigold looked up at him. "You don't need to answer. I'm just making conversation."

His voice was low. "I did, but I lost her."

Marigold's features softened as she maintained eye contact. "I'm sorry. That's so hard, isn't it? I've also lost my true love."

Forsaken, more like. He'd been enduringly faithful while she'd opened her heart to someone new. But telling her who he was so plainly would be her death, so he kept the information locked in his chest. The heartache, however, wanted her to taste his pain.

"Devastated you, did it?" Bram snapped.

She raised an eyebrow. "What's that supposed to mean?"

"I'm no scholar, but it couldn't have been a deep attachment if you're marrying another."

Her gasp scattered the birds from the courtyard. Ah, blood and bones. His chivalry had known better days. Perhaps his loss of control was for the best. Marigold would think him a rough orc, and she'd be more motivated to move on.

"You're right—you're no scholar. You're an absolute oaf. It's spectacularly unwise to provoke someone who's about to pierce your flesh. As for the meat of what you said . . ." She cleared her throat, then fixed her gaze on his eyes. "You know me not, Jask. If you'd like to learn more about how the betrothal came about, you'll need to first tell me about *your* lost love and how you dealt with it. I doubt you will, however. In my experience men don't enjoy expressing emotions."

"I'm not a man," he muttered.

"Saints, you know what I mean." With one hand, she pushed the wound closed. With the other, she readied the needle. "Do you want me to keep talking? It may help distract you from the task at hand, though I promise I'll be quick."

"You still plan to stitch the wound?"

"Yes. I'm petty, but I'm not *that* petty."

He was, indeed, an absolute oaf.

"Keep talking."

She nodded. Concentration tightened her features, and her disarming tenderness loosened something in his chest.

"Here we go," she said. "Saints guide my hand."

Bram grunted as the needle pierced his skin. Not as painful as the vinegar, but not how he'd prefer to spend his morning.

"You have parallel lifelines." Another prick of the needle. "That indicates a person living two paths or two identities."

His fingers tensed.

She glanced up at him. "Sorry. We're nearly done." She returned her gaze to his palm. "Were you not meant to be a farmer, Jask? Were you supposed to join a questing party and seek adventure and steal dragon hoards?"

"Dragons aren't real," he countered.

"Why must you squash my whimsy with reality?" She sighed. "Isn't the world more fun if you imagine there are dragons and unicorns in it?"

He nearly asked if unicorns were still her favorite creature. Instead, he pressed his lips together. She tied off the stitch, then clipped it with her shears.

"There." Marigold sat back on her heels, then reached for the vinegar. "Five stitches. A final wash, then a poultice of honey and thyme."

He sucked the air through his teeth. More stinging. And he'd need to add vinegar to the list for Alfred.

"This next part won't hurt." She drizzled honey from the pot he kept in the kitchen. *Hmph.* The pot was low, and it was his last. In the next week or two he'd gather some from the hive in the orchard.

"Now, a little thyme." She uncorked a small bottle and sprinkled dried herbs on the honey. The peppery herbal aroma filled the air, but she was right—it didn't hurt. "And clean linen to wrap it."

She folded a handkerchief into a square, then pressed that to the wound. Next, she wrapped a thin strip around his hand and neatly tucked the end, then secured it with a brass pin from her bag. "There you go. All done."

He held up his tidily bandaged hand. "Where did you learn to do that?"

"When my true love left me to seek his fortune, I filled my hours to stave off melancholia." She rolled most of her instruments back up and stashed them in the bag, leaving the needle and scissors on the linen. "I studied medical arts. Geography, alchemy, beekeeping, gardening—things like that. I was always in the castle's library or conservatory."

Ah, that was why she'd paled.

"I thought princesses only studied etiquette and protocol."

"Don't forget embroidery." She winked at him.

He coughed to disguise the laugh rumbling in his chest. As she finished organizing her equipment, he drank in the picture she made. Her exterior was the same, but she'd changed since they'd parted five years ago. Compared to his memory, this Marigold was more confident and less prone to dramatic fits.

"You surprise me," he said.

"And you, me. Isn't it delightful to be surprised by a person?" She surged to her feet, then dusted her hand together. "If orcs heal similarly to humans, your hand should be as good as new in ten to fourteen days. Until then, I wouldn't use it too much, or you risk popping the stitches and reopening the wound. Looks like you're stuck with me for the next fortnight."

He'd never survive it.

"Shall we finally break our fast?" she asked. "We could have more brie, or—"

"Please not, for the love of saints." His swollen hand

throbbed. There was no easy way for him to cook, but he craved something heartier.

"As you wish, sir." With her back straight, she sank into a perfect curtsy, then rose again. "Toast, then? I don't know how to make anything else."

He knew that. Princesses rarely spent their lives in the kitchens. They were taught to supervise household staff, not do the work themselves. Not so for knights or their squires.

"Well then, Princess, would you like to learn?"

Chapter 8

The confidence Marigold possessed in the courtyard disappeared faster than Fuzzle during a thunderstorm. From the stiff set of his shoulders, it was clear it cost him to accept help. She couldn't refuse Jask's offer to teach her to cook.

But cooking . . . she was a disaster at anything that involved more than two steps.

The brie-and-blackberry sandwiches represented the extent of her culinary skill. She'd tried to learn at Thornwick Castle, but upon burning a third loaf of bread, the cook kicked her out of the kitchens. From then on, she'd decided she was better suited to eating meals than preparing them. But she was game to try. With a full belly he might at least consider escorting her to Mareval before grunting a no at her.

After washing up at the pump, she asked, "What are we making?"

"Pottage. Easy, filling, flavorful. It's a good first lesson. You'll need this." With his left hand, he reached for a well-worn cutting board stacked on a shelf behind her. Her heart stuttered at the warmth radiating through his shirtsleeves.

Sweet mercy, he smelled even better than his bedsheets.

She cleared her throat. "Was pottage the first thing you learned to cook?"

"No. Egg scramble." He slid a knife from the block. "But

I don't feel like eggs. Fetch ingredients from the root cellar, would you? Carrots, a turnip, an onion, garlic, and cabbage."

"I will." She raised her index finger. "One quick question. Where is the root cellar?"

He wiped his good hand down his face. "You were in it earlier. Across the yard, past the coop. Door stuck in the hill's side. I assume you went in there in search of breakfast?"

"No, I . . ." Might as well be honest. "I thought it might be a fairy house."

He squinted at her. "But the door is full size."

She shrugged as she headed toward the door. "I've never met a fairy. In the stories they're small, but the stories could be wrong."

"The stories often are." Jask snorted. With amusement or derision, she couldn't tell. "Get the vegetables?"

"Bide a moment," she called over her shoulder.

Jask was so hard to read. Because he was an orc? Possibly. Between his tusks and his permanently lowered brow, his resting face was set to grumpy. But there were times where she was sure she amused him. Like yesterday, when he'd opened the door to her, his lips curled in a smile before something had chased it away quickly.

Hopeful chickens clucked as she came near. "Not feeding time, ladies. Sorry."

Not for them anyway. The root cellar door's hinges squealed as she flung it open. Inside, the cool and dry air smelled of the earth. She gathered the vegetables he wanted from the tidy shelves. The way Jask hid his feelings was so strange—she was the opposite, blurting out her emotions at every turn. Much to Bess's chagrin. Her companion endlessly coached her to keep her upper lip stiff and expressionless.

What was the point in that?

It wasn't as if it was a surprise that people had feelings. He certainly had no trouble expressing the surly ones—anger, irritation, exasperation. So why couldn't he admit he liked her? She liked him. She supposed she could see how some people would find him terrifying, with his growly voice and under tusks and mounds of muscle. He could probably pick her up like she was a doll, fling her around, pin her to a wall, and—

She flared her eyes and covered her mouth.

Where had *that* come from? Her heart had died the day the Harvest Hollow squire arrived at Thornwick Castle with the official letter about Bram. The gray numbness that followed convinced her she'd never feel an amorous spark again. Crispin's offer proved her theory when she met his proposal with nothing more than a vague pop of surprise.

With her pruning knife, she snipped a garlic bulb free from its twine.

The court had buzzed about his proposal while she simply shrugged. He was handsome, yes. Anyone with eyes could see that. But everything about his demeanor was overly practiced, like he'd studied facial expressions and optimal angles to present to his adoring fans.

There was nothing genuine about him.

And that was *fine*. Preferred because she'd never be overwrought about someone like Crispin. His contrived gestures, word choices, and overall affect were a contrast to Bram. He never worried about projecting confidence, wit, or courage. Bram simply *was* those things. That was what hooked her from the start—his unabashed *Bramness*.

Oh, and his dreamy, gold-flecked blue eyes.

In his gaze, she felt truly seen, quirks and all, and adored. After he died, she lost the quiet confidence his love provided. She'd allowed her parents to convince her to reduce the volume on her un-princess-like behaviors. No more sneaking out to the marketplace or the wilds of Thornwick. Her appearances were curated, scheduled, and highly choreographed.

Again, that was *fine*.

Then she arrived in Harvest Hollow. Traveling to a new place, shaking off Thornwick, had, much to Bess's chagrin, rekindled her high-spiritedness. And all the things that had been fine were fine no longer.

She closed the root cellar door.

Also not like anyone in Thornwick? Jask. The orc was fascinating. Grumpy, yes. Rude, absolutely. But he didn't eat meat, protected her from the prince, and read more than any man she'd known, including Master Alaric Wyndox, the snooty young tutor her parents hired from Clarus University for Rowan, Beckett, and herself.

A contented huffing signaled Paloma's return. The pig entered her pen, circled a few times, then dropped into the hay.

"Welcome home, Paloma," she said, then latched the gate.

Inside the cottage, she toed off her turn shoes, then delivered the basket to the chopping block in the kitchen's center. Jask had placed a large pot on the stove and stoked the fire underneath.

"What's next?" she asked.

"Washing," he said. "Then peeling and chopping."

She pumped water into the basin, then used the rough brush to scrub the produce. "Is there any way in particular you like them cut?"

"No. But . . . uniformity is preferred, so they cook evenly. The dense vegetables, like the carrots and turnips, should be smaller than the onion and the cabbage. And the garlic should be finely chopped—almost a paste, really."

"So, by 'No'—" she giggled as she peeled the turnip "—you mean, 'Yes, I have firm preferences.'"

"It's not a preference," he grumbled. "It makes logical sense."

"Okay, Mr. Bone-Cracker. But maybe don't watch me lest I ruffle your scales."

"I don't have scales." He set a pot on the stove.

Mirth lightened her tone. "I was *joking*."

With his back to her, he grunted in response. She stifled another giggle. Maybe it was the lack of a full night's sleep or the lull in her dire circumstances, but everything he did was hilarious. Laughing at an orc was likely unwise, but she couldn't help it.

As she sliced, chopped, chunked, Jask drizzled oil into the pot. Once she finished, she added the hard vegetables to the pot with a push of the blade across the cutting board. They landed with a satisfying plop and sizzle.

He added a spoonful of butter and two pinches of salt. "For flavor."

"What about thyme?" she asked.

"Should be ready in thirty minutes."

Oh no, an unstoppable fit was bubbling up inside her. She was powerless against it.

"Not *time*." Her shoulders shook with her laughter. "*Thyme*."

"I don't get it." He folded his arms over his chest.

Marigold fought to stand upright, but her quaking midsection stopped her. "The herb. *T-h-y-m-e*. Thyme."

His rucked forehead smoothed. "Ah. I don't have an herb garden."

"I have some." She exhaled and thumbed happy tears from her eyes, then opened her physic satchel. "It's good for coughs, too. Mind if I add some? And some rosemary? Though you can never go wrong with butter and salt, herbs add a lot to vegetables."

Jask gestured toward the pot. "Be my guest. Give everything a stir while you're at it, then put the lid on so the vegetables steam as well."

Marigold liberally shook in the seasoning, then corked the bottle and set it on the counter. She drummed her fingers. A tisane of rosemary and honey would partner well with the meal.

As she filled the kettle, she asked. "Who taught you to cook?"

He relaxed his shoulders a bit. "My father. It was the two of us, so if he was ill or wanted a break, I needed to learn."

Her heart cramped. Growing up without a mother's care was a difficult wound to heal. Bram preferred not to talk about it, but she'd often wondered if his lack of a mother figure was the root of his fierce self-sufficiency.

"Oh?" Marigold set the kettle on the stove. "I'm sorry—I didn't mean to pry. Would you like to tell me about your mother? You don't have to."

After Bram died, no one spoke about him. While her family's silence was a misguided attempt not to upset her, she felt like he'd died twice because she couldn't remember him *with* anyone. Based on this, she resolved to ask fellow grievers about those they'd lost.

He slid his palm against his neck. "I don't remember much. Only that she was kind."

The vulnerable gesture tugged her heart strings. Almost like she could see the small version of this large-framed person.

"That's its own tragedy." She pulled two mugs from the open shelf above the sink. "No matter when, it's devastating when a loved one dies."

"Has death touched your life?" For the first time today, his gaze was not evasive.

"Yes. My . . ." Her breath whooshed from her. "He was called Bram."

A lump formed in her throat. *Whew, okay.* She'd confessed that without tears.

"You called him your true love, and yet you're betrothed to Prince Crispin?"

She lifted a shoulder. "I'm trying very hard not to be. And you made that point earlier. Are you mocking me?"

"No, but how could you fall for another after experiencing true love?"

As if loving another was possible.

She thwacked the knife through the cabbage head. "I *didn't*."

Jask's grunt drew her attention. With his thumb pressed to his chin, his eyes searched hers. For what, she did not know, and she was too tired to attempt to sleuth it out.

"Does that surprise you?" she asked.

"No. The prince is a loathsome twit. Tell me about Bram, then." Jask lifted the pot's lid. "And add the cabbage and water, then give it all a stir."

"There's too much to say." She slid the chopped cabbage into the mix, then firmly shifted the vegetables.

As Jask sidled next to her with the small pitcher, her back flared with awareness at his proximity. Mere inches separated them. Heat pumped from his body, reaching her through her kirtle. He was warmer than the steam that billowed as he poured the water.

Orcs really did run hot.

He fitted the lid back on the pot. "Then sum him up? I'd like to learn about what made him special to you."

Tears pricked her eyes. She could pretend she was blinking from the steam, but why bother? Jask was a stranger. Talking to him was like telling her troubles to the sea—he'd soak them up, and then she'd sail away, leaving them behind.

"Fair warning—if I talk about him, I'll cry."

Which made people uncomfortable. Mama tolerated the tears, but Papa, Rowan, and Beckett coughed and left the room. Bess, as expected, told her to buck up. To be fair, they all thought Bram was merely her best friend, nothing more. But hugs would've been nice.

"Tears don't bother orcs, Princess. Cats, yes, but never tears."

Marigold laughed despite her breath juddering in her chest.

"Okay, but remember you asked for it. I loved him so deeply that I don't . . . I don't work without him. He was tender but never let me take myself too seriously. He'd bring me small tokens and treats, things to let me know he was thinking of me when we weren't together. A sunflower, a vanilla cake, an exquisite lace kerchief. Nothing that would reveal our relationship to those who'd frown upon it. But it was enough for me."

The lump that swelled in her throat choked off her words.

Jask handed her a fresh linen handkerchief. "He sounds like he was constant."

"He was." She sniffled as she gripped the cloth. "The thing I ache for is having a shared language, someone to whom I can tell all my thoughts, brilliant and silly. He knew I loved him, so I have no regrets on that front, but . . . my world is dim without him in it."

"Did he die recently?" Jask asked.

"Depends on what you mean by recent. Three years, and I'm not sure I want to stop grieving. Missing him means he's still here in some way. Does that make sense?"

"Some," he says.

She blew her nose. "When his squire brought the news to us, I didn't believe it, because they didn't bring home a body. So, I thought the knights of Harvest Hollow must have had it wrong—that he was missing and they were pessimists. When the guard held a modest funeral, I was angry. I thought if we kept faith and hope, he'd return to us. To me."

"What changed?" he said.

She'd never confessed this before. Not even to the clerics.

"Eventually, Prince Crispin paid us a visit. In a private meeting, he gave me Bram's half of our locket." She withdrew the necklace she kept close to her heart. "He hadn't sent it with the squire because he guessed I wanted our affection to remain discreet. Bram would've throttled anyone who attempted to take it from him. There could be no doubt he was gone."

She dropped the pendant back under her kirtle.

Jask started to speak, then stopped and thinned his lips. The fact that he spoke few words made her eager to hear whatever he was fighting to say. Would an orc, reputed to be creatures of low empathy, offer her comfort?

"He could . . ." Jask's jaw bulged with clenched teeth until he cleared his throat. "He could yet be alive, Princess. You said it yourself. There was no body."

No, there was no comfort in that.

Marigold held up her hand. "Please don't. Hope hurts. If I accept his death, at least I can function and find some muted joy in life. If I thought he was out there somewhere and waiting for me . . . that would be torture."

Jask's shoulders tensed. His face clouded, then cleared. He turned his back to her, then lifted the lid on the pot. "So, we'll agree your true love is dead and dusted, then." The lid clattered where he dropped it onto the counter. "Add the barley and the beans. Should be ready in a half hour."

Marigold blew out her lips. She'd annoyed him again. By talking about Bram, though he'd asked her to? Or in refusing Jask's suggestion that Bram's alive? That made no sense at all. They were not friends—why would he care about Bram or how she grieved?

No, pain from his injury was the likely culprit for his temper.

The shrieking kettle inspired her. Instead of rosemary and honey, she'd fashion something stronger. "I'll make a willowbark draught. After you drink it, your hand will feel much better."

She hoped she was right.

Chapter 9

Bram sat in one of his rocking chairs on the cottage's porch. He'd fashioned the pair to enjoy the view of the pumpkin fields and, beyond them, the sunflower patch. Who the second one was for, he had no idea. But crafting a single chair had seemed too sad.

The breeze carried the scent of apples from the orchard, reminding him to fill a basket soon. With Marigold staying here, he'd need more food.

Two weeks. He could make it that long.

"Drink your draught," Marigold yelled from the side yard. "I'll secure the chickens."

Bram twisted his lips. From the small table between the chairs, he lifted the steaming willow bark. This was the second draught she'd made him today. He grimaced. The liberal amounts of honey and cinnamon she'd added took the edge off the bark's bitterness, but it was still as pleasant as chewing chalk.

What a damned strange day this had been.

After her tears, their midday meal had been tense and silent. He was angry, but not at her. *Never* at her. While they cooked the pottage and she'd spoken of Bram, it was like attending his own funeral and all he could do was offer her a fresh handkerchief. His one true love had sat across the table from him, and he could reveal nothing.

Monstrously unfair.

In truth, it had taken every ounce of his control to stop himself from sweeping her into his arms. He'd done that dozens of times in Thornwick. Here, though, she'd run screaming from the cottage if an orc attempted the same.

Fuzzle appeared around the corner.

"Go away, cat," he said.

In two leaps, the tabby was on his lap.

Bram rolled his neck. "You have as much respect for personal boundaries as your mistress."

She'd followed him all afternoon, stuck to him like a burr and demanded instructions for the farm's daily chores. Once she caught the rhythm of each job, she was surprisingly capable. Even the deeply unpleasant stuff, like mucking out Queen's stall. He'd thought the dung would send Marigold running, but she'd snatched the pitchfork from him and set to separating the soiled straw from the clean.

He might have been more surprised than the cow.

In Thornwick, she'd carried a pomander of cinnamon to ward off foul stenches. In cities, they were plentiful. Out here, well beyond the cramped buildings, the odors were less concentrated and more earthy. The constant breeze through the pines helped, too.

He took another bittersweet sip.

The Marigold in his memory was proving to be different than the woman who'd showed up on his doorstep—saints, only two days ago? Absorbed as he'd been in his own chrysalis, he hadn't considered she had five years of new experiences without him.

As he set the cup down, the familiar squeak and roll of a cart perked his orc ears. He shielded his eye, then groaned. Yes, there was Alfred, coming back this way exactly as they'd agreed yesterday.

And Bram *still* hadn't harvested the pumpkins.

He rolled his neck. He couldn't afford it, but he'd need to send the carter away with nothing. Harvesting wasn't a one-handed job. Though Marigold was strong and likely willing, it was too much for one human.

"Shoo." He brushed Fuzzle from his lap.

The chair creaked as he stood.

"Ho there, Alfred." His footsteps thudded against the porch stairs. As he strolled over to the cart, he waved with his bandaged hand.

"You're having a rough go of it, Jask. What happened there?"

"A nail got the better of me," he said.

"Didn't think anything pierced orc—" Alfred's eyes widened. "Jask, did you get a wife since yesterday?"

Shite. Sweat broke out on Bram's forehead. Marigold had appeared on the porch. What the hell? Had they not agreed that for the duration of her stay, she'd remain indoors when strangers were around? Alfred was a gentle soul, but he was the *worst* at keeping secrets.

"She's a childhood friend." Bram clutched the side of the cart. "She needs a place to stay. Discreetly. Her life is at risk, Alfred. So please—keep this to yourself."

He searched the older man's wrinkled eyes, pleading. Trust didn't come easily to Bram since the night Crispin betrayed him, but he had no choice.

"Say no more." Alfred tapped his nose to signal an agreement.

He believed Alfred, but the quiver in Bram's stomach was hard to settle. All that stood between Marigold and discovery was the willpower of a notorious gossip.

"Hello!" Marigold beamed and held out mugs to him and Alfred. "Care for a blackberry-leaf tisane? It's refreshing."

"Can't turn down an offer like that, miss." His smile revealed his scant collection of teeth. "Name's Alfred. And who might you be?"

Bram held his breath as he sipped. *Please let her not be so naive as to give her real name.*

Without hesitation, she said, "Meg."

He choked. Meg was the alias she used to run around Thornwick's city center unnoticed.

"Everything okay, Jask?" she asked.

"Fine," he wheezed.

"Never seen you discombobulated before," Alfred said. "You must be keeping him on his toes, Miss Meg."

"I guess I am." She rocked on her feet.

"He could use it." Alfred drained his mug, then handed it back to Marigold. "That *is* refreshing, Miss Meg. Thank you. Jask, if you can load up the pumpkins for the market, I'll be on my way."

"About that." Bram palmed his neck. "I still haven't had a chance to harvest them."

Alfred twisted his lips. "Ah. Too bad—market's tomorrow. You'll miss out this week."

Too bad was an understatement. When he'd tumbled to the earth as Jask, he'd retained the gold acorns stuffed in his pocket. The cottage and outbuildings had been here, but he'd since acquired everything else—the animals, the materials to expand, the seeds—courtesy of that cursed harvest. Only a morsel of gold remained. Pumpkin and apple sales were supposed to keep him afloat through the winter, but it would be hard to make up for a week's lost income.

Tension banded around his forehead. "Blood and bones."

"Can't we harvest them now?" Marigold asked. "I'll help."

Bram held up his bandaged hand. "This'll slow me down."

"And I can't wait long, Miss Meg. Sundown's around the corner, and the forest's not fit for nighttime travel. I don't want to mix it up with the autumn sprite."

She cast her eyes toward the trees down the road. "There's really an autumn sprite? I thought that was a fairy tale to keep the children out of the woods."

"Indeed," Alfred said. "Any soul that crosses his path is changed for the worse."

Bram could confirm that but held his tongue.

Marigold eyed the empty cart. "How many pumpkins does your cart hold, Alfred?"

The old fellow glanced over his shoulder. "Forty, give or take?"

"We can make that work." She touched Jask's arm, and a sizzle jolted through him. "Get the egg basket," she said to him quietly. "I'll shrink the pumpkins, we'll gather, then I'll resize them. Easy peasy."

That . . . *would* work. He didn't love the casual use of magic but had little choice.

"Alfred, give us ten minutes, and don't tell anyone what you're about to see."

Alfred shielded his eyes to glance at the sun, nodded, then leaned back in his seat. "Deal, as long as I can get another one of those blackberry-leaf whatnots?"

"Oh, I'm so glad you like it!" Marigold took his emptied mug. "I'll get you a refill, and Jask, you get the basket?"

By the time Bram returned from the coop Marigold stood at the edge of the field. She closed her eyes and breathed deeply. With both hands held aloft, she snapped three times. Blue sparks rained on a quarter of the tidy furrowed patch, and the pumpkins shrank to the size of plums.

"Sweet mercy," Alfred muttered.

"Yes! I've never done so many at once before." Marigold bounced on her toes, then twisted toward Bram. "I'll use the apron; you use the basket. First one back with twenty pumpkins wins. Go!"

She arrowed into the field, bending, plucking, and moving down the furrow. With the basket looped over the elbow of right hand, he awkwardly gathered the adorable pumpkins with his left. As a farmer, he always competed against fading sunlight, squeezing in work before the night closed in. This was much more fun. He'd forgotten the joy of trying to outrun, outwit, or outlast an opponent. Once his basket was full, he raced back to the cart where Marigold was already emptying her apron.

"I win!" she crowed as she pumped her fists in the air.

He'd also forgotten how much he disliked losing.

"I wasn't ready," he complained.

"Too bad." She grinned. "Luck favors the sharpened blade."

He leaned against the cart as grief and nostalgia rolled through him. His foster father, Sir Patrick, had barked that phrase a million times while training up Bram alongside the Marigold's brothers, Rowan and Beckett. Sir Patrick alternated that nugget of wisdom with *For a future king, you need more spine.* That last one was only directed to the princes. Bram had heard neither since Sir Patrick died.

"You all right there, Jask?" Alfred asked. "You're looking a little green. A different green, I mean."

Jask shook it off. "Fine."

"Don't worry, Jask. The pumpkins will enlarge with no trouble." Marigold touched his biceps, and saints, the fire caused by her touch whipped through him.

This was intolerable.

"I'm not worried," he ground out.

She popped her hand on her hip. "You *look* worried."

"How can you tell?" Alfred joked. "He always looks like a vulture shat on his breakfast to me. If you'll pardon my language, Miss Meg."

As though she was the one he insulted?

"Pardoned. And if you really want to know how I can tell he's worried, look there—" she pointed to the bridge of Bram's nose "—a crease that could hold an acorn between his eyebrows."

Bram snort-hmphed. Hard. He'd like to tell Marigold she couldn't possibly know what a worried orc looked like because she barely knew him. But then *that* would contradict what he'd told Alfred about her being a childhood friend. Now he wasn't worried, he was mad.

"Can you restore the pumpkins?" he asked impatiently.

She snapped thrice, and the pumpkins swelled to their full size with another impressive display of blue sparks. The cart lurched and sagged with the sudden weight, and Alfred held tight to the startled horse's traces. The control she had over this magic, much as he distrusted it, gave him an idea about her request for a bath.

"You're a hoot, Miss Meg," Alfred said. "This is the most fun I've had at this stop since Jask moved in."

Hadn't been aware he was supposed to entertain the carter.

She curtsied. "Happy to be of service. How often do you pass by, Alfred?"

"Every few days, minimum once per week. I cart mail, packages, and goods to town for those who can't go themselves, then bring back their profits. You ask around—there's no one fairer than me."

"I believe it," she said.

Alfred withdrew his pipe from his shirt pocket. "Anything you all need next week besides the usual?"

"Vinegar," Marigold said. "And house slippers? I forgot mine, and the mornings are chilly."

Bram pressed his lips together. He'd stoke the fire harder this evening. Might mean sleeping in his braies, but it'd be worth it for her comfort.

"Anything else?" His pipe's bowl glowed orange as he drew in the smoke.

"Do you carry letters?" she asked.

"Yes, miss, but only along my route. Any farther and you'll need to hire a carrier. If that's the case, I know some reasonable fellas."

Marigold nodded. "Thank you."

Letters originating from Grimroot Farm were an exceptionally bad idea. Paid carriers hardly respected the sanctity of the seal. If they opened it and could identify her by name, content, or handwriting, they'd earn far more coin alerting the palace guard to her location than they would successfully delivering the letter. Bram would argue with her about the insecurity of correspondence after Alfred left.

"For next week, what do you think?" Bram asked. "The same number of pumpkins? Or more? We're getting close to the festival."

Which happened to be his best sales of the season.

"Maybe none." Alfred shook a few more dried dreamleaf buds into his pipe. "Rumor's going around that the royal family's canceling it."

Marigold tilted her head. "What's the festival?"

"The Goldenmoon Festival's our harvest celebration, Miss Meg." He struck a match and dipped the flame into the pipe's bowl. "Three of the best days of the year. Corn mazes, pumpkin carving, candied apples, cider presses—the works. It's capped off with dancing and bonfires under the full Hunter's Moon. The royals host it, but they say planning the prince's wedding calls for all the local resources and laborers."

"Oh, that's awful." Marigold furrowed her brow. "Why

would the prince schedule a wedding against such a popular event?"

"According to one of his knights in the Laughing Gourd, the Thornwick princess insisted on a fall wedding under a full moon. Sounds like the prince has his hands full with that one."

Marigold's face reddened. "That's the most irredeemable piece of gossip I—"

"Keep me posted, Alfred," Bram cut in, lest she lose her grip on her secret. "You'd best be on your way before dark."

Sunset wasn't the drawn-out love affair they enjoyed in the height of summer. No, at this time of year, the sun's dip below the horizon was fast and determined, like a newlywed diving into bed.

"Agreed." Alfred blew smoke rings over their heads, then tipped his cap. "Pleasure meeting you, Miss Meg."

"Likewise," she said.

As Alfred disappeared around the bend, Marigold turned to him. "You don't own a horse."

The sudden change of topic caused his brain to bump against his skull. "That's correct."

"So, is it that you can't go into town or you *won't* go into town?"

If he shared the truth—that he couldn't leave this farm—she wouldn't stop asking questions. Marigold was tenacious when things didn't add up. Easy to see she'd unravel the rest quickly. Dishonesty rankled. It ran rough against his training and the code to which he swore an oath.

But her death would rankle more, so to protect her, he told a plausible lie.

"Won't. I got tired of the looks from the city folk." He picked up the egg basket.

"I know that feeling." Marigold walked with him to the coop, her tone softened. "Like you're an animal in a menagerie. When I was younger, I disguised myself so I could walk among my people without notice. Isn't that strange? Royals are supposed to shepherd their kingdoms, and yet we're divided from our citizens."

"Doesn't have to be that way," he said.

"I agree." She pinched her chin and stared in the distance.

Uh-oh. That gesture meant she was about to lob an amazing and terrible idea at him. Diving from Piney Falls into Amberglen Lake, for example. Or trying dreamleaf in the castle's hedgerow maze and giggling like idiots looking for the very simple escape.

"What are you thinking about?" he asked.

"I'm always thinking about something, Jask." She blinked and was present with him again. "Are you not?"

Eventually, she'd spill it. Another Marigold habit—she couldn't keep her amazing/terrible ideas to herself for long. He doubt she'd last twenty-four hours before telling him all about it.

"I had an idea for your bath." He hung the basket outside the coop. "Would you like to take one after supper?"

She clapped. "Oh, yes, please."

His heart warmed at the sparkle in her eyes.

Chapter 10

Tell me about this brilliant idea for a bath." Marigold walked through the door Jask held open. Inside the cottage, she toed off her shoes, then asked, "Do you need help with your boots?"

"No, I'll manage." He sat on the bench by the door.

With his left hand, he managed to coax one boot halfway off before cursing under his breath. She pressed her fist to her mouth to suppress a giggle. Men were always so reluctant to ask for help, as though the world didn't operate on mutual support networks.

"Are you sure?" She pumped water onto her hands and washed up with the pine-scented soap.

"I'm *fine*."

His grunts said otherwise, but she respected his determination. At the stove, she stirred the pottage. They'd left it on a low heat so it would be warm for supper, and its heavenly aroma made her stomach rumble.

There was great satisfaction in eating a savory meal after a long day of honest work. The kitchen staff at Thornwick and Brambleton dished out delicious, intricate recipes, but she'd take this simple fare over elaborate meals any day. She ladled portions into waiting crocks, then set them on the table. Spoons, knives, butter, and hunks of bread. Next, two mugs of spring water.

"Supper's ready," she said.

Jask, finally free of his boots, pumped spring water onto his uninjured hand. Before she could offer to help him wash, he lathered by rotating the soap in his palm. Ingenious, but part of her wished he didn't feel like he needed to be quite so independent.

At the table, he sat across from her. "Sorry. 'Bout earlier. 'Twas rude."

Apologies were hard for Jask apparently. The words came out like a bull through a buttonhole. She just wished she knew what he was apologizing for.

Marigold raised an eyebrow. "Why?"

"I said little when I should have been thanking you for preparing the midday meal." He dipped his spoon in the bowl. "Thank you for then, and now. It turned out well."

His words made her feel taller, somehow.

"Thank you. I like it, too." She dragged her bottom lip between her teeth. "And thank you for the apology, but there's honestly no need. You ripped a hole in your palm. I assumed you were in pain and grumpy."

He sipped his drink. "That's generous of you."

"I'm nothing if not a benevolent ruler." She spooned another bite of the vegetable, barley, and bean stew that tasted more delicious for having made it herself. "Now back to my bath?"

"I'm thick for not thinking of it earlier, but you could use the laundry tub. Not as nice as a royal copper, I'm sure, but it's large enough and worn smooth."

"Jask, I will bathe in a rusty bucket if it comes down to it." She pushed back from the table. "I'll put a kettle on to boil for the bath."

"This'll take more than a kettle—the two large pots are better. Before you do that, though . . ." He topped her hand with his. "I need your help."

Delight sizzled through her. At his touch or his admission,

she wasn't sure. No, she was sure—it was both. But mostly the large, warm touching.

"I'm at your service."

"Can you minimize yourself and the tub? I'm leery of magic, but it'll save water and you have command of your power, so it seems safe. And I shouldn't carry anything that heavy."

She might melt with all these compliments.

"It's safe, I swear." She clapped. "But I'd prefer not to minimize myself. It gives me the heaves. A reasonable trade in an emergency, but for a bath, not so much."

He held up his hand. "I didn't realize. Full-size, then."

"I can't tell you how much I'm looking forward to this."

He tore the bread and dredged it through the last of his pottage. "I thought you might. We'll fetch the tub after supper."

She shoveled food into her mouth, tossing her robust etiquette training out the window. The sooner they finished their meal, the sooner she could set up a bath. This morning's basic washing and change of linens was nowhere near enough to remove the grime she'd accumulated during her trek through the darkened wood. After the fastest meal of her life, she put the pots on to boil while Jask lit a lantern.

"It's so nice out," Marigold said as she opened the back door to the cool night. No cloak required yet, but the bite in the air was sharper than it had been during the day. "Ooh, the fox!"

The small creature's paws blurred as it skittered across the courtyard. He paused to look at them, then sniffed the air. Oh, sweet mercy, he was the most adorable thing.

"Clear out!" Jask roared, making both Marigold and the fox jump.

The fox disappeared into the shadows, and her heart threatened to burst through her ribs. "That was unnecessary."

"Unnecessary till you find a pile of feathers instead of Primrose, Heather, Daffodil, or Bluebell."

"Did you . . ." Her laugh caught Barnaby's attention. "Did you name your chickens after flowers?"

Jask checked the latches on the chicken yard. "I like flower names."

"So, you like *my* name?" She bumped her shoulder against his biceps.

After a beat, he said, "It's a nice name."

"I may swoon. Thank you, Jask Bone-Cracker. So is yours." She sniffed. "Does the air smell like cinnamon? Or am I imagining that?"

"That'll be the birch trees." He held the lantern up and led her behind the byre. "The inner bark smells like wintergreen and cinnamon. When bucks scrape their antlers against the trunk, the bark peels and it releases the scent."

The sun had sunk behind the tree line, and the first stars popped on like freshly lit candles in the purpling sky. She sighed deeply. If she lived here, much like the hooting owls, she'd never remain indoors at night.

"There," Jask said. "The bucking tub's under the lean-to."

Beneath the lean-to's canted roof stood a neatly organized collection of equipment. Amid the plow, a device with a crank, ladders, and a laundry pot dangling from its three-legged stand, stood a bucking tub the size of her trousseau trunk.

"It's perfect." Her blue sparks shrank it to the size of a shoe. After tucking the tub under her arm, she skipped back to the house. Inside, she slipped out of her shoes and moved the crate from the center of the bearskin rug.

"I'll manage the water," Jask said.

With great reverence, she centered the tub in front of the hearth. Her blue-sparked snap returned it to full size. As Jask poured the soup pot of boiling water into the tub, Fuzzle scampered up the stairs.

"It's not for you, cat," she called after his tail.

When she turned her attention back to the tub, only three fingers of water rippled within. That was barely enough to wet her ass.

She pursed her lips. "This'll take a lot of boiling."

"Which is why I bathe in the lake." He refilled the pot and returned it to the stove. "It's cold but gets the job done."

"I was told that's not an option for me."

"I stand by that." He folded his arms across his chest, which caused his forearms to bulge. "Too many prying eyes out there."

"Whose? It's you, me, and the animals."

"Ramblers cross these borders all the time, Princess," he said. "And there's Alfred."

"Alfred? He's half my height and width. He's harmless."

"No one in the hinterlands is harmless. Can we please agree that you'll bathe inside the cottage as long as you're here?"

She pressed her hands to her heart. "I swear on my father's crown I will not attempt to bathe in the out-of-doors."

"You do that a lot—swear on your father's crown."

"Do I?" She pursed her lips. "I suppose it's because I wouldn't be sad if he lost it and Rowan, Beckett, and I lost ours along with him. It would make life a lot safer. Easier, too."

He shouldered the support pillar under the loft. "For you."

"Yes, for me." She sifted through her herbal kit, searching for ingredients that matched Jask's scent. "Do you have pine resin?"

"Yes." He retrieved a bottle from the drawer above the kitchen's corner cabinet, then handed it to her. "Tell me, Princess, about this need for a safer and easier life. Do your diamond shoes hurt as well? The tragedy of clean sheets and regular meals must be horrible."

Jask's tone was friendly. Well, friendly for an orc. But the angle of his argument set her teeth on edge.

"Ha ha. Obviously, there are advantages. But overall, I don't want them. My father's position makes targets of us all and prevents me from living the life I want. Royalty complicates my freedom to choose things for myself."

His gaze was as focused as an archer. "What weren't you free to choose?"

She licked her lips. Why dodge the answer? She'd been more honest with Jask in two days than anyone else in her life for the past five years.

Rot it, she'd tell him the plain truth.

"My father's crown distressed Bram. Even before Papa took the throne, Bram thought my parents would deem him unworthy of me. Beneath my station. Good enough to fight under their banner, but not good enough for their daughter. Which is—was—ridiculous. He was so self-confident about a great many things, but he refused to believe me when I said they'd accept him. They would have, I swear it, because he was expert in what they considered the most important predictor for a good, loving match."

After a pause, Jask turned from the stove. "What was that?"

"Bram saw *me*." She turned toward the bath with aromatic herbs in her fists. "As a person, not a princess. And he loved me for my quirks, not despite them. My laugh that cuts through walls, my inability to dance, that I curse without hesitation and mix medicine as well as any apothecary. I don't care a flipping fig for court intrigues and am besotted with the moon."

Jask poured more steaming water to the tub, then rolled his neck like he was weighing his words. "That's romantic, I'll grant you. But surely a princess deserves to be cared for and to—"

"Stop right there. Ugh, you sound like Bram." As she shook dried cloves and juniper berries into the tub, the near-boiling water released their calming fragrance. "It was the one vexing thing about him."

"Just one?" Jask returned the pot to the stove.

"Yes, but it was a big one. He thought he knew how the world worked better than me and intimated my hopeful nature is rooted in naivety. Hope is a choice—a *hard* choice—but I make it every day. And I did my best to learn *exactly* how the world worked by slipping the palace guard at every turn. I longed for the day I'd prove him wrong. But then . . . he died."

She truly believed tears were healthy, but Marigold would *not* cry in front of Jask twice in one day. Blinking faster than a hummingbird flapped its wings, she probably looked like a demon clutched her soul, but she'd accept that risk.

"And you . . ." Jask's cleared his throat. "Lost your chance."

"I didn't *lose* it. My chance—my true love—was ripped from me and left a gaping gash behind. As much as loving him hurt in the end, I'd do it again without hesitation. Some go a lifetime without love like that. I was blessed to have it."

If she wasn't mistaken, pity filled the orc's eyes.

Unable to face him, Marigold poured the final pot of heated water into the tub. It had not yet boiled, but that was fine. As much as she ached for a hot bath, she preferred not to cook herself.

"I respect you for that." Jask slipped back into his house shoes. "I'll wait outside while you bathe. Let me know when you've finished?"

"Wait—soap?" she asked.

"Oh, sorry." From under the bench by the door, he grabbed his kit, then thrust it at her. "Here."

From the kit, she extracted the soap. Yes, this was the source of the addictive scent that had bedeviled her last night.

"Cedarwood," she said. "And, if I'm not mistaken, geranium and . . . bergamot?"

"And birch bark." He folded his forearms. "Do you not

like it? I can get you something else. Perhaps the pine from the kitchen?"

Marigold widened her eyes. "The opposite. I like it very much. Why would you assume I didn't?"

His brown eyes searched hers. "Because you noticed it. To be noticed is to be targeted. Why would you comment on it if you weren't criticizing it?"

Her hands were full, or else she'd settle a reassuring one on his arm. "Recognition can mean admiration, too."

As he backed away, he said, "Not in my experience, Princess. But you have a nice bath."

With the door firmly shut, Marigold shifted her weight. He'd hinted at something—what? The uneasy undercurrent to their exchange could be a ripple or a riptide. Impossible to know what he meant, but the longer she stayed here, the greater the chance she'd find out.

As she shed her clothes, her skin pebbled with exposure to the cool air. Slowly, clad only in her bathing shift, she dipped her foot into the water to test its temperature. *Ah, perfection.* With a sigh, she slipped the rest of her body into the steaming bath. Surrounded by Jask's scent, she closed her eyes in the relaxing water and plotted her next move.

Journey to Mareval as soon as possible?

Or write another letter to Rowan and bring him here?

Both had their advantages. She sighed. If only she'd been allowed to study Machiavelli's *The Prince* or Caesar's *Gallic Wars* with Rowan and Beckett. Perhaps that wasn't necessary, though. The gamesmanship of who was courting whom among the house staff could be just as complicated, and she was well-versed in that.

She'd walk through it in her mind, step by step.

For the journey option . . . Crispin's men might yet be

about, which was a concern. Jask would protect her from both the palace guard and whatever befell them in the Shivering Dales. But he was wounded, and on foot, travel would take at least two days in one direction. With no one to tend the animals, Paloma, Queen, and the chickens would suffer.

Letters to Rowan it was.

With the decision made, her muscles unclenched. Tomorrow, she'd write to Rowan, find reliable carriers, wait here for a response, and help a grumpy orc whether he wanted it or not.

Chapter 11

Bram sat on the front porch, forehead braced by the palm of his good hand, very much trying to ignore the fact that Marigold was bathing on the other side of the door.

Nope, nothing for it. Despite his throbbing hand, he needed to whittle something, anything, to occupy his jumpy mind. She hadn't fallen in love with Crispin. Ever. The joy that bolted through him when she confessed her dislike for the prince suffused every inch of his body, had turned up the brightness on his world.

Hence the need to distract himself. He circled to the back of the house and entered the byre. He kept his tools in the stall next to Queen, who mooed as he entered.

"Go to sleep, girl," he said. "Big day tomorrow. Marigold will milk you."

Her tail flicked as he scratched between her eyes.

From the next stall, he collected his carving knife. Instead of heading back to the porch he delved into the root cellar and dipped a cider from the barrel within.

An hour later—saints, how long did it take to bathe?—he was nearly finished the miniature orc carving and well into his second cider. The beverage was welcome and tasty. It had taken many tries to get to a decent formula. His first attempt, when he was fresh to his orcness and hungered for oblivion, had produced a barrel of fizzy apple juice.

This year's batch was less sweet, crisp, and potent.

His ear twitched. Another difference when he'd been reskinned as an orc—his hearing was sharp. Noises blended into a pleasant background hum of life in the hinterlands had caused him alarm when he'd first turned. With practice, he'd learned to ignore the scratch of a squirrel or the clattering thwip of a locust.

But novel sounds demanded his attention.

Like Marigold's soft sigh an hour ago as she'd settled in the bath's steaming embrace. Or the splash and trickle as she washed herself. Curse his memory and his fertile imagination. In the years since he'd last held her, her body had ripened further. The plains of young womanhood had been replaced by curves he ached to explore.

Not that she'd have him like this.

Nor would he expect her to.

Maybe he should grab a third cider? Before he rose from his rocking chair, Sir Patrick's voice echoed in his mind: *Drink never solved anything better than a frank conversation.* The old man had sayings about everything, and damn, if they weren't wise.

Inside the house, the sound of water cascaded. Must've been Marigold rising from the bath, and mercy, he shouldn't have imagined that picture. He focused on the pumpkin patch in front of him and tried to call any vision to mind that would help him ignore the sound of her sloshing as she stepped over the side of the basin.

And a grunt and a thump as she slipped and fell.

He dropped his knife and burst into the cottage. "Marigold?"

"Over here." She raised an arm from where she lay betwixt the divan and basin.

Mid-stride, he paused. "Are you decent?"

"Enough. But I'm okay." The arm disappeared, and the

sound of shifting cloth sounded from her spot. "Correction. I am tangled."

Sensitive to her modesty, he asked, "May I approach?"

As Bram, he'd seen, caressed, and tasted all of her. But Marigold thought he was Jask. The orc did not have her consent to see her in a state of undress, and she might scream if he pounded toward her without permission.

"I may permanently reside on the floor if you don't. Your linens have become an epic Gordian knot."

Because personal injury was the time to trot out Greek mythology.

He found her on the floor, swaddled in damp linen and her bathing shift. Though they remained opaque, the linens molded to her and did not hide the luscious hills and valleys of her body. Which, as a courtly gentleman, he should do his best not to see as he lifted her to the divan. This was another benefit to his orc body—even with a damaged hand, he possessed the strength of three men.

"Are you hurt?" he asked.

"Mortified, but otherwise hearty." In the firelight, her typical pale skin had whitened further. "The water stayed quite hot. Or maybe it was the fire? Either way, I stood up too fast."

"Uprightness is a hazard." He covered her with a quilt, then lit a taper in a chamberstick. Her pale skin deeply contrasted with the dark russet of her wet hair. "Look at me?"

She turned to him, and saints, she stole his breath.

He brought the flame close to her blue eyes. "Are you nauseated? Or have a headache?"

During tournaments, some knights who'd been knocked from their horses were stunned to the extent that they sought dark rooms and buckets to catch the contents of their stomachs. One telltale sign that they'd suffered a serious blow was the irises' lack of response to light, but Marigold's pupils shrank to pinpricks.

"No on both counts," she said. "The bruises are solely on my ego. And perhaps my ass."

The tight fist of fear around his heart eased. Jokes meant she was fine.

He set the candle down. "Would you like some water?"

"My embarrassment calls for something stronger." She lay her head back on the divan. "Whiskey?"

Hmph. He hadn't gotten around to building a stillroom. "All I have is cider."

She nodded. "Then cider it is."

"Don't move," he said as he surged to his feet.

"Wouldn't dream of it," she said. "But I'll take care of this for you."

In a flash of blue sparks, the bucking tub reduced to the size of a porringer. Magic still raised his hackles, but he was growing accustomed to hers.

"Thanks," he said.

He tossed the water from the tiny tub into the kitchen's wash basin, then grabbed a tankard from the kitchen. Outside, he set the tub on the trestle table that doubled as a work bench, then made short work of dipping a portion for Marigold.

On his way back to the cottage, he glanced upward. It was nice to see the night sky through her eyes earlier. Forced to live here, he rarely allowed himself to appreciate the hinterlands' beauty. The stars had grown bold as the evening darkened and twinkled nearly as brightly as the fire within the cottage.

Quietly he opened the door, then rejoined her on the divan. His chest warmed at the sight of the locket around her neck. Just as he'd carried her image with him in Harvest Hollow, she'd carried his with her. The halves had been rejoined years before the lovers, even if she didn't know they'd been reunited.

"Here you are," he said.

In her hands, the tankard was enormous. "None for you?"

"No, I've already indulged enough for the evening."

"My lady's companion warned me never to drink alone, but I believe rules are meant to be broken." She sipped. "Oh, that's lovely. How many ciders before you feel tipsy? With your size, I'd imagine it takes twice as much to satisfy you as it would a human man."

He turned that over in his head, looking for the critique, but found none. It was an honest question about the differences between orcs and humans. One meant to learn, not mock.

"Thrice, actually," he answered. "I eat and drink at a ratio of three to one."

She furrowed her brow. "But we eat the same amount at meals."

He twisted toward her. "I wanted you to have enough."

"Oh, Jask, that's so sweet." She laid a hand on his knee, and the sizzle when straight to his cock. "But please, eat your fill. I'd speak up if I wanted more. You must be starved."

"I'm fine," he said.

His stomach rumbled at the most inopportune time.

"Sure, you are," she laughed. "Go, eat."

He swung his legs to the floor. "I'll put a snack together for both of us. Don't move—give your humors a chance to settle."

In the kitchen, he sliced apples, then added a chunk of fresh cheese, roasted pumpkin seeds, a few dried apricots, and a dollop of the blackberry jam Marigold had left in the cabinet. He knocked the bread against the counter. Stale, but it would make excellent bread pudding. No matter—the rest should suffice as a snack for the two of them.

"Here." He set the tray on the divan between them. "Have some."

"You first," she said. "Bram couldn't function if he was hungry."

It was so odd, hearing about himself this way. Like earlier, when Marigold had cried over her lost true love and listed his qualities. He'd blushed at her praise, and his tenderness wanted to wrap her in a hug. His desire for her, however, had encouraged distance.

At that, he'd failed.

He reached for a thick apple slice. "How so?"

"It became his sole focus. Me? I acknowledge hunger but can keep myself together until I eat. Bram, though—he treated everything that stood between him and a meal at the appointed time as a villain. He was often locked in existential battle with people who had no idea they were playing the role of opponent."

She . . . wasn't wrong. But he thought he'd hidden it better. The sweet-and-savory blend of the apple slice slathered in fresh cheese and sprinkled with pumpkin seeds took some of the sting out of her observation.

"Why were you with him if you disliked this about him?"

She blasted him with her laugh. "When did I say I disliked this? I loved him as he was. Since the age of seven, honestly. As we grew older, I suggested he have a snack instead of burning the world down. Don't you think our quirks, our flaws are what endears us to people? I always felt like I was privileged to see and know the things he tried to keep from the world. It's in the knowing that true love blossoms."

Hmph.

She might've had a point. The fashionable princess with the shining crown was beautiful, but this kind of quiet moment—Marigold bedraggled from the bath and sipping homemade cider—was where he'd fallen most deeply in love with her. Why shouldn't she have fallen for the less-than-perfect version of Bram?

"Do you truly believe that?" he asked.

She sighed and ate an apricot. "I truly, truly do."

He'd tried *so* hard to be the perfect knight. Skills and strength and courtly manners. Appearance mattered, too. Carefully brushed teeth and hair, frequent visits to the barber for shaves and haircuts, polished boots and armor—all of it designed to prove that he, a foundling fostered by Sir Patrick Duncan, was worthy of a princess.

Worthy, full stop.

But here was sweet Marigold, reminding him that none of the artifice had been necessary for her. She'd seen Bram, truly and well, and had loved him. He'd been too thick to realize it at the time, had convinced himself that she wanted only the handsome knight, not the rough boy within.

"I'm sure he would've loved to know you felt that way." He reached for another apple.

"I *told* him." She slapped the divan, making the remaining bits of food on the cutting board bounce. "Many times. But he didn't believe me. This is what I meant earlier about him thinking I don't know how the world works. I *do*. Our society constrains women, but the system does a huge disservice to men, too. The daily message to them is their value is in how much coin they earn and how well they protect their people. As though we only love men for what they can do for us. That it's impossible to simply love a man for who he is and delight in sharing a table, a hearth, and a home with him."

This was, in fact, a familiar complaint of hers.

"Come now," he scoffed. "You'd be content to be partnered with a weak pauper who couldn't support you?"

She laid her hand atop his, then tipped back more cider. "See how far-reaching that backward philosophy is? It's gotten to you, too, all the way out here on Lonely Hermit Farm."

Ouch. *In vino veritas*. Or, in this case—in cider, certainty.

"It's called Grimroot Farm," he mumbled.

"And yes, I do believe it. That men are for more than money—they are for comfort, conversation, and love. My mother's family is of the merchant class, and the women have as many business responsibilities as the men. If a husband takes ill and needs to stay home, it's fine because his wife is as well versed in the work." Her volume increased, as did the reach of her gestures. "Also, if a man wants to protect the home, he should do laundry."

Saints, he'd missed Marigold rants.

Bram hid his laugh as he turned his hand underneath hers. Palm to palm, but without lacing fingers. That would be a step too far. "The cider's gone to your head."

She shook her head in the slow dramatic way of someone who's crossed over to tipsy. "Bess told me about it. The laundry. Physicians have noticed disease springs up in clusters, like your pumpkins." The cider sloshed as she gestured toward the door. "But less so in places with robust laundry services and scrubbing routines. Disease kills more than war or raids. So, if men wanted to protect the family, they'd do laundry."

The tankard slipped from her grip.

Jask caught it before the last drops spilled. "I do laundry."

"I *knew* you were a good one." She clapped, then pressed her fingertips to her forehead. "Oh. The world is swirly. Can we trade bunks tonight? I'll sleep here. You take the loft."

She flopped back down on the divan, then burrowed under the quilts. This would not do. He grasped the logic of her laundry argument, but his protective instincts demanded she take the less vulnerable loft. If Crispin and his knights returned, Bram wanted Marigold upstairs and tucked into his bed, leaving him down here, ready to fight.

"Come on." He tugged at her hand. "I'll help you up the stairs."

She giggled as she slipped from his grip. "I can't possibly make it."

Her bones were as limp as stewed pears. He agreed she couldn't climb under her own power. Luckily, as an orc, he had power for days.

"Then I'll carry you." With nary a grunt, and careful of his wound, he lifted her. As Bram, he'd capably carried her, but in Jask's arms, she was light as a butterfly.

"Put me down." She batted at his chest. "You'll pop a stitch."

He could feel his pulse in each of those five stitches, but there was no strain in his palm. "I'll be fine."

"You'll get all wet." Marigold laid her head against his shoulder. "Wow, orcs really do run hot, don't they?"

He grunted in response. She didn't know the half of it. At the stairwell, he turned sideways. Fuzzle followed, the evil beast twisting himself around Bram's ankles.

"Do you want us to break our necks, cat? Shoo."

Marigold glanced up at him with her huge blue eyes. "You pretend to be all surly, but you're a big marshmallow, aren't you?"

"No." He turned at the landing.

"Okay, not a marshmallow. But definitely marchpane." She held his chin and squeezed. "Squishable."

"Stop that," he sighed. "You're the only person on the planet with the audacity to put her hand near an orc's mouth."

"Because you won't hurt me." She patted his chest. "I know it."

Saints, but this was a test of his willpower.

At the top of the stairs, he turned, then ducked under the slanted beam as he crossed to his neatly made bed. With ease, he kneeled on the bed's edge, then deposited her gently.

"Thank you." She fluttered her eyes open, then tilted her head. "You remind me of him."

The scant light up here was from the moon and the ambient light that crept upstairs from the fireplace. Both worked together to lend her an angelic glow.

"Him who?" He held the bed's post.

"Bram. Something in the way you carry yourself. And you always seem to know what to do." She sat upright and loosely gestured toward her trunk. "Can you get me a fresh shift? There's nothing better than falling asleep after a bath in clean clothes and a comfy bed."

With a hard gulp, he pivoted.

On some deep level, Marigold recognized him. Despite everything—the changed form, color, voice, eyes—she sensed something familiar under his skin she could trust, and she didn't need to fear him. She couldn't allow herself to consider he might *be* Bram. Who could?

But she liked the orc—that much was clear. And that would need to be enough.

He sorted through her trunk, ignoring her undergarments. As he pulled a soft linen shift from among her dresses, a handheld looking glass tumbled out with it. He'd long rid the cottage of these to avoid his reflection.

Today the orc didn't frighten him as it once had.

After tossing the glass in her trunk, he took the shift to Marigold. "Here."

She flashed him a beautiful, muzzy-faced grin. "What would I do without you, Jask?"

Probably have been captured and dragged back to Brambleton Castle. His insides slithered with the thought.

"Good night, Marigold."

The floorboards creaked under his feet. Downstairs, he thumped onto the divan and tucked his arm behind his head and trained his gaze on the loft railing. In two full days, he hadn't come close to confessing his true name to Princess Marigold of Thornwick. Bram, in her mind, was well and truly dead. She'd never loved Crispin, but her openness . . . the way she talked to Jask . . . touched him . . . Might she might be able to love him *as* Jask? No, that was ludicrous.

That was too ambitious, even for him.

Chapter 12

For all of Marigold's education and etiquette, "Ow" was the most cogent response she could muster to the shards of pain drifting through her skull. She pressed her palms to her eyes to block out the sunlight suffusing the curtains.

Wait, full sun. She'd missed morning chores.

She sniffed the air, picking up a delicious scent against which her stomach rebelled. Had Jask cooked? And with his hand . . . He was probably out there right now, working and risking further injury. She hurried into her homespun, washed her face, neck, and under her arms, then brushed her teeth in the ewer—had Jask replaced the water while she was asleep? She hurried down the stairs to the bench by the door.

Unbelievable. Day three and she was already acting like a spoiled princess. Abed until midmorning because of excesses the night before, missing chores, not helping.

She yanked on a boot. Her thumbnail snagged and split to the quick. "*Dammit*," she grumbled as she shook out her hand.

"Princesses curse?"

She startled and stood upright, the pressed her hand to her sternum. Jask hunched at the table tucked behind the stairs, watching her. How long had he been there?

"You scared me," she said.

"Mmph," he grunted, then scraped his fork against his plate with the last of his meal.

"Not because you're an orc," she clarified. "Because you were silent as a ghost."

"I'll be louder." Jask gestured toward her place at the table. "There's breakfast."

A sour taste rose to the back of her throat. She pressed her fingertips to her mouth to hold in a noxious belch. "No, thank you."

"Eat." He gestured toward her place again. "You were in your cups—this'll help. And I want to talk to you about something."

In all of history, has any good conversation started that way? Cautiously, she approached the table. He'd set out a wedge of savory tart, a mug, and the kettle sat on a trivet on the table.

Gingerly, she sat. Saints, it was as though her body were made of Venetian glass. One sudden move and she'd shatter. Jask poured the kettle's contents into her mug.

"What's that?" she asked.

"Willow bark. For your head." He swirled in a spoonful of honey and a dash of cinnamon, as she liked it, then pushed it toward her. "Barnaby didn't wake you?"

"I'm as surprised as you are." With her fingertips pressed to her temples, she asked, "What was in that cider? A curse?"

As his scowl ridged his forehead, he set his forearms on the table. "Just apples and yeast. But it's aged—I forgot it would be strong for a slight person such as yourself."

She sipped the willow bark and grimaced. This was worse than the chicory. "I'm quite tall and hearty, I'll have you know."

"Comparatively—" he gestured between them, then pushed the plate toward her "—you are small. Eat the tart. It'll quell your stomach."

"I doubt that very much, but I'm desperate." She lifted a bite. Queasy though she might be, she sighed with appreciation. Egg, brie, onion, and an explosion of herbs. Delicious. Flaky, buttery, with the right amount of chew to it.

Jask raised an eyebrow. "You moan when you eat. It's troubling."

"I only moan when the food is this good. Epic poems should be written about this tart." She dabbed her lips with her napkin. "Will you show me how to make it?"

"We need to talk, Princess."

Again, suspicious phrasing. Fear swirled through her, and she set down her fork. Was he about to tell her to leave this oasis of a farm? Something worse?

"About what?" she asked. "Tell it to me plain—I insist."

"Farm duties. There are the normal, everyday tasks that I showed you yesterday. I milked Queen. She would have been in pain had I not. But now I am the one in pain."

Her chest tightened with guilt. "I'm sorry. I should've woken earlier and done it for you."

"Keep your apology—I'm partly to blame. Shouldn't have given you the cider, and I should've woken you. What's done is done. But I realized the rhythm of the work is all in my head, and you'd benefit from a list. Can you write it down?"

Relief flooded through her. "You're not kicking me out? When I arrived, you were insistent that I leave the next day."

"No, I'm not kicking you out. Not so long as this throbs." He lifted his hand.

The willow bark seemed less bitter. "Do you have ink and parchment?"

He nodded, then pushed up from the table. With his back turned, she was free to admire the linen shirt's drape over his broad shoulders. He rustled through his desk, then returned with a quill, inkhorn, sand, and parchment. Another thing the fairy tales got wrong—orcs were portrayed as creatures of war, not letters.

Lucky for her, as she had letters to write.

"Here." He pushed the writing materials toward her. "We'll draft the daily chores first, then the ones fixed to certain days of the week. Are you ready?"

She trimmed the quill with her knife and cut a fresh slit. "Yes."

As he dictated the schedule and she transcribed, the quill scratched against the parchment. At the end of twenty minutes, it was filled with a tidy—and extensive—schedule.

"That's a lot of work," she said.

He stretched. "That's running a farm. Anything you want to add?"

She scanned her handiwork. Baking, both bread and pies, was on the schedule for tomorrow. Laundry was later this week, as was splitting and stacking firewood. Though the pain was receding, a twinge forked across her temple.

"Cider," she said.

"I would've thought you'd had your fill."

Under a new column titled *Other*, she wrote, *Pressing cider.* "I have, but I'd like to press a lighter vintage so I don't feel like this again while I'm here. Ooh, and braiding onions and garlic. I saw them in the root cellar. Genius way to store them and save space."

"Cider takes longer," he said. "That's all you want to learn?"

"For now," she said. "I'm sure I don't know what I don't know, and the list may grow. But I'm not completely useless. I already know how to sew, sweep, gather herbs. Dishes as well." Her face lit up. "Oh, there is something else."

She added, *Carving pumpkins, Dancing.*

"Those aren't really chores. But your jack-o'-lanterns were amazing. We should replace the ones Crispin's knights destroyed."

"And the dancing?" The divot appeared between his

scrunched brows. "A princess who doesn't know how to dance is like a knight who can't mount a horse in armor. I can't believe you need me to show you the steps."

"That's where you're wrong." She flapped the feathery part of the quill at him. "I know stiff courtly dances. But townsfolk always look like they have way more fun dancing during festivals. That's what I want you to teach me, assuming you know them?"

Jask dipped his chin. "I do, in fact. Anything else?"

"Building a gazebo, eventually." Yes, she was adding *Gazebo* to the list. "You *must* have noticed the farm is crying out for a gazebo. Between the pumpkin patches and the meadow, near the sunflowers. It would be perfect for reading or al fresco meals and would make a natural stage for any minstrels."

His snort sounded suspiciously like a laugh. "You're a constant surprise, Princess."

She scattered fine sand across the parchment to soak up the excess ink. "While you're in a state of surprise, I need to share my plans for removing myself from Grimroot Farm. Once you've healed, of course."

The scrunchy ridges returned to his forehead. "But you've been begging to stay. And it's not safe on your own."

"Agreed, which is why I'd planned to ask you to escort me."

"I cannot." The contents of his mug sloshed over the side as he slammed it on the table. If it was chicory, she'd done him a favor. "It's too—"

"Calm yourself." She touched her fingers to his wrist. "After observing you these last two days, I know you can't abandon your animals for the two days there and back."

"Where is *there*?" he asked.

She dragged her lower lip through her teeth. The plan had been her secret for weeks, held closer to her heart than her locket. Something shifted in her chest. She could trust Jask with this information. She'd been on the brink of asking him to escort her to the place, hadn't she?

"Mareval. I've a contact there who will shelter me until my rescuer arrives." She pinched a crumb of tart crust from her plate. "Your cottage was a beacon in the night, Jask, but not my planned destination. May I use your parchment and ink to correspond with my rescuer? He'll be worried, and Alfred said he could find a carrier for me."

His shoulders stiffened again. Mercy, what had she said now? He'd been quite clear he didn't want her staying here for an open-ended period.

"Who is *he*?"

"My twin brother." She twiddled the quill. "Before my dash from Brambleton Castle, I'd sent him word—coded so only he'd understand—that I'd wait for him in Mareval. I knew the palace guard would watch the roads betwixt Harvest Hollow and Thornwick. Less so the roads leading south. He'd meet me at my sanctuary, then escort me home."

"Clever." The bench creaked as Jask shifted his weight.

"Thank you. You see? I'm not just a pretty face. But now I must send word again, both to his position on the northern front and to Mareval in the event he's already there. If you're amenable, I'd like to tell him where I am. Discreetly, of course."

Jask thumbed the divot in his chin. "Only if I read the letters to ensure they're coded deeply enough. I must keep my farm—and everyone in it—safe."

This was a reasonable request.

"Yes, of course," she said. "Now, let me tend to your hand, then we'll get started with the day's chores. The letters will keep until after the animals have been tended."

If Marigold ignored the fact a horde of knights and an angry prince were looking for her, she was happy in the easy rhythm she and Jask had fallen into over the last few. If she wasn't mistaken, the orc was warming to her presence. Her clue? When they spoke, he held her gaze with his magnetic brown-and-gold-flecked eyes—a marked improvement from when she'd first arrived and he'd looked above, beyond, or through her.

Perhaps her capable help with the farm while he healed brought about his change of heart? Or the coins she insisted he take for room and board after Alfred declined an additional pumpkin shipment to market yesterday? After slipping the carter the letters to Rowan that Jask agreed were impossible to decipher, Alfred shared the latest Harvest Hollow news and gossip. On the news side, sprite activity had picked up in the Shivering Dales. As for gossip, according to the *Harvest Herald*'s chronicler Isolde Fenlow, Princess Marigold was suffering from an ague.

Interesting deflection.

Despite the princess's reported "illness," her wedding to Prince Crispin remained scheduled for next weekend. A bold feint, as Crispin had no bride. Dangerous, too, as the prince's bluff likely meant he'd redouble his search for her.

And if that happened . . .

Marigold blinked, then shook her head. No, she was safe here. If found, she'd hide as she did before. All she had to do was stay out of Crispin's reach until Rowan came for her. She mustn't overthink it. Much like she shouldn't overthink bread-making or the fact that flour dusted her from her neck to her hips.

"Shoo, Fuzzle." She lifted the cat from the trestle table and dropped him to the floor.

Indignantly, he marched toward the hearth, tiny white paw prints in his wake.

She eyed the stubborn dough. "I think I hate baking."

From where Jask sat reading at the table, he lifted his eyes. "You did well with the pie. The crust held the apples and the pumpkin with integrity."

"That's the mouthwatering description I aimed for." She laughed as she kneaded the dough. "Pie with integrity."

"It's quite tasty." He was eating a slice to conclude his midday meal. "You were right about the rosemary complementing the apple."

Her chest expanded with his praise. During this fortnight of learning, while his hand healed and she'd taken over much of the cooking, he'd been liberal with his compliments. She soaked up his kind words like wool in a rainstorm. Besides Bram and Jask, the only other person free with praise had been Vera, the cunning woman who'd taught her to control her minimancy.

Not that minimancy helped with breadmaking.

"Glad you're enjoying it." Press. Fold. Turn, repeat. "How will I know when I'm done with this part? My arms ache."

He closed his book. "When it smooths out and is no longer shaggy. It helps to pretend the dough's an annoying person."

"That's good motivation—thank you." She pressed with renewed vigor. "Prince Crispin Batten-Forge, meet your doom."

Jask choke-laughed on the last bite. In addition to looking at her, the orc was far less grumpy than when she first arrived. Obviously, that was partly because she was a damned delight. But he must have been *so* starved for company. Trips into town would be uncomfortable if people truly stared at him the way he said they had. But he'd grown to trust her—maybe he could build a rapport with others, too? Mixing with people would be good for him.

Complete isolation worked for no one.

Jask drained his mug and set it on the table. "I've no love for Crispin, but what went wrong between you and the prince?"

"I reject the premise." She yanked up her too-long sleeves, then folded the dough again. "Nothing was ever right between us. He wanted a queen who'd project the right image as she stood beside—though slightly behind—him. I thought I was up to the task. My reasoning was this—if I would never be happy again, then what did it matter if I sacrificed myself for a marriage that would benefit my home kingdom? Be advised, making huge life choices while melancholic is . . . not great."

"What made you come to your senses?" He approached the trestle table, then rested his hip against it.

Saints, between the oven and his hot-bloodedness, she'd break out in a full body sweat and need a tisane of meadowsweet to bring her temperature down.

"Several things. First, my numbness thawed." The dough stretched as she worked it. "Coming to Harvest Hollow, seeing the things Bram wrote about in his letters with my own eyes . . . it healed me. I suppose I'm grateful for Crispin's proposal, because it brought me here. But he measured so poorly in comparison to Bram. I couldn't spend my one precious life with him. I'd bear him children he'd ignore, care for his aging father without a whit of gratitude, entertain his guests and be treated with less respect than his favorite horse. No, sir, that couldn't be me."

"You said *several things*. What else?"

"Is that not enough?" She blew an errant curl from her face, but the stubborn thing drifted back in front of her eyes.

"Not for a devoted princess of Thornwick whose kingdom has much to gain from this alliance." He tucked the curl behind her ear, his nail lightly scraping the delicate skin behind it.

Her body flipped from overheating to shivers.

"I . . ." She gulped. "Discovered a plot. Knowing more may put you at risk."

He stared down at her, his gold-flecked brown gaze like a sunbeam. "You're worth it."

Despite his words turning her knees to aspic, the ground was more solid under her feet. To no longer be alone in this knowledge would be like shedding the too-heavy ceremonial robes that nearly made her faint at her father's coronation.

"Do you swear you'll tell no one?"

He laid his injured arm across his heart. "Solemnly. I keep secrets well."

Something wistful passed over his face. The moment stretched between them, taught as a bowstring. Underneath the tension, another sensation skated through her.

Affection.

Grumpy as the orc was, he was kind. He took her in when danger was at his door. Fed her. Carved with the skill of a craftsman and cared for a bevy of creatures. Highest in her esteem—he had the good sense to loathe Crispin.

"The prince is allied with the mountain sprites—with Alfred's news today, I wouldn't be surprised if he was similarly allied with those in the Shivering Dales. Regardless, he intends to use the mountain sprites to murder my brothers. With their demise, I become the sole heir to the Thornwick throne. After I succeed my father, Crispin plans to confine me to Scarlet Spire. Per our marriage contract, if I become incapacitated, he'll rule as regent. His goal is to unite the kingdoms of Harvest Hollow and Thornwick, then strip Thornwick of its precious metals and render it a barren wasteland."

Jask's grunt sounded as though he'd taken a blow to the gut. As he ground his jaw, his tusks pressed against his upper lip. "That base, contemptible wretch."

"I chose more colorful words when I learned of it. The next day, I posted a coded letter to Rowan, then ran at my first opportunity, which is how I ended up on your doorstep."

His gaze softened. "You're quite brave, do you know that?"

Her cheeks heated. "You're kind to listen."

"It's my everlasting pleasure," he said.

Her blood froze.

As children, Bess took her and Bram to see a traveling troupe of players stage a romance. At one point, the hero's lover thanked him for rescuing her. While pumping his eyebrows, he answered, *It's my everlasting pleasure*. She and Bram, then twelve, had dissolved into giggles where they stood in the pit. Bess hustled them out, calling them rude and disrespectful. From that point on, they'd used it any time the other did the most minor of favors. As they'd grown romantically entangled, it had become a phrase of endearment.

One he'd just casually used.

"What did you say?" she asked.

"'It's my everlasting pleasure'?" Jask palmed his neck with his bandaged hand, then backed away. "Read it in a book."

She searched his face. Curse not knowing him longer—she could swear he was lying to her but had no proof.

With a sigh, she laid a linen over the bowl. "This is ready to rest."

Unlike her mind. She eyed the shelves near the hearth. Had he truly read that line in a book? Perhaps, as she learned new skills around the farm, she could catch up on her reading.

Chapter 13

Bram sipped Marigold's latest tisane—apple and rosemary—as he watched her through the windows. From the moment he'd injured himself, she'd dived into the routine chores of the small farm. After a week, it was as though she'd been born in the countryside instead of a castle. No hesitant opening of gates, wincing at splinters or the sudden puffs of steam from pots. She'd always been a confident woman, but the way she wore it here was more resplendent than any crown.

After finishing in the coop, she found him inside. "What else for today? Everything went quickly this morning."

"How do you feel about apple picking?"

She grabbed his forearm. "Yes, *please*. I've been desperate to know what the rest of Grimroot Farm looks like. Is it far?"

"Not very. A half hour's ramble."

He'd intentionally stalled, suspicious that Crispin's guard might circle back. But the week had been calm, and he sensed that Marigold might like to stretch her legs. She'd never lasted longer than a week in Thornwick Castle before plotting an adventure outside its thick walls.

Within the hour, after gathering the apple-picking bag and the ladder, they were in the orchard. Apples periodically thudded to the ground around them, and many of the previously fallen ones were half-eaten. Clearly Paloma had been here.

Hopefully she hadn't eaten too many of the ones that had gone soft.

A tipsy pig could be difficult to coax into a pen.

"Did you plant these trees?" Marigold asked as they strolled through the tidy rows. "They're so orderly."

The breeze fluttered the green-and-yellow leaves and carried with it a heady fermented scent from the fallen fruit. Within the enclosed orchard, there was a constant hum of eager insects, along with a chorus of cardinal, crow, and sparrow song.

"No." He shook his head. "The previous owner did. From what I gather, he was the last of his family and the land reverted to Harvest Hollow after he died."

At least, that was what Alfred had told him.

"How sad that he died here alone." She clapped her hand over her mouth. "Sorry. Living on one's own is admirable. My words get ahead of my brain sometimes."

He hitched the bag he carried further up his shoulders. "No offense taken. It's the way things have worked out so far. But I loved once, and I may yet take a wife."

Unlikely. A suitable companion would need to stumble into his path without dashing away, screaming. But the worried flicker behind her eyes was too much to bear, so he broke his chivalric code and told the lie.

"Jask Bone-Cracker, I forgot! The deep true love from your palm." Marigold bounced on her toes. "What's her name? What happened? Please, I must know everything."

Saints, how had he fallen into this trap? Second to Alfred, Marigold was the biggest gossip he knew. Never ill-intentioned—just relentlessly curious and searching for ways to be helpful.

"No, Marigold." He stepped from the walking path and onto the sward, then paused in front of a tree laden with apples. "This one's plentiful."

Under the thick canopy of this tree, he felt sheltered with

Marigold. The sun breaking through the foliage dappled her face, which was currently pinched in frustration.

"This is so unfair. I've told you so much about Bram." She clasped her hands together. "I beg. One tiny crumb of a detail? Then I promise I'll leave it."

With a sigh, he withdrew the minimized ladder from the bag, then leaned it against the tree. "Can you do your magic?"

"Yes." Marigold teased her middle finger against her thumb but did not snap. "As soon as you tell me something about your love. And you can't cheat like that first night. I want something specific."

"Now who's being unfair?" he asked. "You can't force a person to be indiscreet about their romances."

"It's very bad of me—that's true." With her chin resting on her fist, she nodded. "Spill."

He pinched the bridge of his nose and streamed a deep breath through his nose, then out through his mouth. Marigold would not relent. Not when she had that gleam in her eye.

"Fine, you win. My sweetheart doesn't live here because I stupidly thought I could make a life for us elsewhere. During our time apart, another asked her to marry him. She said yes."

It was all the truth, though she'd never see herself in it.

"What a churl! Who'd have so little sense to choose any orc over you?" Blue sparks rained on the ladder, and it shot up the trunk. "How did you find out?"

When she showed up on my doorstep ten days ago.

Instead, he wagged his finger. "Our deal was for one thing, and you must honor it. Ready to harvest? I'll hold the ladder."

He gripped a stile with his bandaged hand. The wound had healed cleanly—she'd snipped the stitches this morning. To protect the fresh skin, she insisted he wear a bandage for anything that rubbed his palm aggressively.

Marigold glanced upward. "I could shrink the tree."

"Please don't. It might disturb the root system and cause it to collapse." He removed the picking bag and handed it to her. "Fill this, and we'll have enough for pies and a firkin of cider."

"And apple fritters?" She looped the strap around her neck, then fussed with the sleeves of her dress, cursing them under her breath. "Apple fritters were my favorite at the Thornwick fall festival. Do they have them at the Goldenmoon Festival?"

"Possibly." He held the ladder steady as she climbed, but if she fell, he'd catch her.

"Crispin shouldn't cancel it," she called down the ladder.

"Because of apple fritters?"

"No, because of joy. If people are well fed and have entertainment, the kingdom holds strong. I—"

Her shriek dragged his gaze upward. Right up her kirtle. Blood and bones, he did not yet need yet another tantalizing glimpse of Marigold to stoke him further. He flung himself into Coldpress Lake daily to chill his ardor.

With eyes closed, he asked, "What is it?"

"A wasp." The ladder wiggled as she fidgeted. "Several, in fact. Can you do anything about them?"

"No. They prefer overripe fruit. Ignore them, and they'll fly to more attractive food."

"Easy for you to say." The leaves rustled as she snapped the apple from its branch. "What's this breed of apple? They smell sweet."

"Hollowsnap Reds, famous for their sweet crisp flesh."

The fruit crunched as she bit into it. "Mercy, these are good. You should send your apples to market, too."

"Can't. The royal family also has an orchard, and all farmers are restricted from selling their apples. Apple products are fine, like pies and cider, but the apples themselves are not."

"They restrict commerce, too?" She took another bite. "My parents would never. Free trade and friendly competition suits the customer and lets the best merchant win. But I can see why they're worried. I could eat a dozen of these apples."

"Legend has it if you eat too many, your cheeks carry their color."

"I'll keep that in mind." She held the apple between her lips as she plucked more to fill the bag's large front pocket.

Above them, clouds scudded through the blue sky. He shielded his eyes to inspect it. They were puffy and white, which didn't bode well for rain. Shite, that was too bad. The pumpkins were thirsty.

Soon, Marigold descended, her picking sack full and making her look like a ripe fruit herself. The sight weakened his knees. Many's the time he imagined Marigold as the mother of his children, but they'd agreed that they weren't ready when they were both in Thornwick.

But they were *quite* ready to love each other.

Fortunately, her herbal concoctions prevented conception. For that, he was grateful. Fathering a babe when he was on the brink of leaving would have been unfair to both Marigold and the child. Unlike his own early upbringing, he'd intended for his babes to know the full force of his love. They'd beg him to go away, he'd be so far into their affairs.

But he'd never imagined children with anyone but this woman.

Not that she'd have him.

"Jask? Did you hear me?" Marigold's cheeks were flushed, and she twisted her curls into a bun.

He swallowed the lump in his throat. "Sorry—what was that?"

"Can I shrink the apples at least? They'll be easier to carry."

"Yes, of course." He folded the ladder in half. "And this, too?"

After taking the apples from her, he led them a different route home to draw out their ramble.

"What happened here?" she asked as they passed the blackened and shattered rootstock tree. Wider and thicker than most of the orchard's trees, he'd used the heartwood for many a cottage project.

"Lightning," he said. "Last fall. Struck and split it in twain."

As soon as the words exited his mouth he wished he could suck them back in. How could he forget she was petrified of lightning?

"Do . . ." Her voice faded. "Do bad storms happen often?"

He caught her hand. "They're rare, and never sudden."

She traced the lines of the charred remains. "Do you swear it?"

"Yes," he lied as he squeezed her hand.

Another of his constant stream of untruths. But she would be gone before long. There was no need to worry her while she remained.

"Good," she said, then withdrew her hand. "That's . . . good."

Saints, he'd overstepped. What had he thought, that the unavoidable touches while they lived in close confines gave him leave to hold her hand? His face, neck, and ears were molten, like he'd dipped them into a steaming laundry pot.

In silence, they restarted the journey back to the cottage.

As they approached the verge where the orchard met the open meadow, the clouds of midges enjoying the fallen fruit thinned. The deepening gold of the afternoon caught the occasional dragonfly wing as it arrowed across the meadow.

"Tell me about making cider?" Marigold prompted.

"There isn't much to it," he said. "The bloom—the faint dusty coating on the apples drives the fermentation. After we chop and press the fruit, nature does the rest of the work. All that's required of us is patience as the cider ages."

"So, fermentation changes the apple, but its essence persists in a new form."

His chest tightened. She couldn't know how personal her description felt to him. The lump in his throat made it difficult for him to respond, so he offered an affirming grunt.

"I feel like that sometimes," she said. "That everything that's happened in the past five years—Bram, magic, the not-wedding, being here with you—it's all changed me, my form, but I'm still *me*. The apple doesn't choose the bloom but bears up under its influence. Ooh, those sunflowers are so pretty this time of day. They're my favorite flower."

He knew.

When he first arrived, the farm held little charm or whimsy. Marigold's voice played in his head, suggesting a different paint color here, flowers there. To pay her tribute, the obvious choice would've been marigolds. But she disliked them immensely, considered their primary purpose to keep pests away. Their pungent scent filled Thornwick's hedgerow maze. No, this happy sunflower patch waving in the breeze suited his true love better.

"We all go through periods of change," he said. "But it's true we're largely the same at our core."

"In alchemy, the transformation reveals, rather than destroys, an object's essential nature." She tapped the head of a sunflower as they passed. "The experiments are designed to burn away the dross and bring out the truest form of a thing."

Beyond the neat pumpkin patches lay the cottage, its cozy presence a beacon through the stormy haze of his emotions. Was that true for him? Had the curse worked like alchemy and turned him into his truest form?

He chose his words carefully. "So, in your experiments, you believe the element on the other side is what it was meant to be all along?"

"Theoretically," she said. "But either I am a terrible alchemist or the science is a sham. I never once turned lead into gold. I believe matter can be transformed—the apples to cider, for example. But the cider is still the apple's essence."

The cider is still the apple's essence. Perfectly stated, and if he wouldn't have to explain why, he'd pick her up and twirl her in circles. Cider was a metaphor for what the curse had done to him—changed him into something new, but his essence was the same.

Bram was the apple; Jask was the cider.

Barnaby's muted rooster call heralded their return home.

Around the back of the house, in the courtyard, Bram set the picking bag on the trestle table. "I'll get the press if you sort the apples—firmer ones for baking, softer ones for cider."

As he wrestled the press, buckets, trough, and keeve into place, Marigold divided the fruit. She took greater care than he would, but she'd always been more particular. From the cottage, he grabbed two chopping knives, then joined her at the table to help wipe the apples clean of debris.

"Is it okay if they're bruised?" she asked.

"Perfectly fine." He handed her a knife. "They'll sweeten the cider. The cider apples don't need to be chopped neatly. A rough crush is better for the pressing."

Between them, they made short work of the apples. Her knife skills had improved dramatically these last few days. Her color, too. Days spent working out of doors had transformed her pallor into a rosy glow. With her lip tucked between her teeth, she was beautiful in her concentration.

Her nose wrinkled. "Ew, ew, ew!"

Marigold pushed away an apple occupied by a wriggling worm.

"I'll rescue you." He hurled offending pieces into the chicken yard, then swept the mountain of chopped apples into the bucket. "Now, we give these a mash to help them to give up the juice faster. Grab one of those boards." He gestured toward scrap from last season's fence rail repairs.

"No wonder farmers are content." She jabbed the board into the chopped apples. "You can take your frustration out on all your chores."

She wasn't wrong.

When Crispin had first discarded him here, he'd been wound tight. Between a life as a hired sword and the curse, he'd spent many of those first days shaking his fists at his fate. Eventually, he'd picked up a spade and hadn't looked back. Working the land, tapped into the seasons and currents . . . there was peace in it.

Marigold's soul seemed more settled, too.

An apple chunk flew from her masher and hit him in the chest.

"Sorry." Her laughter startled the chickens. "That one fought back unexpectedly."

He grunted and flicked it back to the bucket. "These are ready for the press."

From inside the bucket with the holes punched in the bottom, he withdrew a linen sack. With two quick shakes, the sack billowed open, and he tucked it into the waiting bucket. "The linen keeps the mash separate from the cider. Dump the apples in here," he said. "Then we load it into the press."

The sinews in her tanned forearms flexed as she upended the bucket. The destroyed apples fell into the lined one he held steady. "It smells good," she said, "but resembles vomit."

"Can we not discuss vomit?" he asked.

"Do you have a queasy stomach?" she asked.

He fitted the linen-lined bucket into the press above the collection pan. "No. I just don't like that word."

His tusks scraped his top lip as he clamped his mouth shut.

Bram also didn't like that word. Plenty of people didn't, but he *must* be more careful.

Her eyes flicked to him, and she tilted her head. "Duly noted. Any other words to avoid?"

"Oh, no, I'll keep that to myself—thanks." He placed the empty bucket below the drainage hole of the collection pan. "You must think me a fool. I've spent enough time with Princess Marigold of Thornwick to know that you'll pepper every conversation with those words."

"What?" She fluttered her eyelids and pressed her splayed fingers to her chest. "Me? I am all innocence."

"You're all mischief." He turned the crank on the press.

"And you adore it," she teased.

He did but could in no way admit it. Instead, he focused on turning the crank until the keeve filled with rich, amber cider.

Her eyes went wide and bright. "This is strangely satisfying."

He reversed the crank to lift the press. "Grab the bucket of pulp and scoop it into Paloma's trough. Be careful—the pulp is moist. Really moist. The moistest pulp ever."

Marigold clapped her hands over her ears. "I hate that word."

With his back turned, he snort-laughed. He knew she hated *moist*. Along with *slurp*, *squirt*, *crevice*, and *mucus*. Perhaps he could find a way to work several of them into future conversations?

"I'll take the keeve to the root cellar. In a few days, the barm should form, and in a few weeks, we'll have your cider."

"That long?" she asked. "I might be gone by then."

His injured palm screamed as he clenched the keeve. "Might you?"

"Possibly?" she said. "I doubt Crispin will call off the wedding and will continue to pretend I'm ill to stave off suspicion.

So, it all depends on how quickly Rowan arrives. You must be glad that you won't have to put up with me much longer."

With a flat voice, he said, "Very."

With all the power his orc body could muster, he pushed himself toward the root cellar so he could take a knee in private.

Chapter 14

After feeding the chickens, Marigold turned to find Jask contemplating the chopping block across the courtyard. It lay beyond Paloma's pit in a nook. Shadows marbled the white of his shirt as he clapped loudly to scare off the fox that peeped at him in curiosity.

Hmph. Jask Bone-Cracker contradicted every stereotype.

Fairy-tale books all described orcs as dull, mean-spirited creatures with a single-minded focus on questing, treasure, and inflicting damage. But Jask refused to leave Grimroot Farm. Did he possess a treasure hoard? Not unless you counted his trove of books. As for damage, she had no doubt he could defend them with that axe, but the maces and flails typically wielded by orcs weren't to be found in the cottage. An elegant sword hung on brackets above the fireplace, as though more of a decoration than practical.

His demeanor didn't fit the mold, either. Although gruff and grumpy to be sure, Jask possessed more self-control than knights and learned clerics alike. And he spoke so lovingly to the animals that she wondered if they weren't his cursed siblings, like in "The Six Swans." She'd looked through his chests and cabinets but found no evidence he was weaving nettle shirts.

Still, something was off about him.

Had she been less caught up in her own drama, she would've noticed it from the moment she arrived on his doorstep. But these last two weeks, as the farm's daily rhythms helped her soul and muscles unclench for the first time since Bram died, Jask's quirks came in greater focus.

Inexplicable coincidences cropped up, too.

That line he'd quoted when they were baking—*my everlasting pleasure*—sent a shiver through her. *Could* he have read it in a book? At night, as they sat before the fire, she read while he carved miniature animals. She was on her fifteenth tale and *still* had not come across that phrase. And sometimes when he looked at her, he shook his head, like he couldn't believe a runaway princess was in his presence. Well, that last part was reasonable, but something in his eyes was familiar.

There was a mystery here—she was sure of it.

She picked up Bluebell. "What do you think, Blue? Have Jask and I met before? I'm sure I would've remembered a tall, broad, handsome orc with kind eyes. Or perhaps he's the long-lost son of an orc king, doomed not to remember his place in the world?"

As she cuddled the chicken, the rooster scratched his way around the corner. Barnaby raised his head when he noticed Bluebell in Marigold's arms, then puffed his chest.

"Barnaby, don't do it. I'm serious. If you—"

Barnaby screeched, and Bluebell startled from her arms and flapped to the hay-covered earth. With high-stepping feet, she bustled into the coop and away from the rooster.

Marigold sneezed in the cloud of dust and feathers, then chuckled. She didn't blame the hen for running away. After she let herself out of the chicken yard, she stretched her arms. Her muscles no longer ached like they had the first week. She'd nearly used up her supply of comfrey in her baths, but it helped her become accustomed to the demands of the work.

Carefully, she crept closer to Jask.

From behind the golden-and-red maple, she watched him.

Today's breeze held a bite and played with her blue skirts. It did the same with Jask's shining mane of black hair. He tied a leather thong around it at his nape. The gathered tail hung past his shoulder blades, neatly bisecting the back of his ivory shirt.

Jask reached for the axe.

She cupped her hands around her mouth. "Don't you dare."

He yanked his arm back like he'd been stung. "Blood and bones, Marigold. There's work to do, and I'm healed. Stop sneaking up on me."

"I'm *not* sneaking." She had been, but sneaking wasn't dignified, so she'd never admit to it. "And you're barely healed. I'd like very much for you not to split the seam like you're a cheap flour sack."

"Saints, you paint an image." He gestured to the tree rounds. "We need firewood. We've gone through more logs in two and a half weeks than I do in a month. We'll run out at this rate."

She maneuvered herself between him and the chopping block. "A few more days won't doom us. And orcs run hot, right? If I get cold at night, I'll sit near you."

As he tilted his head and raised an eyebrow, tingling swept up her nape and across her cheeks, as though every one of her freckles had caught fire. What in blighted blazes had she said?

She must change the subject—now.

"I need herbs. Mint, rosemary, sage, and comfrey specifically, but I'd like to see what else is out there," she babbled. "Despite the mist, midmorning's the best time since the dew will have dried. Will you come with me?"

He shifted his gaze betwixt the axe and her, then sighed. "Fine, we'll forage. I know a few mint patches." He glanced skyward, sniffed, then pivoted toward the cottage. "Wait here while I get the herb basket."

Where else would she go?

Within moments, he returned with a wide, shallow basket in one hand and her cloak in the other. As he draped it around her shoulders, his heat warmed her back.

"The rain'll hold off," he said, his rumbling voice tickling her ears. "But the darkened wood feels like winter."

"Thank you." With nervous hands, she fastened the cloak's clasp.

As they set off down the path, Jask handed her the basket. "While we're in the wood, Princess, stay close. Dangers lurk within."

She remembered well the night of her escape. The eyes, scurrying, the spiders. *Especially* the spiders.

She slung the handle over her arm's crook. "I promise."

As they entered the forest beyond the pumpkin fields, the loamy chill against her cheeks was welcome. Ten minutes ago, she babbled about snuggling with Jask at night. Now she couldn't divine a single topic of conversation. The weather? Saints, how boring if she could only speak of the weather.

She sniffed the air. "Is that mint?"

Marigold closed her eyes. Amazing. Her conversation skills were as dull as one of Master Alaric's penmanship lessons.

"Beneath the ferns." Jask leaned against a white birch, the scrape of his large back releasing the cinnamon scent.

On her knees, Marigold readied her pruning knife. After digging up a small section to plant at the cottage, she sawed a clump of the delicate herbs free for tomorrow's tisane of mint and meadowsweet. The movement unleashed its sweet green scent, which provided her with a conversation topic at long last.

As she tied the stems with a ribbon, she said, "Did you know mint accents pea soup well, too?"

He held up his hand. "Impossible. I love all things green, but that sounds horrid."

"I swear it's delicious. During a visit to my aunt at Mareval, it was a banquet course. I'll make it, and I promise you'll eat your words."

"I'd rather eat my words than minty pea soup."

She laughed, then tucked her knife back into her belt. As he had often done since her first bath, he offered her a hand. She'd grown accustomed to his calloused grip, and his assistance meant she practically defied gravity as she rose to her feet.

"What else were you looking for?"

The truth of who Jask Bone-Cracker was.

"Parsley and sage," she said instead.

Their feet swished through fallen leaves that littered the trail like wrinkled butterflies. When she escaped Brambleton Castle, she'd thought the forest her enemy, tripping and scratching her at every turn. Today, with Jask, was different. He said danger lurked within, and she believed him, but she felt safe in his company. The ancient trees' golden leaves glowed like beacons in the mist.

What would these trees say, if they could?

Ahead, a fallen tree blocked their path. Before it, Jask knelt like he was about to declare his undying love. As he reached his hand toward her, Marigold's heart hammered in her chest.

"Step on my knee to climb over. I'll steady you."

The hammering stopped.

What was *wrong* with her? Jask was not romantic. He was practical to his core. And she did not want romance. Not from him, not from anyone. She couldn't deny her body flared around him. But those days were behind her. When she returned to Thornwick, she might join the Order of the Quiet Sisterhood.

Though she had trouble with the quiet part . . .

"Mare?" he prompted.

That snapped her back to attention. One person was allowed to address her by that epithet—anyone else, she'd remind them that a mare was a horse, not her. She searched Jask's face. So different to Bram's.

And yet . . .

She took his hand. "I'll dirty your breeches."

"You can launder them later." He averted his gaze.

"Oh, joy." Her ankle flashed as she placed her foot on his leg.

Having never stepped on an orc, she wasn't prepared. His thick thigh was as steady and solid as a boulder. If she could linger here for an age, she would. She pushed off to climb onto the fallen tree, then paused. The drop to the other side was steep.

"Stay there," he called.

With a grace and agility, he ran at the tree and vaulted over. The thick carpet of leaves trembled under his landing. Steady on his feet, he reached for her waist. "May I?" he asked.

She nodded. "Yes. But careful of my knife."

With her hands on his shoulders, he wrapped his hands around her middle. The scorch was instant, overwhelming, like she was iron gone orange in a blacksmith's fire. Gently, as though they were dancing, he slowly swung her around and set her on her feet.

But he didn't let go.

In her mind's eye, she'd held a collection of moments that made her feel seen, loved, adored. Desired. Those memories featured Bram. This one, deep in a golden forest with a dark-eyed orc, left them behind.

For three heartbeats, they locked gazes.

"Sorry." He withdrew. "Thought you needed to be steadied."

He was correct, but not in the way he meant.

"Don't apologize," she said.

Another smoldering look from Jask, and—wait, no, he was fixed on something behind her.

"Goldcaps," he said.

"What?" Was "goldcaps" a nickname? She glanced at her chest. Nothing golden happening there, but maybe—

"Mushrooms." He crouched near the log, then brushed aside leaves. "Plenty here for dinner."

She knelt next to him. "Are you sure this isn't a fairy village?"

"No fairies here, though there's a little magic." Jask plucked one of the horn-shaped fungi, its saffron flesh a lovely contrast against his, then held it out to her. "Smell."

She sniffed. "Pumpkin?"

"More like apricot." He tossed the mushroom into her basket, then snapped a few more. "Never eat a mushroom unless you check with me first. Poisonous varieties closely resemble the edible ones."

Add another curiosity to the Jask Bone-Cracker list.

"When did you learn about mushroom varieties?"

"During guard training." The small under tusks dented his upper lip, and he clenched his jaw.

Aha, she knew there was something here.

"You were in the guard? Where?"

"My home kingdom. My captain taught us the basics as he didn't want the company held captive by their bowels." He dusted his hands together. "Let's find the other herbs."

She had no fewer than a thousand questions, but the set to Jask's jaw meant she'd receive zero answers. Patience was not her best virtue, but her proximity to nature was helping. Since she'd been on the farm, her frustrations weren't as sharp, her worries as deep.

Jask, on the other hand, grew more terse as they ventured through the forest. In short time, they found both the sage and parsley. As a bonus, yarrow as well. As with the mint, she dug up a small portion from the moist earth for planting, then tied a ribbon 'round the stems of the freshly cut batch.

"That'll do," she said.

As she rose to her feet, she saw the mists clearing ahead. In the distance, the forest opened into a meadow. At its center stood an enormous tree crowned in crimson, orange, and golden leaves, with a base as big around as Jask's cottage. This was the tree she encountered during her escape, where she'd wanted to rest under the light of its orbs.

She took a step toward it.

Jask followed her gaze and grabbed her shoulder. "Hold, Princess. That's the Lantern Oak, home to an autumn sprite. We must let it be."

Rage, sharp and quick, sliced through her. Let it be? She'd tear it down to find the sprite and get answers about Bram. She dropped the basket of herbs and launched into a run toward the oak.

Pounding steps caught up to her. "Marigold, stop!"

Jask belt an arm around her waist and sealed her to him. Her skirts flared as he turned her away from the tree.

"Let me go." She pounded at Jask's iron grip. "That's—that's where it happened! Bram. The sprite."

Her attempt to wriggle free was thwarted by his unrelenting arms. She raised her fingers to snap, to minimize him and dash to the tree, but he let her go and wrapped his fists around her hands.

"Marigold, stop."

"Please. I need to know what happened." Tears threatened but did not fall. She was too angry. At the sprite, and at Jask for stopping her. "There were no details in the letter, and I couldn't ask Crispin without making it seem like I doubted the match between us. So, please, let me go."

Jask kinked his knees, his eyes level with hers. "Hear me, Princess. This won't end well. Like a cat that tortures a mouse, sprites play with humans for their amusement. Do not poke at him for answers. All you'll achieve is more misery."

"I'd sacrifice everything to know what happened."

"Would Bram want that?" His gold-flecked gaze searched hers. "Or would he want you to live your best life, even if he couldn't be a part of it? From what you've shared, I'd wager it's the latter."

In her bones, she knew he was right. But she hated it.

"Okay," she exhaled. "Okay."

They did not speak on the way back to the farm. Her eyes barely tracked the path, and her thoughts ran too deep for light conversation. The night she'd run from the castle . . . Had she unwittingly traced Bram's final steps? Rested where he'd died? Had he been the reason she'd arrived at Jask's door none the worse for wear?

As they emerged from the forest, they found Alfred in his cart in the front yard, enjoying a pipe of dreamleaf.

"There you are." Alfred tipped his cap. "Afternoon, Miss Meg."

Marigold set her basket down. "Are you here for more pumpkins? Won't take but a minute for us to harvest them again."

"Afraid not, dear. But I've the goods Jask requested."

Alfred hopped down from the driver's box, then circled to the cart. Amid the parcels and baskets, he fished out a bundle wrapped in paper and tied in string.

"Here you are." He thrust them toward Marigold. "Two homespun dresses."

A soft, pleasant ache pulsed under her ribs. "For me?"

Jask nodded as she took the garments from Alfred.

"Your kirtles' sleeves and lacings seem to frustrate you." He slid a palm against his neck. "Thought you could use more practical options while you're staying here."

"Thank you." As she hugged the garments and met his eyes, the pleasant pulse thumped harder.

To be seen was to be loved.

And after the feel of Jask's hands on her hips, she knew as surely as she knew his name that she'd make things awkward if they were alone together. A solution to that particular problem stood before her.

"Will you stay for dinner, Alfred?" she asked. "We've pumpkin-and-apple porridge left from breakfast. Humble, but satisfying."

Alfred lifted his cap and scratched his head. "That's mighty nice of you. I've been cycling through here for years, and this is the first invitation I've received."

Jask shrugged, looking embarrassed. "Never felt like fit company, but you're welcome to break bread with us."

"Tether your horse to the maple, Alfred, and come inside. I'd love to hear all the town's gossip."

Chapter 15

In the cottage, Bram showed Alfred where to stow his shoes while Marigold sorted out lunch. He cut a glance her way as she ladled the porridge onto toasted trenchers. Her body language was stiff. *Please* let her heed his advice about the autumn sprite.

After he and Alfred washed up, Bram filled mugs of water for the three of them.

"I know it's customary to set the trenchers directly on the table," Marigold said as she set full plates and spoons in front of them, then sprinkled the dishes with cinnamon, drizzled them in honey, and added a knob of butter. "But I'd rather wash plates than the table."

Both he and Alfred remained standing until Marigold took her seat on the bench.

"I'd never question you, Miss Meg." Alfred dug into the porridge with his spoon. "Delicious. Much better than the hunk of cheese and venison jerky in my satchel."

"Glad you like it." Marigold dashed an extra sprinkle of cinnamon onto her porridge. "Now, tell me all there is to know in Harvest Hollow. Isolde Fenlow's gossip column has nothing compared to you."

"I'll take that compliment." Alfred raised his mug of water. "The sprite activity in the Shivering Dales continues. You have a new neighbor to the west. A widow and her boy have moved into the caretaker's cottage at Kindlewood."

"Is that a country estate?" Marigold asked.

Alfred shook his head. "Cemetery. Other than that, the only other news is the Goldenmoon Festival has officially been canceled in favor of the prince's wedding celebrations."

Bram cut his eyes to Marigold, whose color had drained from her face. Alfred, deep into his porridge, seemed not to notice her distress.

"The wedding is still going ahead?" he asked.

"Yessir," Alfred said. "The second banns were delayed until yesterday on account of Thornwick being so far away. Need to give local parish folks more of a chance to object, though I can't imagine why they would. The princess is quite beautiful."

He exchanged a glance with Marigold.

Her mug trembled slightly as she sipped.

"Have you seen her?" Bram ripped a corner from his trencher and sopped up melting butter with it.

"Not with my own eyes, no," Alfred said. "But the royal guard have been describing her to those in the marketplace. Tall and strong, they say, which makes all the biddies crow about children. Hair as fiery as a sunset, and eyes the color of a clear sky. Not unlike Miss Meg, here."

Alfred pointed at her with his spoon.

Bram closed his eyes and prayed Alfred's dreamleaf kept him from connecting the dots between the missing princess and the woman sitting across from him. The royal guard wasn't in the habit of waxing eloquent about a princess's beauty. They were obviously canvassing for her whereabouts.

"Thank you, Alfred." Marigold's grip on her spoon tightened. Only those who knew her well would pick up on it.

Bram was one of those people.

"Meg?" he asked. "Would you mind refilling my water?"

Wordlessly, she nodded and rose to collect her nerves along with the pitcher from the counter. Crispin would often dispatch him and the other knights to gather information through casual conversation at the Laughing Gourd, Brumet's Books, and around the *Harvest Herald* newsstand. This would be no different.

"Are others talking?" Bram pressed. "Do they say anything of her demeanor? It would be wonderful if Harvest Hollow had a future queen with a charitable heart to balance the prince's mean spirit."

Marigold snorted as she refilled his mug with spring water.

"Mostly the guard, at least within my hearing. There was one other—an older woman. Tall, slate-gray fringe, a face that looks like it's made of blades, and the sharpest mouth in Harvest Hollow."

Bess. Bram's throat dried.

She was not to be trifled with—whip-smart and nimble, she'd nearly caught him with Marigold mid-tumble more times than he could count. Bess would want to find Marigold too—as a lady's companion, her job was to keep tabs on the princess. But why would she be working with the palace guard?

Bram drummed his fingers on the table. "A royal wedding is exciting, but I'm sure it causes headaches throughout the kingdom."

"Believe it," Alfred said. "The delay didn't help. Inns are already full from here to the Marches, so people are forced to pay a premium they can ill afford. Truth be told, Jask, you could pocket some decent coin by hosting a lesser noble or two, though that'd mean you sleeping in the byre. Since the pumpkin trade's down, want me to put out the word for you?"

He grunted. "I'd rather remove my tusks with pliers."

Alfred laughed through his last bite of lunch, then dabbed his mouth with a napkin. "No need for dramatics. Just thought it worth mentioning. That was as fine a dinner as I've ever had, Miss Meg. I'm much obliged."

"Happy to have you, Alfred. Were it not for your appetite, the remainder would've gone to the chickens."

Alfred scooted back from the table. "Anything you need for next week 'sides the usual?"

Nothing he'd share in Marigold's hearing. Bram threaded his hands together. "No, we're well stocked. Meg? Anything you need?"

"Not at present, but—"

"Plague take it!" Alfred exclaimed, clapping a hand to his forehead. "I nearly forgot, Miss Meg. Must've indulged in a few too many dreamleaf buds."

From inside his jerkin, he withdrew a folded piece of parchment. "This came in fresh to Elenor Brewster's tavern this morning."

Bram's eyes widened. A letter.

"Already?" With shaking fingers, Marigold lifted the letter. "I'd hoped for a fast return, but I thought a few more days . . ."

"I'm as surprised as you," Alfred said. "I popped into the Laughing Gourd for a bite before my morning deliveries, and there it was."

The seal was cracked—someone had read the letter already. The Laughing Gourd's patrons were generally good people, but there was money to be made trading information. The lack of an attempt to conceal the violated privacy pointed to a petty criminal, not the palace guard.

Still, thank the heavens she and her brother had a code.

Marigold's russet brows knit in concentration as she read the letter's contents.

"What does it say?" Bram asked.

"I'm to stay here until my brother arrives." She folded the note and tucked it into her pocket.

"How long?" Bram's cage of ribs was two sizes too small for his thumping heart.

"Undetermined." She shrugged. "But he was *very* clear I'm to remain here. I doubt it will be overly soon. Consequently, Alfred, I amend my earlier statement. I'll need a rug for the loft. The floors are cold in the morning, and my new house shoes do naught to stave the chill."

Undetermined, she'd said.

So much joy and dread in one word. The last two and a half weeks with Marigold had been a gift, one he did not take for granted. He'd made his peace with offering her protection in the calm oasis of Grimroot Farm for as long as fate determined. But this afternoon's foraging adventure made it plain his rebellious, greedy hands would find ways to touch her.

And, saints preserve him, with each touch, he wanted more.

This was how things had started between them all those years ago—innocent brushes of flesh, caught hands, lingering hoists onto horses. Would he be able to dance on that razor's edge of chivalric help without losing his mind? She liked Jask—that much was clear. But the fondness with which she spoke of Bram might drive him mad.

Alas, she could not know they were one and the same.

With a hearty sigh, Bram pushed back from the table. "A rug it is, then. Come, Alfred, I'll see you to your horse."

Outside, he glanced over his shoulder to ensure Marigold wasn't within earshot. "There's something else I'd like from the market. Sunday next is Meg's birthday. Pomegranates are her favorite fruit. Pick up a few, if you can? They should be in season."

Alfred climbed onto the driver's box. "You surprise me

again, Jask. You sure your last name is Bone-Cracker and not Cuddle-Pie?"

Bram snorted. "Off with you, then."

Marigold reveled in quiet birthday celebrations. Now all he had to do was cajole Marigold into revealing her birthday to "Jask" so he could surprise her with a gift.

Autumn sank deeper into the flesh of the Harvest Hollow. They'd done their best to shake off the news Alfred had shared yesterday. All they could do was wait for the wedding to blow over. The indecisive weather matched Marigold's moods. In the sunshine, the outdoors was temperate. In the shadows, winter had already arrived.

Dark mood or not, there was laundry to be done.

He tapped his good hand with the battledore.

"That's too fine a dress for this work," Bram said as Marigold joined him in the courtyard.

After setting her book down on the table he'd carved from the rootstock's heartwood, she glanced down at herself, then shrugged. Her kirtle was more brilliant than the scarlet oaks that divided the pumpkin fields from the forest beyond.

"My new working clothes are in the pot." She gestured toward the cauldron of soiled laundry that had been simmering overnight. "This is all I have left. Besides, no clothing is too fine for working."

Marigold held a healthy skepticism about the division between royalty and everyone else, and he'd loved her for it as a younger man. There was joy in rediscovering her, that time and circumstance had not dimmed her refreshing intelligence and humor.

"Fair, but it'd be a shame to ruin it."

"I've nowhere else to wear it. If a ruined kirtle doesn't offend you, we'll be fine." With her hands on her hips, Marigold turned toward the washtub. "What do we do next?"

"Nothing pleasant. You're about to discover why laundry's my least favorite chore." With a sanded and sealed wooden stick, Bram poked at the sodden pile soaking in the mixture of water, lye, ash, and herbs. "Saints, you go through a lot of clothes."

"Your pile was as large."

"Because I'm bigger."

As he stirred the steaming cauldron, his shirts, braies, hose, and stockings, mixed with her shifts, corselets, drawers, and dresses. Their enmeshment was oddly intimate and mimicked the way he and Marigold had once similarly been enmeshed.

A time better left unremembered.

As he dipped the flat side of the washing stick into the heated low tub, a gasp of lavender-scented steam rose from its depths. She'd insisted on adding the flower to the pot because it calmed the soul and might help him sleep instead of tossing and turning on the divan. What she didn't—couldn't—know was fantasies about her had kept him up later than his worries about Crispin returning.

He gestured toward the trestle table laden with laundry tools. "Grab a battledore. Lift what you can, then drop it into the washtub."

She nodded. "It would be my everlasting pleasure."

His battledore clattered against the fieldstones.

"Wasn't that what you said the other day?" She jabbed the flat paddle-like tool in the steaming water. "I liked the sound of it."

Bram pressed his lips together. *Dammit.* He'd hoped she chalked his use of the phrase up to coincidence, but her mind was sharper than that. He didn't know what she suspected, nor could he ask. This moment called for nonchalance.

He shouldn't—couldn't—react.

"I'll beat you again, slowpoke." Marigold zipped ahead

of him to deposit garments into the bucking tub, then flitted back to the pot.

He slid his battledore into the soapy pot. "It's not a competition."

"I'm winning," she trilled as she flew by with sopping clothes.

Though his legs itched to do the same, he calmly delivered the last of the laundry to the wash basin, then placed the bucking board across half of it.

"What's next?" Marigold asked.

The flush that whorled over her freckled cheeks was a gateway to the universe of Marigolds he'd known. The childhood best friend, the adolescent crush, the grown lover, and now this version, a woman fully settled into her adulthood yet meeting challenges and adventures with the bright, unbroken spirit she'd possessed as a girl.

"Jask?"

"Soap." He cleared his throat. "Add more to the areas where grime collects—collars, cuffs, underarms." He lifted a shirt from the bucking tub, then painted the collar with the jelly-like substance he'd made earlier this season from lye, linseed oil, and water. "Bundle it up, slap the bundle on the board, and then knead it like dough to squeeze out the water and grime."

With his forearm, he swiped the squeezed-out water back into the tub. Marigold followed his lead with one of her shifts. She paused mid-squeeze, then unbuttoned the sleeves of her dress to roll them up.

"Next." He lifted his battledore. "The beating."

Her laugh startled the chickens. "What?"

"We beat the water out of the garment. If it has buttons, fold those under to protect them. Then have at it, like so." With a might thwack, he smacked his shirt. Water shot out of it, sprinkling them both. "If it helps, imagine . . ."

"Someone I don't like? My theory about farmers using chores to vent their frustrations holds." She whacked her shift, spraying Bram. "But is this *really* the most advanced laundering method? With all the great mechanical minds in our world, why are they fantasizing about flying machines and diving suits? If someone were to invent a machine to do this work, people would line up the world over to acquire one."

"A good question," Bram grunted as he smacked a pair of breeches.

"I suspect if men were responsible for washing clothes, they'd leverage the same innovative spirit that gave us trebuchets and well drills."

"You're probably right. I'll work on one in my free time." He tossed his shirt into the next basin. "After the beating, we put the garment in the rinse water. On and on we go until we've washed everything."

"This is tedious." Marigold tapped the battledore against her open palm, her eyes shifting between the bucking tub and the rinse. "I fully appreciate you want me to learn the correct, labor-intensive laundry process. For that I'm grateful, because now I understand how desperately I've undervalued the laundresses who serve in the castle."

"But . . ." He smacked an impressive amount of water from his hose.

"Can I not minimize these garments to the size of doll's clothes? I'd wager we can be finished in a quarter of the time and maybe, possibly, have a little leisure time this afternoon for reading or games."

He furrowed his brow. Smaller clothes would make for less work. Though he was wary of magic, Marigold's minimancy had been nothing but useful.

"Go ahead," he said and stepped back.

She focused her attention on the clothes in the wash basin,

then snapped a shower of blue sparks over them. The clothes shriveled until they looked like fancy doll clothes. She reached for her cloak, then squeezed and kneaded a bundle the size of an apple.

"See? So much easier."

He reached for his breeches. "These look like they'd fit you now."

"Scandalous, a woman wearing trousers."

As they worked their way through washing and rinsing, they pinned the garments on the line that crisscrossed the courtyard. Fuzzle took one look at the tub and bolted back to the front of the house. After they finished the colored garments, Bram explained smalt and starch, then showed her how to lay out the whites on the field of grass next to the byre.

"You're teasing." She clutched a fine shirt. "After all that work, why would we lay the garments on the ground?"

"To brighten them." He spread his now-tiny shirt out in a T. "The sun will bleach the front. And the grass breathes out a bleaching agent from underneath."

She laid her shift next to his shirt. "Grass breathes?"

"Yes. All living things do."

Once they laid out all the whites to dry, Bram dried his hands on a nearby linen, then handed it to Marigold.

"What'll you do with all your free time this afternoon?" he asked. A frisson rippled over his skin—Grimroot Farm had a visitor. A rambler, hopefully, but he pricked up his ears.

"Read or gather honey from the hive." She lifted a shoulder. "Maybe later we can play a game?"

His pulse kicked up a notch. "Which game?"

She winked at him. "I'll figure something out."

His instincts told him he'd be on the losing side of whatever that might be.

Chapter 16

As Jask set about his afternoon chores, Marigold collected eggs from the coop. She'd skipped the chore earlier in favor of laundry, then put it off till after lunch as they'd laughed over pumpkin soup and fresh cheese sandwiches fried in butter. For all the banquets she'd attended, she'd never tasted a meal so fine.

Marigold transferred the eggs to the counter basket.

Over the weeks since she'd arrived, she'd grown to identify which chickens laid which color—Primrose's were an off-white; Heather's were slightly pink; Daffodil's showed a yellowish hue; and Bluebell's were, of course, blue. Tonight she'd make a dish featuring eggs, mushrooms, and caramelized onions, topped with fresh chopped parsley.

Ambitious, maybe. But she'd learned a lifetime's worth of lessons from Jask and Grimroot Farm. Odd, how her training had taught her to care for a kingdom, but it wasn't until she'd arrived here that she learned to care for a person. After washing up, she reached for the linen that hung under the nearby cabinet. As she dried her soap-roughed hands, she glanced through the window.

Shock dissolved her knees.

Jask Bone-Cracker was shirtless.

A lady would look away, but she was incapable. The landscape of his body warranted careful study. He was all boulders and mountains, muscles that rippled with each thwack of the axe. The furrows of his midsection clenched as he swung the blade, once, twice, and the round split. After kicking half of the round away, he split the remaining half until they'd reduced to wedges sized properly for the hearth.

Marigold blew out her lips. Saints, he was beautiful.

Round after round fell apart under his might. The hands raining destruction on the wood had rendered nothing but tender care to her. Picking her up when she fell after the bath, putting her to bed, helping her over dead trees and down ladders. All too easily, she pictured herself leaping into the safe harbor of his thick arms, letting him twirl her until she was dizzy and laughing. Carry her inside.

Then carry her upstairs.

She twisted the dishrag. In his large and luxurious bed, this gorgeous person would peel her clothing free, caressing her body, climbing on top of her, nudging her knees apart and—

Jask glanced up from his work, then locked gazes with her.

She dropped from sight.

Why, oh why, had she done *that*? She sat on the floor. With her arms wrapped around her bent legs, she rested her head on her knees. Since Bram died, she hadn't given another man a second glance. Even when her parents accepted Crispin's proposal, she'd only considered that it would have been her duty to bear Crispin's children.

But the prince of Harvest Hollow never made her heart hum.

Or the flesh between her legs throb.

Bram had unlocked both, and here she was, feeling this way for another. Jask, with his reliable, helpful, patient presence had, without her knowing it, done the same. She felt for the locket, comforted by the small lump under her kirtle. Was this unfaithfulness?

The front door creaked.

"Marigold?" Jask asked. "Are you all right?"

"Fine," she said into her knees. "Just having a moment."

Without looking, from his heat, she knew he squatted next to her. Still shirtless?

"Anything I can help with?" he asked.

Shirted, actually—he'd thrown the linen on. *Damn.* She lifted her chin and dragged her gaze from his collarbones to his eyes. So familiar were they after these weeks, she felt like she'd been staring into their deep, gold-flecked brown for a lifetime.

"No. I . . ." *Absolutely could not tell him the truth.* ". . . needed to sit for a moment."

"On the floor?" He tilted his head. "Though multiple chairs are within reach."

"Jask, it's fine. I'm fine. It's . . ." She hated this lie, but it was honestly the only one that caused men to back off and leave her alone. "My courses."

"Ah," he said. "Shall I brew you some willow bark?"

Blood and bones, he was the sweetest, kindest person. "No, I'll be fine. You can go back to the firewood. Felt a bit chilly while we were doing laundry, and we're almost out."

He threaded his fingers together. "If you're sure?"

Embarrassment wasn't a mortal wound, or she'd have died many times over in her life.

"I'm sure," she said.

"May I help you up?"

She doubted he'd leave until he saw her up and off the floor.

"Yes." She took his hands. His warm, large, calloused . . . *Stop that.*

"Thank you," she said. "Sorry to interrupt your work."

"Never a bother. I'll stack the wood on the porch, then tend to the animals. You can take it easy in here." He gestured to the bookshelf as he backed toward the door. "Plenty of reading, though I can't say it's all good."

After the door closed, she pressed her palm to her forehead.

Thank the saints Jask was gracious, or that could have been much more mortifying. She reached for the herb basket. Grimroot Farm taught her that rough and prickly feelings were best sorted through talk, nature, activity, food, or water. If combined, even better.

Outside, she set the basket on the courtyard's trestle table. She shaded her eyes to peer at the sky—swirling gray meant rain. This job wouldn't take long. Under the lean-to, she found several small gardening pots and a trowel.

As the chickens murmured contentedly, she scooped rich earth from the nearby vegetable bed into the pots. At the table, she transferred the clumps of mint, rosemary, and thyme into their new homes, then patted the soil. If they embraced the pots and root shock didn't set in, these plants would thrive year-round. Assuming they were cared for properly.

Her stomach squeezed. Who would care for them?

Inside the cottage, she set the lot on the hearthside window, which enjoyed full sun in the morning. At the fireplace, she ran her fingers over the shorn bundles of herbs that she'd hung yesterday. The scents lingered on her hands, married together in sharp green harmony.

All that remained in the basket now was the yarrow that she'd found alongside the rosemary. Its soft feathery leaves were a contrast to the sturdier stalks of the aromatic herb, and she'd happily cut a fistful to bring to the cottage.

Her stomach fizzed as she glanced at Jask's pillow.

Vera, the cunning woman who'd taught her to control her magical gift, had also educated her on herbs' various usages. Some were best used as flavoring; some possessed medicinal qualities. Still others, such as yarrow, could be used for divination. When slipped under a pillow, yarrow caused a person to dream of their true love, Vera said. Bram had visited her frequently while sleeping, always out of reach. She twirled the herb between her fingertips. But these recent yearnings for Jask . . .

If they were just physical, surely she wouldn't feel *this* guilty?

And how was she to know if he felt the same? His touch, while always respectful, had begun to linger longer than strictly necessary. His gaze as well—she'd catch him tracking her as she moved about the house and the yard. Plausibly, he might say he was checking that she was performing a task correctly. But she'd bet the tiara she left in Harvest Hollow that there was more to it.

Maybe he needed a sprig of yarrow in his pillow, too.

She tucked her nose into the cluster of tiny yellow blossoms. Subtle, slightly bitter. Jask's sense of smell was keen, but he might not detect it among the other herbs tucked in his pillow's down. After she worked the yarrow into the feathers, she caught another glimpse of Jask stacking firewood on the log rack.

There was nothing for it—she needed to walk off the desire boiling within her.

After dropping the pillow onto the divan, she swirled her cloak around her shoulders and grabbed the apple-picking bag. She wrenched open the door. "I'm off to the orchard!" she called. "We're running low."

"I'll come with you."

"Don't be silly. I'll be back before you finish."

This was an ill-thought-out adventure, but it was better than watching him flex and wonder what it would feel like to be pinned under all that strength. The heat blooming in her cheeks drizzled down her chest, through her stomach and pooled between her thighs. She jogged more than walked the distance to the orchard, grateful for the distraction of her burning lungs.

Without the ladder, she was forced to pick the low-hanging fruit.

Luckily, the wasps had cleared. Unusual, but she would not look a gift horse in the mouth. The fizzing desire had calmed as she worked, but only slightly. If she knew the direction of Coldpress Lake, she could fling herself into its chilly embrace and cool this attraction. Yes, a nice long swim in frigid water would—

A branch snapped nearby.

"Paloma?" she called.

No happy huffs or snorts in reply. Instead, laughter seemingly without source ricocheted among the trees. The hairs raised on her nape as Marigold swiveled her gaze around the orchard. The sky above was bruised with the clouds that had rolled over the farm. No one was here besides— No, wait. She squinted. There, beyond the orchard's edges.

A shadow. A *man's* shadow.

With her heart banging against her ribs, she called, "Hello there. Are you lost?"

The man stepped forward, still half in shadow, but revealed enough to make her gasp. *Rowan*. She dashed across the distance, hopped over the brook, and leapt into his arms, crushing dozens of apples between them. Tears sprang to her eyes as she laid her head against his chest. He must have journeyed long—he smelled of clinging cold and damp earth, the kind of scent found only in the deep forest.

"I can't believe you're here." She sniffled. Unladylike, but Rowan had seen her in far worse states. "I've been so worried. How did you get here so quickly? Why didn't you come directly to the cottage? I'm eager for you to meet my orc friend, Jask."

Her brother said nothing as his arms tightened around her beyond the point of comfort, and her feet lost contact with the earth.

"Rowan?" She tried to push out of his embrace. "What are you—"

Marigold screamed.

Where her brother had been now stood a creature taller than Jask, with pale gray skin. Its beard was made of grass and tangled with leaves, with eyes a luminous green. It threw her over its shoulder and ran great loping strides that bounced the wind from her lungs.

Terror threatened to claw her brain.

No. Marigold refused the terror. She had been through too much for a damned forest creature to be the thing to take her down. Later tonight she could break down in a bath in front of the hearth or in Jask's arms, but right now, she needed to get it together and focus.

With a snap of her fingers, she rained blue sparks on this tree creature. As it shrank, she tumbled and bounced against the earth, the world spinning as she came to rest against the base of a pine tree. Where was the nasty little thing? She'd lost her cloak but luckily not her knife. She fumbled at her hip for her gardening knife and unsheathed it, scouring the needle-strewn earth for her would-be kidnapper.

Her search soon ended.

With a fibrous creak, the creature shot back to full size. No, wait—bigger. The thing continued rocketing upward until it was as tall as the pines surrounding them. Where *was* she? Jask had never brought her to this part of the farm.

From above, the creature's laughter boomed. Marigold surged to her feet. The earth shook as the thing stomped toward her. Little good her gardening knife would do her in this situation, but it was all she had.

"Stop!" she shouted and held up her palm in defense.

An orange orb of light erupted from her hand and flew at the creature. *What in sweet mercy?* It shimmered as the orbs collided with his brambled leg, but nothing happened. *Great.* A fresh magic unlocked in a moment of panic, and it did nothing.

"Marigold!" Jask shouted as he hurtled toward her, a death grip on his axe.

Gratitude ballooned in her chest. But there was no time for it. The first order of business was to escape this creature. Her magic didn't work on it, and the giant was currently seven times her size. She ran toward Jask, lungs and legs screaming. But her feet found no purchase as they were now uselessly kicking in the air.

Oh goddammit. He'd pinched her up by the straps of the apple-picking bag.

Below her, Jask continued his sprint and leapt into the air . . .

. . . and bounced from something, then landed on his back with a grunt.

She blinked. With what had he collided? More of the creature's magic?

No time to figure that out. She cut the straps of the apple-picking bag and plummeted back to earth. Luckily, the thick pine needles cushioned her fall. She kept her limbs loose and rolled with the impact.

"Lead him to me, Mare," Jask shouted.

Lead? Why should she need to lead? It wasn't like a forty-foot tree creature was hard to spot. Still, she scrambled to her feet and ran. The quaking earth nearly knocked from her feet three times as she hurtled toward Jask.

As she passed him, he cried, "Timber!"

With a mighty swipe of his axe, he cleaved the creature's foot from its leg. Sap sprayed across Marigold's face. *Ew, ew, ew.* This was doing naught for her dislike of forests.

The hobbled tree man fell to its knees.

She wiped the sap from her lips with the back of her hand. "What is that thing?"

"The Leshy." Jask brought his axe down on its wrist this time. "Can you shrink him?"

She snapped her fingers to rain down the sparks. "The magic doesn't last long on him. I don't know why."

"All I need is a minute to restrain him so he'll listen."

As the Leshy dwindled to twigs, she asked, "Listen to what?"

"Me." He picked up the flailing creature in a language of sounds that cracked like split timber and hissed like wind through a canopy far above.

She understood none of it and somehow all of it at once. Jask knew the Leshy, or at least he knew its kind, and this was a negotiation. After a few minutes, he set the creature down, then took several steps back as it regained its height. Its missing foot and hand had regrown, too.

With a nod to Jask, the creature disappeared in a swirl of leaves.

Jask turned to her, then plucked a leaf from her hair. "Are you well?"

She was many things, but well was not one of them.

"No. I'm hurt, I'm scared and befuddled." She poked him in the chest. Harder than he deserved, but not as hard as she wanted. "What in the five kingdoms is that thing? Do all orcs speak tree? And what knocked you down?"

In the distance, thunder rolled, low and angry.

His chest ballooned with his breath. "I'll explain at the cottage. The rain's about to start."

The heavens opened while they were yet forty yards from the cottage. Marigold glanced in the direction of the thundercrack, tightness climbing from her throat to her jaw. No, she would not let the fear consume her.

Inside, they shucked their shoes and their sodden clothes dripped on the floor. Jask reached behind himself and tugged his shirt off by its scruff, then hung it by the hearth.

Honestly, she should get a prize for not staring. She dashed up the stairs to the loft to change into a dry shift and homespun, then returned with her wet kirtle and shift to hang next to Jask's clothes. Nothing to be done for her soaking hair, though. The wet tresses would need to dry on their own.

Downstairs, she found him as modestly wrapped in linens as a friar was in wool.

"Mind if I retrieve clothes from the loft?" he asked.

Over the last few weeks, she'd insisted he not move his entire life from his bedroom to the first floor. He kept a few things downstairs—his brushes, braies, and thongs for his hair—but the rest remained neat and tidy in the wardrobe. Which she knew because she *might* have accidentally opened it to learn more about him.

"Be my guest," she said.

The wind whistled outside, and the fire flickered in the hearth.

Above her, the floorboards creaked under his feet. She tracked his movements to the armoire, then back to the stairwell. As he descended, he rolled up his sleeves to reveal his forearms. All respect to the women who wanted men who were fair of face and long of limb.

Marigold, apparently, was weak for forearms.

"Better?" she asked.

"Much," he said. "Though I wish Paloma had returned already. She ignored my calls, but she does love a good wallow."

"I'm sure she's happy. She loves an escape more than me." She dusted her hands together. "Shall we talk as we prepare supper?"

"Yes." In the kitchen, he reached above her to the infuriatingly high shelf and retrieved the dish for the egg bake she'd planned. "I'll slice the onion?"

"Please." Onions made her weep but had no impact on him. "Tell me, please, what is the Leshy? Another friend of yours?"

"Acquaintance. As for what he is . . . first and foremost, I'd call him a guardian. I don't know its exact territory, but it's several hectares of the forest to the east of the orchard. He knows every plant and creature in his domain and is protective of them. He's also a shapeshifter."

"Which explains how he looked like Rowan."

Thunder rolled above them, but her busy hands and the conversation gave her ample reason to ignore it and the lightning that preceded it.

"As well as why your minimancy didn't persist. Your magic against his is like putting shackles on a strongman—you can do it, but it'll hold them for only so long."

In the small space they were well choreographed, anticipating where the other would move and avoiding collisions. So different from the first time they'd cooked together, when she'd needed his instruction on how frequently to stir the pottage.

"But how did he know to look like Rowan, or even what Rowan looked like?" Patiently, she stirred the loops of onion through the sweating stage in the rich melted butter in the pan. "Is he a mind reader?"

"No—that's what he and I were discussing. The Leshy and I met when I first moved here, and we've developed a mutual agreement to ignore each other. I told him you were with me. He apologized for nearly kidnapping you, by the way."

She shivered. "I'll thank him the next time I see him, which I hope is never."

Jask snort-laughed. "He told me Crispin has been meeting with magical creatures across the hinterlands, showing them your family portrait, and offering rewards to anyone who found and returned you to him. The Leshy guessed your brothers would be most likely to appear in the forest and liked Rowan's face better."

"Well, he was spot on." The onions softened and turned golden. "I wish Crispin wasn't so cozy with magical folk around here."

Jask chopped goldcaps. "He's not cozy with them, but he's respectful. And he's won their favor by rejecting any movements to outlaw magic."

"That may be his one good quality." The onions in her pan shrank into a deep jammy amber. "But they know it's so he can get something out of them, right?"

Jask threw in thyme with the sautéed goldcaps. "Yes, but it's symbiotic. From him, they get safe quarter."

She turned that over in her mind. Much like Jask gave her safe quarter, she could grudgingly respect Crispin for welcoming magic in Harvest Hollow. This might be an area where Thornwick could learn from its western neighbor.

"If Crispin has spoken to the magical creatures around here, then that's even more reason for me to stay put on your farm. Are there others I should know about?"

Jask palmed his neck. "I've heard rumors of a phoenix that guards Kindlewood. With my own eyes, I've seen fairies flit about Coldpress Lake and a kelpie who inhabits it."

"Is *that* why you won't let me go there?" After transferring the onions to the baking dish Jask prepared with oil, she whipped eggs with the cream he'd skimmed from this morning's milking.

"That and wayfarers like to fish there."

"You're too cautious. I'd love to see fairies and kelpies." She poured the egg mixture over the onion and mushrooms, then sprinkled the top with rosemary. "Haven't I proven I can handle myself with both magical and mundane creatures?"

"You have. I'm well-impressed that you stalled the Leshy long enough that I could catch up to you. But I still worry—your scream made my heart lurch."

As Jask slid it into the open wood-fired oven, Marigold flipped the sandglass.

"Yet you stopped from crossing into the Leshy's territory."

"I didn't stop—I *was* stopped. There's a difference."

She wrinkled her brow. "But what stopped you? I crossed into his forest, so there was no magical barrier."

"Not on his territory, no."

"So, there's one on yours," she said. "But people cross the border of Grimroot Farm all the time. You said so yourself."

"I did," he said, crossing his luscious forearms yet again.

She pursed her lips. This was like Master Alaric's lessons. He favored the Socratic method, believing his job was to guide his students as they pulled knowledge from within themselves. She told him her education would go faster if he gave her the answers.

Today she saw the wisdom in his tactics.

"If there's a barrier on Grimroot Farm but it doesn't keep people out . . ." She covered her mouth as the realization dawned. "It keeps you in. *That's* why you don't go into Harvest Hollow proper. Why? Are you a criminal?"

"No, nothing like that."

"What is it like, then, Jask?" Her brain buzzed with possibilities.

The orc worked his tusks against his upper lip. "I'd rather not get into it."

Much as she wanted answers, she wouldn't push. He'd respected the pace at which she shared information with him. She should do the same. But refraining from an interrogation was like trying to hold in a sneeze. She needed *something* to distract her from both the unanswered question of the barrier and the coming tempest.

She glanced at the sandglass. "Shall we play a game while we wait for the eggs to bake?"

Jask lifted a shoulder. "I would, but alas, I have no games."

"Incorrect." She opened a cabinet below his bookcase. From behind a collection of spare farm equipment parts, she withdrew a wooden box containing her favorite game of all time. "You have Tables."

He frowned. "Surely that hasn't been here the whole time?"

"It was quite dusty when I found it." She knelt at the crate in front of the hearth, then unfastened the latches to lay the board open. "But all the pieces are here. I checked. Do you know how to play?"

"Yes, but I don't want to. You'll beat me."

"Where's your confidence?" She separated out the discs and dice.

"You always—" He abruptly cut himself.

After a beat, she raised an eyebrow. "Always what?"

"Surprise me."

"I'll take that as a compliment. Now sit."

He sighed and dropped onto the divan across from her.

Twenty minutes later, she rattled the dice a final time and let them tumble. *Yes*, exactly the roll she needed. Jask groaned as she walked her discs safely home, stacking them where he could no longer touch them.

"Congratulations." She stuck out her hand.

He pumped it. "For what? I lost, as predicted."

"For correctly guessing the future." Her laugh shook the support beam. Insulting? Yes. Unseemly, unladylike, and unbecoming as well, but damn, she loved winning. Never would she flip a game board if she lost, but winning was glorious.

"You're the worst," he said. "Such a sore winner."

"The worst?" She flipped her palms upward. "How would you know? This is the first time we've played."

"I can tell," he said. "Would it kill you to be gracious?"

"At Tables? Never."

"Well, in my house, the winner tidies up."

"A price worth paying." She swept the pieces into their burlap bags, then tightened the drawstring.

Wind buffeted the house, snuffing her calm mood.

She glanced at the roof. Since she was a child, raging storms frightened her. She'd been caught outside once, terrified by the lightning, convinced it would slice through her if she strayed from her hiding place in the hedgerow. Bess had found her and, instead of comforting her with a hug, lectured her on making her worry.

Jask rested a palm on her shoulder. "It's okay, Marigold. The cottage is sturdy. I've weathered storms this bad and worse."

"I'm not afraid," she said, too quickly and with a tremble.

He smiled indulgently, the ass. "Obviously."

She shoved the game in the cabinet and slammed the door to hide her shakiness. Perhaps food would help calm her. The scent of earthy onion, mushroom, and eggs filled the cottage. A glance at the sandglass confirmed what her nose told her.

"Supper's ready. Slice the bread, please?"

She grabbed the long-handled peel and slid the flat paddle under the dish. Tamping down her unease, lest she upend their meal, she slowly turned and deposited the hot dish onto the butcher's block. Jask sliced the last of the bread and set them on plates as Marigold preferred. She spooned the egg concoction onto each trencher, and they carried them to the table. The hearth light did not reach this corner of the kitchen, so Jask lit a candle and set it between them.

Were it not for the screaming winds and pounding rain, she might have thought this romantic. A cozy cottage and a candlelit meal after a hard day's work and dramatic rescue from a giant tree creature. Really, what more could any woman ask for?

Touch, a voice said.

Quiet, she responded. She'd ask Jask a neutral question, something about his childhood, to squash her thoughts of him in rain-slicked linens or coming to her aid while wielding an axe. Nothing about his sweetheart, true love, or the knave who'd stolen her from him. Or why he couldn't leave Grimroot Farm. *Hmph.* That narrowed topics down to the point of silence.

"This is delicious," Jask said. "A recipe from Thornwick?"

"No." She blew on a steaming bite. "One of my own devising. It seemed the flavors would blend well. Since I've cooked you a delicious dinner, will you indulge me by answering a personal question?"

He raised an eyebrow. "One."

"It's very personal and sure to rattle you."

"I can handle it."

"Where did you grow up? And no answering vaguely, like 'far, far away.'"

As the smile died on his face, he drew his brows together.

"Please, Marigold." He backed away from the table. "I can't answer that. I fear you know me well enough to detect a lie, but I cannot tell you the truth."

"Yes, you can, Jask. You can trust—"

With a great, thunderous crack above, air blasted through the chimney. The fire in the hearth went out, plunging them into darkness.

Chapter 17

Marigold's terrified yelp spiked through his chest. This poor woman. What else was she expected to go through today? A near kidnapping by the Leshy, and now her biggest irrational fear was playing out in the sky above them. She scrambled toward him and clung like she'd been cast overboard from a ship and he was a buoyant barrel.

He slipped his arm under her legs, then carried her to the divan. When he tried to set her down, she refused to let him go.

"I'm sorry. I—" Her breathing shallowed. "I can't . . . the lightning . . . Will you sit with me? I can't . . . catch . . . my breath."

He sat with her in his lap, smoothing his hand over her curls. They were softer under his palm than he remembered and smelled more like pine than apples. "I'm here. I'll stay."

This had happened before.

The first time was ten years ago. On a bright fall day, they shirked classes and duties at Moonfall River to skip stones and catch fish. Not long after arriving, an unexpected thunderstorm rolled in, and Marigold lost her shite. She explained the only place she felt safe in a storm was deep in the bowels of the castle.

Out here in the hinterlands, he was fresh out of castles, so all he could do was hold her. He took deep breaths, hoping to transfer his calm to her. There was something else he could do, the thing that had been effective when they'd been by the lake. The thing that had kindled their affection into a full-blown love affair.

But that was a last resort.

In his arms, she trembled, shivering until her teeth chattered.

He pulled his quilt over her. "I've got you, Marigold. You're safe."

"No one's safe!" she fretted. She shook her head violently and tried to push away. "Not me, not you, not—"

Looked like it was time for the last resort. He twisted toward her and, saints help him, pressed his lips to hers. Gentle, chaste. Meant to shock her senses. He prepared for her to leap from him. Instead, his sweet Marigold stilled, then sighed with pleasure, like when she ate fresh-baked bread slathered in butter and black-raspberry jam.

Saints, he was undone.

She shifted until she straddled his lap, her lips still pressed to his. As she cradled his head, she swept her lightly calloused thumbs along his cheekbones. He allowed his hands to roam the length of her thighs, her waist, her back. Heavens help him, he ached for her breasts, but his control was already at a breaking point. He had to stop this—he'd truly kissed her to pull her back to herself. Not press an advantage. This was going too far.

"Marigold—"

"Yes, Jask?" she whispered. He recognized the whiskey in her voice, knew that meant she was on the verge of melting in his hands.

She revived the kiss he sought to end.

He held her face. "Marigold, please."

The picture she made in the dithering light of the candle stole his breath. Hooded eyes black with desire, chest heaving, mouth swollen . . . for Jask.

"Please what?" she asked. "Please you? Because I'd like to."

Saints fucking preserve him.

"You don't mean that." His eyes pleaded with hers. "I can't . . ."

"Liar." She rolled her hips against his length. "There's evidence to the contrary."

Aching, insistent evidence. His only release since he departed Thornwick had been self-pleasure, and every time he'd pictured *this* woman. To have her in his arms, wanting him was both a dream and a nightmare. But he couldn't have her. Not like this, when she was using him to distract her from the storm.

His fault, because he started it.

That said, he didn't have to finish it.

He pressed his forehead to hers. "I meant I can't because I respect you."

The arch in her back deflated. She sat back and drifted her hands from his hair. "Do you not respect women after you've loved them?"

"Of course I do. What I mean is today has been a lot and the storm has made you anxious." He tucked a rebellious curl behind her ear. "You're being rash, and you may have regrets in the morning. I don't want you to . . . regret me."

She still mourned Bram. How could she not compare a new lover to her true love? Tomorrow she'd wake up next to his large green frame and wonder what the hell she'd done.

Fire entered her eyes. "Do you think you know my mind better than I do?"

Not better, but almost as well as he knew his own. And anger was a tried-and-true antidote to her fear. Desire was more pleasant for all the obvious reasons, but anger would do.

"Yes," he said.

She slid from his lap. The heat in her eyes twisted and intensified. *Ah, balls.* He'd gone straight past anger to fury.

"How *dare* you." She clenched her hands into fists.

He held up his hands in peace. "Marigold, I—"

"Hush." She drew herself to her full height, and her curls waved like a gorgon's snakes. "For my entire life I have been *managed* by people who thought they knew what was best for me regardless of what I wanted. My parents, my lady's companion, my teachers. Even my true love left me, against my wishes, to make himself worthy, whatever the hell that means. And it cost us both our happiness in this lifetime."

Her words were darts to his heart.

Flawlessly, painfully true darts. Anyone on the periphery of the Thornwick court understood they'd use Marigold to stitch their kingdom to another and, in so doing, strengthen their hold on their own throne. Cold perhaps, but strategic. There was no advantage to be gained if they'd allowed her to marry a lowly Thornwick knight, unless they counted the swoony legends that might arise and stir the hearts of their people.

But swoony legends did not strengthen Thornwick's defenses.

Bram folded his arms but remained seated. Now was not the time to intimidate her with his size. "Because he had to, did he not? To win your parents' favor?"

"Now you dare to speak for *him*?" Her skirts whirled as she flounced toward the stairs. "You are too bold. I shared my past with you so you could understand me, not use it against me. For the record, the only favor he ever needed to concern himself with was *mine*."

"I'm merely offering a different perspective."

"To what end? To convince me I should not feel the way I feel about what he did? I'm not stupid, Jask. I understand the logic of his choices. But I do not—and will never—understand why we couldn't try speaking forthrightly to my parents and, if that hadn't succeeded, running away *with* me instead of leaving me behind."

The candlelight caused the tracks of her tears to glisten.

Cold moved through his chest. Marigold would have gone on the run with him. This he knew in his bones. But his pride had been so great, he wanted to show her parents, perhaps show himself, that he was exceptional.

And yes, worthy.

But her opinion should've been the only one that mattered. Not her parents, not the court. If Marigold deemed him deserving of her love, that should've been enough.

Above them, the storm ceased.

He rose from the divan. "From the depths of my soul, I am sorry."

She couldn't know his apology extended all the way back to when he'd disappeared from Thornwick. That, if she'd let him, he'd make it up to her every day of his life.

She searched his eyes. "What did you say to me?"

The silence between them was louder than the thunder had been.

"That I'm sorry."

"No, before—" She held up a hand. "Never mind. I am tired. Good night."

She took the candle with her, leaving him in the dark.

Chapter 18

Marigold's emotions thundered harder than that storm. Upstairs, in the low glow of the candlelight, she prepared for bed. Before removing her kirtle, she checked her pockets. Yarrow. She stuffed the flower into her pillow. The herb shouldn't go to waste, especially when she was confused about Jask.

He'd kissed her, and it had lit an inferno in her.

Then he'd apologized, from the depths of his soul.

Which was *exactly* how Bram apologized when he blundered grievously. For missing a secret assignation in the hayloft because he could not evade his chores when squired to Sir Patrick . . . forgetting her birthday . . . assuming all the chocolate biscuits were for him.

She'd never heard anyone apologize like that, before or since.

It could be a coincidence. Bram leveraged rhetorical flourish to lend weight to his apologies. Terse as Jask usually was, she would've expected a quick *Sorry*," then silence.

Still, she might've written it off as a coincidence.

Then she'd looked into his eyes.

Truly, deeply. Perhaps madly.

In them, she saw Bram. Because she wanted to? The shape was different and devoid of a hedge of lashes envied by young women all over Thornwick. But the flecks of gold were there, and the soul beyond them bore an undeniable resemblance to her true love.

She gathered her hair in her fist and squeezed.

Wishful thinking.

Another instance of her *wanting* something to be true that was impossible. After the squire delivered the message about Bram, she dreamed of him often. In those dreams, he hadn't died. She sensed he was alive and well but unable to come to her. Bess told her to keep these dreams to herself, lest her parents call for the surgeon to balance her humors.

The world was not always as it seemed, however. Her magic was evidence of that. As she paced, she allowed herself to consider the possibility that Jask Bone-Cracker, orc of Grimroot Farm, was Sir Bram Duncan of Thornwick and Harvest Hollow.

Why would he not simply say who he was?

That was an excellent piece of evidence that he was not Bram. As was his mysterious inability to decamp from Grimroot Farm. Her Bram wouldn't have been able to keep these secrets from her or his hands to himself.

She rubbed her temples. What madness to consider for a moment that the mountainous creature downstairs was the boy she'd loved?

She blew out her lips.

And yet . . .

No, she refused the notion. She'd buried Bram. A marble marked his empty grave, and a cleric offered comforting words. They'd wept and eaten a feast in his honor. Beyond the rituals, in her heart, she'd said goodbye. False hope would break her to pieces all over again.

She flopped onto the bed.

So *what* if Jask apologized the same way Bram had and possessed golden-flecked eyes? She was no mathematician, but the sheer volume of words and eyes in this world must've meant there were two creatures with similar vocabulary and irises. Surely that was possible.

Fuzzle leapt onto the bed, then cuddled against Marigold's side.

"I'm okay, Fuzz," she said. "Just cursed with hope."

With a quick pinch of her fingers, she extinguished the candle. The callouses she'd developed since she'd arrived were helpful in this way. If only she could thicken the ones around her heart.

Jask was not Bram.

And as vexed as she was with him, she could not deny what she felt when he kissed her. Now that the seal had been broken, the want was undeniable. Had he made a pig's ear of their encounter?

Without a doubt.

Would she forgive him? Yes, also without a doubt.

The fiery feeling of his palms on her backside drifted between her legs. Tomorrow she'd make the Maiden's Mercy silphium infusion that kept her courses at bay and prevented pregnancy. If there was any chance of intimacy, it was best taken early to work its way into her humors. Another thing her magic mentor, Vera, had taught her.

Babies are blessings, she'd said. *But it's ideal not to be surprised.*

Marigold woke with sweat snaking from her temple to her neck. Fuzzle touched a concerned paw to her cheek.

"I'm okay."

She hugged the cat to her. In her yarrow-infused dream, she'd sat in Jask's chair in front of a crackling hearth, sipping hot cider with a curl of cinnamon and flipping pages of her favorite book of fairy tales. She was all cozy contentment when she felt a gentle hand on her shoulder. A low, rumbly voice invited her to bed. When she swiveled her gaze to smile at her beloved, it was Bram.

And *also* Jask, as though they were layered one atop the other.

She pressed her palms to her eyes. The stupid yarrow must've brought on false visions. Assuming Jask slumbered and hadn't stayed up all night, had the yarrow affected him?

Jask, who rejected her advances.

Jask, whom she'd encounter as soon as she walked down the stairs. There was no avoiding him in a cottage this size. After washing up, she whispered the speech she'd spent half the night crafting in her looking glass.

"While I stand by everything I said last night, I know you were trying to be honorable when you thought me impassioned beyond rational thought. Hear me, Jask. My honor's my own to keep, and there's nothing more rational than what I feel for you."

There. If it didn't knock him over, he must've been stone hearted.

She glanced at herself in the looking glass. *Excellent.* Despite a lack of sleep, her eyes were clear and twinkling, their color brought out by her pale blue dress. She'd chosen this one because Jask seemed to favor it, perhaps because it hugged her breasts like an eager lover.

Anything to tempt him.

Since last night's kiss, she could not shake the sensation of him between her thighs. Nor did she want to. This was an ache that could be satisfied in one way, and she was determined.

Was it scandalous for a woman to have desires?

For some, probably. But who wanted to live in a world where women simply tolerated lovemaking when there was so much joy and pleasure to be found in it? She'd not felt this bloom in her body for a long time. Its reawakening assured her that her heart was resilient.

The stairs creaked under her feet. With a deep breath, she rounded the corner, expecting to find him at the table.

It was empty.

Hmph. Sort of spoiled her dramatic entry.

On the table, he'd left a vase of sunflowers. They grew tall on the other side of the pumpkin patch, so he must have been up and out early. Underneath the vase lay a note.

Sugared oats are in the pot. Back by nightfall.

She blinked at the message.

Once, twice, then burst into laughter. One big argument and this tough, strong orc ran away. She wouldn't begin to know where to chase him down. With another giggle and a shake of her head, she tied her apron around her waist. As the kettle boiled, she dished out oats, then dug the dried silphium from her herbal-remedy kit. Once the kettle whistled, she poured the boiling water over the silphium and flavored both the draught and the oats with honey.

While she ate, she read through her fairy tales.

Next, the chores. Keeping busy would keep her mind from Jask.

After scraping the remainder of the oats into the pig trough and opening Paloma's gate, she collected eggs, then milked Queen. Next, she swept the yard clear of the twigs and leaves that littered the cobbles after last night's storm.

She peered up at the trees.

Though still heavily garbed in foliage, more patches of the sky were visible betwixt the branches. She tugged her cloak around her shoulders. They were on the cusp of winter.

Next weekend was to have been her wedding day.

She could honestly say she was happier sweeping the courtyard than enduring final fittings for some elaborate golden gown. She gathered twigs into a basket for kindling and took them inside.

What next?

They were also running low on butter, so she climbed atop a stool to retrieve the mason jar and mechanical churn from the shelf. Fuzzle followed her, meowing. He'd grown to sense when a second breakfast might be in the offing.

"Patience, cat."

She crossed the courtyard to the dairy where she'd stored this morning's strained milk. The scraped cream went into the mason jar, and she ladled a portion of milk into the flat dish she kept nearby for exactly this reason.

"Enjoy," she said as she scratched Fuzzle's ears.

At the trestle table, she capped the mason jar with the crank device. Here, sitting under the bright blue skies and golden leaves, listening to the robins' birdsong, churning butter they'd enjoy later with bread that she'd baked with her own hands, she was content.

Once the butter and the buttermilk separated, she carried everything back inside. A pinch of salt and herbs mixed into the butter to taste, then she pressed it into the butter crock.

Satisfaction spread through her.

Most of her royal duties were intangible, invisible. Greet this diplomat, attend that party, visit these charities, shake those hands. She had no doubt of the importance of those events, but she couldn't point to it as a thing she'd accomplished.

Not like she could with this butter.

Queen provided the milk and cream, but without Marigold, the butter wouldn't exist. She *made* that. After toasting yesterday's bread, the butter melted as she slathered it across the slice's surface.

Heaven.

No sooner had she finished the midmorning treat than Paloma ran across the yard, belly swaying under her. She must've been stuffed with the acorns she'd foraged this morning. Chasing her back into the pen was normally Jask's job, but with him gone who knew where, it would fall to Marigold. From the corner, she grabbed the broom and stepped outside.

"Paloma!" she yelled. "Into the pen."

She swished the broom toward the pig, who trotted through the open gate. Her contented *huff-huff* noises made Marigold smile. With all the essential chores complete, she was alone and possessed hours of free time.

Time to figure out what her new magic could do.

Chapter 19

Bram emerged from Coldpress Lake, shivering. He'd awoken lusty and frustrated. Lusty because he'd had a realistic dream of Marigold riding him like she was atop a galloping stallion. Frustrated because when he opened his eyes, all he held was a pillow.

He could not spend another cozy morning with her, not when his libido raged. Best to spend the day elsewhere on the farm, away from her and temptation. When he left the cottage before dawn, the chill had frosted the ground.

Winter would come soon.

Hopefully it would quench the fire that ran through his veins for Marigold. Last night, he should've worded things better. Her blood was already up, and he'd made it worse. Early this morning, before starting his journey to the far ends of Grimroot Farm, he snipped a few sunflowers as an apology. Luckily, she was still abed, so he left her a note, the flowers, and oats on the stove.

Cowardly? Yes, but the flowers were more eloquent than he.

Quietly, he packed food and washed linens into a haversack. Within the byre, he scratched Queen between the eyes and fixed his tool belt to his hips. With a deep breath that plumed in the chill, he set out to review and repair the integrity of the fences surrounding all forty hectares of the farm. He hoped the spine-breaking mundanity would quell his lust.

Those hopes were dashed.

The monotony allowed his memory to run wild, replaying Marigold hot against his hips while the storm raged. Then imagination took over. As he reset rails that had come loose, he pictured himself peeling her clothing free, laying her down, teasing and stroking her flesh until she fell apart in his arms.

In this body. With this form.

They wouldn't fit together as they had before. He wasn't mythically huge, more like the size of an intimidating soldier, and his member was proportional. With preparation, they'd be possible. Love play was a joy with Marigold, and he knew how to soften her petals.

Bram leaned his forehead against the rail in frustration.

A day spent working out the mechanics of making love to Marigold had resulted in the cold dip in the lake. He couldn't return to the cottage with his trousers tented like an adolescent.

At the lake's edge, the distorted visage of Jask Bone-Cracker rippled in the water's surface. In her eyes, he wasn't a monster. Not once had Marigold flinched from him. No, from the first moment she showed up on his porch, she'd smiled.

Maybe he wasn't the monster he thought himself to be.

His ears twitched. A lone horse clopped nearby. He'd fastened his belt when a lone man dismounted, then approached. If the shiver that signaled someone crossing the boundary had been triggered, he'd mixed it up with the one caused by the cold lake. A possibly fatal mistake since the knight bore Crispin's crest.

His heart thudded like a galloping horse.

Marigold was alone.

"Hold." He growled—might as well lean into the monster bit. "Keep your distance if you know what's good for you."

"I, uh—" the knight stammered. "Sir Bram?"

Bram narrowed his gaze. Who *was* this? And how did he

know he was—oh, shite. The knight's bright eyes and dark hair with the spark of silver gave him away.

"Coby?" He yanked on his shirt. "Is that you, lad?"

Coby broke into a smile. "It is. I was knighted last month."

Bram searched the boy turned man from top to toe. Coby did not seem to suffer any ill effects from the curse. The sprite had said death was instant if he revealed himself. But . . . Coby had been there that night and already knew his identity. The young knight called him Bram, and yet here he stood, hale and hearty. And last night, Marigold deduced that a curse prevented him from leaving Grimroot Farm, also with no ill effects.

Was there a loophole to the loophole?

The sprite hadn't said as much . . . then again, sprites weren't known for being forthright. Crispin was the only other person who'd visited the farm and knew his true identity. But the slippery eel had never used Bram's name.

"Congratulations." Bram bound his wet hair with a thong. "Does Crispin know you've ventured this way? Or your captain?"

"You mean Sir Kevin?"

Bram snorted. "Saints, Crispin made that lunkhead captain of the palace guard?"

"Yes, he's captain." Coby grinned. "But *I* can't say he's a lunkhead."

"I can," Bram said. "Do they know you're here?"

"They've sent a half dozen of us into the hinterlands to search for Princess Marigold, which I can say since the guard already told you as much that first night. The others don't know I'm in this specific part, though. I'm the only one on your farm."

Though Bram was glad to have this intelligence, he'd taught the boy better than to reveal he was alone. A lesson that others should've reinforced. Once again, the lax protocols of Harvest Hollow would kill knights. If Bram wanted, he could rend this young man limb from limb and toss the pieces into the deep of the lake. Lucky for the boy, he was not a murderous monster.

He hooked his damp linen on his haversack. "Why have you ventured this way?"

"I've been following you, sir."

"Call me Jask, in case ears are about." Bram folded his arms. "I'm impressed. I didn't detect you, even with my superior hearing."

He couldn't help but be proud of the young man. Coby was also a foundling who'd been made a squire in the prince's guard. Given their similar circumstances, he'd taken a shine to the boy and taught him much in the time they'd served together.

Color rose in the young knight's cheeks. "Thank you, sir."

"Can we return to the point at hand? Why are you following me?"

"To apologize." Coby's lips formed a grim slash. "For what happened three years ago."

A heaviness settled on Bram's sternum. Saints, had Coby carried the weight of the curse on his shoulders? It always seemed the people least responsible bore the most guilt.

"Lad, no." Bram clapped a hand on Coby's pauldron. "You have nothing to apologize for. 'Twas my hubris that put me in that situation, and it was Crispin's fault for invoking the curse. You are innocent of any misdeed."

The young knight's brows knitted. "But—"

"No, I won't hear it. What could you have done? Argued with the prince? He would've had the sprite curse you as well."

The young knight's shoulders shuddered with a deep breath. "Thank you, sir. I mean Jask. And I want you to know—it was me who delivered the notice about . . . about Bram . . . to the princess. She, well, if you don't mind me saying so, she was devastated. Her lady's companion had to catch her to keep her from falling to the floor."

Bram's heart ached at the image. "I'm grateful it was you. But tell me, have you risked your station to apologize when you should be part of a search party?"

"Yes. I mean, no." Coby scratched the back of his neck. "The person we're searching for—it's Princess Marigold. Besides the prince, her lady's companion, and six of his knights including me, no one in Harvest Hollow knows she's gone missing."

"I hardly believe that, Coby. Surely you know if eight people are in on a secret, at least one of them has leaked it to others. My gold would be on Kevin."

Coby's lips twitched in a smile. "A safe bet, I agree. But I wanted to warn you that Grimroot Farms has been mentioned several times, for obvious reasons. The initial inspection the night she disappeared tempered the prince's suspicions, and the search goes on elsewhere. I'm loyal to the kingdom, sir, but the prince . . . he's not honorable, and in this, I do not wish to help him. So, I had an idea. If you had something of Princess Marigold's, I could deposit it elsewhere in the kingdom. Perhaps nearer the Marches, to throw off the scent, so to speak."

Bram shifted his weight as he considered the knight before him.

Coby had been a delightful squire. Absorbed lessons like a sponge, respectful, early to bed, early to rise, and skilled with blades and lances. He saw much of himself in the young man, including his ambition. Much as he wanted to trust Coby, giving him an item of Marigold's would be a confession that she was on Grimroot Farm. There was a chance the young knight might leverage Marigold's . . . recovery . . . to raise his station within Crispin's circle.

So, he would not agree to it.

"A strategic plan," Bram said. "Alas, I've nothing to offer. I've not seen Princess Marigold since our days in Thornwick."

"Are you certain?" Coby searched his face.

Bram kept his features firm. "Yes."

Coby nodded, then stepped back. "I need to return to avoid suspicion. The offer stands. If you change your mind, my patrol takes me here on this day every week, though usually in the morning. Farewell for now."

Stones crunched under Coby's feet as he departed to mount his horse.

With all the restraint he could muster, Bram pulled on his boots at a normal pace. Herons glided overhead, calling to each other, but the rapid pulse thumping in his ears drowned them out. Marigold was at the cottage, alone, because of his messy feelings.

What had he been thinking, spending the day away from her?

Her safety was, would always be, his priority.

As he walked away from the rocky shore and visible to unknown eyes, he kept his steps unhurried. The moment he was under the forest's cover, he ran. The earth rumbled under his footfall, the fallen logs crouched in fear as he leapt over them, until finally, *finally*, his cottage lay ahead. Windows aglow, chimney puffing warm smoke.

He slammed the door open, then closed and latched it.

The warm scent of fresh bread greeted him, along with something savory. The sandglass trickled the cook time of whatever was in the oven. He tossed his bag and tools onto the bench, then swiveled his gaze, but the cottage was empty.

Not in the kitchen, the dining area, or before the fire.

"Marigold!" he called. "Where are you?"

No answer. Fear shot through him as he tore through the back door. She'd tidied the yard and set the laundry for tomorrow's wash day. The animals were all penned and fed, but he had no time or patience to admire her handiwork.

"Meg?" Out of doors, they agreed to use her alternative name.

Only the wind through the trees answered.

Saints, she wouldn't have gone foraging alone, would she? Not without her basket. He ducked back into the house to check, panic rising in his throat.

Her cloak hung by the door, and her basket sat on the bench.

"Marigold?" He barred the second door, pleading in his voice.

"Jask?" she answered from the loft. "What's wrong?"

She was safe. Relief flooded through him as he kicked off his boots and bounded up the stairs, where he found his princess knuckling her eye.

"Did I burn supper?" she asked. "I fell asleep while reading."

"I'm sorry." He hauled her to him, needing her body close to his to prove she was here and whole. "I'm so, so sorry."

Her eyes flew open. "For what?"

"Last night." He cupped her cheek and searched her eyes. "And leaving you alone today."

She knit her brows together. "I'm not dreaming, am I?"

Her pinch was sharp on his chest.

"Ow. I believe you're supposed to pinch yourself."

"This way's better." Her arms were caught between them, and she slid her palms up to his shoulders.

"Why did you ask if you were dreaming?"

"Because . . ." She traced the line of his collarbones. "I've dreamed this scenario several times now, and then I wake up before . . . Well, you don't need the details, but it's getting a bit . . . frustrating."

Desire pooled between his hips. He was desperate for her, but he needed her to take the lead. Yesterday he'd botched their encounter and would not repeat that mistake.

"I *do* need the details." He brushed her curls from her forehead. "To help ease your frustration. Tell me, what happens in this dream?"

"First, you kiss me," she said.

"Like this?" He curled forward to brush his lips against hers. A tease, then more. She tasted of mint and honey. Of promise. This wasn't enough—small bites and nibbles of her were *never* enough. He swept his tongue across her lips, and she opened for him.

Merciful heaven, she was his favorite flavor.

The vibration of her soft moan set his blood aflame. His daydreams had hardened him, but this turned him to rock. With her arms locked around his neck, the soft mounds of her breasts flattened against his chest as she lifted herself on her toes. He dropped his hands to her rounded ass, pressed her close so she could feel her effect on him.

He broke the kiss, desperate for his next instruction. "Then what?"

She shivered as he licked the delicate shell of her ear. "You lift me, then carry me to the bed."

There was never an order in life he'd wanted to perform more. With an easy bend and scoop, he carried her to his generous bed. There, he knelt on the edge and laid her gently down upon it. The unabashed desire in her eyes momentarily stole his breath.

"And then?" He kissed her again.

"That's the frustrating part." She slapped the coverlet. "Barnaby normally wakes me before we go further."

He trailed his finger against her neck. "What do you *wish* happened?"

"I wish . . ." She caught his hand and kissed the palm she'd healed. "I wish you'd untie my garters."

To himself, he thought, *It would be my everlasting pleasure.*

Slowly, he slid his hands under her skirts. Up the smooth swell of her calf, then tugged at the thick ribbon holding her hose in place above the knee. The bow slipped cleanly free.

He savored the slide of his skin against hers as he repeated the job on the other side. With great care, he peeled the hose from her, then dropped everything on the floor.

"Next?" he prompted.

"You take off your shirt."

The linen joined her hose on the floor before she finished the sentence. Through the window, the setting sun beamed on him, giving her a chance to see him plainly. He stilled, silently offering her a chance to back away from this, from him.

She raised herself onto her elbows, then raked her gaze down his body, then back up to his eyes. "I thought yesterday, while you were chopping wood . . . or last night, when you were soaked . . . I thought you couldn't be more beautiful, but I was wrong."

Her admiration choked him. His highest hopes had been that she wouldn't be frightened by him. But to find him beautiful . . . It didn't resolve all that tightened his chest, but it was a good start.

Marigold swiveled her legs to the floor. "Help me from my kirtle?"

She caught his hands, then pulled them to the lacings that ran up the garment's front. Blue like her eyes, this fashion offered tempting peeks of the tops of her breasts. Especially when she kneaded bread dough and they swelled against the fabric as she moved. One of the reasons he'd happily handed over that chore to her. With trembling hands, Bram slithered the silk ribbon free from the eyelets.

As the panels splayed open, the tight rosebuds of her breasts peaked the thin shift she wore underneath. He slipped his hands beneath her kirtle's shoulders, then pushed. The blue wool pooled at her feet, and saints, now she wore naught but the shift. In fading gold daylight, the outline of her body was clear.

All that stood between him and glory was a thin shield of linen.

She reached behind her neck and unfastened the clasp of her locket. Gently, she laid the necklace on the bedside table, her fingers lingering briefly, then turned to him.

He kissed her forehead. "Are you sure?"

"More than I am of my own name." She reached for his belt, then unfastened the buckle.

With a swiftness, his pants and braies fell to his ankles, soft as fresh fallen leaves. Bold and curious, Marigold reached under his braies. He gasped as she found and stroked his shaft.

"Seems you're sure as well."

He braced himself against the bedpost. "Saints, Marigold."

"Leave the saints out of it. They're busy elsewhere." She raised herself onto her toes to find his mouth, then wrapped her free hand around his shoulder to steady herself as she worked him.

His busy hands mapped her body. The shape of her was fuller than it was in Thornwick, like she'd bloomed and was ripe for the plucking.

And oh, how he wanted to pluck her.

He bunched the fabric at her hips in his fists, then pulled the linen over her head. The movement caused her to stop her caresses, but that was for the best. Much more of her attention and he'd never last. Stepping out of his clothes, Bram walked her backward until the bed bent her knees.

As she lay back, she reached for him. "Be with me, Jask."

The name stuck like a burr. But to tell her was to ruin her, so he left it uncorrected. He was still her Bram, and she wanted him. In that, he took comfort.

He braced his arms on either side of her head.

"You don't know . . ." He kissed her, delighting in her sweetness. "How hard it's been day after day, working side by side with you."

"Tell me," she said with a smile.

He cupped her breast, ran his thumb over the stiff peak. "Every day I fantasize about bending you over the kitchen table and taking you before breakfast."

He licked her tight bud, the way she'd enjoyed many a time back in Thornwick. Under his attention, she stiffened and shivered. He switched to the other breast, lest it get jealous.

"And again, in the yard, I've wanted to lay you down on the trestle table more times than there are stars in the sky." As he teased her tender flesh, he laid a palm on her belly and skated it slowly toward the heat between her thighs.

There, he found her flesh swollen, eager, and moist.

Not that he'd use that word around her out loud.

"Where else?" she gasped as he circled the nub the way she'd taught him.

"The tree where we found the goldcaps," he said. "Upright, like animals. The bark scouring your back as I pin you to it."

"*Yes,*" she said. "Let's do that. All of that."

He nipped her ear. "I swear it."

Her breath caught as he slipped a finger inside her, then two. Eagerly, she accepted him, her body softening like rain-soaked earth. Fuck Thornwick. This was the only homecoming he wanted, and he could wait no longer.

"Wait," she said.

His breath caught. This was where she came to her senses and told him to go. He'd respect her wishes, but blood and bones, it would kill him.

"Let down your hair," she said.

He found he could breathe again. With a quick yank he untied the thong. As he leaned forward, his black hair curtained over her. "Better?" he asked.

"Yes." She tunneled her hands into his strands and cradled his skull, pulling his face back to hers. "Now will you *please* love me?"

Always. He didn't know how he would feel or how he would feel to her. But she was waiting for him, ready. This was no time for second-guessing. This was time for overcoming.

Slowly, patiently, gloriously, he entered her.

Her delighted gasp was *everything.*

"Okay?" he whispered.

She smiled. "Perfect."

He rolled his hips, mind blanking with her pressured heat. Criminal that he'd been without her for three years. That he'd ever risked parting from her, thought anything was more important than being with the woman he'd always loved.

Would always love, from this day forward.

He bent to worship her mouth. As she moaned, she hooked her heels around his thighs. He broke the kiss, needing another look at her. If this was the last time they were together, if she woke in the morning with regrets, he wanted this memory. Her rolling body, swaying breasts, hooded eyes.

With her gaze on him.

He adjusted, bent his knees so they were under her thighs, opening her to him further. With one hand hooked on her hip, he placed his palm over her heart. The beat beneath her ribs was fast and strong.

The sweet coiling tension gathered in his lower back. He refused to give in, not until she'd had her pleasure. He rolled the tight bud between her legs, with slow, steady pressure, the way she liked.

Steady, steady, steady.

Her breath caught again, and her telltale low keen began.

Her little death was imminent.

The movement of her hips grew more insistent, and soon, the keen turned into a wail. She lost herself to pleasure, had achieved her pinnacle. The greedy squeeze of her core undid him, and with a roar, he joined her in shared oblivion.

His thighs trembled as he rested his head against hers, determined not to press his weight onto her overmuch. She locked her legs around the small of his back, pulled him to her.

Powerless, he collapsed, then rolled to his side.

She twisted her face toward his on the pillow, pressed her palm to his cheek, then kissed him. "That was amazing."

"Agreed, Princess."

She traced a circle on his chest. "But we can do better."

Chapter 20

Marigold woke before Barnaby's blood-curdling call. With a satisfying stretch, she turned and smiled at Jask's sleeping form. Much better to find him there, unlike the mornings that followed her dreams of him in her bed.

This time it was real.

She felt tipsy, but without the ill effects. Happy and languid, unable to count the number of times she and Jask made love. That was what last night had been. Not a tumble, this.

Love.

She resisted the urge to brush free the curtain of hair covering half his face. His chest rose and fell with deep, rhythmic breaths. She also stayed her hand from tracing the lines of his rounded muscles beneath the lone bedsheet covering him.

Because orcs, in fact, ran hot.

Were he awake, he would not enjoy the same view of her. Snuggled under a pile of blankets, this might've been the coziest any person had been in the history of time. Light rain pattered the panes, she was warm—but not too warm, didn't yet need the privy, and slept the glorious deep slumber brought about by rigorous exercise and a clear mind.

Jask had been the exercise, and as for the clear mind?

She'd reached a decision.

She wasn't returning to Thornwick.

No, she'd stay here in the hinterlands with Jask on Grimroot

Farm. She'd never thought her shattered heart would mend after Bram's death. But it had, in the unlikeliest of places, with the unlikeliest of people. She wouldn't take this feeling for granted. Not again. No, she'd hold on to it with both hands and never let go.

Saints, she wanted him again.

Was it healthy to feel this much desire? *Eh, fuck it.* If her humors were out of balance, she liked them this way. At court, Bess had expected her to be reserved, to dim her light so as not to outshine the menfolk. But Jask enjoyed her sharp wit from the first. Encouraged her questions and asked several in return. Never mocked her for enjoying fairy tales. No, he simply quietly sat and carved while she turned pages.

Compatible, blissful.

And in bed, they were fire.

That, she hadn't expected. Had hoped, of course. But with Bram, it had taken ages to learn what pleased her. He'd been a game partner, but it had taken experimentation. Not Jask, though. He knew exactly how to please her without awkward learning period.

She frowned. *Wait. How—*

Barnaby shrieked at the faint glimmer of light in the sky.

Jask took a deep breath, then fluttered open his eyes. He rolled toward her and smiled. "Good morning."

"How many lovers have you had?" she asked.

With a snort, he said, "That's not the greeting I expected."

"Good morning, my lusty Hercules. I hope you slept well. Now, how many?"

"Besides you?" He propped his head on his pillow, then traced her shoulder. "One."

Much as she wanted his touch, she shook it off. "Don't lie to me, Jask Bone-Cracker. I'm a grown woman. I can take the truth. Dozens?"

He laughed.

"Hundreds?"

He scooped and flicked his shimmering hair over his shoulder. Curse the bouldered beauty of him.

"What inspired this line of questioning?" he asked.

She blew out her lips. "The little death. I experienced it no fewer than four times and didn't instruct you *once* on how to bring it about."

"Perhaps I'm a natural?" He dipped his hand under the sheet and found her breast, running his thumb over the beaded tip.

"See? This is what I mean. You know exactly how to—" she gasped as he lightly pinched her nipple "—excite me."

"I may have only had one lover, but we loved often." He scooted closer, then kissed her neck. "She taught me well."

Jealousy flamed through Marigold. Which was completely hypocritical. She'd shed tears about Bram in front of this man. They were both allowed to have people in their past.

"What was her name?"

"I'll never tell." Jask removed her blankets, leaving only the sheet.

"Please, I must know."

"Sorry to disappoint you." He slipped below the sheet, then spread her legs and positioned himself between them. "Allow me make it up to you."

Her toes curled as he licked her like cream.

She gasped as he alternated between long and short strokes. "You . . ." Her gasps turned to panting. "Are avoiding the question."

"Correct, Princess. Now allow me to help you come."

Marigold was depleted in the best way possible.

Each of the last three days, she awoke to Jask's hardness and happily helped him relieve it. Romps occurred when the moment carried them, which was often and unpredictable. Of the places Jask listed that first night, the goldcap tree in the forest remained, but she had high hopes for her foraging plans tomorrow.

After years of walking about half-dead, this was a joyful rebirth.

She sniffed the air—the buttermilk biscuits were ready. As she removed them from the oven, the door opened. Jask was returning from his lake bath. He'd no sooner hung his linen than he curled himself around her back, nuzzling her neck.

"Miss me?" He palmed a handful of her behind through her homespun dress.

"Every minute. Though I'm productive when you're gone."

"I'd prefer you were so besotted that you spent every minute wishing I'd return."

"I can do both," she said. "Sit, and we'll eat."

She'd made a mushroom-and-barley soup. Seasoned with thyme, of course. They each dished out their portions and seated themselves when the familiar bells of Alfred's horse rang from their front yard.

Jask dabbed his lips with the napkin. "I'll receive the delivery."

"Invite him in while you're at it," Marigold urged.

Jask pushed back from the table, then crossed the front door. A pumpkin-scented breeze from the ripe fields curled through the home. "Ho, there, Alfred. Care for dinner?"

Alfred called back, "Indeed I would!"

Marigold rose to scoop another serving of soup into a bowl, added a biscuit on a plate, and set it on the table. As she upended the pitcher of the cider she and Jask had pressed two weeks ago, bubbles rioted into a light foam in the waiting tankard.

By the time she'd set his portions on the table, Alfred entered the house. "Welcome, Alfred. Any news from town?"

Jask closed the door and tucked a small sack of flour into the cupboard.

"Not much. The festival's still canceled, but no new wedding date's in sight." Alfred hung his hat by the door. "Seems the princess's ague has worsened."

"That's all it is?" Marigold asked. "An ague?"

"Rumors run wild. The townspeople have diagnosed her with everything from melancholia to plague. I'm taking bets on ergot exposure. Rémy the baker sold some bad rye lately." Alfred slathered his biscuit with herbed butter. "He can't compare to your delicious goods, Miss Meg."

Much could change when she put her mind to it—a month ago, she couldn't bake a bean.

"Thank you," Marigold said.

"To the princess's recovered health." Jask held his tankard aloft, and both Alfred and she clanked theirs with his.

From behind her tankard, she glared while he hid a snort. The honeyed fizz of the bright cider gently prickled her tongue. Unlike the orc-strength cider, this was meant to refresh, not blind, the drinker.

"That's nice." Alfred sniffed his cup. "What do you call it?"

"It's Miss Meg's Hollowsnap Red–cider recipe," Jask said. "She calls it Crankle's Finest. Light enough to enjoy at midday without compromising the afternoon's work."

"Would you like to take some with you?" Marigold asked. "We pressed far too much, and it would be a shame for it to go to waste."

"I'll take you up on that, if you're sure," Alfred said.

Marigold spooned up her soup, then blew on it. "We'll call it a fair trade for your reporting."

The rest of the meal passed with tales of the market's quieting business and mounting frustration with Crispin's stance on trade, and laughter as Jask stoically endured Fuzzle's leap onto his lap.

When his soup was gone, Alfred folded his napkin and placed it beside his dishes. "I need to get going to my other stops. Thanks for your hospitality, friends."

Jask stacked their dishes. "I'll get the firkin."

In the courtyard, Marigold and Alfred watched Jask dip a pitcher into the light cider barrel, then pour it into the firkin's funnel.

"You're good for him, you know," Alfred said. "I've been out here every week, sometimes more, for three years. It's hard to tell with orcs, but this last month's the happiest I've seen him."

"I'm pleased to hear it," she said. "He's lovely but easily misunderstood."

"On that, we agree. At first, I stopped here out of habit—the previous farmer, Halvard, and I were good friends, rest his soul. Gruff as your fellow is, he struck me as a solid sort. Capable, and set much of Grimroot's disrepair to rights. Busy as all get-out, like he was trying to escape his own mind. He's calmed, though." Alfred fiddled with the brim of his hat. "I hope you don't mind me saying so, Miss Meg, but for Jask's sake, I hope the princess never, ah, recovers from the so-called ague and you stay here with Jask."

Sweat prickled Marigold's brow. "I don't know how that's related."

Alfred chuckled. "Don't you, though? You needn't worry. I'm the only one who knows you're here, and I'm no gossip."

"That's demonstrably false." She bumped shoulders with him. "Every time you're here you tell us the latest from Harvest Hollow."

"Well now, that's just making conversation." Alfred winked. "But what I see in the hinterlands stays out here. Especially with your fella. It's my personal life philosophy never to piss off an orc."

Jask tapped a stile into the side of the firkin, then hoisted it onto his shoulder. As they walked around the cottage to the front yard and the cart, he said, "You'll want to store this on its side. The cider's still fermenting a bit, so I didn't plug it."

He wedged it amid the other goods to reduce jostling on Alfred's journey back to Harvest Hollow proper.

"Thanks, friend." Alfred untethered his horse from the maple in the front yard. After he seated himself in the driver's box, he tipped his cap. "Till next week."

As his cart disappeared, Marigold tangled her fingers.

Jask slung an arm over her shoulders. "Something troubling you?"

"How could you tell?"

"Your fingers are knotted tighter than your kirtle's laces." Jask squeezed her shoulder. "You do that when you're anxious."

She parted her hands, then stared at them. "Do I?"

"You do." Fuzzle twined himself around Jask's ankles. The orc scooped him up, then scratched under the cat's chin. "What's got your fingers in knots?"

"I really thought they would've canceled the wedding and accepted that I was gone by now, or that Rowan would have arrived to escort me home so we can alert our parents to Crispin's schemes. But now with us, I don't want to leave . . . and I'm sure this lie about me being ill is to buy time to find me. I don't like it."

There. That was all true, but not the whole of it. Nothing about Alfred guessing her identity. And certainly nothing about her new magical ability. She preferred to wait until she knew more about it before sharing it with him. During her brief periods of solitude, she'd lobbed orange orbs at the byre, the trees, and herself, but nothing came from it. If they were simple illuminations, they were useless since they lasted all of ten seconds.

"I admit it would be better if Crispin accepted the situation. But he's a prideful prick and won't release you until he sees the advantage in it for him." He squeezed her shoulder. "They've already searched for you here once, and they've attempted to conscript magical creatures to find you. If they come 'round again before Rowan comes for you, we'll handle it."

She wished she could be so sure. But if Alfred saw the goodness in Jask and how good the two of them were together, perhaps more people would see it as well. Like the common folk of Harvest Hollow. And Rowan. Maybe even her younger brother and parents.

Strength lay in numbers.

Like that fairy tale of the princess protected by seven little people—alone, none of them would have been able to protect her from the evil queen, but together they succeeded.

Marigold tangled her fingers.

Well, not succeeded, exactly. She still ate a poisoned apple, and the little people preserved her until a passing prince could help.

But the point was to survive, they'd need allies.

Chapter 21

Bram's breath plumed in the crisp air. "Are you sure about this?"

He was game for most physically demanding activities, but he couldn't believe he'd agreed to this.

"More than sure. Let's get started." Marigold rubbed her hands together. "Where do I touch you?"

"You don't—not yet." He placed his hands on his hips to survey the courtyard. "Dancing is more fun with music."

Fuzzle curled up on the chair facing nearest the firepit, his diamond-shaped face swiveling between Marigold and Bram as they faced off.

"Well, we're fresh out of minstrels." She tightened her cloak around her shoulders. "Stop stalling. What do I do first?"

"This." He sketched a bow toward her. "Now you."

"So respectful." She curtseyed.

"The respect rarely lasts." He held out his hand. "This dance is called the Sway. Master it, and you'll fit right in with any field or folk party. The key is to remember this kind of dancing is faster, more fun, and less concerned about propriety than courtly dancing. Don't get in your head about it—just have a good time. Ready?"

"As ever."

With clasped hands, they turned to face the pumpkin fields. "For the one-step version of this dance, start with your weight on your right foot, then step to the left, and bring the right foot to meet it, but in a tapping pose. So, step left, tap with the right, step right, tap with the left."

She followed along, colliding with him only slightly.

"You know left from right, yes? That's integral to this dance."

"*Yes,*" she huffed. "I only occasionally mix them up."

"Now reverse it—right, step, left, tap."

More bumping. Not that he minded.

When he paused, she said, "Your rhythm's off."

"Never heard you complain about that before."

She slapped his biceps. "Be serious."

"I am. Dancing is deadly, deadly serious."

"It *is.* Men are allowed to look foolish, but women are held to a higher standard." She squeezed his hand. "Let's try again?"

He'd practice all night if it meant holding her hand. They repeated the steps—left, then right—again and again until they didn't bump into each other.

"Is that it?" she asked. "A lively sidestep and hop?"

"Not quite. Those are the basic steps—after we string six together, we turn toward each other, then kick our feet. You—right, then left, and me—left, then right. All together it's *step-tap* six times, then *kick-kick.* Got it?"

As with battle maneuvers, describing it made it seem complicated. Seeing it was a different story. Fuzzle was unbothered, licking his paws.

The flames from the firepit sparkled in Marigold's eyes. "We'll find out."

"Then we go." He led them into the routine.

The *step-tap*s were fine. At the *kick-kick*, she nailed his shin.

He grunted and rubbed at the spot.

"Oh, sorry. Did I mix up the kicks?"

"I refuse to name names. Let's try again, but maybe this will help you remember which leg is your right."

He knelt before her, then lifted her skirt.

"What are you—*oh*," she said as he licked a trail along her right thigh. "That tickles. And is chilly."

"Now you'll remember." He rose again and held out his hand.

Side by side, they hop-skipped as he hummed a tune, turned to each other, and this time their kicks alternated, saving his shins from further bruising. As they caught their breath, his was stolen again by the dramatic light and shadows playing on her face.

"Now what?" she asked. "A staring contest?"

"A lift." He lifted her hands to his shoulders, then wrapped his own around her waist. "You jump, and I assist. On the count of three. One, two—"

She jumped.

"*Marigold*. I said on the count of three."

"I was eager." She shimmied and shook out her fingers. "Okay, nervous energy cleared. Count of three."

Bram's chuckle rumbled his chest. "One, two, three."

She jumped, and he lifted her as though she weighed no more than a pillow. With her hair shrouding them from the night, he couldn't resist spinning while holding her upon the pedestal of his body. There were many things that displeased him about his orc form, but he enjoyed the strength from the start.

"Like it up there?" he asked.

She lifted her arms to the sky. "There are so many stars out tonight—it's like they're out here dancing with us."

After a few more turns, he slowly drifted her down his body and back to the courtyard. The friction of her homespun on his linen set his blood alight. Many a night in the Laughing Gourd, he'd overheard men complain about their wives, referring to them as the old shackle. But Marigold was the first person he wanted to talk to in the morning and the last hand he wanted to hold at night.

He'd never tire of her.

"Can we do it again?" she asked. "I want to practice until we get it fully right and then keep going until I never get it wrong."

"Luck favors the sharpened blade," he said.

"*Exactly.*" She squeezed his hand.

On they went, dancing the line back and forth and back again, with turns and kicks, jumps and lifts. His arms never wavered, as though their sole purpose was to support her.

"I feel ready," she said, chest heaving.

He dropped into the chair next to Fuzzle. "All you need is a festival."

"About that . . ." She opened the root cellar and dipped cider for both of them. "I had an idea. Grimroot Farm is the perfect place for a big celebration."

Aha—was this the moment she confessed that tomorrow was her birthday? The crown made an enormous fuss about Rowan every year, since he was the heir apparent. She, in contrast, preferred to celebrate with a picnic. Perhaps that had changed?

"Do you, now? And what would be celebrate?"

"The Goldenmoon Festival, of course. What about hosting it here?"

Cold flashed through him as he gripped the chair's arms. "Mare, what? All those people? You can't be serious."

"Hear me out." She handed him a tankard, then sat on his lap. "You said the townsfolk gawk at you, so you don't feel comfortable around them. How will that ever be repaired if you never go to town?"

The cider's bubbles scrubbed his tongue as he drank to buy time. He'd been a fool to hope this wouldn't come up again.

"You have the space, Jask. People deserve a celebration.

They'd be so happy if you step in where Crispin stepped aside. And if it's the expense, I can—"

"No." He sets his tankard on the ground, then stood, careful to set her on her feet. "You're too trusting and optimistic. I don't want the entirety of Harvest Hollow here. Not when you're in hiding—"

The words stuck in his throat. The idea of Crispin locating her and spiriting her back to Brambleton Castle was more than he could bear.

"Just . . . no, Marigold."

"Please? It would be so good for you." Her eyes widened. "Also, Crispin's search for me is exactly the reason you *should* host it. It's a feint. Why would you invite everyone here if you were really trying to hide a person? I could shrink. Not even be here."

"Oh, really? You'd hunker down in the cottage, after you've gone to all this trouble to learn to dance? You know the first fiddle that comes out, you'll be in the center of the circle."

"You are completely . . ." Her laugh echoed over the fieldstones. Barnaby squawked in response. "Right. You're right—I would. But I could wear a disguise, Jask. A wrap to cover my telltale hair. Mistress Meg, at your service."

He waved off her curtsey. "Why do you want this?"

"Because you're wonderful, and if you do this, everyone in Harvest Hollow will have a chance to know you. It isn't healthy for a person to live in such solitude. And since you can't leave, we should bring Harvest Hollow to you."

He warmed at her kind words but bridled against the stratagem. "That's a lot of opinion for someone who's been here a month."

"It's empathy for your situation, Jask. Not judgment." She raised her chin. "I did the same thing when Bram left. I hid in my tower, reading my books, convinced a world without him had nothing to offer me. Then he died, and I blacked out the windows until my parents and brothers dragged me from my isolation. Looking back, I would've healed sooner if I'd allowed myself the company of people."

He pinched the bridge of his nose. Was it mad to be jealous of himself? As Jask, he resented that she tossed out Bram's name as frequently as drunkards toss dice in a tavern. As Bram, he was jealous that she was happy and with someone new. He was both the ghost and the possessed body, locked in despair.

Today Jask's jealousy won.

Through clenched teeth, he asked, "For someone who claims to have enjoyed the miracle of true love, you seem to regret the length of your mourning period often. Did he not mean as much to you as you claim?"

She shrank from him. "Did you really just say that to me?"

The air smelled of cinnamon, pine, and his cavernous regret. Holding her to account for how she processed her grief was unfair. She didn't know, couldn't know, who he truly was or what it cost him every time she spoke glowingly of Sir Bram Duncan.

He ran his hands through his hair. "I'm sorry. That was thoughtless."

"It was." The crackling snap of the firepit filled the air. "That's the second time you've used what I've shared about my past to wound me, Jask. Do not do it a third time. Especially when you are so reticent about your own history."

She whirled on her heel and stomped into the cottage.

Chapter 22

Marigold paced the loft. How *dare* he say that to her?

Even if . . . she blew out her lips . . . he had a point.

Despite all her academic achievements, she'd never figured out how to mourn Bram properly. She felt like a widow with a forever-altered future, but she wore no black, nor did she receive a folded banner to honor his service. With no public acknowledgment of their relationship, she grieved in solitude for years.

To honor him.

But she had regrets, which was why Jask's question was like a poke to a sore tooth and sent a painful shock through her body. She didn't regret the duration of her mourning—never that, because it took as long as it took.

No, she regretted the loneliness.

Without people to lean on, she turned to the grief itself for comfort. Before, she didn't know who she was without Bram. Now she didn't know who she was without the grief.

She tangled her fingers together.

Saints, she was a mess. Jask was the first person she'd told the truth about her relationship with Bram. Finally, here was a stranger to whom she could tell her troubles. He didn't flinch—he listened. Then things changed between them.

Was it possible that people did not, in fact, have a single true love?

The way she felt with Jask was a mirror to what she'd felt with Bram. A sizzling, instant magnetism. But also an easy comfort that allowed her to let her truest self shine around him. Like a flame in her recognized a flame in him, and they called to each other.

Were safe with each other.

"Marigold," Jask called. "Are you awake?"

She poked her head over the loft rail. "You didn't run away this time."

From here, he looked small. Or average sized, at least.

"Are you angry?" he asked.

"No. I'm hurt."

He placed a foot on the stairs. "That's worse. May I come up so we can speak properly?"

"No. This works better for me."

He rested his back against the wall. "I'm sorry."

She narrowed her eyes. "For?"

"I shouldn't have said anything about the way you've mourned . . ." He swallowed hard. "Bram. You've been clear how you felt about him, and grief is complicated."

"It's . . . I won't say it's fine, but I forgive you. I'm still sorting out my feelings. Part of the grief was that I didn't know until weeks after it happened. I was convinced we were connected by a heartstring that, if clipped, would tug mine from my body. Do you know what I was doing the day the squire arrived to tell me he'd died?"

Jask shook his head. "Tell me."

"We were banqueting with my mother's cousins from Mareval, eating a honeyed pumpkin tart. My lady's companion, Bess, gestured for me to leave the table and follow her. In the withdrawing room off the great hall, a squire asked if I was Princess Marigold."

"Was he kind, this squire?" Jask asked.

Well, that was an odd question. "Very. With tears in his eyes, he handed me a letter and said he was sorry. He turned on his heel and hurried away. It was sealed with the royal Harvest Hollow signet, and I *knew*."

The first line of the letter caused her knees to turn to aspic. Bess had been helpful to Marigold in that moment. Her lady's companion helped her to her rooms, offered a prayer for Bram's immortal soul, then left her in the dark.

"That must have been difficult."

"To say the least."

"What did the letter say?" Jask asked.

"Prince Crispin had personally written to say that his company had encountered an enemy, and that he'd spare me the details but wanted me to know that Bram had been courageous. That Crispin had tried to save him, but Bram ran ahead, fearless and foolish, and disappeared."

"That craven wretch," Jask uttered.

"Bram?" She held firm to the railing. "Or the prince?"

"Always the prince," Jask splintered a staircase spindle.

"So, to respond to what you said—"

Jask held up a hand. "You don't owe me a response, Marigold. That was mean-spirited jealousy talking, and I'm embarrassed I said it."

"No, Jask, I want you to hear this." The railing bit the backs of her fingers. "I didn't give people a chance to know my pain and let them stand with me. To help me through it. But I should have. This time here with you . . . you've taught me that people are good for the soul."

"Not all people." He folded his arms.

On this, they could agree. "No, not all. But many."

He closed his eyes, then rolled his neck. "Hosting a festival here will enrage Prince Crispin. He'll take it as a challenge to his minimal benevolence."

"True." Her smile widened.

"Which is a point in its favor." He climbed a step.

She descended one step. "It will bring people who may gawk."

"A point against." The next step groaned under his weight.

"It will also bring children and their sense of wonder."

His rigid back softened. "I've not seen a child for a very long time."

"I promise you they are as appealing as ever."

He climbed another step. "Two points in favor."

Her heart thumped an extra beat. She had a weak spot for people who liked children.

"There's one more thing that'll seal your opinion in favor." She descended. With their height difference, they now saw eye to eye. "I'll get to show off the dance I've learned."

She slipped her hands onto his shoulders.

He belted his arms around her waist. "Then we shall host a Goldenmoon Festival of our own. I'll ask Alfred to secure a headwrap for you."

Chapter 23

Bram tapped the head of the hammer against his thigh. It was a testament to how much of a pig's ear he'd made of things last night that he'd agreed to host the Goldenmoon Festival next week and let all of Harvest Hollow trample his farm.

He'd worry about that later.

Today was all about Marigold's birthday. Which she still did not know that he knew. He raked his hand down his face. He'd figure something out—maybe tell her she talked in her sleep. Which she didn't. She giggled though, and it was charming.

He stood at the chicken-yard fence, waiting for Marigold.

If all went to plan, he'd stay behind to finish repairing the fence and she'd forage for herbs. In truth, he'd use the time apart to bake the cakes and make the pomegranate frosting. Yesterday's pomegranate delivery waited in the cabinet—Alfred had cleverly hidden them in a flour bag so Marigold wouldn't notice.

He was uneasy about her venturing far on her own, but she knew Grimroot Farms and its pumpkin fields, orchard, lake, and wood well. Should anyone cross the threshold, he'd sense it and she could deploy her minimancy powers.

"Jask?" she called as she exited the cottage. "I'm ready."

Saints, she was beautiful. Her red curls spilled along her shoulders. Under the cloak, she wore the homespun that revealed her ankles. For a moment, he was tempted, but he needed to bake the birthday surprise.

"This split is trickier than I thought it would be, and I'd like to finish it before dark. I need to stay behind."

She wrinkled her brow. "I really hoped for your company. What if another tree tries to kidnap me?"

"The Leshy and I squared our agreement, and the herbs are not in his territory regardless. This needs to be complete today," he lied. "I found fox scat in the pumpkin field. Can't have him getting access to the chickens."

"Oh. No, I suppose not." She slid her basket further up her arms. "I'll be gone for an hour or so—if you finish early, I plan to harvest more goldcaps. I know it sounds odd, but I had an idea for an onion, mushroom, and spiced apple pastry that I'd like to try."

"No odder than peas-and-mint soup," he said.

Her laugh startled the chickens. "You'll never get over that, will you?"

He caught her around the waist and kissed her deeply. "To remember me by. And don't forget—avoid walking through fairy rings."

"I promise," she called over her shoulder.

He waited for her figure to disappear into the wood, then hurried into the cottage. As fast as he could muster, he lit the oven, then removed the bowl where he'd mixed the flour and spices this morning while she slept upstairs. Next, he whipped together eggs and melted butter, then folded it into the batter.

Fuzzle leapt up onto the block to inspect his work.

"She'll love this, Fuzz."

The cat meowed and hopped to the floor, uninterested.

After greasing six baking hoops, he placed them on the baking sheet. Next, he carefully filled them halfway with batter, then slid the sheet into the oven and flipped the sandglass.

Now for the frosting.

From the cabinet, he withdrew the pomegranates and set about splitting one for the seeds. When they were teenagers, he'd questioned her love of the fruit. The memory replayed in his mind's eye as though he were watching it happen today.

"First of all," she'd said as she cut into it with her gardening knife. "You clearly don't know your Greek mythology."

"Try again. Persephone, Hades, Demeter, winter. Chew on that."

"Fine, you know your mythology."

"Thank you for recognizing my greatness. Pomegranates are a lot of work for an insubstantial reward."

"Insubstantial?" She dribbled gem-like seeds into a small dish. "This is a treasure chest of delight. A trove. A hoard."

"Your tutor's been teaching synonyms again, I see."

"Perhaps." She pushed a dish toward him. "Try them."

"No, thank you." He stubbornly resisted food from the royal kitchens lest he prefer it to the plain, filling food Sir Patrick had taught him to cook.

"Bram, you must."

He lifted a shoulder. "I can do without."

The gleam entered her eye. He knew it well, and it always meant trouble. She counted out six seeds.

"What are you—"

She leapt onto him, nearly knocking him from the bench as she flattened the seeds to his lips. The tart rich juice seeped inside his mouth. He held on to her to keep her from falling to the ground, then licked his lips.

Damn it, she was right. They were delicious.

And she was in his lap.

"Saints, Bram." She giggled. "You look like you've caught a bloody flux."

This was it—this was the moment he could do what he'd been dreaming about for a while now. He leaned forward and pressed his lips to hers.

The kiss was chaste.

Until she held firm to his face and devoured him.

Fuzzle leapt back onto he counter.

"Saints, cat!" He lost his grip on the fruit's slick skin. Ruby-colored seeds scattered across the butcher's block. As he collected them, he felt the chill of someone crossing the boundary without his permission.

Marigold.

He dashed to the door, grabbed his cloak from the peg, and ran down the cottage's front steps. The path to the woods was damp with this morning's melted frost, giving him excellent footsteps to track. He was halfway to the trees when he remembered—*shite.* The cakes. Burning down the cottage wouldn't do, either. As he pivoted on his heel, the familiar clang of Alfred's bell rang in the distance.

But Alfred didn't trigger the chill, and this visit was out of schedule. He wasn't due for another few days. Jask shaded his eyes and peered.

His hammering heart calmed.

Crisis averted.

A woman sat beside Alfred—wait, he recognized her. Elenor the Brewster, the formidable alewife of Harvest Hollow. She ran three taverns and was known for unapologetically booting anyone too soused from her establishments. He'd knocked back plenty of ale at the Laughing Gourd as Sir Bram Duncan. But he'd always been respectful.

He'd helped her kick out Kevin a time or two as well.

He raised his hand in reluctant greeting. She wasn't the first Harvest Hollow resident to visit Grimroot Farm. Alfred, obviously. Wayfarers and ramblers, too, some of whom he'd known as Bram. Every time, he wondered if they'd see through the autumn sprite's magic and perceive the man within the orc—but none did.

"Salutations," Alfred called. "Jask, meet a potential customer."

"You need pumpkins?" Bram asked. "Apples?"

Elenor tipped her head back and roared with laughter. "Mercy no! The cider."

"What cider?" He helped her down from the driver's box.

She glanced over her shoulder. "What did you call it, Alfred? Crankle's Finest?" She turned to Jask. "Strange name."

Crankle had been Rowan's nickname for Bess after she'd swatted a pint of cider out of his hand at a banquet. Admittedly, the prince had been young, but he took it personally.

"Alfred offered me a sample," Elenor explained. "It's the lightest, frothiest cider I've ever had the pleasure to drink. I want it for my taverns."

"We haven't produced it at scale."

"Even better," she said. "If it's scarce, folks'll prize it more. Do you have any you can part with?"

"A firkin, at best, but it belongs to my . . ." He ached to say *wife*.

"Ward?" Alfred offered.

"Friend," Bram countered. "She'd be upset to find it gone."

Elenor nodded her kerchiefed head. "I'll make it worth your while. We've brought back the firkin my customers emptied. The prince's guard are a thirsty lot. How much are you asking?"

With the lack of pumpkin sales this season, another stream of income would be useful. He did the math in his head—what he'd paid while in her tavern, multiplied by the number of pints that fit in a firkin, compared to what it cost him to produce.

"Thirty sous," he said.

"Twenty," she countered.

"Twenty-five."

"Done." Elenor stuck out her hand to shake. As she pumped his hand, she looked him in the eye. "Do I know you?"

"No, ma'am," he said.

"Don't call me *ma'am*. Either Elenor or Brewster'll do, but the husband's gone, so the *ma'am*'s gone with him."

"Yes, ma . . . Elenor. I'm Jask Bone-Cracker."

So hard to keep a straight face when sharing that name.

She narrowed her gaze. "No, I suppose we haven't met. I don't recall meeting an orc, and I never forget a face. Still, though—something about your eyes is familiar."

"I get that a lot." He shoved his hands into his breeches' pockets to hide their trembling.

"Out here in the hinterlands?" She put her hands on her hips and let another laugh rip. "You're a funny one. Alfred said you never come to town. Why's that?"

"I've got everything I need here." He gestured for them to follow. "Cider's in the root cellar out back."

"Shame you don't bring your wares to Harvest Hollow. The market's bustling most days. You'd make a killing."

Bram opened the root-cellar door, then loosened the barrel's lid. "I don't need to make a killing. Just enough to get by."

"Alfred said you make otherworldly pies, too."

"And bread," Alfred said. "And butter."

"Sounds like Alfred talks a lot," Jask grumbled, shooting Alfred a look.

Elenor elbowed Alfred in the ribs. "He's got your number."

"I'm not a gossip, if that's what you're getting at," he said.

Bram and Elenor burst out laughing.

"I see it's Let's Be Rude Day here on Grimroot Farm," Alfred said. "But I'll overlook it if you have any pie."

Bram tapped a spile into the firkin, then wrapped it in honeyed cloth to prevent spills. "We have a few slices we can spare. Oh, shite, the cakes."

He dashed into the cottage and rescued the pans from the

oven. Thankfully, they hadn't burned. More done than he'd like, but he'd cover them with the pomegranate frosting.

At the back door, he shouted, "Come in this way."

He sliced a few wedges of the pie he and Marigold had made yesterday afternoon. It was a twist on the standard pumpkin pie—they'd finished it with a toasted pumpkin seed and maple-sap topping.

Elenor dropped her head back dramatically at the first bite. "This is like autumn on a fork. If I chased it with the cider, I'd feel like I'm double-dipping on the season."

"Thanks?"

She pointed her fork at him. "Are you *sure* you won't set up a market stall? Rémy's retiring, and we could use another baker."

"Not a baker," he said. "I'm a—"

Knight. But that was no longer true. And while he carried the training with him, he wasn't sad about losing that warrior identity. He had been, once open a time. But no more.

"—farmer."

"This pie would argue," Alfred said. "As would those cakes on the counter. But you could be both if you'd allow visitors."

"That reminds me." Bram snapped his fingers. "I need your help. We're planning to hold the Goldenmoon Festival here."

Alfred blessed himself. "Saints, you've been possessed."

Bram crossed his arms. "It's Meg's idea. She thought since the festival's been canceled, we could invite Harvest Hallow to celebrate here. Apple picking, caramel apples, bonfires, dancing, pumpkin carving, pumpkin decoration, pumpkin throwing. Maybe a hay-bale maze? Things like that. Anyone who sets up a stall could sell their wares, too."

"One week is tight," Elenor finished her pie. "But I'd love to stick it to the prince. Imagine canceling the most joyous day of the year for most in the kingdom without so much as a by-your-leave. If I put the word out and get you minstrels, I can run the beer garden?"

"Be my guest," Bram said. "And thank you. Alfred, can I ask you to circle back this way in three days' time with a pound of nails?"

Alfred nodded. "Can do. What for, if you don't mind me asking?"

Bram chuckled to himself. "A gazebo."

Chapter 24

Marigold stomped through the damp forest, angrily appreciating the beauty around here. Golden fingers of light streamed through the leaves, and the orange-and-yellow carpet of their fallen brethren glowed in the sun. A perfect backdrop for a romantic romp.

But Jask had chosen a railing repair over her.

"Nature is soothing, my ass," she muttered.

She'd been out here for a half an hour and was no calmer than when she'd left. She understood wanting to protect the chickens—she'd be horrified if anything happened to the girls. Barnaby, too, she grudgingly admitted.

But it was her *birthday.*

Not that he knew she turned twenty-nine today. As the date approached, it felt increasingly awkward to bring it up out of nowhere. But now she wished she had, because it was a normal piece of information you provided to the person you loved.

She stopped and leaned upon a tree as the realization wrapped itself around her soul.

Love. She'd fallen in love with Jask?

With her hand pressed to her chest, her stomach swirled. Saints, she *had* fallen in love again. Her young love with Bram was all sunny possibility and the conviction that all would work out well in the end. Her feelings for Jask were more rooted.

This Marigold understood that life contained shadows but found the courage to open her heart again.

To the love, yes, but also to the pain.

How would a love match with an orc work? She clapped her hand over her mouth to stifle a giggle. Not that she believed it of them, but if Bess believed her parents frowned upon her marrying a knight, what in the five kingdoms would she counsel about marrying an orc? Would any children be added to the line of succession?

A blur rolled past her, leaves crackling underneath it.

"What in sweet mercy?" She whirled and held out her hands as a small creature ran at her. Orange orbs of light erupted from both palms and flew at her attacker, twisting and twining around each other as they went.

Oh no. Oh no no no.

This wasn't a creature—this was a child.

The boy shimmered as the orbs collided with him. For ten seconds, however, a faint crown rested upon his head. Marigold looked at her hands with astonishment, then back to the boy. Except her magic no longer crowned the knobby-kneed boy.

"What in thunder?" Marigold stared at her unblemished palms. "Those lights didn't hurt you, did they? Are you well?"

"Yes, mistress. Have you seen my hoop?" He scanned the area near her feet. "It got away from me on the hill."

Ah, that was what had ripped past her.

"Over there." Marigold gestured to a curve in the path. "I think it leapt between those trees. What's your name, lad?"

"Bastien." The boy crashed into the brush in search of his hoop. His driving stick poked from his breeches' back pocket. At his age, her brothers had begun their military training. Playing hoop and stick in the woods seemed like a far more reasonable use of a young lad's time.

"Are you alone out here, Bastien?"

"Maybe. Are you Old Mother Ash?" he asked. "My ma said she lives in the woods and eats little boys who ask too many questions."

Marigold hid her laugh in her fist. The boy might not have known it, but the words were obviously from a woman desperate to slake her child's curiosity. She'd not met Bastien's mother, but she already liked her.

"I'm neither a mother nor old," Marigold said. "So, no."

He emerged from the woods, clutching his hoop. "You're kind of old."

Hmph.

"What's your name?" he asked.

"Mari—" She coughed. "Meg."

He tapped his hoop with his stick. "Marimeg is a strange name."

"It's just Meg." She shifted the basket dangling from the crook of her elbow. "Where are your parents, Bastien?"

"My ma's at home updating burial records." He jerked his thumb over his shoulder, then pointed up. "And my da's in heaven."

Her heart shifted in her chest. This must've been the son of the new caretaker at Kindlewood Garden of Rest. The widow Alfred had mentioned a few visits back . . . Marigold sighed. This poor lad was far too young to lose the steady hand of his father.

"I'm sorry to hear that."

"Thanks." Bastien shoved his hand into his pocket. "We moved here last month. I don't know anyone yet. Are you *sure* you don't have kids?"

The hope in his voice made her heart pinch. "I'm sure. But now you know me. And my friend has a cottage through the woods. His name is Jask."

"Are you married?"

"No," she said. If they were, that would solve one of her current problems. "He's a great big green orc and the kindest person I know. You can meet him, and then that would be two people you know."

The boy lifted his shoulder. "I'd rather know kids. Or a puppy?"

Affection washed over her. If she had a puppy, it would be his.

"No luck there, either. But I have a cat, Fuzzle, whom you're welcome to visit." She crouched so their eyes were level. "Anytime."

"Okay." The hoop bolted ahead as he struck it with the bow stick. "Bye, Marimeg."

"Bye, Bastien." She raised her hand to wave at his receding back.

Once he'd disappeared, she lifted her hands to inspect her palms. For minimancy, she kindled the magic by snapping her fingers. She was still learning to control this new power, whatever it was, but it answered her call when she flipped her palm quickly forward.

But what, exactly, did it *do*?

On her, nothing. Same with the Leshy and the various buildings around Grimroot Farm. Bastien, however, briefly transformed into a man and seemed none the worse for wear. She dusted her palms together. Without Vera and her vast knowledge of magical gifts, Marigold would be forced to experiment like she had during her alchemical pursuits.

She needed to try it on someone else.

Marigold steepled her fingers and pressed her pointers to her lips. A large, green opportunity could be found back at Grimroot Farm. He claimed to hate magic, but he'd grown comfortable with her minimancy. She called forth an orb on her palm and gazed upon its heatless light. During her alchemy studies, she'd conducted strange experiments on stubborn metals. She could convince him; she was sure of it.

After all, it *was* her birthday.

Didn't he owe her a present?

Chapter 25

Bram put the plate of frosted cakes into the cupboard, pleased with the cakes, the pumpkins he'd prepped, *and* that he'd figured out a plausible reason he knew today was her birthday.

He stilled.

The frisson of someone crossing the border skated along his spine. A new arrival? Or Alfred and the alewife leaving? It couldn't be Coby. He wasn't due back until tomorrow.

Marigold burst through the door.

"What's wrong?" He glanced at her empty basket. "Where are the mushrooms?"

"Shite, I forgot—well, I didn't forget. I was distracted." She lifted her hair from her neck. "I had an encounter."

Bram's neck tensed. "Are you hurt?" *Please don't let her be hurt.*

"No, just frightened for a moment." She peered into the kitchen. "Do I smell cakes?"

He reached for his cloak. "Tell me where."

"By the tree covered in goldcaps." She turned back to him as he plucked the sword from its bracket above the fireplace. "You don't need to storm the wood, Jask. I met a little boy. Your neighbor—the widow caretaker's son. He's adorable, and he might want to visit. But first, there's this—will you marry me?"

Surprise and delight whirred through him, despite the impossibility. Few in history had approved a union between a princess and a commoner, much less an orc.

"What precisely did you speak with this boy about?"

"Old Mother Ash. Answer the question. Will you marry me?"

"I believe it's customary for the man to ask for a lady's hand." He slipped an arm around the small of her back to pull her in for a kiss.

She laid her hand on his chest. "We've never been customary."

"True. But why have you asked me tonight?"

"Because if I'm already married—" she lifted onto her tiptoes to kiss him "—then I can't marry Crispin. Brilliant, isn't it? Can we summon a cleric right now?"

Heaviness settled in his sternum.

He couldn't doom her to his fate. Grimroot Farm was his world, but it didn't need to be hers. As much as he'd love to marry her, for her sake, he wouldn't.

Deflection was the coward's way, but he had no choice.

"I think the opportunity has sailed for today. The sun sets soon, but I still have a celebration in store." He kissed her forehead. "Happy birthday."

Underneath his lips, her forehead puckered. "How do you know it's my birthday?"

So many lies this evening.

"The night you drank my cider. You said the first time you'd been in your cups was on your birthday, the eighteenth of October, when you and Bram overdid it on perry."

She pulled a face. "I still can't look at the stuff."

"As far as alcohols to ruin for yourself, you could have done worse than pear cider. Sparkling wine—that would be a loss."

"I can't believe I told you all that and have no memory of it." She placed her palms on his chest. "I promise I will never touch orc-strength cider again. I prefer to retain control of myself and memories. And thank you for being a gentleman that night."

For a moment, he was confused, thinking she referenced the pear-cider night. On that birthday, years ago, he'd helped her up the secret stairwell through the kitchens, tucked her in, and left a mug of water by her bedside. But she meant the orc-cider night, when he'd done the same.

"I'm nothing if not a gentleman," he said. "Now, go upstairs. I need to ready the surprises I have. I wasn't expecting you back so soon."

"Okay." She bounced on her toes a bit. "Have I ever told you how much I like surprises?"

Many, many times.

"Once," he said. "I'll call you down when everything's ready."

Chapter 26

In the loft, Marigold changed into her blue dress. The sleeves were dotted with soap stains, but she didn't care. In Jask's eyes, she felt pretty in everything. But in this, she felt magnetic.

She held up her looking glass.

Her hair was wild, as usual. And the sparkle in her eyes was back. Roses bloomed in her cheeks from the sun and running home from the forest. This was a happiness she'd not known in years. She inspected her feelings, turned them over like rocks. There was no sadness.

No guilt.

Everything she'd told Jask about her numbness, her grief—that had all been true. But she'd been the only one to know the depths to which she carried that burden, couldn't share her troubles with anyone without revealing her true relationship with Bram. She'd played the sunny, bubbly princess Thornwick expected when forced into public.

Here, with Jask, she'd been able to be herself.

Let someone else, for once, see her tears.

"Marigold, you can come down now." Jask's voice rumbled up the stairs.

Eagerly, she descended. As she rounded the turn on the stairs, her heart skipped a beat. Perfect pumpkins of varying sizes lay scattered across the kitchen table. The hearth oven's flames lent the kitchen a lovely glow, and something aromatic—cottage pie, her favorite—baked in its warm embrace.

"Happy birthday," he said. "Besides the gazebo, jack-o'-lanterns were the last thing on your list. Ready to learn?"

She applauded and skipped toward the table. "Show me everything."

"Start by selecting a pumpkin." He lifted one and contemplated it. "I stare at it for a bit to allow the shape to inspire me."

"I like this one." She picked a medium pumpkin with some bumpy spots along its crown. "It reminds me of you."

"I'm not sure I feel flattered."

"Because of this side." She rotated it. "See? A green patch."

"What is it you want to carve?"

"A portrait of you."

He groaned. "That is very complicated."

"Why? On the night I arrived, one of the pumpkins had a realistic rendering of an apple tree. You can't be more complicated than that."

"Then I'll render you." He selected the largest pumpkin.

"Hey," she said. "Now who is not feeling flattered?"

"I need a larger canvas to capture your personality."

"I'll accept it," she said.

He handed her a sheet of paper. "Next, we sketch. Easier to render an idea on paper and transfer to the pumpkin than to go straight to the pumpkin."

She sat at the table across from him, in her usual seat. "Sit still."

"I'm not moving," he said as he sketched.

"You're looking down."

"To draw you as I put chalk to paper." He laughed. "These will not hang in a banquet hall, Marigold. Precision isn't necessary."

"But I want it to be good."

He reached for the ten-minute sandglass they kept near the stove. "That's the beauty of jack-o'-lanterns. Even when they're terrible, they're good."

"Now who's the optimist?" She laughed.

Jask grunted in response, then set the sandglass on the table "Ten minutes, chalk down, and we carve whatever's on the parchment. Agreed?"

"Agreed," she said.

In silence, as the hearth fire crackled, their chalk whispered across the parchment. Fuzzle prowled among the pumpkins on the table, then butted his head against her biceps.

"I'll get your dinner in a minute, Fuzz." She had to add one of Jask's ears, the one with the double hoops.

Fuzzle complained but slunk away again.

Jask cleared his throat. "Time. Now we lightly score the designs onto the pumpkins."

"Mine . . ." She twisted her lips. "I don't know if it'll work."

Jask circled from his side of the table. "I bet it'll be—oh."

He drew his brows together as he contemplated the warped sketch. She glanced from him to the sketch. She'd accurately captured the shape of his head, but everything else was too big, too small, or warped. Saints, had she given him a third eye? Still, Jask said nothing.

"You said it didn't have to be perfect."

Jask erupted into laughter. "Is that—" he snorted "—is that how you see me?"

"No!" She hid her face in her hands. "I told you I'm no artist. Stop laughing—I know it's terrible."

"It's perfect." He lifted the drawing. "I must frame it."

"Ha ha. Let's see yours, Mr. Perfect." She snatched his paper from across the table and . . .

Oh.

It was like she was staring at herself through different eyes.

Not overly detailed—there hadn't been time for that—but in this rendering, she glanced over her shoulder, a mischievous glimmer in her eyes, a smile on her lips, and a cascade of curls down her back.

"You did this in ten minutes?" she asked.

"I've had a lot of practice."

"When? All I ever see is you doing chores."

"The nights when I can't sleep. I prefer to occupy my hands. Drawing, whittling, carving, cooking—though I've done that last one less since you arrived. Fritters at three a.m. seem rude when a guest is sleeping."

"Fritters at three a.m. seem like a gift, and I resent you for never having awoken me with them." She tapped her finger on the corner of the portrait. "But Jask, this is . . . You're so talented. I knew that before, but this is more proof. Running this farm, carving, furniture making, cooking, baking . . . is there anything you can't do?"

"I'm sure there is, but I haven't found it yet."

"And humble." She laughed. "Shall we carve?"

With awls in hand, they scored the designs into the rind. *Hmph*, this required more pressure than Marigold expected. Resilient things, pumpkins. With each stroke, the amber of the pumpkin's flesh emerged. When they'd completed the design transfer, Jask handed her a shepherd's blade.

"Now, we eviscerate the pumpkin. First, saw through the top, like so." He jabbed the knife into the top and circled around the stem with rhythmic movements. "When your cuts make a circle, lift the top. But be careful not to break the stem."

As he lifted, stringy pulp clung to the rind. The thick pumpkin scent, like a garden damp with fresh rain, flooded the kitchen. He grabbed a sturdy metal spoon, then scraped the fibrous strands free from the top's underside.

"Now, it's a lot of scooping. Dump the innards into the

bowl." He flung them into the largest mixing bowl from the kitchen. "We'll sort the seeds for roasting and comfiting, then feed the pulp to the livestock."

Marigold plunged her knife into the pumpkin and sawed a circle. "Do the animals turn orange if you give them too much?"

Jask scraped another pile of pumpkin guts into the bowl. "From the pumpkin? No, they'd need to eat a good deal of it before it would have that kind of impact."

"I turned orange once." She freed the cap of the pumpkin and yanked the stringy strands free. "Yuck. You didn't say they were slimy."

With a twist to his lips, he said, "I'd even say they're moist."

She pointed her spoon at him. "Say it again and suffer the consequences."

After his chuckle died down, he asked, "When did you ever turn orange?"

"I was still in leading strings. According to my parents, my favorite foods were carrots, sweet potatoes, oranges, apricots. One day, I aggressively hugged Rowan, who was a shade of pinkish white, and seeing my skin against his they realized I had turned the color of the inside of a pumpkin shell. Though Bess fed me endless greens to counteract the effect, my father relished calling me *pumpkin* from that day onward."

Bram roared with laughter. "How have I not heard this before?"

"We haven't known each other all *that* long," she said. "I'm sure you have stories you haven't told me yet."

He continued quaking with laughter.

"It's not *that* funny," she said. "My pumpkin's empty. Now what?"

"You carve out the design," he said. "Some like to hack at a pumpkin with bigger blades, but the smaller ones work best for me. Gentle, patient movements. Like so."

Her heart shifted watching this titan delicately tease slivers of rind and flesh from the pumpkin. She followed suit.

"Where did you learn to do this?"

"Here as well. The nights can be very long. I've filled my solitude with lots of hobbies. I competed with myself to improve."

Sadness laced his words—no, not sadness. Melancholy, with which she was too familiar.

"It must have gotten lonely." She removed a large chunk to reveal the pumpkin version of Jask's smiling mouth.

"I managed. The same could be said for you, right? You said you closed yourself in your tower for a long time."

"I did." She sighed. "But I mostly read. Old letters, books, especially fairy tales. The stories seemed closer to my real life than anything else I read. Bad things happening to people by chance. Not because they put themselves in harm's way or because they deserve a comeuppance, like in fables. Nope. They just happened to piss off a fairy and, bloop, now you're a hedgehog."

Jask's shoulders stiffened, and he dropped his knife.

"Is something wrong?" She sawed out the whites of one of his pumpkin eyes.

He shoved back from the table. "I need to take the pie out of the oven."

Liar. If he was any more tense he'd snap a tusk. But she'd learned these moods of his blew out as fast as they blew in.

"Do you have a smaller knife?" she asked. "I need it for your earrings."

"In my whittling box," he said.

She ventured to the fireplace and knelt to where he kept the box. Its hinges creaked as she opened it. Inside, a dozen knives were slotted into the velvet-covered rack. Various figures in progress were jumbled in the kit's well. She grabbed a small knife from the end but couldn't resist inspecting figures. More of Jask's skilled handiwork. These thumb-sized creatures were adorable. Here was a bear, there a squirrel, and there, under a few others, a . . .

A unicorn. Rough, much less skillfully crafted than the others.

Her blood pounded, and her vision clouded at the edges. She stood, though she wasn't sure her legs would continue to hold her.

"Marigold?" Jask stood behind her. "Did you find what you needed?"

Slowly, she turned with the figure in her palm. "Is . . . is this my unicorn?"

Green though he was, he paled.

Marigold's mind reeled back to the night before her true love departed Thornwick to seek his fortune. They'd met in the hayloft at the witching hour, and she'd given him the rough-hewn charm, half of their locket, and her handkerchief.

All on loan so he could keep her close.

Not to worry, Marigold. A confident smile played upon lips she'd kissed a thousand times. *I'll be back with a fortune and, with any luck, a title. I'll ask for your hand, and we'll have our happily-ever-after. Like the people in your fairy tales.*

Cradled against his steady heart, she'd believed him.

What if . . . what if he *had* come back to her?

She rubbed the figure's mane with her thumb, the way she always had. With her gaze trained on Jask, she squinted. Tilted her head, then squinted again and looked at him, her mind whirring.

The gold flecks in his eyes . . . the expression, private jokes from their past . . . the gentle teasing . . . and the skilled pleasing in his bed. Saints, how had she not seen it before? Felt the tug on her heartstring?

She laid a hand on his face. "Bram? Is it you?"

"What? I— What, Marigold?" He stepped backward, his leg knocking into his chest, making him stumble and thud onto the divan.

The panicked set to his features confirmed it. Any time she'd caught him in a half-truth, this was the expression he wore. Certainty settled on her shoulders like a cloak.

"You're Sir Bram Duncan of Thornwick, my childhood best friend, sweetheart, and true love."

His grin was more of a grimace. "Did you get into my cider?"

"Don't you joke with me." She thrust the precious unicorn into her pocket, then knelt before him. "This is not the time."

"I'm not him." Panic laced his voice. "You must believe me."

She grabbed his left hand. There, at the base of his thumb, was the scar from the deep self-inflicted wound from when he carved the unicorn for her eighth birthday.

Tenderly, she kissed the scar. "It is you."

Not a question, a statement.

"I won't let anything happen to you." Anguish carved lines in his face as he pulled her onto his lap.

"I know that." His embrace squashed her nose to his chest. "But I need to breathe."

"Oh, sorry." He released her. "But wait. You're all right. You're all right? You're not dying?"

"Sweet mercy, no. I'm fine." She leaned back from him. "I'm well. Are *you* well?"

His glistening eyes searched hers.

"Bram?" She placed one hand on his cheek and the other on his heart. "Why didn't you tell me?"

His chest swelled with a long, slow breath.

"We'd better talk."

Chapter 27

The fear that gripped Bram and hadn't let go from the moment Marigold arrived dissolved like spun sugar in the rain. She was alive. She knew he was Bram, and she was alive. For the first time in years his true love looked him in the eyes and called him by his name.

"Yes, we'd better talk." With tears shining in her eyes, she twisted in his lap to straddle him, then rained kisses upon his face. "Later. First, I need you to love me. Now."

He wouldn't wait for her to make a second request. With eager—nay, frantic—hands he undid her laces. Marigold was gorgeous in any setting, but with the flickering fire picking out every gold strand in the wild curls loosed around her shoulders and the ghost of her rosebud nipples beneath her shift . . . She was a goddess.

"You're my favorite person, Marigold."

"You as well . . ." She knit her brows together. "What do you prefer I call you?"

"Edmund," he said. "I've always liked that name."

She laughed. "Be serious. Bram or Jask?"

"I am both," he answered. "But I was Bram first. Honestly, Marigold, you could call me an ass and I'd still happily respond."

"Noted." She pulled her shift over her head. "Ass."

Bram's heart thudded against his chest in time with the

blood rushing to his cock. She was too beautiful for words, and he was no poet. But he'd be damned if he wouldn't show her how well he loved her and write poems with their bodies.

He caressed her perfect breasts, knew the weight of them as sure as he knew the weight of an apple from the orchard, and hungered for them just as much. As he licked and swirled one tight rosebud with his tongue, he rolled the other between his fingers. She gasped and rocked against him, then tunneled her hand through his hair.

She tugged at his shirt. "Off."

He obliged, and she curved against him. The feel of her warm flesh against his, all that soft strength hungry for him, for his body, blanked his senses. No longer was he a man trapped in an orc's body. He was only a powerful potion of feelings swirling together.

Want, need, lust.

But above all, love.

With her grasped in his arms, he rose from the divan. She wrapped her legs around him as he desperately untied his breeches and shoved them to the floor. As her mouth devoured his, he thought about taking her to bed upstairs.

No, his need was too great.

The wall.

As a man, he might not have had the strength, but in this body, he could hold her up all night. He raised her so her hips were higher than his, then pinned her against the wall. After notching himself at her entrance, he pressed into her. With a soft gasp, she melted as he hooked his arms under her legs and rolled his hips.

They locked gazes, and her eyes were blown black.

She bucked into his thrusts, meeting each one. This woman had given him everything. Her heart, her mind, her body. And curse him, he wanted it all, and more. The rules about who could be together mattered not. He would marry this woman, she who'd asked Jask to wed, all smiles, no hesitation.

Still, he'd been starved for her to know she'd found her Bram.

Now that she did, his happiness would never end.

He pulled her away from the wall, still joined together. He needed more, deeper, harder. With a roar, he kicked the crate from the rug in front of the fire. He knelt, then gently lay her on the plush bearskin. With her hair spread out like sunbeams, she was an angel.

A devilish angel.

"Don't stop." Her breath was shallow, her cheeks and chest flushed, her eyes blown black.

"Never." He pulled her ass onto his thighs, then lifted her legs to his shoulders. The way her hips rose with his touch thrilled him. She reached for his legs, caressing his thighs as he flexed.

"Slower," she said. "I want to savor you."

As though saying that didn't make him want to come right now. But she was his princess, and her wish was his everlasting pleasure. With torturously deliberate movements, he eased into her, causing her body to sway in a way that would be burned into his memory for the rest of his days.

A smile played on her lips. "This . . . is my . . . favorite birthday."

"Mine, too." His voice was rough as he belted his forearm across her shins to keep her locked in tight.

With a gasp, she rolled her hips. "I changed my mind. Faster."

Obedient as ever, he obliged. Control slipped away as fast became furious, and the sweet tension built in his spine, coiled between his hips. He held it off, until, until, until. . . .

Princess Marigold of Thornwick fell apart in his arms.

He allowed his own pinnacle to meet hers. One, two, three thrusts as its echoes coursed through him. He stilled, as senseless as if he'd been knocked from his horse in a joust. His chest expanded as he caught his breath, then released a contented sigh.

"Come here." She reached for him.

Gently, he withdrew from her, already missing the sensation of being overwhelmed by her. He lay next to her before the fire. She used his chest as a pillow, and he wrapped his arm around her waist, tucking her close to him.

"Why didn't you say anything?"

"I couldn't." He trailed his fingers along the curve of her hip. "It's the curse. I'm forbidden to reveal my true identity to anyone, upon pain of their death. It's also why I can't leave Grimroot Farm. The rules were quite clear. Perhaps because you guessed who I am—"

"Who cursed you?" she demanded.

"The autumn sprite."

"But you hate magic. Why would you engage with a sprite?"

"Starry-eyed ambition on a foolish quest led by Crispin. For a title, I was to gather golden acorns from the Lantern Oak. After I filled a haversack, the sprite challenged me with a riddle."

Marigold nodded with understanding. "And you got it wrong."

"No, that's the thing—I got it right."

"And he cursed you anyway?" She drew her brows together. "That's unfair."

"It was at Crispin's behest."

Her mouth formed an O. "But . . . why?"

"At the time, jealousy motivated him." He sighed as he swirled his fingertips against her soft shoulder. "Harvest Hollow cheered me more than him. Now, given what you told me of his plot with your brothers, I wonder if removing me was the first step in his plan to acquire you."

"Yuck." She pulled a face. "I don't care to be described as an acquisition."

"My humblest apologies." He hissed her forehead.

"Accepted. Why would the sprite obey Crispin's command? He's made no secret that he's magic-tolerant, but I doubt a sprite would do his bidding from simple gratitude. I've been a spectator to royal authority my entire life, and that's simply not how it works."

"That, I do not know."

Her hand fisted. "I will throttle the prince."

"I love that you're fired up on my behalf, but there's no need to attack him. I made my peace with it."

"Why make your peace? Crispin should pay for this. He's stolen years from us."

"It's partially my fault," he said.

She blinked at him. "Explain that part."

"I was a knight, Mare. There are virtues we're supposed to uphold, like humility. If I had, I wouldn't have cozened to Crispin so much and made myself vulnerable. I should've known better than to try to win a negotiation with a sprite."

Her eyes grew shiny in the firelight. "Bram, Crispin did this to *you*. The shame is his to bear, whether he owns it or not."

"But I—"

"No." She laid her hand on his heart. "You trusted him, and he violated that trust. This is not your fault, and he should be held to account."

Bram sat with that. Whenever misery befell someone, most often the conversation centered on what the poor soul had done wrong, how they'd put themselves in a position to be harmed. The default assumption was a villain sought opportunity and everyone else must defend. A lack of defense was the victim's fault.

But Marigold reframed it—he was a survivor, not a victim.

"Why put ourselves through that?" Bram asked. "I've already won. You've left him, found me, and fell back in love with me. This is, in fact, the best way this could have unfolded."

"And he . . ." She circled her hand in the air above them. "What? Gets away with it?"

"It'll stain his soul, along with any other injustices he's enacted."

"But people should know."

"You do." He cupped her cheek. "And for me, that is enough."

"So how do we break the curse?"

"I . . ." Bram pursed his lips. "I don't know. During the transformation, I was ill. I'm not sure I paid close enough attention, but he said true love would fix it."

She frowned. "But you've always had true love."

"For which I'm grateful," he said. "But I took it to mean that my true love has a key role in ending the curse."

Marigold's eyes flared why. "Ooh, I have an idea!"

She pushed from him and scurried up the stairs. Much as he enjoyed the sight of her behind, he'd rather she stayed by his side.

"Where are you going?"

"To look for instructions!"

"For curses?" he called.

"No, not curses." She hurried back down the stairs and, with a flourish, presented her book of fairy tales.

"Mare, those are fictional."

"Are they, though?" She lay beside him and flipped through the leather-bound tome's pages. "They're morality plays in some cases, cautionary tales in others. They may not contain hard facts, but they offer learning through imagination."

"But it won't tell us anything about breaking this specific curse."

"Yes, it will—look." She pointed to a picture of a woman sleeping. "This one is reversed by true love's kiss. *Hmph.* Your curse would've been broken a thousand times by now if that were the solution."

She flipped the page, this one featuring a frog. "In this, she throws the frog against a wall and it kind of stun-starts his transformation. Want to try that? I could shrink you."

"I think not."

On the next page, a woman puckered up to another hairy beast. Marigold frowned. "I'm realizing these tales may be propaganda crafted by unattractive men."

Jask laughed.

She flipped again. "Oh, this one's closer. A sister silently weaves shirts from nettles for her cursed swan brothers but can't speak all the while. Right before she's set aflame for witchcraft, she throws the shirts on the swans, and presto—they are again men."

"You're no sister to me." Bram nuzzled her cheek as he palmed her strong thigh, she flipped another page.

"Closer still!" A man-sized hedgehog glanced up from the pages. "The princess kept her promise to marry him and not ask questions, and delighted in him when he shed his hedgehog skin at night and came to her as a man. One night, she burned the skin and set him free. Now *that* is more like it."

"Alas." He skated his hand higher. "I do not shed."

"And thank the saints for it." She kissed him. "But I mean taking action. This princess understood she shouldn't sit and wait. I must speak to the autumn sprite."

"There's no casual conversation with a sprite, Marigold. It's always a gamble, and very rarely does anyone besides the sprite win."

"But I—"

"Do not go to the Lantern Oak, Marigold. Promise me."

She pursed her lips. “Don’t you want to be yourself again?”

“I am.” He arched an eyebrow. “Can’t you love me like this?”

“I already *do*, Bram. I’ve loved every version of you I’ve known—the boy, the youth, the man, and the orc. This isn’t *right*, though. The world’s out of balance while an innocent man lives under a curse. And don’t you want to leave Grimroot Farms?”

“For years, I was desperate to leave. Tried everything I could to escape, including flinging myself through the sky on a trebuchet. The farm isn’t a prison to me—it’s a perimeter. Every inch of it is knowable, manageable, mine. The crops behave according to predictable rules, and a pumpkin doesn’t stab me in the back, unlike my brothers-in-arms. Aside from all that, the reason I was desperate to find an escape knocked on my door in the middle of the night, and I’m more content than ever to stay.”

“I swear, you are the sweetest marshmallow.” She kissed him, then broke out into giggles. “You must’ve been shocked to see me.”

“That’s an understatement.”

She laughed harder. “You tried so hard to get me to leave.”

“And you wouldn’t. Your stubborn reputation is intact.”

“*Delightfully* stubborn,” she said. “And aren’t you grateful?”

“I am.” He kissed her cheek, then pushed up from the rug. “If you’re up for it, there’s one additional birthday surprise.”

He held out a hand to help her up, then Marigold followed him, both naked as the day they were born. Appropriate, given they were celebrating her birthday. After washing up, he reached into the cabinet where he’d hidden the cakes.

“Close your eyes,” he instructed.

Marigold sealed them shut. “What is it?”

He fitted a small taper into the center of the apple-sized cake, then set it in front of her. "Happy birthday, Marigold."

She opened her eyes, then covered her mouth. "I *knew* I smelled cakes!"

He nodded. "Vanilla with pomegranate frosting. I made it while you were foraging."

"You did this for me?" She swiped away a tear.

"Why are you crying? Are pomegranates no longer your favorite?"

"These are happy tears. I have missed this *so* much." Her wobbly smile steadied. "I took the way you see me, *really* see me, for granted. If you asked my parents, my brothers, Bess what my favorite fruit is, they wouldn't know. They'd think it a silly question."

"All the better that we found each other again." He lifted the cake to her mouth. "Dry your tears, Princess Marigold. They don't mix well with birthday cake."

She giggled, then bit into the cake. "Delicious." She licked her lips. "Now you."

The frosting was sweet, the honey, pomegranate, butter, and cream perfectly whipped. The cake underneath was moist and spongy, the way Marigold preferred it, even though she'd never use the *m*-word to describe it.

"My compliments to the chef," he said.

"You still have frosting on your lips."

He swept her into his arms, then kissed her. "Now you do as well."

"How do you . . ." She traced her fingers on his chest. "Feel about returning to the rug?"

"I feel excellent about it."

And once again, in front of the fire, he wished Marigold a happy birthday.

Chapter 28

Two things became more obvious than ever for Marigold the day after Bram's revelation.

One, she'd venture to the Lantern Oak to give that miserable autumn sprite a piece of her mind. And two, Prince Crispin could not be allowed to get away with betraying Bram. Ruling through magical threat was a dangerous path that had warped many a sovereign. Though she didn't want to be queen of Harvest Hollow, she cared about the common folk.

As for that first item . . .

She'd need to check the proportions with Bram, but the map of Grimroot Farm that she'd drawn on a large sheet of parchment seemed accurate. Ostensibly, the rendering would help her visualize the best layout for the Goldenmoon Festival. It served a dual purpose, however, of learning precisely where the imp who'd upended their lives lived. There was the wood, which led to the cottage, the pens, the coop, and the pumpkin fields. Farther down, the sunflower patch, the meadow, the orchard, and beyond that, Coldpress Lake.

Fuzzle leapt onto the table to inspect her handiwork.

"What do you think, Fuzz?" She hovered her hand over the orchard. "Apple picking will be here, obviously. And pumpkin decorating and carving either in or near the pumpkin fields. But what about the dancing? And the vendor stalls?"

The telltale creak of the stairs signaled Bram's descent. His orc-yawn shook the cottage's very foundation.

As he came around the corner, she sighed contentedly.

Was there anything more delicious than rolled up shirtsleeves on his muscular forearms?

"Good morning." With his chest to her back, he slipped his hands around her waist and nuzzled her neck which, if her looking glass was true, featured a lavender love bite. "You're up early."

"The festival waits for no one." She pressed back against him. "I've already done the eggs and milked Queen, and Paloma's living her best life in the woods. Porridge is on the stove."

"Sounds like I can go back to bed." He rested his chin on her shoulder, then gestured to her scattered parchments. "What's all this?"

"A map of your property. I'm trying to figure out the logistics for the festival. We can also make copies for Alfred to take to the city to help people find their way."

"Trust me, everyone knows how to get to Grimroot Farm." He kissed her cheek, then released her. "Wayfarers have walked the paths thin. They claim the farm's energy is magical—something about ley lines, though all I've noticed are boulders to pluck out of fields. Coming here's also a rite of passage for young ones to visit and have me roar at them. But we don't have to host the festival, Mare. Crispin's continued search for you worries me."

"But I don't want to disappoint the townspeople."

"They'll live. Your safety is my greater concern." He poured himself a mug of her chamomile tisane, then topped up hers. "You're not worried Prince Crispin's people—or the prince himself—will attend?"

"I'd be surprised if they did." Marigold blew the steam from her mug. "What kind of prince skips off to a festival when his lady love lies suffering from an ague that prevents their nuptials? If he and a lance of knights storm the farm, though, I can shrink us in a snap. We have an edge."

He stirred the porridge pot and ladled out a portion to break his fast. "Still, the unresolved question of your betrothal and the announcement that it's been delayed, not canceled, feels like a sword of Damocles."

She beamed at him. "You *did* study your Greek mythology."

"The only stories you love more are the fairy tales." He sat at the table and spooned up porridge.

"Incorrect. Romances first, then fairy tales, then Greek mythology." She spun the parchment toward him. "Did I get the placement and scale right?"

"It's close." Bram tapped his finger on the orchard drawing. "If an inch equals a hectare, then the orchard needs to move an inch to the west. The pumpkin field, the cottage, and the yards are more or less correct. Coldpress Lake should move to the east, maybe an inch and a half. The brook that runs through the wood is a bit farther south. And that's the wrong spot for the Lantern Oak. It's farther north."

She bounced on her toes. That was *exactly* what she wanted to know.

Bram snapped his gaze to her. "Marigold."

She fluttered her eyelashes. "Bram?"

"Absolutely not."

She sat and rested her chin on her latticed fingers. "*Absolutely not* what?"

"Don't go to the autumn sprite."

"Why would I do a thing like that?"

He pinched the bridge of his nose. "Because you're headstrong."

"You're lucky for it. Otherwise I wouldn't be here."

With narrowed eyes, he searched her face. "Please, don't risk our happiness for so little reward. We're content, are we not? I know I am. But if you're not, tell me."

She reared back. "Why would you ask me that?"

He shoved back from the table. "Nothing. Forget it."

With a great clatter, he tossed his dishes into the sink.

"Don't avoid me, Bram." She placed a hand on his shoulder.

"Bringing people here, trying to break the curse. I get that if you had the choice between this—" he swept his hand down his midsection "—and the gregarious handsome man I was in Thornwick, you'd choose him every time. But it's not worth it, Marigold. It's not worth *you* to try to change me back."

"Oh, Bram. Is that what you think this is? That I want you back the way you were?"

"Yes." He crossed his arms as he looked down at her. "Do you not?"

Her heart folded on itself. Did he really have such a low opinion of her?

"I fell in love with *you*, Bram. No matter what you look like, what form you take. I desire a chat with the autumn sprite to free you from Grimroot Farm."

"Because you grow bored of it."

"Please stop twisting my words. I want you to have the choice to stay *or* leave. If you can't choose, this is a prison. A lovely, rustic prison, but a prison nonetheless."

He tilted his head. "I like it here."

"So do I," she said. "But was Rapunzel content to stay in her tower? Or Persephone in the underworld? You've done an admirable job keeping yourself occupied while you've been here, but you deserve the freedom to come and go as you please. Seek adventures, quests, and the like."

His eyes dimmed. "I'm not the man you remember."

"Yes, you are. Just as I'm the same woman."

He gripped her shoulders. "No, you're not. Neither of us is the same. Once upon a time, I dreamed of a bigger life. I'd tasted it, and yes, at first, I felt trapped here. But as the seasons changed, I fell in love with Grimroot Farm. If I, or this place, are not your choices, I'll understand. But please, what I have here—what we could have here—is good without trying to lift the curse. Do not let perfect be the enemy of good."

He melted away from her, then grabbed his cloak from the peg beside the door. "I'll return."

"When?" she asked.

"Later." After a beat, he closed the door.

His footsteps on the stairs rattled the house. As he walked the path, his figure grew smaller until you'd never guess he was an orc. How had she fumbled that so badly? Did he truly not believe that she loved him in all his forms? Her goal was justice, not aesthetics.

Marigold paced the cottage.

She needed fresh air. On the porch she scanned the horizon. It was devoid of Bram—wait, no. There was movement. She focused on the shadow moving through the pumpkins. It lifted its head and . . .

Marigold exhaled as her fear blew away as a leaf on the wind.

A young fox sniffed the air. From what she'd read, the young ones were kicked out of their mother's territory in the fall to find their homestead. They wandered until they found a hospitable place to call their own.

To say she identified was to put it mildly.

She tapped her fingers against her lips. Bram said Crispin ordered the autumn sprite to curse him, despite answering the riddle correctly. Why? Sprites were notorious mischief-makers and did not respect human hierarchies. Rather, they mocked them.

That was the mystery here.

One that she'd need to resolve before she'd feel safe. Even if she convinced the sprite to return Bram to his human form and untether him from Grimroot Farm, Crispin could compel him to curse them both.

Despite all Bram's warnings, she had no choice.

She must seek out the sprite.

Chapter 29

The cold slapped Bram's cheeks as he stood at Coldpress Lake. The water offered him no wisdom. He blew out his lips. He'd been far too harsh with Marigold. He believed that *she* believed the form he took did not matter. That she loved him as an orc as much as she had the man.

But surely, she lied to herself.

His breath plumed in the air as he waited. Cottages dotted the lake's rim in the distance, their windows faintly glowing like beacons on this gloomy autumn day.

Footsteps crunched the rocky shore behind him.

A hundred yards . . . fifty . . . twenty-five . . . ten.

He twitched his ears. "Hello, Coby."

"Sir . . . I mean, Jask." The young knight stood next to him.

Bram folded his arms. "No one's about. Call me what you prefer. How do you fare?"

"Well, thanks," Coby said. "You?"

He was brimming with turmoil and fret.

"I'll do." Bram ran his hands through his hair, then cradled the back of his skull. "That's a lie, kid. It's been a devil of a day."

"It's eight a.m., sir."

He twitched an ear toward Coby, listening for any shifts in breathing pattern. Anything to help discern if the young knight spoke with truth on his tongue. "Can I trust you, Coby?"

The kid took a quick breath. Still in the realm of normal, though. Not the heave of someone who was about to lie to you. "Yes, sir."

Bram sucked in a breath. Coby had never broken his trust, but it felt like the world had when Crispin betrayed him. With Crispin maintaining the ruse of the wedding . . . His gut told him another plan was afoot. To protect Marigold from whatever might come, he needed more allies.

"If I need to reach you without attracting attention from the rest of the guard, where can I leave word?"

Coby rubbed his chin. "The Laughing Gourd, I suppose. The tavern nearest Brambleton's keep. These days, most of the knights prefer to indulge at the Black Dragon."

The Laughing Gourd was Elenor Brewster's tavern. Handy, that.

"Good," he said. "Next—would you be willing to keep an eye on Sir Kevin?"

"How do you mean? I shouldn't like to cross him."

Bram crossed his arms over his chest. "I suspect he'll return on the prince's orders. Crispin typically bloodies his hands by proxy, and he was . . . dissatisfied with the search of Grimroot Farm the night Princess Marigold disappeared. I wouldn't be surprised if he seeks another opportunity to ransack my homestead via Kevin."

With his brow lowered, Coby scratched his jaw. "But you said the princess is not here."

"I stand by that," he said. "As part of the prince's guard, the less you know, the better. All I'm asking is if you notice or catch word that Kevin is planning another visit to Grimroot Farm, send word to me."

"That I can do. But how? Sending a messenger would raise suspicions, wouldn't it?"

"The royal falconer," he said. "Garrick Hale. He and I were

friends once—hunted together on our off days. He loathed the prince."

"Based on the comments he utters under his breath, he still does."

Bram was oddly comforted that despite the years he'd lived in seclusion on the farm, some things remained as they were in Harvest Hollow.

Coby wrinkled his forehead. "But falcons are birds of prey, not messengers."

"These are. Garrick trains them to deliver messages because Crispin prefers their look. Says they are more intimidating than pigeons. He pays a mage a monthly sum to work a spell that makes them fly true along ley lines."

Coby rolled his eyes. "What a waste of money and magic. All for aesthetics?"

"That, unfortunately, is how Crispin makes most of his decisions. He slots people into places based on their looks and not their merit." Bram tossed Coby a silver sou from the stash he'd earned from the cider sale to Elenor. "Grimroot Farm's cottage is a nexus point for ley lines. Pay Garrick to send the falcon screaming when Kevin makes a move. I'll hear it."

Coby offered his hand. "You have my word."

Chapter 30

A twig cracked to Marigold's left. She held her fingers aloft, ready to snap herself small and hide. *Ah.* It was Fuzzle. That was odd. Fuzzle was less of a fan of the out-of-doors than she'd been when they first escaped the castle.

"What are you doing out here? Are you worried about me, too?"

Fuzzle meowed, twitched his ears, then shot off into the underbrush. Okay, then. Not worried. Bored, more like.

Marigold swooshed through the fallen leaves carpeting the path, then paused to review the rough map she'd drawn this morning. She was not far from the goldcaps tree. Based on the adjustments Bram suggested this morning, the Lantern Oak should be across the brook.

The trees held their breath as she leapt across the gurgling water.

She wobbled for a moment on the bank but caught her balance.

"Ha!" She pumped her fists. "No distressed damsel here."

She stepped forward, and *hell*. Her left-turn shoe stayed behind, sucked from her foot by the squelching mud. She crouched and reached, but the shoe lay beyond her fingertips. Minimancy wouldn't help here, nor would true face.

A stick, on the other hand . . .

Marigold grabbed a fallen branch and wiggled it into her

boot, then coaxed it free. The boot popped from the muck and straight into the brook. As the water swept it away, she swore she could hear it laughing at her.

"Damn it all," she muttered.

No matter. She'd make this work.

Her gait was uneven as she pushed through the flexing scrim of willows branches. The papery leaves caught in her hair and whispered along her cloak.

"*Pthtt.*" She spit out a leaf that found its way into her mouth.

Once again, she loved being outdoors adjacent, but the *actual* out-of-doors, however, could rot. She paused to brush the leaves and burrs from her skirts. The stubborn vegetation refused to fall free.

She'd deal with it later, back at the cottage.

When she'd have to confess to Bram that she'd taken this risk.

As she looked up from her skirts, goose bumps fanned over her skin. She understood why the autumn sprite chose the Lantern Oak as its home. The tree's cloak of fiery leaves was resplendent as it swayed in the autumn breeze. In today's gray gloom, the orbs glowed a welcoming orange, inviting her into the branches.

Maybe that was part of the sprite's magic, luring people into the tree's embrace like a siren calling sailors to crash upon rocks? She knew little about sprites. Fairies, gnomes, pixies, witches—these she'd read about in detail.

Sprites on the other hand . . . She knew two things: That they preferred to align with natural elements—seasons, terrains, trees, waters. And that they were quick to vanish.

Since Marigold decidedly did *not* prefer natural elements, that explained why she'd never crossed paths with them.

So, she'd need to be fast to catch him.

She tilted her head back. Bram said he'd climbed the tree

to collect the acorns, and that was where he'd met the sprite. Her spine curved as she took in its full height. This . . . was a tall tree. Life would be easier if she'd grabbed the ladder. All she'd brought in the pack basket was food and drink.

Welp, no time for dillydallying.

The lowest limb was chest high. With bent elbows, she placed her palms on it, then leapt, hauling herself up. She swung her legs over the thick limb and scooted forward, bark scraping her thighs, until she grabbed another limb to pull herself upright. On and on she went—up, scrape, up, scrape—until she reached . . . the middle.

Enough of this.

She cupped her hands around her mouth. "Autumn sprite?"

No answer. The sting on her thighs was deeply unpleasant.

"Sprite?" she called again. "Please talk to me."

The wind blew in response. Around her, the air charged, like before a lightning strike. Marigold's stomach swam at the idea. A flutter tickled her hair, like a hummingbird trying to sip from her ear. She screamed, and her flailing hands connected with something solid.

"Ouch! And what was that for?"

A luminous orange creature hovered above the branch in front of her, rubbing its forehead. His features were sharp but perfect, like the sculptures pocketed in the alcoves of Briarveil Cathedral. Instead of pale marble eyes, however, his were large, golden, and zeroed in on her.

"Are you him?" she asked. "The sprite?"

As he fluttered to a fresh branch, gauzy light trailed and fizzled behind him.

"Go on, then, Red, and make it good." He held up his pinched thumb and index finger. "I'm this close to turning you into a cardinal, so I am."

She pointed at him. "You've got a lot of nerve."

"*I've* a lot of nerve? Bold, you are. Climbing my tree and smacking me about, trying to steal my gold."

She shook her head. "I don't want gold. I want answers."

"About what?" The sprite's gossamer hair waved in the breeze.

"Sir Bram Duncan."

"Who, now?"

She wiped her hands down her face. "You ruined his life, and you don't even remember him."

"Now listen, Red. I don't go about ruining lives for sport. If something ill befell your man, I'd wager he brought it about himself. Isn't there someone always up my tree, helping themselves to what's mine? If one gets away, they'd tell any who'd listen to give it a go. Can't have that, no, I can't."

The hair raised on her arms as he moved faster than her eyes could track. She twisted to find him again among the leaves.

"But he didn't deserve it."

"Sure, and that's what they all say." The sprite flung his hands into the air. "What'd I do, lass? Turn him into an apple?"

"No." She gasped and clutched her hands together. "Did you do that to someone?"

"Not that I recall." He wagged his tiny finger at her. "But I could, and you'd best not forget it."

"An orc. Three years ago you turned Sir Bran Duncan into an orc. Yes, he tried to take your gold, but it was at someone else's behest. You challenged him to a riddle, and he answered it correctly, so you should've let him go. But Prince Crispin told you to curse him anyway. That's cheating."

The sprite paled as he backed away. "I haven't a clue what you're on about."

"Oh yes, you do." She pursed her lips. "I can see it in your face."

"You know me not, lady."

"Princess, actually." Maybe he was intimidated by royals, and that was why he did Crispin's bidding? It was worth a shot. And in case he wasn't . . .

She nabbed him by the feet and held him upside down. A challenge, as the sprite's skin was slippery as moss.

"D'you have no sense, Red?" he said. "I'm fierce cranky. The Hunter's Moon's nearly upon us. When the sun rises after it, I'll be off to slumber till the next equinox. Put me down and be on your way, or I'll be forced to do something drastic. And mind your arse on the way down."

"Can we talk like civilized people?" she asked. "I brought cake."

He flapped his wings, curious. "What kind of cake is it, then?"

"Vanilla with pomegranate-cream frosting."

The sprite raised an eyebrow. "No funny business?"

"All serious business. Baked goods and answers—that's all."

The sprite flitted closer, the buzz tingling her ear. "No one ever brings me anything."

"Clearly a lack of proper upbringing." She set him down and withdrew a cake wrapped in linen from her basket. "Here."

He took it, sniffed at it, then unhinged his jaw and ate it in one bite.

And she thought Jask had rough table manners.

"Meh, I've had better," the sprite said. "Is there more of it?"

"Plenty." She handed him another cake. "Do you have a name?"

Crumbs filled the air as he spoke with a full mouth. "Oh, you'd like to know that, wouldn't you?"

"It's polite to use someone's proper name. Did the cake help your memory?"

"A bit," he said. "Better take another cake to be sure."

Like the others, he ate it with nary a chew. The sprite's belly, if possible, rounded further.

"I might remember your fella." The sprite drummed his fingers against his belly. "Blond, was he?"

She sighed. "Like the sun in June."

"Dimple? Blue eyes?"

"Like the early-morning sky, after the pink has faded."

"You're full lovestruck, aren't you? A plain yes would've done the job." The sprite tilted his head, and his hair wisped about his ears. "Are you the true love he mentioned?"

"He spoke of me?"

"Yep. Seemed dead certain if he got the riddle wrong, you'd come to his rescue to break the curse." The sprite looked her up and down. "All in all, I guess he was right."

She shifted her seat to ease the chafe on her thighs, but there was nothing for it. "So there *is* a way to break it?"

"There's always a way." The sprite flipped his palms to the sky. "Every trickster's required to provide a loophole."

"What is it for Bram's curse?"

His orange eyebrow shot skyward. "Careful now, Red. That's how you start a bargain."

Bram's voice nudged her brain. *Never bargain with a sprite.*

"Forget I asked." She withdrew the last cake from her basket. "But I'd like some information, if you're willing to give it freely."

He took it from her. "You've been generous, so I'll give you a hand. Only one question, mind, so make it good."

She could ask about Bram's loophole to return him to his true form and free him from Grimroot Farm. But she'd meant what she said earlier—she loved him no matter what. And if they broke this curse, what would stop Crispin from visiting some other misfortune on them with this sprite's magic? His hold over the sprite was the greater mystery—*that* was the answer she needed to keep them safe from the prince's shenanigans.

"Why did you do Crispin's bidding, even though it contradicted the bargain you made with Bram?"

The sprite whistled, long and low, the pitch drifting into notes that caused her skin to break out into goose bumps. "Fair play to you—that's a honey of a question. Crispin true-named me. That means he can force me to his bidding until someone else cracks my true name. That takes him out of the game, and once a true-namer's bumped out, he's done."

Marigold wobbled as wind gusted through the tree, then caught herself. "I don't suppose you'd be willing to tell me your name?"

The sprite fluttered closer. "Would that I could, and its pure class of you to ask instead of trying to trick it out of me. I can see why Crispin wants to steal you from Bram. He said so that night—snatched your guy's necklace and said he was making a play for you. You haven't married him, have you?"

"No." Her hair whipped around her face. "I ran away."

"Good. He's a prick. Any more of those cakes, then?"

Her basket was empty. "All gone."

"Pity." He alit on the branch above her. "It's a right nuisance to climb down in a skirt. Tell me you can do it without breaking your neck?"

"Uh . . ." She peered at the forest floor below the tree. "Maybe?"

"I gotcha." He tapped her on the forehead, and in a blink, she was standing on the forest floor, staring up at the sprite.

She cupped her hands around her mouth and shouted, "Thank you!"

"Welcome, Red. And I hope I never lay eyes on you again."

Chapter 31

Bram rocked on the front porch, whittling the block of wood into a ring. As he waited for Marigold, he needed to keep his hands busy to stop himself from punching walls in frustration. Had he been kinder, more understanding, she wouldn't have left the cottage and put herself in danger. The frisson he felt when strangers crossed the border of Grimroot Farm had been quiet today, which held his panic at bay.

There was a chance she was simply foraging.

But there was a better chance she went to talk to the damn sprite. He looked up from the ring emerging from the block to scan the horizon. Empty. Back to the whittling; curls of wood rained on the porch.

Back up again, and—

He froze.

Marigold, looking much worse for wear, approached. His knife and the wood clattered to the porch, and the porch steps shook as he bounded down them to meet her. Twigs and leaves clung to her hair, and mud spattered every inch of her. Beneath her cloak, she was missing a shoe.

"What happened to you?"

She sighed. "I think we both know I went to see the sprite."

"Dammit, Marigold. I *told* you—"

She held up her hand. "Please, Bram. All's well. We made no bargain. We merely chatted civilly."

"How did you manage that?"

"Help me set up a bath, and I'll tell you."

Within twenty minutes, Marigold, skin pinked and steaming, relaxed in the tub in front of the fire. As her scrapes met the water, she'd hissed, but claimed she was now in a perfect state of bliss. The cloves and pine released a soothing scent, and she leaned her head against the pillow he'd made from a linen roll.

"Now will you tell me?" he asked.

She sighed and leaned forward. "Scrub my back for me?"

"Delaying is very dramatic."

"I'm processing." She moaned as he sluiced water over her shoulders. "That feels wonderful."

The soap lather hid the border between her suntanned and ivory skin. "Marigold, you're driving me insane."

"My technique is simple. I took him birthday cake."

He dipped the linen back in the water. "That's it? Cake?"

"Yes. Did you not take him cake?"

"Well, no. I climbed the tree under cover of night hoping he wouldn't wake."

She tsked. *Men.*

"You . . . filled him with sugar, and he talked to you without trying to bargain for your first-born child?"

"That's it." She rested her forehead on her tented knees. "He was quite friendly. Seemed a bit lonely, if you ask me."

"What did you talk about?"

"Mostly why he does Crispin's bidding."

He scrubbed her shoulders. "And?"

"Could you massage my neck? I got a kink when I climbed the tree."

Bram exhaled. Compliance would get the information faster. Once again, she erupted into soft, breathy moans as he worked the knot below her neck and to the left of her spine.

"That's the spot." She lifted her head back up. "The sprite said he does Crispin's bidding because he true-named him. If we can figure out the sprite's true name, then he'll have to do *our* bidding. But we don't even have to do that. He said he gave you an out when he cursed you. What was it?"

Bram's hands stilled. "Did he?"

"Yes." She twisted in the tub. "He was adamant. Do you not know the loophole?"

Bram's stomach hardened. "So, hm. I . . . whew."

"Oh, Bram. Did you do that thing?" She scrunched her nose. "Where you don't pay attention to the middle part?"

Bram's cheeks heated. "I was full of adrenaline."

"Well, is there anyone we could ask?"

"Like, who, Marigold? The prince who ordered the sprite to curse me? Or the knights who witnessed it and ran away with the golden acorns, leaving me in a quivering, retching heap under the Lantern Oak? Or . . ."

Oh, shite. There *was* someone who might remember the loophole.

"What is it?"

"There was a squire—he's now a knight. He has no love for Crispin, but he's beholden to the prince for his job."

She curled her fingers over the edge of the tub. "Can we trust him?"

"We?"

"You and me. We're in this together." She twisted toward him. "You get that, right?"

A breath shuddered out of him. He truly wanted to believe her. But he couldn't shake the feeling that she stood firm on this because she wanted her blond knight in shining armor back. After three years in this skin, he didn't feel like that man anymore.

But he didn't feel like an orc, either.

No, he existed somewhere between the wide-eyed young

man who aimed to conquer the world and the grumpy orc who'd been beaten by it.

Marigold loved him—that, he could believe.

But there was no way she would stay here with him. Nor should she. Grimroot Farm would cage this princess destined for a bigger life, just as it had caged him. He'd coped within the borders because the circumstances of his birth were humble. He'd love to have the freedom to step past the farm's borders, feel the snow-capped chill of the Gildfall Mountains or the ocean spray of the Sea of Red Tides. But not if it meant putting Marigold at risk. No, he'd sacrifice himself ten times over if it kept her safe.

"Bram?" She nudged his shoulder. "Where'd you go?"

"Lost in thought." He dried his hands.

"I see." Like Venus, she rose from the bath, water cascading over her curves and hollows. His body gravitated toward her, like sunflower to sun. "You could use a bath as well," she said. "Join me?"

"There's not enough room."

"This basin is as big as the public bath pool in Thornwick." She tugged him to her by the belt. "There's room."

Once again, his body won over his brain.

He shucked his shirt, then slipped into the hot bath. "Saints, how do you stand this heat?"

She knelt between his bowed legs. "I thought orcs ran hot."

"We do. This is steaming for me, so it must scald you."

"I like hot things." She lifted the linen rag, lathered it with his soap, then roughly scrubbed his chest.

"Ow," he said.

"Sorry." She eased the pressure. "Are you anxious about breaking the curse?"

"Did you invite me in here to ask uncomfortable questions while I'm captive and vulnerable?"

"Yes, obviously." She dragged the linen across his shoulders, then down his arms. "I'm incapable of deception, Bram. You know that. Emotions show up on my face as brightly as gold leaf on an illuminated page."

He caught her hand to the center of his chest. "It's one of the things I love best about you."

A shy grin played on her lips. "You love me? Still?"

His insides melted faster than the pine soap. As transparent as Marigold was with her feelings, he was opaque. Feelings were a luxury in his childhood and in the guard, which was why his friendship with Marigold was such a bright treasure. She was all feeling, and her free expression in turn unchained him in their private moments.

Since his hermitage, he'd regressed.

"Always, Marigold. Always and forever." His heart was a thick thump under their joined hands. "Have I not told you?"

"Not recently," she said. "I love you, too. Always."

For the first time since she'd arrived, the bricks he'd stacked around these last three years heart shook, and a few tumbled free.

Before daybreak, after writing a note for Coby, Bram wrote another for Marigold. *Contacting my friend. Back by dinner.* Upstairs, he'd left her tucked in bed, lightly snoring.

A detail she'd deny.

Too bad, because it was one of the intimacies he cherished. In Thornwick, he thought he knew her through and through because she'd shared her sarcasm and her sadness, traits the royal family would never allow her to exhibit publicly.

Because princesses must be kind, beautiful, and generous.

They didn't curse when they stumbled over a rock. They didn't disguise themselves to barter in the marketplace and argue with a baker that they'd been shortchanged. And they certainly didn't sneak into the hayloft with a young knight of the realm.

All those moments were evidence that she'd let him in. But this Marigold? The one who shared his home and let him see her make mistakes as she learned? Allowed him to tend to her scrapes and scrub the mud from her back?

This was a woman who allowed herself to be known by him.

The frost melted as he crunched his way toward the hazy border of the hinterlands and Harvest Hollow proper. Over the last three years, he'd scoped out all the places where contact with others might be possible. During the first year, he'd taken a run at various parts of the border that seemed thin, hoping that *this* time, he'd push through.

No such luck. Each time he tried to breach the boundary, whether he wielded an axe, a sword, or his own brute strength, he collided with an invisible barrier, bruised and angry. Never the best student, it took him far too many attempts to accept the magic wouldn't let him through.

There was learning, however.

For example—he could throw things across the boundary. His voice carried as well. Understandably, the average man was terrified of an orc randomly roaring at them and tossing boulders in their direction. Several times people fainted at his mere appearance.

Most sprinted away from him.

Today he was hoping to entice someone to fetch Coby. He didn't have time to wait for their weekly covert meeting. Marigold's encounter with the autumn sprite had inspired him. If Coby remembered the loophole, he might yet be able to break the curse without endangering Marigold.

Beneath his boots, the fallen golds and reds softened his footsteps. As he approached the crossing where Marigold reported meeting the new neighbor boy, the hair on his arms raised as it always did near the boundaries. Sweet luck—the shape of a child moved through the trees beyond the boulder that marked the border of his land.

Deliberately, he made noise to catch the attention of the boy.

The young one sliced a stick through the air as though it was a broadsword. Bram had been a boy like that once—playing at knighthood and glory. He relaxed his shoulders and slouched, doing his best not to appear intimidating. A lost cause, he was sure.

Because green, muscled, and tusks.

But worth trying. He rearranged his features into what he hoped was a gentle smile.

"Ho there, young man." To his own pointy ears, his voice was gruff. "My name's Jask."

The boy snapped to attention. His eyes widened, but he didn't run. Stunned, perhaps?

"I know," the boy said. "The lady I met said she lived with her orc friend. My ma warned me to stay away from you."

Wise mother.

The boy remained rooted to his spot. "We live here for free because no one else wants to live in a graveyard next to an orc's farm. Do you eat children?"

"Not on Tuesdays," Jask said.

The boy giggled. "Then I'm glad it's Tuesday."

The sun shone bright as Bram's heart shifted in his chest. Saints, the frothy sound of a child's laughter was a magic unto itself.

"Can I ask you a favor?" he asked.

The boy pointed his stick-sword. "Ma says no adult should ever need a child's help."

Bram's respect for the boy's mother grew by leaps. "That's true, but—"

"I'll get her." The boy scrambled from the boulder. "Ma! Mama! Ma!"

Blood and bones! All he wanted was to send word to Coby that he needed to meet. *Deep breaths, relaxed stance.* If the boy returned with his mother in tow, he couldn't scare them with a prickly attitude. They might be his only chance to deliver a note quickly since Alfred didn't have a set schedule.

The swishing sound of leaves on the other side of the boundary caught his attention, as did the soft voice of a woman.

"Bastien, honestly, I'm up to my ears in—" The woman came around the path, then stopped short. She pushed her son behind her, then whispered loudly, "You didn't tell me it was *him* who needed help."

Bram held up his hands in peace. "I mean no harm. I need to convey an urgent message to a knight. Discreetly."

She quirked an eyebrow. "Why can't you convey it yourself?"

A wick in his mind caught flame—the sprite had said he couldn't reveal his true self to anyone, but the particulars of his entrapment were fair game.

"Magic binds me within the borders of Grimroot Farm. I cannot leave."

She eyed him. After a beat, she asked, "What do you offer in return? This boy eats as though he's a man, and I cannot pay for food with gratitude."

"I have some coin." He flipped a sou to the woman, who caught it easily. "And my orchard is full of apples, more than I can use. Pick your fill."

The woman bit the sou, then slipped it into her apron pocket. "How do I know you won't eat *us*?"

"You have my word as a knight," he said.

She cocked her head. "Since when do they let orcs into the knighthood?"

"I was knighted in Thornwick."

"*Thornwick*? That's the other side of the five kingdoms. What brings you so far from home?" she asked.

"Originally, ambition and fortune." Bram lifted a shoulder. "Now all I seek is a simple life."

"Life's simple out here, all right," the woman said. "Far cry from my customary homestead. What's your name, neighbor? I'm Matilda."

The curse was still in effect, so he introduced himself in the least lethal way possible. "I'm Jask Bone-Cracker."

"Pleased to meet you." Matilda nodded. "Now, what's this message you need me to pass along?"

"Here." He approached the barrier and held up the folded and sealed parchment. "Leave this with Elenor at the Laughing Gourd. It's a message for Sir Coby."

The note within was innocuous.

Sir Coby—

If you remember, tell me what the loophole was?

I'll wait by the lake.

—Your Favorite Knight

Plain, but vague. Anyone breaking the seal wouldn't guess its meaning. He hoped.

Matilda plucked it from his grasp. "That's it, then? Deliver this, and I can pick apples?"

Bram nodded.

She spun the note between her index fingers. "Done. But please don't cross me, Mr. Bone-Cracker. You won't like what happens."

"Jask," he said and bowed. "And I would never, Matilda."

Chapter 32

By the time the sun hung high overhead, Marigold had planned the whole of the Goldenmoon Festival. The activities, space for vendors, beer and cider garden, location for the minstrels, and the dancing—it was all organized. She stepped back to admire her handiwork.

Not only had she mapped out the logistics, but she also drew broadsides.

She had no talent for drawing, it was true. But her penmanship was *excellent*, and these broadsides clearly listed the date, time, location and entertainments on offer. Some might wonder why a few sported inky paw prints, but there was little time to redo them.

The cottage door swung open, and Bram entered. "You left again without waking me," she greeted him.

"You seemed peaceful." He hung his cloak on the peg.

"You know I prefer you wake me before you go. I had something I wanted to talk to you about."

At least he had the decency to look apologetic. "I'm sorry. I'll reform." He kissed the back of her neck, causing her to shiver. "What's all this, then?" He leaned over her shoulder to peer at her work.

"Broadsides for the festival." She patted his cheek, then stepped away from his embrace to dish out their midday meal. "Wash up, and I'll get you something to eat."

She withdrew a flatbread topped with melted cheese and finely diced vegetables from the oven, then plated their portions. He sat farther down the table from his usual place, which was currently occupied by two dozen broadsides.

"Thank you," he said. "What was it you wanted to discuss over the breakfast I so rudely skipped out on?"

She tangled her fingers together. "One itty-bitty thing I keep forgetting to tell you about. I, uh . . . It seems I have a new magic."

Bram set down his fork. "What is it?"

She understood his hesitancy. Magic had caused more harm in his life than good. Bram had only warmed to minimancy because she used it to help with chores around Grimroot Farm. For a moment, she'd been tempted to keep this new magic a secret.

But hadn't she been grumpy with him for keeping secrets?

Best to show the way by example.

"I'm not certain what it does. At first, I thought they were just benign lights." She showed him her empty palms. "When the Leshy attacked me, in my fright these orange orbs popped off my hands. The same thing when Bastien surprised me while I was foraging, but unlike the Leshy, the boy appeared different—there was a ghost of a crown on his head. So then I thought it was a future-telling magic and tried it on myself, but I appeared the same."

Bram caught her palm and kissed it. "I doubt it's nothing. Want to try it on me?"

Not the reaction she expected. "You'd be willing to serve as an experiment?"

"I trust you," he said. "You tried it on yourself, you said, and again with the Leshy and the boy with no ill effect."

"If you're sure." She flipped her palms toward him, flicking her fingers like she'd flung soap suds at him when they'd done their first batch of laundry together. The orbs flattened and popped against him.

As with Bastien, Bram shimmered.

And underneath the shimmer, retook his human form.

Mostly.

Marigold rucked up her eyebrows.

"What?" Bram asked.

"You're . . ."

Bram once again possessed his enviable blond curls, blue eyes, strong jaw, and skin the color of a newborn fawn. The vertical dent between his confused eyebrows was new, though. Then the orc face shimmered on top of the human. The same confused wrinkle slashed from his forehead to the bridge of his nose, but this was the emerald face she'd come to love.

She stepped closer and laid her palms on his face, turning him slightly to inspect him. "You're both Jask and Bram. How . . . What is this magic?"

He stared at his hands, turning them this way and that. Under the shimmer, they were both Bram's and Jask's, peach and green, large and huge. He scrambled up the stairs to the loft to find her looking glass. By the time he located it, only the orc looked back.

He whirled, desperation naked on his face. "Do it again."

"Bram—"

"Please," he begged.

Like Narcissus, this couldn't be good for his heart or mind, but she was powerless to deny his request. With a deep breath, she held her hands aloft. The orange fizzed and sparked in her palms, then bloomed into orbs. With a gentle motion, she flicked it toward him.

As before, they popped on his skin, then shimmered as the

magic spread over him. Once again, his form danced between human and orc, sliding back and forth. He lifted the looking glass and the tendons stood out on his neck.

He dropped the glass. "What is this?"

"I don't know its name." Marigold took his hands. "But it may reveal a person's truest self? And raises questions about Bastien."

The color left his face, like a candle being snuffed.

"So I'm both a knight of the realm and a farmer orc? How can a person have two true identities?" He set the mirror on the mantel, directly under his sword. "Saints, I don't know who or what I am anymore."

"You are Bram." She caught his hand and kissed his knuckles. "And I love him."

He tugged her close. After his chest expanded in a sigh, it rumbled with his words. "Brief as it lasts, there's a gift in this magic. We don't need to bother with the sprite or the curse. If you want to see the real me instead of the monster, you can hit me with the orbs."

The real him? She stepped back. "Bram, look at me."

His eyes were feverish in the firelight.

Her insides hollowed. "I'll tell you this a thousand times until you believe it. I love *you*. What you look like has no bearing on my affections."

A sad smile twisted his lips. "I don't believe that, Marigold."

Another step back, as though a wall were pushing up between them.

"I'm not lying to you," she said.

He palmed his neck. "But you're lying to yourself."

"That's . . . I can't . . ." She spluttered. "Bram Duncan, that's the meanest thing you've ever said to me. Do you think me shallow?"

"Mercy, Marigold. No. I think me monstrous."

"You are *not* a monster." She tunneled her hand into the hair at her temples and tugged in frustration. "Is it so wild to imagine that your heart, mind, and soul is who you are, and the rest is decoration? My body will change, too, you know. It already has. The person you knew five years ago is not the person I am today. *Life* changed me. Do you love me less for those changes?"

"Mare," he said. "Let's not deceive ourselves. This is different."

He gestured to his body. His delightful mountain of a body.

She crossed her arms. "I don't see it that way."

"You're being naive."

Heat rushed from her belly to her cheeks. The *nerve*.

"That's the second time in five minutes you've claimed to know my mind better than I, you clay-brained ninny. Do it again at your own peril."

He held up his hands. "I'm sorry. I overstepped. But the offer stands. Whenever you get are weary of this form, you're welcome to change it."

In that moment she resolved never to use this ability, whatever it was, on Bram again. She would, however, do everything in her power to give him the opportunity to be restored to his original form, if that was indeed what he wanted.

Which meant she'd pay the autumn sprite another visit.

Chapter 33

No sooner had Marigold scattered sand on the last of the broadsides than Alfred's bell jingled along the path to the cottage. With less than a week before the festival, they needed to get the word out to as many people as possible. Alfred said the markets were already buzzing with anticipation.

This would be *so* good for Bram.

Harvest Hollow would accept him—of that, she had no doubt. They'd be curious about the hermit orc, too, and many would attend the Goldenmoon Festival to see him with their own eyes. That played into her plans.

With as big a crowd as possible, she could reveal to all that he was Sir Bram Duncan of Thornwick, her true love, and Prince Crispin had forced the autumn sprite to transform him. She wanted *everyone* in the five kingdoms to know of the prince's thin-skinned treachery.

She shimmied with delicious anticipation.

That smug royal blowhard had banished and tethered Bram to this remote farm to clear the path toward making his own play for her. Crispin had probably enjoyed it since his people adored her true love more than they did their prince. But who wouldn't adore Bram? Not because he was handsome or long of limb. No, because of how he made them feel. Ever the gentleman, he was unfailingly kind and put people at ease.

He was like that as a child, too.

Like with Rowan, her shy twin. As boys, Bram was full of good humor and possessed more confidence than he had a right to, whereas Rowan was a secret alchemist who uttered as few words as possible. Beckett, a few years younger, was also a friend, but not as close as Rowan and Bram. The two boys made each other laugh during their instruction in arms and horsemanship so much that Sir Patrick often separated them.

She knew, because she watched their lessons until Bess dragged her back to her needlework and penmanship lessons.

The knock on the front door broke her reverie.

"You in there, Miss Meg?" Alfred asked. "I'm here for the broadsides. Jask asked me to circle back twice as often as you get ready for the festival."

As she opened the door, the wind whipped it from her hand. "Goodness! Does this kind of wind visit Harvest Hollow often?"

"No, ma'am. It's blustering more than my Great-Uncle Glorian, I'll tell you that." Alfred helped her tug the door closed. "Hope it doesn't tear all the leaves from the trees. The festival'll be more picturesque with bright foliage in the background."

"My hopes are the same." Marigold peered out the window. "Did you see Jask?"

Alfred shook his head. "Nice pile of pumpkins in the field, though."

"He harvested them for the activities. There should be three different piles for the jack-o'-lantern carving, pumpkin decorating, and the pumpkin-chucking competition."

"The kids'll love it." Afred sniffed the air. "Is that one of your mint tisanes?"

"Mint and blackberry. I'll pour you a cup."

"I'll thank you for it." Alfred took up his normal seat at the table. "Miss Meg, I've been meaning to ask you something."

"Is it about the vendor stalls? Because we'll have room for a dozen vendors to set up and sell their wares."

"Ah, I'll be sure to tell the nut monger—he was wondering. But no that wasn't my question. I was wondering . . . are you the Thornwick princess?"

She spluttered her drink. "Excuse me, that was unladylike."

"Doesn't bother me." He wrapped his wrinkled hands around the steaming mug. "But are you? The princess, I mean."

Marigold met Alfred's kind eyes. From the first, Alfred wasn't intimidated by the orc who'd suddenly appeared on Grimroot Farm. The carter was a lifeline for Bram from his earliest days here. For that, Alfred would forever have a place in her heart. For now, though, for her safety and Bram's, she needed to deny her identity.

"Don't be silly, Alfred. Would a princess muck out stalls?"

"If she were a good one, yes." Alfred blew onto his mug. "Good folk do what needs getting done, no matter what their station."

"I agree. So, why are you looking for the princess?"

"I'm not. But the palace guards are. More aggressive than before, they are."

She spluttered again, dammit.

The older man lifted a cookie from the plate on the table. "Need me to thump your back?"

"No, thank you," she wheezed.

"Well, so anyway. A flank of knights were carousing in the Laughing Gourd last night. I tried to ignore their conversation. You know me, I mind my business."

Marigold laughed, and Alfred narrowed his eyes.

"I'm sorry," she said. "Go on."

Crumbs caught in his beard. "One of 'em—portly guy—noticed a broadside about the festival plastered next to the taproom. Had lots of questions for Elenor."

"The alewife?"

He nodded. "I inched closer till I could hear what they were saying."

Meg tangled her fingers together. "And he seemed interested in that?"

"Very. Seemed to think the prince would be interested in it, too. And by interested, I mean vexed. The knight seemed to think he might pay a visit to the festivities. But it's okay, right? Because you're not *that* princess."

Under the table she felt the warm glow of an orb on her palm.

"That's right—I'm not." She shook her head. Not quite a lie, because she wasn't the same princess who'd left Thornwick.

Not by a long shot.

Now she was a princess who spoiled for a chance to fight her enemies in public rather than swallow it down. If Crispin came to the Goldenmoon Festival, she and Bram would give him that fight.

And then some.

The effort of prying up the loose stones from the meadow caused Bram to break out in a sweat. Despite the whipping wind, he stripped his tunic free. Better to remove it than soil it and grow the laundry pile.

Thankless work, this. But Marigold declared there must be dancing, so clear the stones he must. He'd already built the gazebo for the minstrels, which he and Meg happily christened under a star-bright sky.

Steadily, he swung the pickaxe side of the mattock toward the earth, breaking the soil to loosen the rock. Next, he used the flat side to pry the stones free. Once the earth coughed up the lumps of basalt, he lifted and heaved the stone into a growing pile.

His aim was accurate—another knightly skill that earned admirers.

After the festival, he'd have enough fieldstone to expand the cottage. Another room to allow Marigold to read in peace, perhaps? He grinned. No—not a reading room. An enclosed space specifically for her bath. He might even be able to rig a pump into the room to siphon in the cold water and add a fireplace to heat it near a permanent tub. Not even castles could boast that kind of ingenious luxury.

He rolled his neck.

If she stayed. That was the delusion he was operating under.

She wouldn't admit it to him, but she seemed determined to coerce the sprite into lifting the curse. To what end, though? After her magic revealed he was both Bram and Jask, what would happen after the curse was broken? Would it restore him? Or create a hybrid half orc, half man, forever mingled, never apart?

Like what the mirror showed him.

That had shocked him more than the first time he'd seen his raw orc face the night he was cursed. At some point in the last three years, the orc had become an indelible part of him. Stitched into him like a squatter that refused to be evicted. The whipping wind matched his mood. His shadow reminded him, with each stroke, he was as much beast as man.

He rested the axe, then stood tall.

Perhaps he was being harsh. This form had served him in ways his human body could not. Take that mountain of stones, for example. Clearing the field would've taken a dozen strong men the same amount of time, if not longer. Orcs didn't tire as easily, nor did they need much sleep. Amazing what a person could accomplish when he only required four hours of rest each night.

If he'd been human and cursed to stay at Grimroot Farm, would he have made it? Or had the orc helped him survive?

Perhaps the sprite had done him a favor with this form.

He dragged a kerchief over his forehead, then sipped his flask of water. What a twist of the mind if *that* were the case. That the sprite had fulfilled Crispin's command to curse an innocent soul but put his own brand of *fuck you* in the magic to keep Bram alive.

The frisson rippled over him.

He swung his gaze to the north—the direction of Brambleton Castle.

No falcon. Which should mean no Kevin.

If Coby delivered the letter and Garrick agreed to the scheme. Before becoming Jask, he'd trusted his fellow guards implicitly. Time and again, the world had shown him most people were good. But the knights he'd been with that night broke that trust.

Please, let him not have granted them misguided trust.

In case he had . . . He ran toward the cottage. His orc speed was another point in this body's favor. As Bram crossed the meadow, the frisson rippled over him again.

Blood and bones, was an army invading? Still no falcon, though.

After trampling through the sunflowers that lined the meadow, Bram leaped over the larger pumpkins at the back of the field. A quick hectare later, the cottage was in view. A palfrey stood tethered to the maple in their front yard, and Marigold was speaking animatedly to a tall, trim man in black whose pauldrons reflected the bright fall sun.

Oh, sweet saints.

A knight.

Chapter 34

Joyful tears sprang to Marigold's eyes. This was no stranger who'd thundered down the path on horseback. This could not be the Leshy, for he was anchored to his patch of forest.

"Rowan!" She flew down the stairs and into her twin's embrace. He was the *best* hugger, arms fully wrapped around and squeezing tight. "Please say you believed what I wrote in my letters?"

"How could you ask me that, sister?" He released her and searched her face. "Of course I did. The devil take him and all of Harvest Hollow for his evil plans."

She tangled her fingers together. "Not the people—they're lovely. Don't blame them for the prince's villainy."

"Fallen in love, have you?" He hooked his thumbs into his belt.

Heat bloomed in her cheeks. She certainly hadn't written *that* in either of the letters to Rowan. "How . . . how do you mean?"

"With the people of Harvest Hollow, naturally."

"Ah, right. Yes, I have." She fidgeted with the tail of her braid. "Have you told our parents of Crispin's plot? With the possibility of an intelligencer lurking in the castle, I didn't feel safe sending a letter. And how go the battles with the sprites of the Gildfall Mountains?"

"No, I came here straightaway." Rowan turned his signet ring, which he'd inherited when he'd been elevated to prince of Cliffward. "Your first letter arrived during a rare calm. Beckett had already left for a respite in Thornwick, so I had none with whom I could confer. I boarded the *Orvale* to set sail and round the Horn of Rashemba, and I came north through their port and Mareval. How do you fare, though? You're well? He did not hurt you? You do not appear sickly like the kingdom's criers and broadsheets claim."

Her throat tightened. She had no armor against kindness and concern. She swallowed.

A smile bubbled her cheeks. "I'm sound. Tales of my illness have been greatly exaggerated. More of Crispin's deceit to explain the stalled wedding. I'm more than sound. Happy, content, well fed. Better than I've been since Papa's ascension. It's all due to this farm."

"Clearly it suits you. I'm glad you've had a chance to escape for a bit and clear your head. Where are your harborers? I'd like to thank them."

"In the fields. We're hosting a festival in a few days, and there's much to be done. It's just one harborer, though. Did you ask the townspeople about Grimroot Farm's proprietor?"

He shook his head. "No. As soon as we docked, I flew here like a longbow's loosed arrow. I've not spoken to anyone in Harvest Hollow."

It might've been easier if someone had spilled the beans.

She beckoned to him. "Come inside. Let's catch you up on—"

An angry, galloping Bram sprinted directly for Rowan. Too late, she yelled, "Bram, no!"

Rowan's whirled around, and his eyes widened. "Bram?"

A green blur collided with her brother, sending up clouds of dust as they tumbled through the yard. Rowan's palfrey whinnied and pranced away from the wrestling cluster of arms and legs. Barnaby crowed nearby, because that was all Barnaby knew to do.

"Stop!" She picked up her skirt and dashed toward the two before either of them could seriously injure the other. She tugged at Bram's arm before he could pummel her brother. "Bram, it's Rowan."

She tugged again. It was much like tugging on a pillar. Capable though Rowan was in battle, at his core, her older brother was a scholar, not a warrior.

"Rowan? Sorry, friend. I mistook you for one of Crispin's flunkeys." With a grunt, he raised himself from the pale Rowan, then held out his hand to help her brother rise.

Rowan brushed off the offer and pushed himself upright. With his hand on his hilt, he locked his gaze on Bram. "Twice she called you Bram."

Marigold rested her hand on Bram's shoulder. "Because that's his name."

"What are the odds . . ." Rowan shifted his gaze to her, but his grip remained on his sword. "You'd meet another by that name?"

She blew out her lips. For a scholar, Rowan lacked imagination. Which could explain his failed alchemical experiments. Delighted as she was to see her rescuer and grateful as he might be that Bram had kept her safe from Crispin, he might not be the picture of happiness that she'd taken up with a commoner . . . who was now an orc.

This required a plainspoken explanation. And *that* required privacy. While she was fairly confident there were no spies about, she'd rather not tempt fate.

"Let's discuss it inside over hot cider." She climbed the porch steps and opened the cottage's front door. "Rowan, sit on the divan. Bram, take the rocking chair."

Because people were less intimidating in a rocking chair. Even orcs. Especially when a tabby cat leapt onto their lap and made biscuits on their broad chest until the orc relented and scratched the cat's chin.

"Feel free to chatter!" she trilled.

They did not. She filled the kettle with cider and set it on the stove. The quiet was unsettling. Credit to Rowan for not staring at Bram, but his gaze flitted about the cottage. Instead of the quaint love nest she'd come to adore, she was seeing it through his luxury-tainted eyes. The frayed upholstery, the slightly uneven mantel, the homespun curtains.

No. She wouldn't allow her family's upturned nose to spoil this.

She dropped cloves and cinnamon sticks into the tankards, then added the steaming cider. The aroma soothed her rough nerves. Simple pleasures were the only pleasures she cared to have for the rest of her days. Which included, above all, Bram.

Who was indeed a pleasure but definitely *not* simple.

In her pursuit of a life with him, she could use an ally.

On a tray she carried the tankards, along with comfited pumpkin seeds and last night's dessert wafers, then set them on the crate in front of the divan. She handed Rowan the unchipped mug, Bram another, then took the third and sat on the squashy chair she preferred for reading.

"So," she said.

"So?" Rowan answered.

"Rowan, at long last, I have found Sir Bram Duncan." She gestured across the space to Bram. "He's been cursed by an autumn sprite these last three years."

Bram pinched the bridge of his nose. "Marigold, I'm not supposed to tell anyone, or the curse will kill them."

Rowan stiffened.

"Relax, Ro." She sipped her cider. "Loophole. He can't tell

anyone—" she gestured to Bram "—but if someone figures it out on their own, like me, or if *I* share the information, it's fine."

"How many experiments have you run to test this?" Rowan asked.

"Including you and me?" She made a big show of counting in her head. "Two."

Rowan blanched. "Sister, are you sure you haven't been deceived? What proof—"

"For a future king, you need more spine," Bram grumbled.

"Is that necessary?" Marigold asked.

Cider sloshed from Rowan's cup as he slammed it on the table.

"It *is* you." Rowan's bright eyes sharpened. He rose and held his arms wide. "Come here, you crafty rogue. I thought I'd never see you again in this lifetime."

Marigold's thoughts didn't line up. "Why do you believe him now?"

"Sir Patrick endlessly chastised me that way." Rowan laughed as he thumped Bram's back. "If I winced as a wooden sword thumped my leg—I needed more spine. Didn't seat my horse perfectly—more spine. Slow to strap into my armor—spine. Only Beckett, Bram, and I would know that."

She beetled her brows. "I'm offended."

"Don't be. I require evidence before believing anything." Rowan stepped back to clamp his hands on Bram's shoulders. "How did this happen? A sprite, you said?"

Bram gestured to Marigold. "You'd better tell it. To stay within the loophole."

She nodded and tucked a curl behind her ear. "When Bram came to Harvest Hollow seeking fame and fortune, he outshone Prince Crispin one too many times for the prince's comfort. Crispin also had designs on me, for all the reasons I wrote you in my letters—to marry, get me with child, murder you and

Beckett, put me away at Scarlet Spire, and, ultimately, unite and rule both thrones and despoil Thornwick. So, under the guise of harvesting the autumn sprite's gold acorns, which grow in the Lantern Oak, Crispin set a trap for Bram to engage with the sprite."

"That sounds exhausting," Rowan said. "But sprites only bargain with willing souls, don't they?"

"I was willing," Bram huffed. "Crispin promised me a title and a share of the gold I harvested if I accepted the challenge."

Rowan twisted his signet ring. "Oh, friend. That's a dangerous game."

"Trusting a sprite? Or persuading your parents of my worth?"

"Both." Rowan reclaimed his seat and his mug. "I take it you lost?"

"He won." Marigold set down her tankard, then stood next to Bram. "Crispin has control of the autumn sprite and ordered him to transform Bram and tether him to this farm. While the curse is in force, he can never leave."

Rowan shifted his gaze between them. "Do I detect an attachment between you?"

For once, her brother's observations were accurate.

"Yes." She reached for Bram's hand. "I love Bram, and he, me."

With his ankle crossed over his knee, Rowan jiggled his foot. After a few quiet seconds, he seemed to arrive at a conclusion and nodded. "When did this . . ." Rowan gestured toward them. "Kindle?"

Marigold kissed the back of Bram's hand. "In Thornwick. Before Bram left. It's *why* he left. To improve his circumstances so he could ask for my hand."

"You were discreet. I knew not of this."

Rowan wouldn't have noticed unless she and Bram had

cavorted nude in front of him. Her sweet twin noticed the tiniest of details or big walloping facts but rarely anything in between.

Fuzzle switched allegiances and leapt onto the divan next to Rowan, then sniffed at the tankard.

"So, what is it you want to do, Marigold?" Rowan slid a palm against his neck. "Shall I spirit you to Mareval, then Thornwick, so we might inform our parents in private council? It seems you're happy here on this farm—"

"Deliriously so." She wrapped her arms around Bram's waist.

"But you're still a daughter of the House of Ashford. Our parents' blessing is required if there's to be anything . . . permanent between you. Is there any chance of reinstating Bram to normal?"

Something pulled tight across her chest, like a bow about to let an arrow fly.

With calm, protective anger, she said, "He *is* normal."

"I didn't mean to be rude," Rowan said quickly. "The crown could grant him land and a title in reward for his knightly service giving safe harbor to you. Marriage to a commoner is a scandal but manageable if he's human. To an orc, though? Unthinkable. You'd need to give up your claim to the throne and remain here."

Everything he said, she already knew. He meant well, but her brother was yet another person trying to school her on the ways of the world. He could not fathom that she understood the mechanics of noble society and would simply . . . opt out.

"Well, think it, Rowan."

Bram lifted her chin, his face soft. "Marigold, love, I never intended for you to walk away from the crown itself."

"I'm walking *toward* you, Bram." She cut her gaze to Rowan. "What if I died?"

"What?" Rowan asked.

Bram lowered his brow. "Yes, what?"

"For a month now, Prince Crispin's claimed I'm too sick to marry. We obviously need to hold him to account for his dastardly murder plot, but would it be such a stretch for everyone to believe I'd died?" She bounced on her toes. "Yes. Death *may* be the solution. I could fake it like one of those poison-apple princesses. Then I'd be free to live as I choose. Mayhap we could fix the blame upon him, too, and add that to his crimes."

"No, Marigold," Bram said. "I've lived the last three years of my life as another person. Not being able to own my name has clawed at me, and I would never ask you to do the same."

"But I—"

They swiveled their heads toward a knock at the cottage door.

Chapter 35

Bram's pulse hammered in his ears. The shadow cast upon the drawn curtains at the window nearest the cottage door was unmistakably Coby. Their previous encounters allowed them to maintain plausible deniability of any kind of alliance between them. He'd simply been an orc bathing in the lake. Coby had been a knight on patrol.

Words were exchanged—that was all.

Arriving on his doorstep was a different matter. Harvest Hollow knights rarely knocked on farmers' doors for a friendly chat. Coby did not know for certain that Marigold was here, and he'd prefer to keep it that way. He doubted Coby was accompanied by other palace guards, but if by chance he was . . .

"It's one of Crispin's knights," he said to Marigold and Rowan. "Stay here, and do not follow. I'll deal with him."

He slipped out of the cottage. After closing the door behind him, he trod down the porch stairs and hooked a finger through the air. "Come with me."

"Did you get a horse?" Coby eyed Rowan's mount as he followed. "Looks a bit small to carry you."

Bram ignored the question as he led Coby to the byre. Queen mooed in greeting. At the final stall, where his tools lay, he turned to the young knight. "Why are you here? For your protection and mine, our connection should remain secret."

Coby looked confused. "But I got your note."

"And the idea was you'd write back. The guard will notice your absence, won't they? Might get curious about where you've gone."

"They think I'm sick—I pretended to vomit."

Bram flinched at the word.

"I'd planned to send word back with Alfred, as you'd asked." Coby reached into his brigandine and withdrew a folded square. "But thought I should encode it in the event someone nosed through my communication. But I couldn't encode it because the answer itself is coded. It all felt quite complicated in my mind, so I gave up and brought it to you directly. Here."

Bram plucked the proffered note from Coby's hand.

With trembling fingers, he opened the letter that contained his curse-breaking salvation. His eyes scanned Coby's neat handwriting.

Once, twice, a third time.

"This can't be correct." He glanced at Coby. "You're sure?"

Coby nodded. "That's what the sprite said. I repeated it during the long walk back from the Lantern Oak. As soon as I got back to my cot, I scribbled it down. But I can't say I understood it."

"What the hell does it mean?"

Coby shrugged. "I wish I knew, sir."

His hopes fizzled and shrank. He wished freedom from this curse was as simple as bringing sugared treats to the sprite. But if what Coby had written was accurate, Marigold must return to the Lantern Oak on his behalf. He stood by what he'd said to her earlier—engaging with the sprite was inherently dangerous and not worth the risk to her life.

No, they would not go down that path.

Bram folded the useless note and tucked it into his breeches' pocket.

Alas, he'd hoped for an easy solution. Marigold insisted

she'd be happy with a life here at Grimroot Farm, but Rowan was right—the world would not let them be happy together if he remained an orc. An impossible situation.

"Thank you, all the same." Now to gather intelligence from the young knight. "How goes the search for the princess?"

"Fruitless. They've combed Harvest Hollow from the Gildfall Mountains to the Marches and have turned up nothing. The crown continues to tell us that Princess Marigold has taken to her bed. Prayers are requested in the cathedral during every service, and the people have covered Brambleton Castle's gates with well wishes and her favorite sunflowers."

His heart ached for the good people of Harvest Hollow.

The deserved better than Prince Crispin. The popinjay was probably seething with jealousy that his people lavished the unknown princess with attention. No, the prince was not fit to lead these compassionate folk—his plots, lies, pettiness, and the coffers emptied for his personal benefit were more than enough evidence.

Bram pinched his nose, then stared at the byre's roof.

He might've been a farmer with more personal shite to contend with than was fair, and he would love not to care about communities beyond his borders, but he was also a trained knight devoted to the chivalric order, and this kingdom was in distress. Part of the plot Marigold overheard involved sending her to Scarlet Spire to gain control of Thornwick's throne.

What if Crispin had done such a thing before, to his own sister?

"Sir Coby, I've a thought. Princess Rosamund—has she ventured to home for the royal wedding? Or is she still languishing at Scarlet Spire and taking the seaside air?"

"There's no news of her traveling. I believe she's still there."

That tracked with Bram's suspicions. "Then . . . I think you must undertake a quest."

Coby raised an eyebrow. "Is it noble?"

"The most noble." Bram clapped him on the shoulder. "Travel to Scarlet Spire and inform Princess Rosamund of what's happening in Harvest Hollow. Writing it down would put you in danger, but the list is this—the king is in his dotage, and the prince spends wastefully. His taxes squeeze the people to madness. To quash dissent, he leverages the magic of a sprite. He will not listen to advisors and keeps his own counsel. The prince's betrothed has run away, and he's yet to find her. For all these reasons, it's vital Princess Rosamund return and take her rightful place as the head of House Batten-Forge. Offer to escort her back—her people need her."

He left out the Thornwick murder-and-throne plot. The rest of the list should be enough to shake any sovereign out of their convalescence.

Coby widened his eyes. "I'm to say all that? Royals don't receive truth well."

Bram snorted. "Trust, I'm aware. Can you do this?"

"Yes?" Coby's gaze softened as he ran the scenario in his head. Then, with greater certainty, he said, "Yes. The Scarlet Spire is a two-day ride. If she doesn't have me brained on the spot for my candor, we may be back by week's end."

"If she's like her brother, she'll be quick to decide." Bram folded his forearms. "But let's hope she is not, in fact, like her brother in all ways. I have faith in you, Coby."

The lad boosted his shoulders. "I'm grateful for the vote of confidence."

"If all goes well, you'll be back in time for the Goldenmoon Festival, and the day will be full of nothing but merriment."

"But what if Prince Crispin attends? He's right vexed it's happening, and—"

"Pardon the intrusion." Rowan appeared at the doorway. "I couldn't help but overhear your conversation."

Bram squeezed his fists. The House of Ashford should swap their family crest's unicorn for a mouse or a mule, because their silence and stubborn streaks ran as wide as his fields. And his sudden appearance was most inconvenient. Explaining this prince's presence at the farm would be as easy as shoving a pumpkin through a fence knothole.

"Go away," Bram said. "This does not involve you."

"I'd say it does, old friend." Rowan stepped forward, spreading his hands wide. "All I offer is help. It'll be easier for another royal to gain access to Scarlet Spire and Princess Rosamund than a knight." He nodded at Coby. "No offense."

Coby briefly bent his knee and bowed his head. "None taken. Those are facts. Prince Rowan of Thornwick, I believe?"

Annoyed as he was at Rowan's presence, Bram was pleased with the young knight's keen mind. The Thornwick royal family's likenesses had been shared in the broadsheets along with the announcement of the betrothal.

"Indeed," Rowan said and shook Coby's outstretched hand.

"So the princess is here, then?" Coby shifted his gaze between Rowan and Bram. "I'm glad of it. I'd worried that she'd got lost in the Marches or, worse, the Shivering Dales."

"She's safe," Bram said.

"Leaving me free to accompany you," Rowan said to Coby. "We must relieve Crispin of his throne, and two have a greater chance of success than one."

Bram turned the offer in his mind, looking for the catch. "Your involvement will raise tensions between the kingdoms, possibly the entire Lunara Peninsula."

"Then so be it." Rowan rested his hand on his hilt. "The threat to Thornwick, and to my family, is too great not to act."

Bram saw Rowan in a new light. He was not just a friend—he was an ally. For so long, Bram had shouldered his plight alone, braced for the impact of another blow from fate.

Since Marigold returned to him, she'd shown him that more hands make the load lighter. That he could place his trust in others.

He held Rowan's shoulder. "For a future king, you have the spine."

Rowan grinned. "I'm aware."

After thumbing a tear from his eye, Bram clapped a hand on Coby's shoulder as well. "Rowan, my oldest and dearest friend, allow me to introduce you to Sir Coby Goodwin, who may be the truest knight of the realm. Together, we may yet save my future and, as a side quest, save Harvest Hollow."

Chapter 36

Marigold's stomach fizzed. Today was the day of the Goldenmoon Festival. The importance of the day hummed in her bones. Many of the people who made Harvest Hollow a charming, warm kingdom would meet Bram today. His tenderness and humor would shine through, dissipating their misperceptions of the orc's surliness. Even if he never again stepped foot from Grimroot Farm again, he would not want for company.

She cared not a whit for the plan Bram, Rowan, and Coby, the adorable golden retriever of a knight, had hashed out at the kitchen table yesterday while she fed them pumpkin crumble and hot cider. No, all she cared about at the moment was the festival. The day would be full of merriment, drink, and food.

She opened the door to the porch and frowned.

Hmph. The day, in fact, was full of clouds.

The swirling gray taunted her from above. "This is a disaster."

Bram's arm curled around her back. "It's not a disaster, my love."

"It *is*." She thrust her hands toward the field. "This is an outdoor event. Meant to celebrate the resplendence of the season. Mud is not resplendent."

His hand played at her hip. "Paloma would argue with you."

"Paloma is a pig."

"An *intelligent* pig."

Marigold elbowed him. "Stop trying to make me feel better."

"It'll be fine. Common folk are hearty folk. Nothing holds us back from a celebration, even if it means dancing in the rain and mud. Better yet, the possibility of muck will keep Crispin in his castle and we needn't worried about him gracing us with his presence. Now, will you please minimize the tables so I can distribute them to their various stations?"

He gestured to the dozen tables he'd built in the last weeks. They were his own ingenious design, with legs on hinges so they could be folded and easily stored in the byre's empty stalls when they weren't in use.

"Yes." She snapped, and blue sparkles rained until the tables reduced to the size of a deck of playing cards.

Bram gathered them into a haversack. "Thank you. I'll let you know when they're arranged so you can enlarge them. Elenor's note said she'd arrive in an hour to set up the beer garden, and the other vendors will soon follow. We'll be set for the noon start."

She eyed the clouds and muttered, "Hope those burn off by then."

As Bram headed toward the pumpkin fields, Marigold disappeared inside to check her preparation list. Ah, yes—next was to wrap her identifiable hair in a scarf on the chance any of the palace guard might attend the festival. A wimple was more fashionable these days, but she couldn't fathom swaddling her chin and neck in volumes of fabric.

Fuzzle leapt onto the counter and butted her hand, greedy for pets.

"Feeling lonely?" She scratched behind the cat's ears. "Sorry. We've been so busy these last few days."

Fuzzle leaned low and tapped the pull for the catchall drawer. He went after it like it was catnip. Which, *ew*, might mean there's a mouse in there? Or a large spider? Between the two, she'd prefer the mouse.

"Don't bring me anything dead as a prize, please?"

Marigold tugged open the drawer. Fuzzle batted something around in it until a folded piece of parchment flew free. As he sat to lick his paws, she picked it up to put it back.

"Is this what you wanted?" she asked.

The parchment was fine stuff, very much like the parchment she'd been provided at Brambleton to write to her family back in Thornwick. She rubbed her thumbs over its surface. She shouldn't open it. This was not addressed to her—was not addressed to anyone, in fact. But no good ever came from reading someone else's correspondence.

Then again . . .

"If Bram *really* hadn't wanted me to find this, he would've hidden it better. Right, Fuzz?"

The cat meowed in agreement and continued cleaning its paws. Satisfied she had one ally to her snooping, Marigold unfolded the parchment and laid it flat. The spiky hand was not sophisticated, and words were oft misspelled. But as she read, she widened her eyes. *List all that true love does, not swears; the quiet works, the patient cares . . .*

Saints, this was the loophole.

The instructions were simple enough. Where had this come from? Why hadn't Bram told her about it? She bit her lower lip, then glanced out the window as he happily worked in the pumpkin fields. The Hunter's Moon was tonight, and come sunrise, the sprite would slumber until next year's equinox.

Outside, she spied him crouching to place tables in the cleared part of the pumpkin patch.

Did Bram not want to break the curse?

As the late-afternoon sun hung low in the sky, Marigold admitted to herself that Bram was right. She needn't have worried. The clouds had burned off by midmorning. Vendors and guests started arriving not long after. Now, as the day shifted to evening, people outnumbered the pumpkins at Grimroot Farms. Marigold wove around the pumpkin-decorating tables, admiring the children's clever handiwork. At the end of one table, Bastien sat with a woman her age—his mother, most likely. Singing an off-key tune, the boy put finishing touches on his pumpkin.

"Enjoying yourselves?" Marigold asked.

"We are." She raised her tankard of cider in greeting. "It's nice to celebrate the changing seasons with a festival. I'm Matilda, the new caretaker at Kindlewood Garden of Rest next door. This here's my son, Bastien."

Marigold shook Matilda's rough hand. "I'm Meg. Welcome. Your boy and I met last week in the woods."

"So *you're* the lady with the cat who lives with Jask? Until I met your farmer, I thought Bastien pulled all that from his imagination."

"I am indeed the lady with the cat." She skipped her gaze over the crowd. "He's around here somewhere. An orange tabby. If Fuzzle crosses your path, he's a glutton for scratches behind the ears and on the belly."

"Do you do this every year? Seems popular." Matilda gestured to the crowds circulating from the pumpkin activities to the vendor stalls and beyond to the meadow and the orchard.

"To be honest, I'm new around here, too. This is the first time the festival's been held at Grimroot Farm—it's usually in Harvest Hollow proper. But I'm told it's a favorite tradition."

"I can see why. Bastien's had a great time." Matilda tousled the boy's hair.

"I'm glad to hear it. May I take a closer look at your pumpkin design?" As she crouched, she felt like she'd gulped an apple whole. The pumpkin's painted face bore a strong resemblance to the autumn sprite, wispy hair and all. "Is that someone you know?"

The boy nodded. "I saw him last night. He was singing and dancing around a fairy ring in the wood, near the Lantern Oak."

A fairy tale flashed in Marigold's memory. Something about a girl who spun straw into gold and was able to dissolve her bargain with an imp.

"Bastien!" Matilda clasped his shoulder. "You're never to go there. You know that."

"I was chasing my hoop." The boy scratched his knees and looked down, scolded.

Marigold couldn't let the boy shut down. Not when she needed information from him.

Marigold tapped Bastien's pumpkin. "Do you remember his song?"

Bastien nodded eagerly. "It was silly."

"Can you sing it for me? Please?"

Bastien looked to his mother.

"What's this about?" Matilda asked.

"This creature—" she tapped the pumpkin again "—is a sprite who cursed someone dear to me. If we don't break the curse tonight, we'll be forced to wait until next year. Fairy tales lead me to believe the sprite's song could be a clue."

Matilda whispered to her boy. He nodded, nodded again, then smiled.

"Mama said you'd give me a sweetie if I sing for you."

"I will give you ten sweeties."

"Three," Matilda countered.

"Three." Marigold wouldn't dare push a mother's sweets limit.

Bastien cleared his throat. In a quiet, wavering voice, he sang,

"Cleverer far than king or jack,
Guess and gamble, lose your stack,
None outwits old Grindlethwack."

Marigold's insides vibrated like a struck blade. It was a perfect name for the rotund little creature. Her limbs felt light enough she could take flight. Handy, that, since she'd need to scale an enormous tree.

"Grindlethwack," Marigold asked. "Are you sure?"

Bastien nodded. "He sang it twenty times."

"Clever boy! Thank you." She gave him a small bag of comfited pumpkin seeds that she carried in her apron. To Matilda, she said, "You're welcome to visit any time. I make lovely tisanes and enjoy conversation."

Matilda laughed. "I'll take you up on that. So far I get most of my gossip from the carter."

"Alfred has the juiciest reports." Marigold rose to relieve her protesting knees. "He mentioned you recently arrived. How did you come to Harvest Hollow?"

"Ah, that's too long a tale," Matilda said. "But the short of it is I was to work in a noble house—a favor from a friend of Bastien's father. His missus didn't like the look of me, though, and that was that."

This poor woman. When Marigold thought she'd lost Bram, she was as hollow as the jack-o'-lanterns decorating the cottage and tables in the field. To mourn, solely parent a child, move house, and earn a living as well—Matilda might as well carry the world on her slim shoulders.

"I'm sorry to hear that. But their loss is my gain in a good neighbor. Should you need anything at all, please don't hesitate to ask."

The thick beat of a hand drum from the brigade of recently arrived minstrels pulsed through the crowd. Beyond the blaze of sunflowers lay the meadow that Bram had cleared of large stones and, within it, the new gazebo. The fiddle's bright, resonant tone was like ribbon wrapping around her and pulling her toward the field.

Bram knew her so well. As he'd predicted, the first fiddle, and she was off to dance.

"Care to join us for dancing in the meadow?"

"Soon as I've finished my cider," Matilda said.

Marigold squeezed her new friend's shoulder. "I'll see you out there."

As she scampered toward the music, she passed by clusters of people enjoying themselves. Children squealed from within the haystack maze, and young men congratulated the stout lad who'd won the pumpkin-chucking competition.

A delicious swirl of aromas from the warren of food stalls made her stomach rumble. Strongest was the roasted chestnuts dusted with sugar. From a small fire, the seller fished out the nuts with tongs as they popped and cracked. Marigold had already indulged in a candied apple from the next stall, which she'd been granted in exchange for a dozen Hollowsnaps they'd traded the confectioner. The cheesemonger's business was also brisk, as was the spit roaster's.

Coins tinkled into the tills as she passed by.

Excellent—she wanted their trouble to be worth it in earnings. A few vendors said the royal guard offered them a bribe not to put up a stall here today. But they took their chances that today's event would bless their pockets. The more money they made, the more likely they'd return next year. Because she'd already decided they were hosting again next year.

Hmph, she should probably inform Bram of that, too.

Speaking of, where was he?

She shaded her eyes from the powerful streaks of setting sun—ah, there he was. Standing by the sunflowers and watching the minstrels in the gazebo. On her way to him, she passed Elenor's beer garden.

Seated under the pergola, Brother Oswald called, "Hello again, Miss Meg! This is a fine celebration of the harvest!"

She tipped her head and couldn't hold back a smile.

Brother Oswald had been one of the first to arrive and hadn't been without snack or drink since. With his frequent booming laughter and bawdy jokes, he was a welcome change from the prim Archbishop of Briarveil.

Across the meadow, Bram caught her gaze, then waved. The day had been a success. The night would follow suit—especially when she slipped away to pay a follow-up visit to the autumn sprite. A diversion would be required, however, or Bram might give chase.

She was sure she'd think of something.

For now, though—dancing.

Chapter 37

For once in his life as an orc, Bram was not running hot.

Hundreds had crossed Grimroot Farm's threshold, sending constant shivers along his spine. The pace had slowed in the last hour, thank the saints. Otherwise he might've needed a second cloak.

The minstrels played a lively song, the lyrics just skirting the edge of bawdy. Many a Hollower kicked up their feet and danced in the meadow. As Marigold threaded through the crowd toward him, the music shifted to a different beat. Instinctively, the crowd split into lines to begin the Sway.

She grabbed his hand. "Shall we show them how it's done?"

His grip tightened around hers. "We shall, so long as you remember your left from right."

She bumped her shoulder to his biceps. "Ha ha. Keep a tight grip on me? With this headwrap, an ox could be charging at me and I wouldn't know. But at least I'm demure."

The music began in earnest, and Bram led her through the steps. Saints, he'd forgotten how much fun dancing within a crowd could be, the infectious nature of joy. The dance lines shifted and curved, and now they were dancing in circles wrapped round each other. He held hands with Marigold on one side and Beatrix Brumet, the bookseller's daughter, on the other. As Bram, he'd purchased many a book from her father to keep his mind occupied while away from Marigold, but tonight was the first time she'd met Jask.

As the minstrels sped up the tune, the circle gallivanted faster, until it was time for the final turn, kick, and lift. In the center of the field, Bram lifted Marigold into the air. The setting sun lit her with its bold streaks of crimson and orange.

Her smile, which was all for him, outshone twilight's pageantry.

The seconds stretched like a century. He wanted to hold on to this bright feeling forever. And, depending on what she said about the ring in his pocket, he might just be able to. As the crowd's applause exploded, Bram lowered Marigold, savoring the slide of her body against his. Yes, after the crowds dispersed tonight, he would ask his princess to be his bride.

Above him, a falcon screamed.

The scarlet jesses streaming behind signaled the raptor was one of Garrick's. The brief joy he'd felt in the dance curled inward like the petals of a fading chrysanthemum.

Grim determination took its place.

"We must go." If Sir Kevin or any other knight wanted to whisk Marigold away, they'd have to go through him first. "You need to hide. Sir Kevin approaches."

"When?"

He pointed at the circling falcon. "Soon."

She followed his gaze. "How does a falcon herald Kevin's arrival?"

"I struck a bargain with the royal falconer."

"I have many questions." She raised herself onto her toes and kissed him. "But I won't scurry into the dark, Bram. I prefer to walk in the sun."

"It's twilight."

"I didn't mean literally." She clasped his biceps. "I am a

princess, which comes with privileges and authority. Kevin is not, in fact, the boss of us. And I have magical gifts, which grants me power beyond laws and protocols. Before my time here, I didn't have the confidence to carve my own path. Now I do."

This stubborn, beautiful woman.

"Was it the baking or the laundry that boosted your confidence?"

"'Twas the butter. If I can churn cream into golden deliciousness, I can do anything, including facing down the prince's thug." Marigold's eyes searched the crowd. "Where is he?"

"He's not here yet—the falcon was a warning."

The lute player cupped his hands around his mouth. "We're taking a brief break. After we enjoy a pint of Elenor's finest, we'll return with plenty of vigor!"

With a smattering of applause, half the crowd drifted toward Elenor's beer garden with the minstrels. A flourish of trumpets split the air, startling him. Whispers rose among those who remained in the meadow. Courtesy of his height, Bram had a clear view of the heralded arrival.

Their newest guests turned his stomach to stone.

Prince Crispin and his personal guard had arrived. Accompanying him were King Matthias and Queen Elowen of Thornwick—Marigold's parents. Trailing just behind them was Bess, Marigold's lady's companion.

"Marigold, they're here." His breath came fast as he tugged her toward the cottage. Beside the pile of quarried fieldstones, he paused. Here, they were alone. "Crispin, his privy circle of knights, your parents, and Bess. Run. Shrink. I'll keep them busy."

"But in order for us to remain together—"

He held her face. "I adore your optimism that they'll support our love match. They may, but this is not the time nor the place. Rowan's right. Marrying a commoner orc is unthinkable. Crispin will make a meal of this, delight in making a big show of how much they approve of him before we can tell them the truth of his plot. They cannot discover you with him orchestrating the conversation. 'Tis simply your word against his, and so I say again: Run, Princess."

Marigold furrowed her brow. "But—"

"It's not your parents you should worry about," a low, thick voice said.

Bram shielded Marigold's body from Kevin's brutish gaze. Blood and bones, no evidence of a soul danced in the eyes of Crispin's man-at-arms.

"You'll come with me, Princess." Kevin drummed his sausage-like fingers against his sword's hilt. "I've a gentle way or an ugly way—choose."

From behind Bram, she said, "I choose neither."

Marigold squeezed his hand twice, then let go. Behind his back, Marigold's body heat fizzed, then disappeared as she shrank herself.

Bram clutched a pumpkin-sized stone. "Looks like it's the ugly way."

"A poor choice." Kevin slipped his sword from its scabbard. "I told Crispin we should've killed you that night years ago. After I dissect you, I'll inform the crowd you kidnapped the princess and enslaved her on this farm since the first banns were read in the cathedral."

"I've done no such thing," Bram growled.

Cold mirth lit the knight's eyes. "And who will they believe, orc? Me or a monster?"

"Monster or not, they're my friends, so I'd bet on me."

Bram gestured to the happy lantern-lit faces. Matilda walked by with her exhausted boy wrapped in her arms. Elenor clinked tankards with Brother Oswald. Beyond the beer garden, Alfred gave children hayrides toward the orchard. And there, by the pumpkin carving tables, Beatrix chatted with Coby.

Coby! Bram searched the crowd for Rowan and Princess Rosamund. If the young knight was here, did that mean they'd succeeded in their mission? With Marigold safely on the run, they could strike the flint on the plan to unseat Crispin with the rightful heir, his sister.

Kevin bellowed with laughter. "You're a fool. The day men believe orcs before knights is the day pigs wear crowns."

"That can be arranged, oaf." Bram hurled the stone at Kevin. It exploded against the maple tree behind the knight. "Leave. I won't miss a second time."

"Enough." Kevin charged him.

Bram easily dodged the man-at-arms. Points to the orc's body for its speed as well as its strength. Behind him, Kevin met nothing but air.

"Where did she—"

Barnaby, ever the broken clock, drowned out the knight with a heart-stopping shout.

"Tell me where she is," Kevin snarled.

A familiar *huff-huff-huff* came around the corner. Clever woman. Marigold must've opened Paloma's gate. The pig locked onto Kevin, then scraped a hoof against the flagstones and lowered her head. A challenge.

"Call off your pig," Kevin said. "Fight honorably."

"A lost cause with you as an opponent." Bram hefted another rock. "Paloma, fetch him."

In a clattering flurry of hooves, Paloma rushed Kevin. She collided with his legs as Bram's rock thumped against his chest. The simultaneous blows knocked Kevin from his feet. With his blood pumping, Bram scrambled toward the downed knight.

One kick sent his sword spinning across the courtyard.

Bram lifted Kevin by his pauldrons, then lifted him into the air. Oh, the sprite had indeed done him a service in granting him this form. For all the times the orc's body had felt like he was wearing ill-fitting garb, today he delighted in the fear its speed and strength struck in this small-spirited man's eyes.

"What's the matter, Kevin? Afraid I'll treat you the way you've treated me?"

Kevin's nostrils flared. "What do you want? Set me down and name your price."

Bram gritted his teeth, his under tusks aching to know what it felt like to go for the thick pulsing vein in Kevin's neck. Since his true love arrived on his doorstep, he'd achieved his heart's desire. Withal, he had but one regret.

"I want the time I missed with Marigold back, you wretched cur."

With superhuman restraint, he twisted Kevin 'round, then squeezed his thick green arm around the knight's neck until he collapsed like a marionette with cut strings. Alive, but no longer a threat.

Unlike Crispin and the autumn sprite under his control.

"Coby!" he bellowed. "I've need of you!"

Chapter 38

With the folded note tucked inside her corselet, Marigold fled into the forest with a basket of cakes, cookies, and comfited pumpkin seeds. They might've jumbled as she ran, but she couldn't slow down. Not with Kevin threatening to force her return to Crispin and accuse Bram, known to all of Harvest Hollow as Jask Bone-Cracker, of kidnapping her.

They'd believe it, too.

Why else would a princess betrothed to the—*yuck*—winsome Prince Crispin live at Grimroot Farm? Saints, she had to get to Grindlethwack first. Tonight was the full Hunter's Moon, and upon sunrise, the autumn sprite would slumber until next year's equinox. It was entirely possible for Crispin to ask the sprite to unmoor Bram from the farm so the guard could throw him into Dreadmoor. The prison was known to break spirits as well as backs. She couldn't allow Bram to rot there.

She needed to free him from this curse.

Impossible? Maybe. But she'd accomplished a lot of impossible things since she'd been in Harvest Hollow, so honestly, what was one more? She jumped over the brook rather than run upstream and cross at the bridge. Her ankle rolled under her as she landed. Not exactly a hero's leap, but she'd limp on.

"Princess, on the prince's orders, stop." A stranger's voice reached her at the goldcap tree, along with the unmistakable sound of swords being drawn.

Crispin's knights had infiltrated the Windfall Wood.

Stop? Never. She didn't slow, nor did she look back. Halfway to the Lantern Oak was no time to be snatched up by these ruffians. Princess Marigold Ashford was far too busy.

With a flick of the fingers, she snapped herself small again.

"Dammit," the knight swore.

Hidden in the tall grass, she caught her breath. Small as she was, she'd evade the knights. Except . . . small as she was, it would take a week to get to the Lantern Oak. Perhaps she hadn't thought this through.

The grass swayed with the movement of a skulking stalker.

Shite, shite, shite, she *really* hadn't thought this through.

"Princess, you're surrounded. This is foolish."

The ground underneath her vibrated as steps grew closer.

The swaying grass in front of her parted. This might be how things end for her. The size of a mouse in a forest on the way to bargain with the autumn sprite. She cowered against a rock as a pink nose surrounded by white-and-orange fur emerged from the grass.

"Fuzzle!" she squealed.

The cat twitched his ears as he nosed her small basket.

"I'll give you treats if you get me out of here," she whispered.

He crouched to allow her to climb on his back. With firm grips on his fur, she whispered, "Take me to the Lantern Oak."

Fuzzle was off like lightning.

She'd never been accused of being an expert horsewoman, so it was no surprise she was having difficulty keeping her seat on the cat's neck. Though his stride was smooth, she clamped her fists and legs tight.

Soon, Fuzzle slowed before the glowing golden orbs within the Lantern Oak's branches. It had shed more leaves since she'd last been here, revealing more of its trunk and limbs. At daybreak, the autumn sprite would disappear. They'd have to wait until the wheel of the year cycled back to fall to break the curse on Bram.

At the base of the tree, she snapped herself back to full size.

From within the basket, she withdrew a cream tart, then tossed it to Fuzzle.

"Good man," she said.

As the orange tabby happily dined on the treat, she shed her cloak and scrambled onto the lowest bough. If Bastien got the sprite's name wrong and she tried true-naming him first, he might be too irritated to give her a chance to solve the riddle. But if she tried to solve the riddle first and failed, she had the true-name option as her last arrow in the quiver. And if both failed . . . well, she wouldn't entertain that possibility. Positive thinking only from this point forward.

As she heaved herself upward, she sang a tune to calm herself.

"Bram and Marigold, sitting in a tree."

Heave, grunt, plant her foot, and—shite, she slipped and banged her knee.

"*K-I-S-S-I-N-G.*"

Twist, bend, hook her arm around the limb and . . . yep. There was the kink in her neck again. Hopefully Bram could massage and melt it like butter later.

"First comes love."

She stood on her tiptoes, then stretched for the next branch.

"Then comes a curse."

Her grip slipped, and she whirled her arm until she caught a branch and her balance.

"Then comes grief." She heaved herself up another branch. "And isolation, melancholy, the grayness. Then love again while navigating class-system oppression. Typical girl-meets-boy story."

She breached the surface of the canopy.

"Grand tune, Red." The autumn sprite appeared at her side. "Didn't think I'd see you again. Tell me you've brought more of those cakes?"

"I have."

"Well now, don't be shy." The autumn sprite rubbed his hands together. "I'm hard pressed for time."

She yanked the basket away before he could get under the lid. "Ah, ah, ah. First we talk. Then cakes."

The autumn sprite pouted and held the hand she smacked. "Be quick about it, then, will you?"

She cleared her throat. "It's about Bram."

The autumn sprite sat on a branch. "The green fellow, aye?"

"Cut the shite. You know who he is, and I'm here to break the curse." She shifted her seat on the branch as she reached for the note. "'List all that true love does, not swears; the quiet works, the patient cares. Miss but one, and thorns shall scrape; speak them all, and free the face.' Is that right?"

"Not my finest rhyme, I'll admit. But yes, that's the loophole."

"Great. So, I'm to tell you all the ways my true love is wonderful. Is that it?"

The sprite shrugged and spread his arms. "Can't help you there, Red. The rhyme's open to interpretation. Interpret it wrong, and I get to throw a curse your way, too. Something along the lines of what I dished out to your man Bram. For the fun of it, I could add a twist where he's orc by day, human by night, and vice versa for you."

"That's diabolical." She tucked the note back into her corselet. "I'm trying to undo a curse, not bargain with you."

"I get it's fierce unfair, but that's the nature of the exchange. This here's a magical pyramid scheme."

"A what?" Marigold asked, baffled.

"Oh, Red, you need to get yourself out in the world a bit." The sprite waved his hand. "But I want a cookie, so let's have at it."

She boosted her shoulders and mentally adjusted her crown. Listing Bram's qualities was no challenge. It was a delight.

"My love for Sir Bram Duncan, also known as Jask Bonebreaker, is limitless. It's impossible to sing all his praises before your season concludes, so I'll summarize. From the moment he wakes, I am in his thoughts and he in mine. We are not a fabled couple full of sunshine and tranquility—we argue. We disagree. We debate. But we are rich in repair and always return to each other."

"Is that the lot?" the sprite asked.

Marigold shook her head. She was cooking now. "My true love sees the whole of me, flaws included, and still cherishes me. He believes in me more than I do myself and cheers me on when I succeed, especially in those moments when I misperceive my achievements as obligations. I want to spend eternity in his company in whatever form we take. Whole, bruised, or broken, he is mine and I am his."

The sprite fluttered in front of her like a hummingbird.

Below them the earth thundered. Through the branches she made out Bram's shape carrying a lantern. His noise must have attracted the attention of the knights. "Marigold, stop! Come down from there!"

"It's too late, Bram. I've already started."

He sank to his knees. "I tried to save you from this fate."

"Life with you is all I want," she said. "This is how we achieve it."

The sprite rolled his eyes. "The drama of the two of you. Red, you had me at 'rich in repair.' Well done. I'll break the curse, on one condition."

"What's that?" she asked.

"Not for you—for himself. Hey, lad," the sprite shouted to Bram. "This one's a hoot. She's mad about you. Do you believe you deserve her love?"

Please let him believe it.

Bram's eyes gleamed on the orb glow. "Yes."

"You'd better." Marigold's cheeks were wet with her own happy tears.

"That's it, then." The sprite rubbed his hands together, and glimmering gold sprinkled and swirled toward Bram. He fell to his knees, hidden from view.

"Bram!" She scrambled to descend.

"Which would you have him be? Bram or Jask? Hand on heart, I can't tell if the human or the orc is the truer form. He's found the advantage to both."

"That's not my decision." She dropped to another branch, and ouch, shite, that scrape through her kirtle would need a bandage. "No matter his form or face, I'll love him."

"You hear that, lad?" the sprite shouted. "Pick which you want to be."

The swirl intensified, raged, until it seemed to connect to the heavens. Then, with a snap of the sprite's fingers, the gold shimmer disappeared. Marigold's feet thumped against the gnarled roots of the Lantern Oak in front of her kneeling true love, but her heart thumped harder. Sir Bram Duncan was restored to his human self. Older, with a firmer jaw, laugh lines, and longer hair. The clothes she'd laundered sat loose on his body. He turned his unmistakable gold-flecked gleam to her.

He caught her hand. "Hi."

"Hello," she answered. "So you chose this version of you?"

"It's the only way to see my mother's eyes again, and my father's face." A dimple punched Bram's cheek as he smiled at her. "Is this all right? You'll still love me in this form?"

"In every form," she said. "Always."

He lifted her hand to his lips, then withdrew a wooden ring from his breeches pocket.

"What's that?" she asked.

"A long-overdue ring. I whittled this from the heartwood of the Hollowsnap tree. Encircling it, I've carved a channel and filled it with the last of my acorn gold."

"Whose acorn gold, now?" the autumn sprite asked.

"Hush," Marigold said.

Bram, whose blue eyes shone brighter than the golden moon above, asked, "Marigold Ashford of Thornwick, will you marry me?"

"Yes." She nodded. "Tonight, if possible."

He slipped the ring onto her finger.

"It's a perfect fit," she marveled.

"I took the measure of your finger as you slept." He trailed kisses from her wrist to her elbow, onward and upward until they rose and landed on her lips.

One point in favor of his human form—she needed to be less careful of nips from his under tusks.

The sprite cleared his throat. "Hate to be the one to interrupt, but—the cakes?"

Now that the curse was lifted, she could safely try the true-name solution. From the basket, Marigold tossed a pumpkin cream puff to him. "Enjoy, Grindlethwack."

The puff bounced off the sprite's chest.

"You know my name?" His orange hair dimmed. "How?"

"That's my secret to keep." She had the sneaking suspicion that outing Bastien as her informant might rain trouble on the small boy's head. "You're under my direction now, is that right? If so, I have a command."

"Ah, here we go." He picked up the cream puff, tossed it into the air, then gulped it. "Let me guess, now. You want gold? To rule? The adoration of all and sundry? Out with it. I can take it. Humans always use me for my magic."

"I don't need yours—I have my own." She snapped her fingers and shrank herself and Bram to the sprite's size.

When she negotiated, she preferred to look directly into her opponent's eyes.

"I feel sick." Bram bent and rested his hands on his knees.

"Oh, sorry." She rubbed his back. "I should've warned you that the magic makes your stomach a little spinny. It'll pass."

"Well now, Red." The sprite's eyes widened.

"Here's my command." She laid her hand on the sprite's shoulder. "Never honor another human request you don't agree with. In fact, if there's anything you've done at Crispin's behest that you didn't want to do, go ahead and undo it."

Grindlethwack's glow brightened. "Are you . . . are you releasing me?"

"Yes." She nodded. "I don't believe in servitude without compensation of any kind. Also, if you want to come back to Grimroot Farm, the Goldenmoon Festival is still going strong."

He circled his index fingers around each other. "You're inviting me to a party?"

Next to her, Bram found his feet.

"You seem surprised," she said.

"No one's ever invited me to a party." His lips spread in a smile. "Tell me there'll be cakes?"

"Many." She snapped and returned herself and Bram to full size. "I do have a request, though. Not a command."

"What's that?" Grindlethwack cocked his head to one side.

"Crispin's knights stand between the Lantern Oak and the farm."

"And you'd like me to kill them?"

Marigold covered her mouth. "Saints, no. Let their eyes not see us."

"Blind them, then?" Grindlethwack rubbed his hands together.

"*No*," Marigold huffed. "Don't hurt them at all. Render us not visible to them."

"Oh, sure, that I can do." Sparkles swirled around them. After a brief shimmer, they saw through each other to the magical wood surrounding them. The sprite flew ahead, wings fluttering, and his glowing body lighting the way.

"He's nicer than I remember." Bram's warm hand found hers.

"Because I fed him treats." She squeezed his hand. "Always take treats."

Chapter 39

Bram's nerves crackled more than the leaves under their feet as they approached the pumpkin fields. Lanterns and the bonfire loaned the scene a cozy glow, one that made his heart shift. Here was the place where he'd learned to sit still, to rest in his skin, in whatever shape that skin took. But for three years, it was just a place where he lived.

With Marigold, Grimroot Farm had become his home.

The minstrels' brisk tune brought many dancers to the meadow. Sitting apart from the group were the Thornwick royals, Bess, Crispin, and more of Crispin's guard. His stomach churned. Now that he looked like himself again, he was confident her parents would believe them when they informed them of Crispin's plot.

They still might not accept Bram as her husband, however. He was a commoner, after all. They and the hierarchy they represented were the last obstacle to his enduring happiness. Marigold might put on a good show that she didn't need her parents' acceptance. Giving up her crown was one thing—she had no love for courtly demands.

But she'd suffer if she cut ties with them.

As frustrated as she was by the demands of royal life, her love for her parents, and they for their children, was as obvious as a red tree in a green wood. Her parents' eyes shone with pride when Marigold played the virginals for visiting dignitaries or when Rowan took first in the joust. Beckett, born to them later, twenty now and stationed in the Gildfall Mountains, was rambunctious, but he'd amused her parents rather than cause despair. They corrected their children when they'd erred, too. Firmly, but commands were never barked. Before Matthias had been crowned, they'd simply been a lovely family on whose fringes Bram had lived.

All he'd ever wanted was for them to accept him.

Saints, he'd faced battles and monsters, but this confrontation threatened to knock him to his knees. He'd ask for her hand in an honorable way. Her parents might decline, and then Marigold would have a choice to make.

As they approached the royals, Crispin's knights squared up.

"Turn around," a beefy fellow barked.

Yikes. Sir Fergus had aged like milk. Too much ale, too little tilting at the quintain.

Bram boosted his shoulders. "We need to speak to King Matthias and Queen Elowen."

"And I need to take a piss, but we don't all get what we want."

"Enough, Fergus." Prince Crispin pushed past the knight. "Marigold, my dearest, we've been looking for—"

He stopped short as he laid eyes on Bram.

"—you. What's this?"

"The curse has been broken." Marigold stepped forward. "And I need to speak to my parents. Now."

"Marigold?" Queen Elowen, radiant as ever, leapt up from her seat.

Bram stepped aside so she could wrap her arms around her daughter.

"My little pumpkin, is it really you?" The queen rubbed her thumbs along Marigold's cheeks. "You look so well! Crispin said you'd taken to the countryside to cure your ailment."

"That's one way to put it." Marigold narrowed her gaze at Crispin. "Will you tell them the complete truth, or shall I?"

King Matthias joined his wife and daughter's embrace. "The truth about what, pumpkin? And who is this— Wait."

The king blanched as though he'd seen a specter.

With a nervous breath, Bram said, "It's me, sir. Bram Duncan. I didn't die."

King Matthias clasped his shoulder. "And I'm very glad for it. Marigold was despondent her childhood friend had . . . How did you come to be here?"

"May we speak in private?" Crispin's eyes darted from face to face, never landing. "I can explain, but it would be best if—"

"No." Marigold shook her head. "Enough with secrets and shadows. Let's share in the open, shall we?"

Among the gathering crowd, Bram noticed a studious young woman edging closer to their circle. Isolde Fenlow, the chronicler who specialized in Harvest Hollow intrigues. Prior to the curse, when he was a knight in Crispin's privy circle, he'd have chased her off.

Now?

He welcomed her attention and the light her pen would shine. It wasn't his job to protect bad behavior. Nor was the shame his to bear. Crispin was the one who'd plotted, planned, and inflicted harm. The prince was the only one to be held to account here.

Bram cleared his throat. "Three years ago, Prince Crispin of Harvest Hollow bade the autumn sprite who resides in the Lantern Oak to curse me. He transformed me into an orc and tethered me to Grimroot Farm."

"An orc, you say?" King Matthias scanned him.

"I've returned to myself." He glanced at Marigold. "After your daughter broke the curse."

Rowan stepped forward. "It's true. I saw him with my own eyes two days ago. But that's not the whole of it."

Queen Elowen whipped her head to her daughter. "What, then, *is* the whole of it?"

"Honestly." Crispin grasped Marigold's forearm. "Please take this into the cottage?"

Bram sizzled with anger. "Leave off, if you know what's good for you."

"I've got this," Marigold said. "I can shrink him to obscurity if need be." She turned to her parents. "I overheard Crispin plotting Thornwick's ruin. Upon our marriage, he planned to have the mountain sprites murder Rowan and Beckett, then put me away at Scarlet Spire to convalesce in grief. From there, he'd rule both kingdoms and strip-mine Thornwick for the benefit of Harvest Hollow."

King Matthias lowered his brow. "Is that so? In league with the mountain sprites? I've never heard of such a thing."

Grindlethwack fluttered into view, then scrunched his face apologetically. "Ah, that'd be my fault. Crispin had control of me, and I brokered the deal with the mountain sprites. He promised to give them the foothills of the Gildfall Mountains."

"A full quarter of Thornwick's land?" Queen Elowen gasped.

Marigold nodded. "So, you see, I can't marry Crispin."

"No, you cannot." She kissed her daughter's cheek, then glared at Crispin. "I forbid it."

"How's that now?" Crispin laughed darkly. "We have an agreement. A marriage license."

"And you have broken the contract." King Matthias, shorter than Crispin though he may be, intimidated the younger man enough to force him to step back.

"You don't believe this . . . this *fantasy*, do you?" Crispin spluttered. "Why would I, a prince in my own right, engage in this kind of subterfuge?"

"How dare you, sir?" The king pursed his lips as though he were holding back venom. "My daughter does not lie."

Crispin's arched a sharp eyebrow. "Then she told you about the romantic relationship she and Bram carried on all those years ago, did she? You should be grateful I was willing to take her off your hands, knowing what I know about her virtue."

"You go too far." King Matthias fisted Crispin's jerkin. "Apologize."

"Never." Crispin glared at Marigold's father.

"No one should apologize for true love." Grindlethwack flitted around Crispin's head. "The only person who should apologize is you, you great weasel."

Queen Elowen held her daughter's hands. "True love?"

"It's the only kind that breaks the curse." Grindlethwack fluttered above them, swirling them with amber glitter.

Marigold beamed a smile at Bram. "The truest."

"About that." Bram cleared his throat as he shifted his gaze between her parents. "Sir, ma'am. Marigold and I . . . we'd like to marry and would be grateful for your blessing."

The parents exchanged a glance. A silent conversation waged between them until, imperceptibly, Queen Elowen nodded.

King Matthias opened his arms. "We welcome you, Sir Bram Duncan, into our family. You've remained true to Marigold and have done our family and Thornwick a great service in protecting her from this craven lout."

The crowd cheered as the king and queen embraced him. Their clothes were of the finest material he'd touched, but beneath it, their warmth and ready acceptance stole his breath. Saints, he'd forgotten how easy it was to shed tears as a human.

"Stop!" Crispin sputtered. "There's more you should know about your daughter. More of her lies. *Magical* lies."

Next to him, Marigold sighed, then pivoted toward her parents. "I am so tired of keeping secrets. Mama, Papa, let me strip the leaves from your branches. I possess magical abilities."

"What?" her parents said in unison.

Her mother covered her mouth, then removed it. "My darling, when?"

"For the first one, five years ago. Bess told me not to tell both of you—said the laws of Thornwick forbid magic and my talents would put you in an awkward position. The second appeared roughly two weeks ago."

King Matthias turned to Queen Elowen. "You said it skipped a generation."

The queen flipped her hands to the sky. "I'm wrong sometimes." To Bess, she said, "And how dare you encourage our daughter to divide herself from us in this manner?"

Rather than look abashed, Bess lifted her chin. "I was looking out for her in a way neither of you hypocrites seemed to. Crispin embraces magical abilities and would encourage her to use them instead of threaten her with the oubliette. They're well-suited."

"There's still the whole willing-to-murder-my-brothers-by-proxy situation that's hard to overlook." Of her mother, Marigold asked, "And what do you mean, skips a generation?"

Queen Elowen splayed her fingers against her chest in a way that reminded Bram of Marigold. "I, too, possess magical abilities, but I've refrained from using them. As you say, Thornwick frowns upon such things, and Matthias and I were already budging up against propriety since my family is of the merchant class. But I'm eager to know, pumpkin. What are your gifts?"

"Minimancy, but I don't know the second one's name," she said.

"Show me?"

Marigold popped the glowing orbs from her palms and flung them outward.

A stray orb splatted onto Crispin, who shimmered and showed as a small, puckered, ashy creature. The crowd gasped and shrank from him, while Isolde Fenlow frantically scribbled on a pad of paper.

Bram leaned toward Marigold and whispered, "Is he a creature masquerading as human?"

"No, I think that's what he's like on the inside," she said.

After a beat the shimmer faded.

Queen Elowen widened her eyes. "Trueface. I've heard of it but never seen it."

"That's slander." Crispin shook his finger at Marigold. "That wasn't me. You don't possess trueface, you're—"

The autumn sprite fluttered toward Crispin. "Ah, give it a rest. They figured you out."

"You're audacious today, sprite." The loathsome prince puffed up his chest and crossed his arms. "I command you to turn the lot of them into orcs. See how they like that."

A smile spread over Grindlethwack's face. "No."

"What do you mean, no? You must obey me."

"Not anymore. Red true-named me, so she's the boss now. She also told me plain—no more following orders I've no heart for. She granted me agency, you eejit."

Crispin stamped his foot like a toddler. "Don't call me eejit."

"Oh, *Crispin.*" A melodic, disappointed voice cut through the whispering in the crowd. "Have you been misbehaving again?"

A tall woman approached, folding back the hood of her cloak. As the cloth fell around her shoulders, the rising wind snatched at her long dark hair. She narrowed her violet eyes. "Hello, brother."

Crispin blanched. "Rosamund?"

"Oh, shite," Grindlethwack murmured. "What's she doing here?"

"I'll own that," Bram said. "Marigold's brother and a knight friend of mine—Sir Coby—went to persuade Princess Rosamund to return to Harvest Hollow since she, by all rights, should serve as regent instead of Crispin."

"Brilliant, but fair warning—she might be pissed." Grindlethwack swirled his index fingers around each other. "Crispin true-named me right around the time the old king took ill. First thing he asked was to afflict his older sister, too. Nothing fatal, mind. Just enough for her to need the air at the Sea of Red Tides. So *he* could be regent instead. And then Red here told me to undo things I didn't agree with."

"Like making Rosamund ill," Marigold said.

Grindlethwack nodded. "Just so."

"Guards?" Rosamund called. "Please ready the carriage so my dear brother and I may return to Brambleton. We must consult with the High Council about the legitimacy of his regency. Oh, and you there." She beckoned to Coby. "You'll ride in the carriage with us. The rest of you will walk or ride, if you have horses."

Her cloak swirled as she turned toward Marigold and Bram. Rosamund's cool gaze appraised the two of them, dressed in humble farmers' clothing. "I understand I have you two to thank for retrieving me?"

Marigold curtseyed. "Princess Marigold of Thornwick, at your service."

Bram bowed. "Sir Bram Duncan, also of Thornwick."

"Up, up." Princess Rosamund touched their shoulders. "No bowing among friends. We'd be stuck all evening, bobbing at each other like ducks. I fear it'll be a late night for me this evening, but I'd like for us to visit with each other soon."

"I'd like that, too," Marigold said.

Bram remained silent until Marigold stepped on his toe. "And I."

With a great clanging, the palace guard, Princess Rosamund, and Prince Crispin headed toward the corner of the harvested pumpkin patch where carriages and horses had been tethered.

Marigold's curls smelled of pine as he leaned to whisper, "I don't envy him that ride."

"Pumpkin." Queen Elowen reached for her daughter's hands. "We shall plan the wedding of the century."

With an audible huff, Bess stalked away and into the night. Had they been on better terms, he might've warned her she was headed straight for the Leshy's patch of forest.

"Um, actually." Marigold twisted her shoe into the ground. "Could we not?"

With a fizz in her belly, Marigold called, "Brother Oswald! We need your help."

The round monk huffed over to where they stood. "How may I be of service?" he asked.

"We wish to be married." Bram kissed her knuckles. "Tonight."

The full golden moon loaned the pumpkin patch and the meadow an amber glow. A perfect scene for the wedding of her dreams.

"'Tis a marvelous night for a wedding," Brother Oswald agreed. "Where may I do you the honor of officiating?"

"The meadow," Marigold said.

"Pumpkin," Papa said, "there's no need to rush."

"We could take our time." Mama pulled a leaf from her hair. "Tidy up a bit?"

Marigold giggled. "This isn't rushed, Mama." She reached

for his hand. "I've wanted to marry Bram since . . . always. From the moment Sir Patrick brought him to May Day and we played tag."

"You could—" the autumn sprite swirled his fingers together "—and I'm just throwing it out there—you could ask your old magical friend to sort some wedding duds, if you like?"

"Give me one second." Marigold climbed atop the nearest table. "Excuse me, everyone? Excuse me."

A few faces turned her way, but most of the festival goers remained locked in chatter, laughter, or jigging with the minstrels' latest tune. She took a deep breath, then cupped her hands around her mouth. Before she could shout, Barnaby joined her on the table and split the air with his shriek.

All eyes turned toward Marigold.

"Thank you, Barnaby." To the crowd, she shouted, "You're all invited to our wedding, starting in five minutes."

The crowd erupted into a cheer.

Bram helped her down from the table. "Are you sure?"

"*Sure* isn't the half of it." She leaned forward and kissed him. "I am rooted, Bram. In you, this place, our life."

"Ah, ah, ah, you two." Brother Oswald shook his finger. "Save it for the altar. Speaking of which, what will serve as the altar?"

She and Bram looked at each other.

In unison, they said, "The heartwood tree."

"Lead me there?" Brother Oswald said to Bram.

"See you soon." Bram kissed her knuckles.

As soon as Bram was out of sight, the autumn sprite cracked his knuckles. "Okay, Red, you ready for this?"

"Go for it," she said.

The autumn sprite wiggled his fingers, then tapped her on the forehead. From where he made contact, gold, crimson, and orange sparkles swirled around her like a gentle rain. As the magic drizzled, twisted, and turned, her dress changed from the simple homespun and headwrap to a body-skimming ivory confection adorned with autumnal flowers.

Mama folded her hands over her heart. "*That* is a gown fit for a princess."

The sparkles leapt from her hem, then flew and wheeled like a flock of starlings over the farm. In their wake, they left an amber trail of floating lights, marking the path toward the orchard.

"Shall we?" Papa said, offering his arm.

"Wait—sister, your bouquet." Rowan clipped a dozen sunflowers from the blaze that stood at the edge of the pumpkin patch and tied them with his handkerchief.

Her eyes shimmered at the gesture. "Thank you."

The crowd advanced before her, and in five minutes' time, she and her family arrived at the orchard. The sweet scent of apple filled the air. The crowd split, making space for her to find her groom.

Rowan escorted their mother to the front of the crowd. Marigold's eyes followed them and led straight to Bram. The autumn sprite's magic had transformed his clothing to ivory finery, but still with a blue shirt to accentuate his beautiful eyes. When they locked gazes, his face was full of joy. It was like she could see all versions of him at once, smushed together into one delicious person: the seven-year-old boy, the teenager, the young man, the orc, and now this new version, with finer lines and longer hair.

Saints, she couldn't wait to love the versions yet to come.

The minstrels played the start of the traditional wedding march, and Papa patted the hand she'd slipped into the crook of his elbow. This moment, right here, was the dividing line between the last version of herself and the new, and she couldn't wait for her chrysalis.

"May I offer you some advice, Marigold?" her father asked.

She nodded. "Please do."

"There are many people who will tell you marriage is work," he said. "That may be true for them. But with your mother—I've never felt it was a burden because love makes the so-called work easy. Never take the love for granted."

"I won't," she promised. "Ever."

This moment, this life with Bram—it had always felt inevitable. Even in the most impossible moments, like death. But even that could not stop them. Look at him over there, beaming at her like she was the sun and the moon wrapped together. The way her cheeks hurt, she must've been wearing the same smile. She'd felt married to him since . . . forever, really. Tonight was about declaring it in public so that everyone else knew how they felt about each other.

She squeezed her father's arm. "I'm ready, Papa."

With that, Marigold took the first step into the next chapter of her life.

Chapter 40

Good morning, Mrs. Duncan." Bram kissed her nape as he curled his body around hers.

"It is not morning, Sir Duncan. Outside is still pitch." She twisted in his arms and kissed him back. "For the record, it's bullshit that husbands don't take their wife's rank."

"But it doesn't matter, since you've decided to step back from royal service."

"I'd hardly call it stepping back, since I never really stepped forward." She stretched and rolled her back. "I can't believe how late my family stayed last evening."

"I can," he said. "Country parties are more fun than courtly ones."

"My father certainly enjoyed your orc cider."

"Your brother, too. I'm sure they'll need willow bark this morning. Elenor will look after them at the inn. I'm sure they're happier there." He kissed her shoulder. "Brambleton Castle must be awkward as ass right now. I wouldn't want to go within a hectare of the place."

"Although you can now, if you want."

"Thanks to you." He kissed her.

"Thanks to *us*."

"To us." She tucked his hair behind his ear.

Outside, Barnaby shrieked.

Marigold giggled. "Does he ever crow at dawn?"

"Not once."

"We'd best start the day." She flipped back the covers. "I'll do the chickens, you milk Queen?"

"Deal," he said.

As they descended the steps, a full Grimroot Farm breakfast awaited them—pumpkin-apple oatmeal, eggs scrambled with herbs, fresh cranberry scones and butter, and a fragrant tisane of ginger and honey.

"Hello?" Bram called. "Who's there?"

"It's me, kids." The autumn sprite fluttered around their house.

"How long have you been here?" Marigold asked.

"D'you want the truth or . . ." The sprite flapped a hand. "Let's say I got here an hour ago and sure didn't hear anything happening upstairs. Once dawn breaks, I slumber, and I still needed to give you a gift. Morning chores are done, along with the cleanup from yesterday, and breakfast is on the table. Thought you two could use a lazy morning."

"That's really sweet of you," Marigold said.

"'Tis my fault you had a three-year pause."

"I hope you understand you didn't do that of your own free will," Bram said.

"I suppose you're right, but it'll take me a second to wrap my brain around it, though." He peered through the window. "Almost time. Okay if I pop by when I'm back?"

"You'd better." Marigold opened a cupboard and withdrew a covered crock. Inside, she'd stashed the last of the small cakes the autumn sprite adored. "For the road?"

With a grin, he took the cake. "Many thanks, Red. Until next year."

With a pop and a sizzle, he disappeared.

"If the chores are done, what do you say to a walk?" Bram

held her cloak out to her. "I'd like to take this body out for a spin."

"Didn't we do that last night?" she asked.

"Several times." He fastened her cloak around her shoulders. "Walk with me in the pumpkin patch?"

The air outside was brisk.

"Smells like snow," Bram said as they stepped out down from the porch.

She lifted her face to the gray clouds swirling above. "Because it's snowing."

Her hand was warm in his as they walked through the pumpkin patch and delighted in the flakes sifting down from the sky. All the banquets, masquerade balls, fine silks, and intrigues couldn't compare to the life she would create in this place with Bram.

Her Bram, forever and always.

★ ★ ★ ★ ★